I0762054

SCARLET SUNDAY

Also by Alyssa DiCarlo

Catatonic
Switch

SCARLET SUNDAY

Alyssa DiCarlo

Purple Fern Publishing

First Purple Fern hardcover edition November 2021

Edited by Lauren Short
Cover designed by HL Macfarlane
Chapter headers designed by Nicole Scarano

ISBN 978-1-7332480-4-4

CONTENT WARNING

Scarlet Sunday contains frequent visuals of blood, excessive gore, and two instances of suicide.

"The hand that heals is the hand to hold."

The Book of Araedia

c. 1606

prologue

It was everywhere.

All over my hands, my face, my clothes. It absolutely reeked—a scent so strong, so ghastly that it nearly triggered my up-chuck reflex. Only, I didn't have the time to hurl. I didn't have time to do anything, really, except hide. Watch. *Listen.*

They were all dead around me. An unimaginable amount of bodies, more than I'd ever seen in my life. Some were intact; peaceful, almost.

Others weren't so lucky.

I stumbled over a particularly grotesque corpse, one which lacked half of their skull. Their limbs were mangled, moist, and drenched with seeping, scarlet blood. I wondered if some of their blood was on me too, and I wished more than anything that I could fall to my knees beside them and summon the blood back into their veins. To suction my lips to theirs, to breathe life into their still, skeletal frame. But dead was dead, and not even I could bring back the deceased.

Thus, I pressed on—choking back a sob as the lights above my head flickered and flared. Most of the bulbs had blown, leaving behind nothing but crunchy, soot-riddled glass within their wake. It was nearly impossible to dodge the abundance of glass and plethora of bodies, but I did my best, keenly avoiding the very root of the entire fiasco. Only two short hours earlier, every one of these bodies had a heartbeat—had air in their lungs, a drink in their hand; laughter cascading over their lips. The once lively event had succumbed to nothing more than complete chaos.

A shaky hand met the blood spattered wall, trembling digits struggling to steady my wavering weight. I felt woozy and weak, and although I'd been lucky enough to dodge its wrath thus far, I almost envied those who've been freed from such a wild, wicked world. The idea of having to survive beyond this day was something that rattled me to my very core, and although I'd feared death for as long as I could remember, it almost seemed plausible, now. Warm. Welcoming.

The cool white light from the overhead lamps promptly extinguished as my frail frame rounded the corner, cloaking the long, slender hallway in a bitter black fog. A foreboding silence enveloped the area, the overwhelming stench of death filling my nostrils as I struggled to breathe. Something about this area of the residence felt unnerving—*wrong.*

As I'd placed one foot forward in preparation to navigate the inky black hallway, an artificial, unknown light source illuminated the area, and the wind exited my lungs in a rapid, distasteful fashion. I nearly fell to my knees, sucking in a sharp gasp as the haunting whisper cascaded over my ears—an unidentifiable sonance, an unknown tune, but nevertheless unique. It resembled something like a gasp, a sharp intake of breath, and then an abhorrent ringing.

It was inevitable. *They were here.*

When I mustered up the strength to lift my head, I saw *them,* standing there in all their glory, a placid expression slapped across their features.

I couldn't quite miss the blackness of their eyes, regardless of how hard I'd tried.

one

"Come *on,* Freya! I'm going to find out one way or another, so you may as well just *spill.*"

"Nothing happened," I weakly slurred, ignoring Raiden's piercing glare as I continued to dice a multitude of tomatoes. There was an entire box left of the squeaky clean fruit for me to prepare, and at this point, I was sick of both the sight and smell of them.

Raiden wasn't convinced. He rounded the prep table, joining me on the opposite side before poking me in my ribs. "Oh, *c'mon.* You act like I don't know you. I know you like the back of my hand, Frey. I've known you for twenty-three years."

"Oh yeah? And what does the *back of your hand* say about this entire situation?" I teased, bottom lip jutting outward to blow a stray curl out of my eyes. I needed a haircut—*bad*—but Momma was envious of my thick locks. After completing her chemotherapy, her hair never grew back.

"*Wellll,*" Raiden slurred, unable to contain his chuckles. He nearly tripped over his own two feet as he positioned himself beside me, careful not to nudge the arm which held the blade. "My pretty little *palm* says that you *fucked* him!"

I stiffened, readily recalling the events that had transpired just the night before. Myself, Maxwell, a lot of wine, and some unsavory sex. I nearly cringed at the thought of how unsatisfying it was, but nevertheless, I continued to dice my tomatoes as if I were unphased.

Raiden, however, would not let up. He threaded his pale, slender fingers around my clothed elbow, his rosy red lips strung up into a gleeful grin. He was so handsome—Raiden Crow—and although he was an incredibly awkward kid and an even *more* awkward looking teenager, he'd truly blossomed into a charming adult. By the eve of his twenty-fifth birthday, he'd finally grown into his too-large head and filled out his lanky limbs. By now, the messy mop of curls atop his skull had learned how to properly frame his face, his wicked, green eyes bright and beautiful. He was only a year younger than me, thirty-two, and he was chipper as ever; never leaving my side.

"It seriously sucked," I revealed, and Raiden couldn't help but laugh; tossing his head back in amusement before returning to his side of the prep table. His pleased features were partially concealed by a plentitude of hanging pots, and I found myself wanting to wriggle my arm between them and move them aside, *just* so I could look him in the face. In the eyes. Those pretty, emerald eyes.

"Maxwell McKinnon's a total douche canoe anyways. I don't even understand why you agreed to go out with him," Raiden pressed, shuffling through a box of onions. "I need to start chopping these, so prepare to cry."

"Goddamn onions," I groaned. "Goddamn salsa. You know, we should really look into working somewhere that won't leave us smelling like tacos all the time."

"I don't think I could ever give up the free tacos, though," he recoiled, inspecting the row of sharp knives, each of them accented with a vibrant colored handle.

"The blue one's freshly sharpened," I called, and Raiden nodded; snatching the large butcher knife with the blue grip from the magnetized board. "And you're right about Maxwell. He's been practically begging me to come over all the time, and I always leave disappointed. Maybe, I was just lonely."

"How can you be lonely when you have me?" Raiden purred. I mustered up a smile, and as soon as he'd begun to prepare the onions, I heard it—a gasp. It nearly buckled my knees, and I couldn't help but outwardly mimic the sound with my own mouth.

"Shit!" Raiden hissed, the knife falling to his feet. A tasteless bead of blood blossomed upon his forefinger, and the very same finger that adorned my right hand seemed to pulsate with pain. My ears mercilessly rang as I met his side.

Once the ringing ceased, I spoke up. "God, Raiden. You've got to be more careful."

I claimed his bloody finger in my steady hold, a slight whimper slipping off of his mouth as I turned the digit over in my grasp. When I'd slightly squeezed and more blood freely flowed, he hissed; yet the sound that tumbled off of his rounded lips was nothing compared to the sudden racket that emerged from behind us both. Simultaneously, we jumped, glancing over our shoulders to view the source of the sound.

The remaining knives had fallen to the ground, as if they'd been knocked off of the wall. Only, it was seven in the morning, and besides our manager, Sierra, who was out smoking a cigarette—we were the only ones in the restaurant.

"What the–"

"Take care of it, will you?" Raiden clipped, bitterly diverting my attention from the fallen utensils.

Hastily, I obliged; my mind swimming with the thought of the knives just randomly falling. It didn't seem plausible for the magnet to just *give up*—for them all to fall at the same time. Something about the event made me uneasy; nevertheless, I slipped my thumb into the depths of my mouth, sucking sharply on the surface before withdrawing it and gliding it along Raiden's severed skin. He grinned as the flesh immediately sealed itself, as if by the assistance of invisible stitches, and I wiped the blood away against my once white apron.

"Never gets old." Raiden beamed, inspecting the closed wound.

"Probably won't even scar," I said, rinsing my hands in a nearby sink. He did the same before returning to his prep, salty tears coating the apples of his cheeks from the onions' overwhelming stench. As I finished off my box of tomatoes, I couldn't help but ponder over the knives, and how it was possible that they'd leapt off of the wall without warning.

Perhaps, another energy was brewing deep within me.

I'd never felt so abnormal.

two

Raiden was with me the first time someone called me the "F" word.

Freak.

We were young and dumb, a fresh friendship blossoming between us. I met the short, awkward, frumpy boy a day shy of my tenth birthday. He tried to nick a mushy, melted candy bar from the rundown, unnamed gas station several blocks south of our home. A younger Brennan, my brother, had sent me out for some ice cream while Momma and Dad were out working. They always worked long hours. Hell, we hardly saw them most of the time; however, their hard work and dedication provided my brother and me with the best of the best. Name brand clothing, luxury items, the newest technology, gourmet food. Even our housemaid, Blanch, had her fair share of being spoiled rotten.

I'd watched him beyond the shelves, widened, auburn eyes studying the apprehensive boy as he'd slipped a chocolate bar into the pocket of his too-small coat. Although he weighed a fair amount, the boy looked gaunt in his face, sickly, as if he'd been recovering from a month-long illness. I'd wondered if he had that dreadful *tummy bug* that Momma always talked about. She was always scared of seeing Brennan and me get sick, and she made either Dad or Blanch clean up after us so she didn't have to.

When the young boy began to creep towards the door, I'd felt compelled to rat him out. It wasn't fair for him to have such a luxury for free, when my parents worked long hours to give both Brennan and me the things we most desired. I'd clutched the cold carton of chocolate ice cream to my chest and wailed, index finger jutting outward in the direction of the sneaky lad who'd almost made it to the door.

"Thief!"

I wasn't quite sure what outcome I'd expected. After all, it was only myself, a wee-little girl with too much curly hair and the beginnings of a unibrow, arms so thin they resembled twigs; a frumpy looking boy with a too-tight sweatshirt and bulging, green eyes, and a young store clerk; no more than twenty but no less than sixteen, eyes heavily lined with black makeup, lips obnoxiously smacking together as she chewed her gum. For a moment, she just stared; mostly at me. The young thief was frozen in fear near the exit, arms suspended midair as if in surrender. His face was as white as a sheet, and he looked as if he may faint, black bags cradling the big, bright, sparkling orbs that claimed the sockets of his skull.

"Just let him take it, Snitch." The cashier blew a large, periwinkle pink bubble with her gum, a brightly hued magazine pinched between manicured nails as she avoided the boy entirely. "Didn't your parents ever teach you no manners? The kid looks like he's about to drop dead of starvation. If he wants a candy bar, he can have one."

Before I could protest, the kid went to leave; only his departure was interrupted by an uneven set of tiles, improperly laid by the builder. I watched as the toe of his sneaker clipped the tawdry tile, sending the youthful boy face first to the ground. The scene almost appeared to play out in slow motion. With widened eyes, I observed his animated fall; palms gravitating towards his face to shield his bulbous nose. Only, he was half a second too late, and a horrified gasp tickled my tongue as a profusion of blood rapidly escaped his nostrils, the cartilage snapping with an audible crack.

I'd overheard the cashier mumble one of those wretched *sour words* Daddy always warned us about, but my attention was solely fixated upon the starving thief and his broken nose. He looked so pitiful and numb; big, fat tears welled up within his eyes as his severely shaken fingers cradled his ruined nose.

Shocking even myself, I ran to his aid; discarding the suddenly undesired cartons of ice cream onto a nearby shelf before falling to my knees beside him. The crimson blood that steadily dripped from his flared nostrils cloaked my jean-clad knees, but nevermind that—for this sad, little soul was injured, and Momma always taught me to put others before myself.

Use your energies for good, Freya.

"Hey, let me see that." The words had tumbled from my mouth in the form of a low coo, and when the boy refused to comply, a rushed statement nearly slapped him in the face. "I can *fix* it! Come on, now. I can. Just *let* me."

I'd felt the nosy girl beyond the counter studying the situation, her magazine sprawled along the surface as she awaited my next move. To a stranger, it didn't make any sense at all. It shouldn't make sense. How could a kid like myself fix a broken nose, anyhow?

With widened eyes, the boy submissed; sprawled out along his back on the blood-smeared tile, the smushed chocolate bar hanging halfway out of his mustard yellow coat pocket. His nose was so broken that it looked *crooked,* and the sight made my stomach violently churn, but I brushed the feeling aside as if it were nothing but a pesky, little bug beneath my shoe.

"Just take a deep breath," I'd told him, trying to make him smile. At that age, I was unsure of whether or not the healing hurt, for the one thing I couldn't do was heal myself. "What's your name?"

"Raiden," he breathed, his stunned stare studying my every move. He'd watched as I brought my thumb to my mouth, slipping the curled digit between cracked, chapped lips. I could hear the cashier shifting uncomfortably behind the counter, as if she were trying to get a better view of the scene at hand. She was irrelevant, then. The only thing that mattered at that time was to fix poor Raiden's nose.

So, I did. Cockily, I'd cradled Raiden's nose, and as if by magic, the wound seamlessly healed; it looked as if it had never been broken in the first place. Later on he claimed he hadn't felt a thing, but I'd always called bullshit on that one, because my brother Brennan complained that everytime I mended him, the pain was *unbearable.*

Perhaps, he was just a big baby.

When I'd requested a bundle of napkins to wipe the blood from Raiden's face, I was met with a harsh string of words by the horrified shop worker. The worst word of all wasn't even within the slew of obscenities that tumbled from her lips—*no*—it was the bold, brash statement that emerged after, just as she'd taken several steps backwards and away from my shy, small self.

Fucking freak.

She probably thought I would pull a *Carrie* after that, judging by her reaction alone. Raiden was still collapsed along the tile, thoroughly inspecting his healed nose. Although I was nearly ten and rather short for my age, my rage was blinding; and I couldn't help but glow a ghastly red, fists clenched at my sides, and I insisted that she'd eat the words she'd just spilled.

She'd begged me not to crush her to smithereens with my *mind powers,* and out of my pure, pathetic rage, I'd run to the back of the store, yanked open the freezer doors, and stuffed as many cartons of ice cream into my arms that I could. I even beckoned the boy over, shuffling some of them into his own arms.

Raiden and I had fled the premises in a giggling mess, abandoning the frightened worker as she cowered in her loafers.

Needless to say, we'd been inseparable ever since.

three

"You told me you'd quit it with those things," I jabbed, sharply side-eyeing the pack of cigarettes within Raiden's hold. The sun had settled beyond a puffy patch of somber rain clouds in the distance, and if we wanted to beat the inevitable storm, we would need to hustle. After all, the walk back home was just over twenty minutes.

"I will," Raiden murmured, his tone masked by the presence of an unlit cancer stick. Several stringy curls dipped within his line of sight as he rummaged around his pockets for a lighter. When he'd finally found it, I snatched it away; holding it high above my head as I stood on my tippy-toes. I nearly stumbled into a nearby bush, the concrete sidewalk uneven beneath my feet as Raiden bitterly bit down on his cigarette.

"Come *on,* Freya," he groaned, coiling his arm around my waist and yanking my slightly taller frame forward. "I'll quit next week."

My nose nearly smacked against his cheek, the toes of my non-slip shoes waltzing around his feet as I avoided crushing them with my own. His hot, labored breaths danced along the crevice of my jaw, conflictingly cold, ring-clad fingers tickling my wrist as he snatched the lighter from my hold.

He practically shoved me away before I'd even registered what happened; my wide, ebbing eyes fixated on the fullness of his lips as the younger man lit his cigarette with ease.

"You promise?" I croaked, shyly stepping forward to tuck a part of his wild, curly mane behind his ear. "You're going to light your head on fire one of these days."

"Maybe just two more weeks. It's not too easy to stop. Remember when you had to get off your meds?" Raiden dryly countered, sunken cheeks hollowing out as he took a deep drag off of the lit stick. His statement felt like a bitter jab, and I was unfortunately reminded of my pesky depression and the medication I once took to combat it.

"Don't bring up my meds," I pressed, knotting my fingers through the frayed fabric of my aged purse. Ever since Momma got sick, the luxuries dissipated; the spoiling stopped. We were a one-income family, and we still missed the help from Blanch's daughter Emmalein, who was too expensive to keep between our mother's treatments and the severe lack of funds coming in. We were lucky to still have Dad around. Most men would flee at the first sign of trouble, but not him. Never him.

"Listen, I'm sorry. I'll stop soon," Raiden revealed, twirling the cigarette between his fingers.

"You can't just take out your anger on me like that. I'm human, too."

Raiden playfully scoffed, inhaling deeply before releasing a large puff of toxic smoke. "Humans can't heal people with a single touch, Frey."

"Hey, *okay.* I'm like a *fancy* human, then." I chuckled. He refused to meet my stare as we walked; his wide, sleepy eyes instead fixated on his feet, as if to inspect every single step. Something about his aura was off today, and it generated an overall essence of unease within the deepest depths of my heart. I wanted nothing more than to wrap him up in my arms and heal him of his every pain, every insecurity, every fear.

After several minutes of stagnant silence, Raiden spoke up once more, discarding his cigarette into a nearby bush. "Your brother turns thirty in two weeks. Is that party still on?"

"Sure is," I replied, cringing at the thought of Brennan's coming-of-age party. Although none of the guests knew it, it was *way* more than just some lousy birthday party. In fact, it was hardly a birthday party at all. It was a celebration, a *ritual.*

Brennan would become the omnipotent. The thought made my spine tingle—to imagine my younger brother so invincible. He would pave the way for the Araedians to follow. Our children, their children, and the children thereafter would be safe—*secure*—all because Brennan made it to his thirtieth year. Most Araedian men would perish before their thirtieth year, all thanks to the malevolent De Mörka, who had all since disappeared following the Great Clash. Our true enemy was eliminated, and all that was left of the Araedian people was that of my mother and her parents. It was a frightening thought, really, to know that my family was all that remained of a four-hundred year old coetus. If Brennan and I were to die before each of us produced a child, the Araedian bloodline would die along with us, along with our energies.

A guttural roll of thunder vibrated the windows of a nearby parked car, a yappy, little dog barking through the sorry excuse for a slit. For a moment, I wished that I had Brennan's energy, for then I could unravel the window entirely and let the poor animal roam free.

"Where do you go?" Raiden wondered, nudging me in the ribs.

"What do you mean?" I countered, adjusting the strap on my purse before extending my arm in Raiden's direction. Eagerly, he took my hand, threading his fingers through mine as he lightly squeezed.

"When you zone out like that," he clarified, tucking his mangled mess of hair behind his ear. It was almost as long as mine. "I've never quite figured out what planet you go to."

"Saturn," I said. "I tend to hang around the rings. They remind me of the ones circling your fingers."

With a giant grin, Raiden pulled me to him, causing me to nearly trip over my own feet as my nose painfully collided with the curve of his jaw. As I busied myself with massaging the sore, throbbing tip of my nose, Raiden wrapped his arms around my waist, enveloping me in a warm, welcoming hug.

"My *nose,*" I lightly whined, unable to stifle a giggle as Raiden's fingers tickled my jaw, index finger curling beneath the underside of my chin. He forced my head upwards to meet his amused stare, a silly smile etched along his mouth as the pair of us were greeted with a staccato of chilly, wet raindrops. The first drop met his forehead, the size of a pea, and I watched as it cascaded down his pale skin before burrowing itself into the bushy brown hair of his brow, which instinctively arched at the feel. He tore a hand away from my back, drawing it up towards his face as stiff fingers wiped the wetness away.

When I'd looked up to the darkening sky in search of its source, I was met with another drop, one which invaded my sight and turned my surroundings into an irritable blur.

We tore apart, desperately attempting to escape the rain, a plethora of laughs erupting between the two of us. By the time we'd reached our shared abode, we were drenched down to the bone; sticky clothes slick against our heaving frames. We couldn't quite bite back the laughter that cascaded over our tongues, and we even earned an awkward side-eye from one of our neighbors—an elderly woman with hardly any hair and deep-set crow's feet—whilst she checked her mail, a floral umbrella shielding her lanky self from the rain.

Raiden struggled to shove the key into the bulky brass lock, spooled ringlets of drenched hair dangling within his line of sight as I politely pried them away. Inaudibly, he thanked me; slipping the key into the lock before kicking open the door. Per usual, the sunny yellow door shrieked in protest, revealing a trio of wild, wired dogs; all overjoyed at the sight of their owners.

"All right, all *right.* Back it up, let us through," Raiden playfully purred, leaning down to stroke each and every one of their buzzing skulls. I nearly tripped over the largest of the bunch—a Great Dane we called Kelso. I couldn't help but fall to my bottom, enveloping the big boy in a giant bear hug as he feathered an abundance of wet, slobbery kisses along my jaw.

Raiden and I lived together in a townhome just barely a mile west of my parents home. It was small and cozy—only a single bedroom with an adjoined bathroom—but it was warm, and it was home. It had been for nearly a decade now, and deep down, I hoped it would stay this way for an eternity.

Raiden released a groan from the kitchen, followed by the distinct sonance of dry dog food being poured into their allocated metal bowls. Once more, I was nearly trampled by a mass of fur, and as I joined them in the tiny kitchen, I was greeted by Raiden's source of displeasure.

Within his hands was a mangled potted avocado plant, the once blooming bud now nothing but a chewed-up mound. Dirt littered the créme tiled floor, irritably sticking to the slick skin of Raiden's toes as he handed me the plant.

"Look what one of them did," he grumbled, running a hand through his wet hair. "I was *so excited* to eat that damn avocado!"

"I guess indoor plants are a no-go." I frowned, taking one of the chewed-up leaves between my fingers as I inspected it.

"If only you could heal those, too," Raiden replied, stroking Bear's fur as the large chocolate lab nuzzled against his knee.

For a split second, I felt incredibly odd about Raiden's comment—*if only you could heal those, too*—and with a frown, I wandered out of the room, propping the obliterated potted plant up on a high shelf. Our space was crowded and cluttered, an assortment of tables, shelves, and bookcases slapped up against most of the walls. I had more books than I could physically count, and Raiden collected antique objects—ranging from tiny to tall—all of which were on display. Although our tastes differed immensely, we made it work; and the antique, bohemian decor kept us content.

My fingers buzzed as my downcast stare collided with the flushed flesh, an overwhelming amount of energy coursing through my core as I weakly attempted to tame the grievous sensation. It didn't happen often—the flares—but when they did, it usually meant that there was going to be some sort of significant shift. Whether it be a change in my own personal life or with the universe itself, I could never tell.

Raiden's palm met my lower back the second my hands began to burn.

"Hey," he cooed, a bushy brow raised at the sight of my slightly disheveled state. "What's the matter?"

"Nothing," I dismissed, brushing my palms along my wet pants. "Let's get out of these wet clothes. It's borderline torture. Plus, Momma's expecting us all for dinner to talk about Brennan's birthday."

"Oh yeah, that's right. I forgot about dinner tonight," Raiden said. He retracted his touch almost too quickly for my liking, and I suddenly felt colder than I'd ever been before. The burning sensation returned, only this time, it was accompanied by a numbing chill, one which enveloped almost the entirety of my spine.

"Yeah. I just can't believe it's almost Brennan's birthday," I said, leading the way towards the single bedroom near the back of the building. The dogs followed close on our heels, nearly attached to the two of us like pesky fleas. "The big thirty, can you believe it? It makes me feel incredibly old. *Decrepit.*"

"That's because you *are* old," Raiden teased, earning a spiteful glare from me as he pulled his knotted brown hair into a bulbous bun at the bottom of his skull. The pair of us dispersed once we'd entered the room, flocking to our own assigned corners before thumbing through our mismatched dressers for something warm to wear.

"You can shower first, if you'd like," the man offered. I could feel his eyes on me, and I swore that I could physically see the silky black slacks that were undeniably thrown over his shoulder. After all this time, I could read Raiden like a book—I could feel the sensations that riddled his being, whether it be displeasure, fury, depression, glee. Whatever it was—whatever he *felt*—always transpired to me. Momma said it was something I'd picked up over the years I'd spent healing him, as if using my energy on him had created some kind of tether. With each and every event, the bond tightened, and she even teased that one day, I'd lose myself *in* him. It was a frightening thought—to become out of tune with your own self, your own *soul*—but I adored Raiden. He was my best friend, and he was everything I'd always wished to be. Selfless and kind, regardless of the circumstances. He was a people pleaser, a negative trait in some eyes, but a positive one in mine. He made people laugh, he evoked light and life and emotion. He was always the center of attention, and although he hated it, it was just who he was. I'd always envied him for that, for my chemical makeup was that of mostly anger and annoyance.

"You on Saturn again?" Raiden wondered, thrusting me out of my temporary trance. When I'd craned my neck to look at him, my suspicions were confirmed, for a pair of sultry black slacks were laid across his shoulder, slightly wrinkled from being stuffed up in a drawer for so long.

"Sorry," I murmured, ripping my own outfit out from the mangled mess that was my dresser. "I just have a lot on my mind today. My energy feels off."

"Maybe you're getting a new one," Raiden said, his tone light as air. "That'd be cool, wouldn't it? To get another badass power? Or maybe they're transforming, or enhancing. You'll probably be able to heal people without even being in the same room as them."

A weak smile slithered along my lips as I joined Raiden on the opposite side of the room. "You know that once we turn thirty, our energies don't change. What I have now is what I'll have until I die."

His bright eyes sparkled, and I swore I could see the galaxy within his light, lively orbs. "Yeah, I remember. It was just a fun thought. Now, go shower. I'm getting all pruny underneath these sopping wet clothes."

With a sly smile, Raiden excused himself from our shared bedroom, the creaky door clipping closed on his heel. I stared at the bundle of clothes within my arms, my work uniform still suctioned to my skin. Momma was expecting both Raiden and me for dinner in less than two hours, and if we wanted to be on time (for once), I needed to shower, and quickly.

Per usual, the water took too long to warm up, and I stood rigid beside the quaint cubicle, prickly patches of goosebumps trailed along my arms. The en-suite bathroom reminded me of something straight out of the 70's, and if it weren't a rental property, Raiden and I would've ripped the room apart years ago. The shower walls were an ungodly shade of bubblegum blue, some tiles cracked, several missing entirely. The landlord—Tally—told us she'd fix it months ago. She hardly showed her face around the property at all, so we'd given up hope on getting the broken tile fixed.

When the water was finally warm enough, I crawled into the itty-bitty box, allowing the pleasant stream to soak me down to the very bone. Just as I tangled my fingers through my messy mane of hair, the flesh encircling my fingers began to burn once more, only it wasn't from the heat of the water. No—it felt sharp, *stabbing.* With a gasp, I ripped my hands from my hair; widened eyes fixated on the reddened skin of my clammy digits. It felt as if flames were dancing upon the surface, and with each passing moment, the sensation intensified—and to my complete dismay, it *spread.* Dipping down into the innards of my palms, originating in the very center before extending outward. All I could do was stare—dark pupils the size of saucers, jaw agape in a mixture of wonder and horror. I'd never felt anything quite like it, and I swore that I could actually *see* the bright, blue veins beneath the skin of my arms begin to bulge, flushing a deep, dark scarlet. My trembling fingers curled inward, a scream cascading over my tongue as I watched the red, webby ropes dip down the length of my arms.

Before the crimson curse could continue, I tumbled out of the shower; a series of sobs slipping off of my tongue as I refused to look at the horrors that unfolded beneath the very flesh of my arms. I fell to my knees, blinding tears blurring my vision as the searing pain subsided into nothing but a tingle, enveloping the entirety of my right side and numbing my nerves.

I hadn't even noticed Raiden's presence until he was on his knees before me; widened, doe-like eyes fixated on my quivering form as he slid a towel around my naked body.

"What is it? What happened?" His voice was unusually shrill—*sharp.* It cut like knives through my skull, and an additional cry tumbled off of my tongue as I suctioned my palms to the surface of my ears, weakly attempting to ward off the incessant ringing that seemed to emerge from my best friend's lips.

Without another word, Raiden helped me to my feet; slender fingers yanking a mess of soaked curls away from my face as he led me towards the bed. My hands refused to budge from my ears, and I could feel the searing pain cascading down my legs with every step I took. I refused to look, for what I saw may prompt me to lose consciousness.

Originally, our room was divided into two sides—mine and Raiden's, respectively. We each had a full-sized bed, similar to the ones they crammed in cheap motel rooms. When they were apart, the room was incredibly tight, barely any space to move around. Less than a year ago—mainly for fun during a drunken night—we pulled the two beds together to create one big bed, just a tad-bit bigger than a king sized. We spent that night playing an abundance of card games and sharing endless giggles in our new oversized bed. Some found it odd that we shared a bed, but things between us never escalated past platonic.

I missed that night, and I missed what it was like to not be in excruciating pain. It was so severe that I'd almost forgotten what it felt like to *not* feel it. I was almost positive that at any moment, my veins would combust; ripping through my freckled flesh like butter and painting the walls red.

A boxer-clad Raiden helped me onto the bed, gently covering my shivering skin with both the towel and the blanket. His hair was still pulled back into an unbrushed bun, and as I violently shook beneath the covers, he smiled—that white, lovely, shit-eating grin—and suddenly, the pain ceased; a distant, dreary memory. He watched as I retracted my palms, his ring-clad fingers wiping the bulbous tears from my flushed cheeks as he audibly asked what had happened.

"I-I don't know," I whispered, eyeing my arm. The veins beneath my skin had returned to normal, as if nothing had happened. "There was this horrible pain in my hands, and it spread down my arm and my legs when I walked. It almost looked like the veins were swelling. I was afraid they'd burst."

Raiden's grin faded. "Has this ever happened?"

I shook my head. "I think we should call Momma. I don't feel well enough for dinner."

"I'll give her a call," he said. "My cell's in the living room, I'll be right back."

To my dismay, the discomfort returned mere moments following Raiden's departure, only this time, it started at the very tips of my toes. I ripped up the blanket to view the source of the pain, a horrified gasp tickling my tongue as the surface of my bare legs flushed a ghastly blue hue. Just as I'd feared, the veins began to protrude, the vivacious red shade sharply contrasting the blue of my legs. The swollen veins resembled the webs of a spider, inching further and further up the length of my legs, creepily crawling towards my nether regions and above.

Once more, I screamed—animatedly thrashing and kicking my legs beneath the comfort of our checkerboard duvet.

"Shit, *Freya!*" Raiden called, filing into the room with his mobile phone in hand. Instantaneously, I froze; lowering the blanket to view his horrified expression.

"Is it Momma?" I questioned, my glare glued to the phone in his hand. Wordlessly, he nodded; handing the device over to my shaking self as I steadied it against my ear and cried out for my mother.

"Il mio amore!" Momma exclaimed from over the line. The volume of her voice prompted me to pause, and I wondered how on *earth* I'd explain what had happened just moments ago.

"Momma, something weird is happening," I revealed, resisting the urge to peek beneath the covers once more. I didn't want to see it—the veins, the pulsating, the *pain.*

Raiden sat beside me, a genuine look of concern etched across his complexion as he rested a palm atop mine. His thumb curled inward, drawing continuous circles against my knuckles as my mother revealed a series of bewildering statements.

"Rai told me some, but Bren's the same way. Oh, *mia figlia*, I'm so worried! Only moments ago, he started complaining of this horrific pain in his legs, and it kept going *up up up.* He was afraid it would reach his heart and make it explode. I've never seen anything quite like it," Momma spilled. It sounded as if she'd been crying. The poor woman was probably worried sick at the sight of my brother, and now to know that *both* of her children were experiencing the very same phenomenon was probably too much for her frail, little heart to handle.

"I'm sorry if I've worried you, Momma. You aren't well enough for such worries," I murmured, threading my fingers through Raiden's.

"The cancer is gone, *bambina.* I may be sickly and tired, but I'm never ill enough to ignore my children's troubles."

The cancer. I couldn't help but tear up at the thought of it, and how we'd almost lost her to the devilish disease not once, but *twice.* It was only a matter of time before it reared its ugly head once more, and perhaps a third time's the charm.

"I don't think I'll be able to make it to dinner, Momma. I don't feel right. Can we come tomorrow, instead?" I wondered. It was then that I heard Brennan's presence from the other end. What started as a low groan had transcended into a hideous howl, one which made my skin crawl and prompted our mother to coarsely curse in her mother tongue.

"Jesus," Raiden gasped, green eyes widening at the sound of my brother's screams. "Him, too?"

"Ladybug, I have to go. Tell Raiden he better care for you, or he'll be meeting God in the morning," Momma rushed, and before I could reply, she'd hung up.

"It must be an Araedian thing," I simply said, slipping the silent cell back into Raiden's grasp. "Momma told me you'll be meeting God if you don't take care of me tonight."

Raiden snickered, dismissively tossing the phone atop the bedside table before delivering a trio of pats to my bony hip. "I'm not too keen on meeting her God, so I suppose I should take *real* good care of you. Want some warm soup to calm you down?"

"Crackers, too." I grinned, and with a shy smile, Raiden went to fetch me just that.

four

I couldn't quite recall the moment I'd slipped into a dreamless slumber, but it would be difficult for me to forget the way I'd woken up that night.

The moonlight creeped in through the pale, parted curtains, illuminating the room in an ice-cold glow. I was dressed in a pair of silky, periwinkle panties and an overly large t-shirt, the weighty duvet tediously tangled around my now normal legs. The spot beside me was empty—*lonely*—and I could clearly see the bright blue flickering of the living room television, the sleepy, intermixed hues dancing along the stark white wall just beyond the open door. It was probably sometime after midnight, and it was no surprise that Raiden was still awake. He was a night owl; sometimes staying up until half-past three, even on work nights.

Witching hour.

Only, there was nothing ordinary about the way I'd been woken. This time, there was no pain; no burning, no discomfort. No bulging veins and blue legs. No, this time was entirely divergent. Foreign. *Odd.*

It was tricky to identify the sensation at first, for it originated in a very peculiar place, and it was so unlike anything I'd ever experienced. Well, I'd *felt* it, but not like . . . *this.* Not without the assistance of my fingers, or a toy, or a stranger's invited touch.

I pulled my upper body up and onto my elbows, bewildered brows arched in wonder as the warmth between my legs ached and throbbed. Before I could fully process the situation at hand, the sensation intensified tenfold; prompting my neck to roll—*tip*—back, a moan crawling up my throat as the invisible entity continued its gentle assault on the inbetween of my legs.

What in the world–

Curious, I trailed my fingers down towards the culprit, and just as I'd grazed the hem of my underwear, a euphoric, electric shock invaded my torso, climbing *up up up* the slope of my spine.

I felt dizzy—*giddy*—as I attempted to suppress my moans, for Raiden was only just on the opposite side of the wall watching television, and the door was wide open.

Completely dumbfounded (but nevertheless intrigued), I retracted my touch from the entrance of my undergarment, rotating my palms to meet the sheets as I took the material between clenched fists. The sensation was borderline overwhelming, and whether there was a phantom or a ghost or a demon hidden between my parted legs, I wasn't quite sure—nor did I care. It'd been too long since I'd experienced such pleasure, such *lust,* and although the event was wildly unusual, I figured I may as well ride it out as long as I possibly could.

What started out as a slow, sensual massage had totally transformed, mimicking that of the erotic act of intercourse itself. It was impossible—completely *ludicrous*—but it physically felt as if there were someone between my legs, and as I rotated onto all fours on the mattress and buried my face within the pillow, I couldn't help but groan.

This wasn't happening. I was dreaming—it's the only logical explanation. A very odd, vivid dream.

The phantom's pace increased drastically, and with curled toes and an arched back, I lowly gasped; blinded by pleasure as a welcoming warmth washed over me, numbing me from head to toe. I rode the high for a solid minute, head tossed back, lips breathlessly parted as I struggled to maintain my composure. My limbs were shaking uncontrollably, and I felt weightless, *warm.* Everything was just so, so warm.

I collapsed into an exhausted heap upon the mattress, my too-large shirt suctioned to my slick skin as an abundance of invasive thoughts riddled my mind. So many *how's* and *why's* and *wHAT THE FUCK WAS THAT?*

I heard Raiden shuffling around in the kitchen immediately after, and just as I was able to finally catch my breath, he strutted into the room; a pair of drawstring pajama pants snug around his hips. His hair was washed and wavy, the loopy tendrils tickling the surface of his shoulders. He took notice of my alertness, and with a shy smile, he crawled into bed.

Within seconds, our three dogs joined us. The largest of all—our sweet, spunky Kelso—claimed his spot at my feet, giddily lapping at my covered leg. Bear laid beside his brother, resting his chin atop the curve of Kelso's bum as he released an exaggerated exhale, as if he'd had a hard day.

"You're supposed to be *sleeping,*" my human roommate purred, burying himself beneath the blankets. The smallest of the dog trio, a beagle called Mimosa, flattened herself against Raiden's back, just as she'd done every night since we'd brought her home four years prior.

I couldn't help but stare at Raiden, for he looked gleeful; *spent.* It made me wonder what he'd been up to only moments prior, and if it correlated at all with what I'd just experienced.

I opened my mouth to speak, but instead, I bit my tongue—*hard.* A metallic taste filled my senses, dribbling down my throat and prompting me to nearly retch in disgust. A sleepy Raiden took notice of my peculiar actions, and as he abruptly sat up, I waved him away, insisting that I was fine.

"You've scared me to death today, Freya." The words oozed off of his tongue, completely coated with worry. He cared for me deeply—as I did for him—but whatever this was, whatever was happening to Brennan and I, it was something out of his control. When it came to our energies, Raiden served useless; regardless of how much he wanted to help. After all, he was nothing more than an average human being, his aura and soul indefinitely tethered to mine by my mending.

It occurred almost weekly at this point. The healing. He was clumsy, childlike; thus, he was always getting into something he shouldn't, slicing his fingers and toes open, smacking his head against low-hanging objects. It was almost second nature to heal him—I found myself doing it constantly—and just as Momma predicted, with every instance, our bond intensified. Although I was *slightly* still in denial about it, tonight's episode was no coincidence. I'd never felt something so strange, so *erotic.* It was mystifying, almost. The only logical (illogical) explanation had pointed an endless array of fingers in Raiden's direction—*he'd done it he'd done it he'd done it*—and in order for me to feel such a sultry sensation must've meant that–

–had to *mean* that–

Raiden must've been touching himself.

The thought almost made me yelp, and my roommate's eyelids fluttered at the sound of my palms colliding with my gaping mouth. He was curled up beneath the blankets—lengthy locks awry around his skull—and before I could offer an explanation, he sluggishly unraveled an arm from his blanket, inching it towards my stiff self. My eyes must've been huge at this point—unblinking and wide—and an unwanted gasp tumbled over my tongue as his warm fingers danced along my shoulder.

"Go to *sleep*," he grumbled, eyelids sealing once more. He nuzzled his nose into the pillow, slender, ring-clad fingers slipping down my bare arm before encircling my wrist. Just as I'd expected, (for he'd done it a million times, the boy was so damn predictable), he tightened his grip; squeezing slightly before pulling my arm towards him. I knew him well enough to know that this meant only one thing: *come closer.*

Anxiously, I obliged, desperately attempting to brush away the thoughts of Raiden—*fondling*—himself and me *feeling every single second of it!* It made me uneasy, although I loved him to bits. I loved him, and perhaps I loved him in ways that even I'd never *thought* of, but to feel his lust—his *pleasure*—was something that I was having trouble coming to terms with.

Had I liked it?

Raiden outwardly groaned in annoyance when I'd failed to move over, and when he started to audibly complain, I obeyed orders, slowly slithering into his open arms, burrowing beneath the blankets. Instantaneously, he buried his fingers within my unbrushed hair, sweetly circling my skull with his fingertips.

Thus, the lurid thoughts dissipated. Nothing mattered in this moment, for I was safe. *Home.* I huddled against his warm body, planting my nose directly into the hollow of his throat as I'd done countless times before. He contentedly hummed, continuously etching miscellaneous shapes against my skull as the pair of us drifted into dreamland, and the lewd thoughts existed no more.

five

It was half-past two when I'd emerged from my spent slumber. I sat up in a panic; trembling fingers clawing at my itchy chin as I snatched my mobile phone from the bedside table to view the time, for Raiden's absence and the brightness of the room had already confirmed my suspicions: I'd overslept and missed my shift at work.

Why the hell did Raiden not wake me?

A snoring Kelso was still wrapped around my legs, and I quickly dialed Raiden's cell. The thought of losing my job over a few extra hours of unneeded sleep was enough to make my stomach churn. Momma would be happy, however. She claimed that I needed a real, *grown up* job at my age. That working at a Tex-Mex restaurant was inappropriate for someone in their early thirties. She probably wanted me to be an accountant, or a banker, or something more *mature.*

I cringed at the thought of having to sit behind a desk all day.

Just as the line began to ring, Raiden strutted into the bedroom; a bag full of greasy fast food pinched between his fingers. The mobile phone buried within his distressed pant pocket began to buzz, eliciting an annoying chimed ringtone.

"Rai?" I squeaked, immediately hanging up. I was relieved when the tedious tone of his own phone finally quit ringing. "Why didn't you wake me up? I'm going to get fired!"

"Relax, Freya. I let Sierra know that you were under the weather. I went in at six and did all the prep." He tossed the brown bag onto the bed, several dark, wet spheres claiming the surface where the oil from the fries had oozed through.

"My stuff's in there too, so don't be a hog and claim it all," Raiden added, running his fingers through his too-long locks before crawling into the bed beside me. By this point, the rest of the dogs had joined us; all extremely interested in what was in the sweet-smelling paper bag.

"Thanks for covering for me this morning. You must've gotten no sleep," I murmured, dividing up the food as Raiden flicked on the incredibly tiny television propped up on a table at the foot of the bed, a multitude of cords and wires left wonky and visible.

"You know that I can function on hardly any sleep at all," he coyly replied, peeling the paper away from his grilled chicken sandwich; painstakingly plain, just the way he liked it. No lettuce, no tomato, no onion. Only a thin layer of mayonnaise and chicken.

I took a bite of my hearty bacon burger as he navigated the lackluster channels, eventually settling on a rerun of *How It's Made.* Halfway through his food, he spoke up once more; mouth stuffed full with his lunch.

"Your Momma called me while I was walking home."

I raised a brow, shooing Bear away as he begged for a fry. "Oh yeah? What for?"

Raiden heavily swallowed, pausing slightly to prevent himself from choking before continuing. "She said she'd tried your cell twice. I told her you were probably still sleeping, *which you were.*"

"Yeah, yeah," I grumbled, glare fixated on the staticky television. "Get to the point."

"She postponed dinner to next Tuesday. That's when Grammy comes to town. For Brennan's birthday, and all."

I found it comical how Raiden referred to my family as his own. He had his own set of parents—adoptive, he never knew his biological family—but he preferred the company of mine. His parents were significantly older; his father on the edge of seventy-one, and his mother closer to eighty. Raiden spoke of them occasionally, and we went together to visit them when he asked, but I could tell that the topic saddened him. After all, his mother was probably in her final days, and she barely even remembered his face. She'd been suffering from dementia for nearly five years.

"She lives in Ireland now," I said, referring to my grandmother. She was quite the world traveler, even in her advanced age. She was seventy-three—she had my mother *crazy* young, like seventeen or so—but she never let any of life's obstacles slow her down. Grandaddy's death ten years ago only made her more keen on exploring, and everywhere she went, she carried his ashes around in a shiny, silver box. After all, in her old age, her energies were rendered quite useless. It only made sense to be as human as she could possibly be—and to her, being human was traveling the world, eating expensive food, and staying in Mom and Pop inns all over the globe.

"I thought it was Argentina," Raiden queried, but I only shook my head, offering Kelso my last fry when Bear wasn't looking. Bear had too weak of a stomach to eat human food.

"Argentina was three years ago. She never stays in one place too long."

We sat in silence for a few moments, watching the fuzzy television. It was old and decrepit, and we hardly used it, but it got the job done when we needed it.

I couldn't help but glance in Raiden's direction; lanky limbs laid lax against the muted yellow-splashed wall, jean-clad legs stuffed beneath the blankets. It was always ten degrees colder in this room than it was in the rest of the house, and Raiden got cold easily. The poor bloke was almost always shivering; a blanket up to his neck, extremities adorned with long-sleeved clothing. It didn't help that this particular part of Northern Canada was always so cold, too.

Although he was functioning on less than four hours of sleep, he looked bright, lively; lovely, green eyes piqued in curiosity at the content displayed on the screen. His hair was combed and curly, especially around the ears. I teased him about the length consistently, but truth be told—I never wanted him to cut it. He looked damn good with long hair. It framed his face nicely, highlighting his striking features. He was so pretty that it was almost effortless. I envied him and his natural beauty. Others, like myself, actually had to *try* to look attractive. Raiden just rolled out of bed and existed and he just—*was.*

"Are you feeling any better?" His soft, shy tone thrust me from my awkward trance, and I couldn't help but notice how the heat rose to my cheeks. He'd totally caught me staring, and the tantalizing thoughts of *last night* kept tip-toeing their way back into my mind. The way I'd physically *felt* what he'd done to himself. It was morbid—*sick*—and even though I couldn't control what had happened, I felt guilty. *Gross.* Like I'd eavesdropped on something significant, something for *his eyes only.*

"Frey . . ?"

"Yeah." The word emerged like venom, and I noticed the way his lips downturned into a frown at my harsh tone. "Sorry. I'm fine. Just thinking of some stuff."

"If you're well enough, I was wondering if you want to accompany me to Lakeview?"

Lakeview. The nursing home that held and cared for his elderly adoptive parents. The thought of seeing his poor, pitiful mother made me feel slightly sick. Raiden tends to slip into a deeply depressive state after every visit with her. We both knew that her days were numbered by now. It was only a matter of time before one of these visits would be the very last.

I forced a smile and a nod, chest aching at the thought of seeing Ethel Crow once more. It'd been nearly four months since I've seen her, and according to Raiden, she'd worsened significantly. He'd gone alone the past two times, and I'll never forget the way he looked that day when he'd walked in the door—empty, numb; as if Ethel had sucked the life—the *youth*—right out of him. It took almost a week for him to act like Raiden again.

My palm met his forearm, and I couldn't help but genuinely grin at the sight of his smile. "Yeah. Sure. We can go."

six

For some peculiar reason, Lakeview reeked of almond butter. What was once a scent I admired, I now thoroughly loathed, for every time I inhaled the nutty scent, I knew what would follow: a melancholy Raiden, who would hardly leave the bed except to work for days to come.

Before we crossed the threshold, I took his hand; squeezing it tight as the automatic doors slid open, our senses immediately invaded by the atrocious almond scent. A forced burst of air from the doors sent Raiden's long locks awry, whereas my thick hair remained intact; pulled back by the assistance of a pretentious, blue bow. My brother, Brennan, used to tease me for wearing such puerile objects in my hair—*you're a grown woman for God's sake*—but Raiden claimed to like the trinkets, and even assisted me in adding them to my messy mane.

I recognized the youthful man at reception almost immediately; big, blue eyes and wicked, red curls. He was eccentric—*handsome.* I felt the heat creep up to my cheeks when he'd acknowledged our presence, a freckled arm raising as he waved us over.

"Hey, Raiden." The greeting slipped off of his plump lips with ease, and I ineptly diverted my stare as he and Raiden shook hands. Suddenly, my palm felt empty. *Cold.* I missed the feeling of his reassurance, his warmth.

"Afternoon, Baylor. Remember my best friend, Freya? It's been awhile since she's accompanied me." Raiden politely introduced me, a sneaky hand coiling around my lower back. I debated brushing him away in fear of Baylor catching a glimpse, for he'd most certainly misinterpret Raiden's incredibly innocent touch as something more . . . *serious.* Romantic, even. I dismissed the sensation of many brutal butterflies creeping up my spine as I offered up my hand for a small shake.

With a broad smile, Baylor complied; taking my cold hand in his before weakly shaking. He had a pitiful grip. "Good to have you back, Freya. Ethel will be pleased to see you both. They're actually finishing up her shower as we speak, but if you're comfortable with it, you can go ahead and go back there."

"Yeah, great. That'd be great," Raiden murmured, scratching at his skull before grabbing my hand once more. "Hey, uh, who is this?"

Baylor's gaze met the frail, little lady sat snug in a wheelchair beside him, her nimble fingers threading through a plethora of paperwork. She failed to overhear Raiden's inquiry, and instead, she simply adjusted her periwinkle pink glasses and continued on.

"Oh." Baylor grinned, nudging the elderly woman's shoulder with his knuckles. "Nettie, my friends Raiden and Freya want to meet you!"

An unexpected tone emerged from the lithe lady called Nettie; hoarse, heavy. She sounded irritable and slightly angry. "Tell them to come back later. I'm goddamn busy."

Baylor's features flushed, rosy, red lips parted as he ushered a series of apologies our way. Raiden assured him that it was okay—*another time, maybe*—and he started towards the suites, grip tightening around my hand as he led me towards Ethel's room. She resided in

403B, directly beside her husband's slightly smaller space, 405B. From what I'd been told, Ethel and Stephen spent every morning and afternoon together, until retiring to their separate rooms for the evening.

Ethel couldn't even tell her husband Stephen apart from the other elderly men. Most days, Raiden said, she'd even shunned him—repulsed by the idea of having to socialize with some stranger. Only, he was anything but: they'd been married forty-one years.

"Dad says Mom's been having a hard time lately," Raiden began, arriving upon Ethel's sealed door. Her name was etched in a red, cartoonish font along a laminated sheet of paper, suctioned to the door by the assistance of some strong sticky tack.

"Hard time how?" I countered, but as soon as the door opened, my inquiry was answered.

Ethel was stark naked, sagging skin flushed an angry, red hue. She was screaming at the top of her lungs, bitterly batting away the sympathetic touch of her bathing assistant—a tall, thin woman with a blonde ponytail and completely soaked clothes.

"I can do it *myself!* You've already done plenty!" Ethel exploded, palms flattening against the younger woman's chest as she bitterly shoved. The timid lady stumbled and nearly fell over a nearby table, an estranged shout ricocheting off the echoic walls as Raiden ripped out of my grasp.

"Jesus, Ma!" he exclaimed, scurrying forward in order to assist the worker in tending to his adoptive mother. I half expected Ethel to magically recognize her chosen son, but instead, the volume of her yells increased, along with a multitude of painstaking words, varying from *creep* to *pervert* to *get the hell out!*

I felt for Raiden, I truly did. My chest ached as I watched the scene unfold, limbs locked in place near the open door. At this point, several additional workers filed into the room, eyes all widening as they observed a poor, old Ethel hovering over her wheelchair wearing nothing but her birthday suit. Although she wouldn't remember this moment by morning, I felt my cheeks flush at the sheer thought of enduring such an event—to be naked and erratic in front of so many people. I felt sick, and as the additional assistants came to her aid, I excused myself from the room. Trembling fingers encircling the frigid door handle, I yanked the portal closed, encasing both Raiden and his mother in their anxious tomb.

With a small cry, I collapsed to my knees; an unidentifiable sensation consuming me fully as my slick, sweaty nose met the musty carpet. With shaking palms suctioned to my ears, I cried; unashamedly embracing the sudden, sharp pain buried within the cavity of my heart. An abundance of emotions took over at once—humiliation, anger, heartbreak. I knew damn well that the sensations were not mine, nor did I have the permission to feel them so fully. No, these were Raiden's emotions, and I was absorbing them like some sort of sopping sponge.

It was overwhelming, and regardless of how much I tried to block them out, they continued to penetrate my every pore; filling me up entirely until I was nothing but a buzzing ball of Raiden's entire being. It was entirely inappropriate—*so wrong*—but I felt out of touch with my very soul, *no longer in tune.* It was an out of body experience, and I felt as if I were nothing but a spectator, observing my crumbling self on the carpet, diminished to a pitiful, little ball on my knees.

Make it stop.

Block it out.

A blinding array of hues invaded my vision—striking streaks of blue and green, somber and sadness. The blues variated immensely, and with every shade that arrived, I could feel the sorrow—the *hurt*—penetrating down to my very core. I felt helpless; *weak.* In some peculiar sense, it almost felt as if I may be dying. Only instead of seeing some bright, white light, I saw nothing but blue.

His touch pulled me out of it.

It was gentle, *soft.* Warm, wide hands dipped down towards my face, a hooked finger sliding beneath my chin as he forced my gaze upwards. Once our eyes met, the sensations seemed to fade entirely, as if they never even existed in the first place. What was left in their place was a boastful buzz, warming me down to the very tips of my toes as a worrisome Raiden cupped my flushed, sunken cheeks.

"Frey," he breathed, sorrow etched along his expression. A single tear slipped from his left eye, cascading down the apple of his reddened cheek. I bit back the urge to wipe it away. "What is it? What's happened? Is the pain back?"

"Rai," I gasped, unable to control the sudden shakes that consumed my being. Suddenly, it felt impossible to function, and the swirling in my stomach was a warning sign that I'd soon be sick.

"M'gonna . . . *sick–*"

With widened, watering eyes, Raiden let go of my face; scurrying towards the small trash tin halfway down the hall. By the time he'd rushed it to my side, I'd missed half of the can—emptying the contents of my stomach (and the greasy lunch I'd unfortunately consumed) along the hideous, mahogany carpet.

Before I could glance up to view Raiden, he'd disappeared. It wasn't much of a surprise, the poor guy couldn't handle vomit in the slightest. Sometimes, the thought of it alone would send him into a panicked frenzy, and suddenly, I felt as if I'd ruined everything. Not only did I inappropriately feed off of his emotions (unintentionally, may I add), I also managed to completely soil his visit with his mother, who was already in a sour mood as it was. I wanted to scream—to *cry*—for lately, I couldn't even control my own body. It was as if I was slowly draining the life from Raiden—sucking up his every sensation until he was nothing but an empty, cracked shell. The thought of gradually murdering my best friend was enough to prompt an additional round of sickness to travel up my esophagus, and this time, one of Lakeview's workers had the pleasure of watching, whilst calling for a janitor to help clean up the mess I'd made.

By the time my stomach had settled and I was ready to join the land of the living—a cool cup of water in hand—Raiden's mother was completely calm. The pair of them were isolated within her quarters, her caregiver momentarily absent for a short lunch break. The poor soul who cleaned up my wretched mess tiresomely pried, insisting that I stay seated in the waiting room in case of illness. After reassuring the bug-eyed boy that I was—in fact—absolutely *fine,* he finally let me join my best friend, who needed me now more than ever.

Ethel's room differed from most. Her husband Stephen's space, for example, looked and reeked like a stereotypical nursing home—a distinct lack of color, the absence of photographs, love, life. It almost resembled a grand hospital room, tiny television and all. The only thing present in his individual room that actually signified a sense of life was a stack of nearly a hundred newspapers. He refused to toss any out, and Raiden said that Stephen often skimmed over old articles simply out of boredom. On the other hand, his other half—a sweet, red-faced Ethel—lived in paradise: lovingly surrounded by a surplus of framed photographs, almost all of them including Raiden's dapper grin. Strategically placed on the tiny table beside her bed was Raiden's graduation photo; a mustard yellow cap and gown, rolled diploma pinched between loose fingers, and the biggest, brightest smile I'd ever laid eyes on. One so large that it even made his bulging eyes squint.

When I'd entered the premises, Ethel was curled up in bed, her favorite red, knitted blanket pulled all the way up to her neck. She'd always been rather large, but following several illnesses over the past few years, she'd dropped easily over thirty pounds. From what I'd gotten a glimpse of only half an hour earlier, the fickle flesh that adorned her aging frame was wrinkled and warped, the clear evidence of her sudden and dramatic weight loss. Although she was elderly, she looked almost ten years past her age; her dark, diminutive eyes nearly sunken into her skull. Her lips were cracked and dry, and it was difficult to avoid the gaudy, purple bruise that claimed her left cheek. She looked worse for wear, and my heart physically hurt at the sight of Raiden's mother in such pitiful shape.

I wished more than anything that I could cure her from the inside out, but my energy seemed to only work on wounds of the flesh. Something as complicated as Alzheimer's (and my mother's cancer) practically rendered my powers useless.

"Rai," I cooed, my voice barely above a whisper. He was seated beside Ethel's bed, bottom planted firmly in a cracked, plastic chair. He had his back to me, but I could clearly see the way he torturously trembled, elbows suctioned to his knobby knees, reddened face buried within his palms. He'd been crying, no doubt, and Ethel remained unphased; empty, ebbing eyes glued to the whiny television on the wall. I wasn't even sure if she'd noticed my presence.

With a sigh, I dismissively discarded the empty cup into a nearby trash can, cautiously approaching my distressed friend as Ethel remained fixated on some old rerun of a show I'd never come to know. Raiden remained silent, but I knew that the moment he would lift his head, his eyes would be puffy; *swollen.* I was almost afraid to see just how red they'd become.

"Rai, baby." His name tickled my tongue as I fell to my knees before him, quivering digits traveling up the length of his arm before gently prying his fingers away from his face, one by one. Begrudgingly, he obeyed; ripping his hands away from his flushed skin before collapsing against the back of the chair. Just as I'd suspected, his bug-eyed stare was almost as red as his mother's homemade blanket.

"She's pretty upset today. Dorothy, her caregiver, was able to convince her to have a small sponge bath in bed while you were gone," Raiden revealed, his tone low and hoarse. Guilt instantaneously flooded my entire being, and the thought of my mental breakdown nearly an hour prior made me cringe.

I glanced over my shoulder to view Ethel, who hadn't moved an inch since my entrance. She looked empty, cold; like a frozen statue, her features transformed to stone. She was barely recognizable, and the Ethel Crow I'd once known had been reduced down to nothingness. Nothing remained but her physical form, which was deteriorating by the day. Raiden mentioned months prior that she was well on her way to becoming catatonic.

My lips parted in preparation to speak, but when words failed, Raiden spoke. "Come here, Freya. On my lap. I need you."

With words unspoken, I slithered onto Raiden's warm lap, my back suctioning to his front as his long, slender arms warped their way around my midsection. A tender sigh of relief danced along the exposed area of my shoulder, and I couldn't help but slightly smile when I felt his pointed nose bury itself into my skin.

"Have the pair of you exchanged words?" I whispered, threading my fingers through his.

"Barely," he said, the words hot against my neck. "She's only said one word so far: Tubman. I don't know of any Tubman, except like Harriet Tubman I guess. She seems awfully fixated on that episode of Andy Griffith, though. She might remember it, or it's familiar to her."

I turned my head to meet Raiden's stare, the tips of our noses meeting in a small, shy kiss. A blush creeped up my neck as I hastily pulled away, our close proximity sending tingles down my spine. Sure, personal space between the pair of us was usually nonexistent, but something about that moment felt unusually intimate. When I'd diverted my stare, I was met by the ice-cold gaze of one Ethel Crow, thin, peeling lips pulled back into a scowl. At the sheer sight of her expression, our incredibly idyllic moment woefully transformed into a stiff scenario. I almost felt awkward at the fact that I was sat upon his lap, and her statement confirmed my hunch.

"Heather, get off of your brother."

I felt Raiden uncomfortably shift beneath me, his fingers unraveling from mine before settling upon each of my hips.

"Momma, this is Freya, remember?" Raiden sweetly said. "She's been my best friend for over twenty years."

Ethel's expression hardened, and if looks could kill, I'd be dead twice over by now.

I crawled off of Raiden's lap, falling to my knees beside Ethel's bed. I couldn't help but frown when Ethel shot me a scolding glare, and it was evident that she thought I was someone called Heather, and Raiden was evidently Heather's brother. Only, Raiden was a single child. Ethel and Stephen were never able to have any of their own, hence the reason they adopted him.

"Who's Heather, Ethel?" I wondered, fingers creeping up towards her crossed palms. Bitterly, she yanked away; burying her wrinkled hands beneath the blanket. I wanted to suction my palm to her cheek—to heal that horrid bruise of hers—but if she wouldn't let me touch her hands, she definitely would not allow me near her face.

"Aunt Heather," Raiden muttered, saddened glare downcast. I glanced up to view his somber stare, and he flinched when my warm palm met the clothed flesh of his knee.

"What?" I requested, unsure if I'd heard him correctly.

"Aunt Heather," he confirmed. "Momma has a sister named Heather, and a brother named Nathaniel. She must think that we're them. She hasn't seen them in years, so she only remembers them as our age, I think."

"Heather," Ethel grumbled, lengthy nails digging against the frayed flesh of her palm. It appeared as if her eczema was acting up once more. "Heather, Heather, *Heather.* Have you seen my son, Heather? My son. His name . . . *Raiden.*"

Joyously, I met my best friend's empty expression, standing to my feet as I coiled my arms around his neck. However, Raiden didn't seem amused in the slightest, not even cracking a smile at the fact that his name had slipped off of Ethel's lips.

Sharply, Raiden yanked out of my consoling touch, leaning forward to rest his palms on Ethel's bed. "Momma, it *is* me. It's Raiden. Your son."

"Left Canada," she replied, shaking her head. "Left. Left Canada."

"I didn't leave Canada. I'm right here, Mommy. I haven't gone anywhere," Raiden protested, his tone wavering. He was on the verge of tears.

I backed myself up against the wall, arms tautly crossed as I nibbled away at the nail of my thumb. It was a filthy habit—biting my nails—but I did it most in times of distress, and seeing Raiden so worked up over his mother almost always pushed me over the edge. It was only a matter of time before I succumbed to a panic attack once more.

I didn't do well with illness. Death. Despair. It made me uncomfortable, *anxious*. I was a distressed wreck nearly the entirety of my mother's cancer experience, (well, *both* times), and Raiden had his fair share of scooping my trembling, naked body off of the shower floor.

Raiden claimed Ethel's hand in his, a trail of slimy snot dripping down onto the curve of his upper lip as he promptly wiped it away with the shoulder of his shirt. He pressed a sealed-lip smooch to her knuckles, which were cocooned between his gentle, wide hands. Although Ethel thought Raiden was actually her brother, Nathaniel, she seemed happy; content. Her bleak glare softened, a small smile dancing across her lips as she softly spoke.

"Raiden wouldn't leave me. Wouldn't leave Canada. Would he, Nathan?"

"No, Momma," Raiden pressed, his voice cracking over several syllables, "No. He wouldn't leave you. He'll be by your side until the very end."

Ethel paused, glancing my way once more before tugging her lips into a big, broad smile. "I love my son."

A forced burst of air emerged from Raiden's nostrils, a staccato of chuckles easing off of his bulbous lips. He buried his nose into the crook of their conjoined hands, obscenely long locks encasing his reddened complexion as he remained in that position for what seemed like an eternity. Completely content, Ethel allowed him to sob into her lap; brightened, lively eyes meeting my stiff stare. Once more, her lips peeled away to reveal a precious proclamation.

"I love you, Raiden."

seven

As I'd feared, Raiden managed to capitulate to his typical dismal state following our visit with his parents.

We both had weekends off from work, which meant that the next two days would consist of him barely sleeping, hardly eating, and frequently bathing. By the cusp of midnight, he'd taken two showers; drenched, unbrushed hair dismissively pulled back into a knotty bun at the base of his skull and a pair of mismatched pajamas slapped across his lean frame. He lounged across the sofa, a cozy, cerulean blanket tangled around his tiny torso. Usually we'd lay on opposite sides of the couch, lanky legs overlapping beneath the blankets, one or two of the dogs curled into bitty balls atop our laps. Tonight, I avoided the cozy piece of furniture entirely, and instead I sat in an old leather barcalounger, the material ripped and cracked. It was an old piece of my childhood, and regardless of how much Raiden begged me to toss it out, I couldn't bear to part with it. After all, I'd sat in this very same chair since the day my mother brought me home from the hospital, infantile frame wrapped up in the warmth of a charming, orange blanket, one too large for my small size—it had nearly swallowed me whole, and my exhausted mother continuously pried the material away from my face as I slept.

Raiden was watching some old war movie, but I was busy studying him. He hardly noticed, it seemed, and the aging, yellowed book atop my knees was nothing but a prop. I was watching him—slyly, of course—making sure that he wasn't slowly succumbing to his inner demons. He smoked five entire cigarettes on the way home, and the tangy, tobacco scent stuck to his skin like sweat.

He was afraid, and I sympathized with him. He was afraid of losing his mother, the woman who chose him, who *rescued* him. The one who took him in when his own birth mother abandoned him, disappearing without a note, without a trace. As if she didn't even exist. He knew nothing of her—not a face, not a name. She was merely a phantom, a figment of his imagination. Surely he shared several of her physical features, or perhaps he mirrored those of his biological father. It was a fact that he'd never come to know.

"Stop looking at me," Raiden hissed, running his palm along Mimosa's back. He was so dainty, diminutive; people often mistook him for being far younger than he really was. Perhaps it was his height—barely grazing five-foot seven, if even—and his sheer size, so skinny and taut. Naturally fit, with a tone that most would despise him for. I couldn't even recall the last time he'd touched a pair of weights or even ran on a treadmill.

"We don't have to discuss today, if that's what's getting you so down," I pressed, discarding the forgotten book onto the bleak, red-stained table directly beside my chair. The paint was worn and worse for wear, and Raiden was constantly reminding me to take it outside and respray it.

"We don't need to discuss anything," he replied, easing his curled thumb into the depths of his mouth. With a frown, I watched him nibble and gnaw on the nail; a deep wrinkle enveloping the inbetween of his brows. He looked deep in thought, and I couldn't help but wonder what he could possibly be dwelling over.

Mimosa nudged her wet nose at his hand, politely urging him to withdraw it from his clamped teeth. Raiden only grumbled in response, lightly shoving the animal away. I opened my mouth to scold him for doing so, but almost instantaneously bit my tongue. Nothing good would come of it, anyways.

Timidly, I shifted the subject, desperately hoping to get some kind of positive reaction out of the man. "I'm hungry. Want a midnight snack?"

"Nope," Raiden clipped, leaning forward on the sofa to snatch the remote from the spotless coffee table. He increased the volume of the program, and I almost took offense to the thought of him trying to drown out the sound of my voice.

Dismissively, I stood; kicking the recliner closed as all three dogs leapt up from their positions and followed me into the kitchen. I hated this damn kitchen with all of my being—the crusty, old tile, the hideous, lime green cabinets. Oddly, the countertop was made of a dazzling white marble, the only acceptable part of the tiny space. The oven was outdated, old, and difficult to clean. The refrigerator was new, only because the previous one quit working one night and diminished all of our fresh food into nothing but a moldy mess. I was paranoid of the instance recurring, and even though Raiden insisted that this fridge was significantly better than the last, I kept both the fridge and the freezer stocked with thermometers, which I checked every morning before breakfast. Once, the freezer hit a positive two degrees and I woke Raiden up in a frenzied panic—*the fridge has gone bad!*—only for him to dramatically sigh and adjust the controls, stating that they must've been bumped when we were filling the compartment.

We'd been through so much together over the past decade. Momma always joked that we were one person—one soul severed into two separate beings. Although I'd always brushed the statement off as if it were nothing, recent events proved it to be factual. Regardless of how hard I tried to shove the carnal recollection aside, it persisted;

plaguing my mind, swallowing it whole. Admittedly, I'd never thought of Raiden in such a hedonistic way; for we were nothing more than friends—*pals.* Nevertheless, I'd *felt* his late-night escapade as if it were my own. I'd been crushed betwixt the desire to ride out the sensation, or ignore it entirely, and to my dismay, I'd completely ignored the latter and I let it absorb my every atom, reveling in the feel of what Raiden—*my shy, precious Raiden*—had experienced in the very next room.

A delightful heat invaded my belly, dipping down the length of my legs as a tacky, old mug drifted between weakened fingers and fell to my feet; decorating the blackened abyss in an array of chunky glass.

"Freya?" Raiden called, his low tone muffled by the adjoining wall.

"It's fine!" I exclaimed, a tremble enveloping my spine as I blindly avoided the rubble, inching over towards the light switch. "I'm fine! I just accidentally dropped one of those old mugs from the thrift shop that we got years ago."

The luminous, white lights danced along the paper-white walls, the evidence of my error now evident across the floor. I was lucky that I hadn't stepped on any of the sharp shards, and Kelso's lengthy, pink tongue nearly nicked one of the larger chunks.

"Stop, *out!*" The statement emerged as a sharp scold, and Kelso's poor, defeated expression immediately made my heart sink. I was no better than Raiden, who'd bitterly shoved Mimosa away for simply wanting to comfort him.

I fell to my bottom, arms outstretched as I beckoned the big dog forward. Giddily, he skipped into my arms, nearly sending me backwards onto the pointy mound that once was a mug. "I love you. I'm sorry."

By the time I'd cleaned up my mess and returned to the living room—a strawberry frosted Pop-Tart in tow—Raiden had shifted his position on the sofa; his damp, disorderly curls dangled over his face. An amused chuckle crawled up my throat as I studied his surplus of uncombed hair, and I wanted to announce that he reminded me of Cousin It from *The Addams Family.* Hell, his hair was thicker than mine, and I was Italian.

Taking my seat once more—a trio of dogs hounding my spot in search of a snack—I tore open the foil, revealing the tasty treats. With a smile, I broke off three tiny pieces, feeding each of them to the begging, drooling dogs. Raiden still had his hair fanned over his face, slender fingers knotting around the strands as he weakly attempted to brush through the abundance of knots.

"Can I braid it?" I asked, mouth full of the strawberry snack. When Raiden failed to reply, I repeated my question.

"God, Frey," Raiden hissed, smoothing his palm along his hair and removing it from his testy complexion. "I don't feel like talking tonight, okay? Just leave me be. Don't make me sleep on the couch just to have some peace."

A peeved heat rose up to my cheeks, painting my features a wrathful scarlet as I discarded my midnight snack atop the table. Within seconds, a giant Kelso demolished what remained, but my attention was exclusively fixated on Raiden—a pissy, aloof Raiden—and quite frankly, the sight of him made my insides boil.

"What the hell is your problem?" The interrogation arose like vomit, spilling over my tainted tongue as I climbed to my feet. "I get that you're feeling down, and you're upset about Ethel, but you don't have to be so–"

"Shut *up!"* Raiden exploded, clammy palms suctioning to his ears, charming, green eyes screwed shut in angst. I wondered if he were referring to me, or perhaps a slew of unknown voices in his skull.

"Rai–"

I watched with widened eyes as he stood, quivering hands dropping to his sides and contorting into taut fists. I mirrored his actions, fingers curling inward toward my palms, unkempt nails piercing the soft skin. A series of inquiries oozed up my throat and exploded over my tongue, bombarding Raiden as he tightened his grip and released a vengeful shout, one which tightened my chest and generated a flurry of fury to erupt within my being.

Upon the coffee table sat a glass vase, wonky, warped, and sprinkled with a sequence of kaleidoscopic colors. It was one of Raiden's favorite collectibles—aged nearly fifty years, evidently—and it currently held a bouquet of fresh white lilies.

During Raiden's sudden outburst, my attention was curiously diverted to meet said vase, and I could almost feel Raiden's fury, his *rage.* The sensation wrapped around my spine, sharply squeezing—*suffocating*—and as Raiden released that dreaded, sour shout, the ringing began. Low, clamorous. My fists tightened as I whined, a guttural gasp tickling the shell of my ear—*a whisper*—and then, it exploded.

A million tiny pieces, a surfeit of fetid water. Busted bulbs of lifeless lilies, damp petals suctioned to my toes. The carpet was drenched—*soiled*—and there was so much glass around my bare feet that I wasn't quite sure where I could safely step without being cut. The variegated colors were nothing but a memory as they laid demolished at my feet. Thus, the burning commenced; the freckled flesh along my hands and arms lighting up like that of a flickering flame. I openly gasped, and Raiden issued a string of obscenities; excusing himself to the cupboard to locate a dustpan and broom.

Gradually, I extended my fingers; doe-like stare studying the reddened flesh across my palms as I struggled to catch my breath. It was impossible—*preposterous.* I was thirty-three, my energies were solidified, *set.* It was impossible for them to alter this late in the game. I was a Mender, I couldn't move things—*break* things. Something wasn't entirely . . . *right.*

When Raiden returned, I burst into tears.

"Don't move," he whispered, falling to his knees to scoop the glass shards into the navy plastic pan. Although he didn't voice it aloud, I knew that he was upset. Beyond that, even. I'd broken one of his favorite collectibles.

"I'm so sorry, Raiden. I don't know what happened!" I exclaimed, hot tears cascading down the swollen apples of my cheeks. "I don't know what this is. I–I don't know what's happening. I feel so out of control, and I'm not a Shifter or whatever the hell this is . . . I'm a *Mender,* Rai. I d-don't . . . I don't *break* things–"

"Freya, it's fine," Raiden clipped, pausing briefly to glance up at my distressed features. I covered my mouth with my hands to muffle my sobs, but that only seemed to escalate them further.

"I–I need to see my M-Momma. I think she can help."

"Can it wait 'til Tuesday? That's when our dinner is, and Grammy will be there then," Raiden said, ridding the carpet of the remainder of the glass. "I think I got it all. I'll vacuum just to be sure."

I nodded, stepping sideways and away from the crime scene. The tears refused to cease, and as Raiden stood to his feet—a tray full of broken glass in hand—I couldn't resist the urge to wrap my arms around his neck. He stiffened upon impact, a soft sigh tickling my forehead as he awkwardly wormed his free arm around my waist.

"Go to bed, Frey. I'll clean the rest of this up." With that, he practically shoved me away; the sound of shifting glass made me squirm as he disappeared into the kitchen.

I directed the dogs around the soiled spot, leading them towards the bedroom across the hall. I stole one last look at Raiden as he trudged into the living room with the vacuum, his expression unreadable. My heart hurt horribly, and I wondered if he'd hated me for what I'd done to his vase.

Raiden slept on the sofa that night, and I cried myself to sleep against the fuzzy fur of Mimosa's chest.

eight

The elderly engine whined endlessly, signalling that it was near the end of its life. It wasn't much of a shock, considering the car wasn't even new when my parents gifted it to me on my sixteenth birthday. Now, seventeen years later, it was ready to retire, regardless of how much I'd put it off.

"I think it's time," Raiden muttered, twiddling his thumbs. I killed the motor, jerking the keys from the ignition as I glanced in his direction. On his lap was a periwinkle box, accented with a bulbous, white bow. He had a habit of bringing gifts over for my mother everytime she hosted supper.

"Time for what?" I countered, gliding my calloused thumb along the length of a stunning silver key.

"Time for a new car," he clarified, a slight snicker present in his tone. "We have plenty of money for one. Hell, we have enough to buy a brand new vehicle for each of us. Not that we need more than one, but still."

With a wordless nod, I reached over the console, freckled arm dipping down towards Raiden's feet as I snatched up the fallen bag beside his left leg. Half of the contents of my purse were scattered along the floorboard, and with a hefty huff, I slithered across Raiden's lap to retrieve the miscellaneous items.

"Sorry," I grumbled, swiftly shoving everything back into my cheap leather purse. I distinctly felt Raiden's lanky legs stiffen beneath my elbows, and I avoided meeting his certainly gauche glare as I straightened my posture. "But yeah, I agree. Electric's had a good run, but his retirement is imminent. I'm surprised he even starts anymore."

When Raiden failed to respond, I craned my neck; submitting to the overwhelming urge to just—*look.* I felt as if I'd hardly done that as of late. The past few days had been . . . inept. We hardly spoke. We ate our meals in silence in front of the roaring television. Both of us refused to acknowledge the broken vase, and tears still pricked my dark eyes at the recollection of the grievous bundle of white lilies that I'd found at the top of the trash the following morning. I took a long shower immediately after—knees pulled to my chest, curled spine suctioned to the shower wall. The thunderous howl of the shower had veiled my wails, and I could barely look Raiden in the eye that day.

Yesterday was the first time we'd really, *truly* spoken. He was back down to showering only once a day, and the dismal, looming cloud that hovered his skull incrementally dispersed. By now, it appeared to have evaporated entirely, and apart from his inert expression, he seemed to be himself once more.

Hopefully.

"Go ahead and go inside," Raiden whispered, threading his index finger through a particularly large loop in the bow. "I'll join you in just a second."

Words eluding me, I nodded; slithering my arm through the busted strap of my purse. I rotated my upper frame to view the back seat, where a foggy glass baking dish sat, a wrinkled piece of foil stretched across the top. With a nod, I evacuated the vehicle; my purse irritatingly slipping down the slope of my elbow as I struggled to hold the fresh baked dish. I gave Raiden one final glance as I rounded the hood, peering at him through the warped windshield. His gaze was downcast, plump bottom lip pinched between gnawing teeth. Something was bothering him deeply, and I wondered when he'd finally let it spill. Although the vase incident certainly upset him, there was no possible way that he was still *that* troubled over it.

My parents' house was always thoroughly kept; the bright bushes neatly trimmed, the flowers freshly watered. They changed the exterior concrete color every five years, and it appeared as if I'd have to stare at the ghastly, blue walls for at least three more years.

Sigh.

My curled knuckles met the posh front door—mahogany hued, shiny and sweet—and my mother ripped open the entrance before my fist had even left the surface.

She was mid-laugh, her cherry red, artificial curls swept aside by the abrupt burst of outside air. She was taller than I—standing nearly five-foot-nine—and the basic, blue apron flattened against her torso looked like a garment that was specifically made for a child. It barely grazed the curve of her belt, and strutted the simplistic slogan *Kiss The Cook.*

"*Salve, Mammina,*" I merrily greeted, extending my arms to show off the fresh baked goods balanced atop my palms. "I come bearing gifts."

Brushing her realistic false hair aside with fingers full of eccentric rings, my mother, Gaia Gallo, embraced me in a tight squeeze; a staccato of kisses smeared along my jaw as I openly scowled.

"Momma, *Momma!*" I exclaimed. "That's enough, you're smearing my foundation."

"Okay, okay—*mi arrendo.* What'd you bring?" The jubilant woman grumbled, unraveling her arms from my pointed shoulders. A series of splendid hues danced along the shiny foil as her ring-clad fingers pried open the left corner, desperately peeking at its contents.

"Vanilla brownies," I replied, handing over the dish. "With M&M's. They call them blondies."

"Yum," Momma purred, slithering her lengthy index finger and thumb into the platter before extracting a crumb and tossing it into her mouth, careful not to smudge her coral colored lipstick. "It tastes wonderful, honey. Come inside, come! Brennan's on the couch playing God-knows-what, Grammy's freshening up, Daddy's on some silly conference call that'll probably last halfway through the meal. It's a typical Gallo evening, you know the drill. Hey, where's Raiden?"

I kicked the door closed with my heel, not bothering to look over my shoulder to see if Raiden had approached the entrance. I knew damn well that he was still seated in the stuffy cabin.

"He'll be in soon. He's on a call."

Momma raised a bold brow. "Oh! Lovely, lovely. I'm going to put this in the kitchen, go frolic about with your younger brother. He'll be a true, Araedian man in less than two weeks' time!"

With that, Momma rounded the corner and vanished, a lazy hum tickling her lips as she walked. The anxiety that consumed my entire being for the past few days seemed to dissipate the moment I strolled over the threshold, for alas, I was home.

With a peaceful exhale, I discarded my purse, unintentionally knocking over a few of my father's trinkets strewn along the cocoa cabinet. He was a hoarder, the polar opposite of my mother—a woman who would scrub the toilets with bleach even when the virulent chemotherapy left her shaky and spent, weak and worn. She was lucky that Brennan was home the day she collapsed from the fumes after her very first treatment session. Momma got sick once, scrubbed the toilet, then promptly lost consciousness from the strong scent. The memories of her illness and treatment were almost unbearable to recall. We could only hope that she'd remain in remission until her skin wrinkles and sags.

Just as my mother described, Brennan sat upon the hazel leather sofa, elbows balanced atop his knobby knees as his fingers speedily navigated the Xbox controller. He looked like a typical young man, all but for the horde of inanimate objects gradually rotating above his head. The randomized items were spaced evenly apart, revolving around an invisible turntable at an incredibly slow speed. They were completely dissimilar, ranging from a half-eaten apple to a scratched game disk. I was able to distinguish both a dull pencil and a black ball-point pen, and even a partially sipped water bottle. It was random and odd, but it was entirely Brennan.

"You couldn't finish the apple?" I joked, snatching the fruit from the rotating ring. The other objects maintained momentum, continuously spinning as if nothing was missing. Brennan lowly laughed as I took a bite out of the ripe apple, avoiding the spot where his slobber probably still resided. I could barely hear my thoughts over the television's obscene volume, a multitude of faux gunshots echoing within my ears.

"Where's Raiden?" My brother queried, an arm darting up to snatch the apple from my hold. His question was answered the moment his mouth met the fruit, and in came Raiden; a hand in his hair, lips downturned in a frown. The sleeves of his plum button-up were chaotically rolled and hooked behind dry elbows, and the collar of said shirt was slightly crooked. It was only a matter of time before my mother would chant Raiden's name and fix up his haggard appearance. He looked exactly how I felt—troubled. *Cold.*

Upon Raiden's timid entrance, Brennan paused his game; the objects neatly fluttering to the floor around him as he tossed the controller aside and jumped to his feet.

"Rai!" Brennan called, a wide grin slapped across his mouth. He was in desperate need of a haircut—his hair wasn't nearly as nice as Raiden's and grew awkward and rugged—but nevertheless, he refused to trim it, insisting that it looked *just fine.* I chuckled as I watched my brother wrap a significantly shorter Raiden up in his arms, an array of lively laughs toppling off of their lips as they greeted one another. Raiden looked youthful and childlike beside my brother, who towered over his five-six frame at a stunning six-two. He inherited our father's height, but our mother's trademark aquiline nose.

"Is that for me?" Brennan teased, snatching the diminutive box from Raiden's clutch. Before he could rip it open, our mother filed into the room, her stare instantaneously brightening at the sight of my best friend.

"You know *damn* well that present is for me, Brennan. Give it here, *stronzo.*" Gaia grinned, unraveling the neatly tied bow to reveal the gift within. A pleased shriek toppled out of her as she inspected the glossy, green ring.

Not like she needed any more of those.

"This is beautiful, Raiden! Thank you for the gift. You know me so well," Momma cheered, coiling a single arm around Raiden's neck, sending his light brunette curls awry. She planted a fat kiss on his rosy red cheek, heartily examining the jewelry before removing the red ring and replacing it with the brand-new emerald one.

"I like today's hair choice," Raiden mused, threading his fingers through Momma's tamed wig. "Where's Grammy?"

"Right here, *prestante!*" Grammy exclaimed, trudging down the wooden stairs. The sharp sound from her petite heels ricocheted off of the squeaky clean wooden floors, and her dress was adorned with so many variations of roses that she looked as if she belonged in my mother's garden.

With a pearly-white grin, she greeted my friend. "Oh, Raiden! *Così bello!* You are the most beautiful boy I've ever laid eyes on, and you get prettier with age. Come here, give Grammy a smooch."

"Good to see you, Aymeline." Raiden beamed, enveloping my Grammy in his warm, welcoming arms. I playfully scoffed as she peppered kisses along his jawline, smearing cheap lipstick along the smooth, porcelain surface.

"Okay, *okay.* That's enough. *Sheesh.* Give your actual grandkid a hug and a kiss, won't you, Grammy?" I mocked, a hint of sourness present in my tone. Grammy chuckled, pulling away from Raiden and diverting her attention to me. She was half Brennan's height, with a head full of wicked, white hair and the palest, bluest eyes I've ever seen. She was the only one in our family to have an eye color other than a deep, dark brown.

"Ai, it's been so long, hasn't it?" Grammy began, twiddling her posh, dangling earring. "Lord, are you two married yet?"

I felt the heat rise up to my cheeks, enveloping my expression in a stunning, scarlet hue. Raiden's complexion mirrored mine in color, only his was more pronounced—*deep.* He bit his lip before looking away, purposefully avoiding the question.

Dammit, Grammy.

"Eh, only a matter of time," Grammy said with a shrug. She thrust a finger in Brennan's direction before continuing with: "Now *you,* you're nearly thirty. The *big* thirty. As an Araedian, you know that your biological clock is ticking *dangerously* quick. Any fish in the sea, Bren?"

Brennan paled. "Grammy, I'm–"

"*–gay,* I know. But in this day'n age, two men can have babies, too! All you need to continue your bloodline is a biological baby. That's all. It needs to be *soon,* Brennan. I'm serious."

"Hey, why is this all about me?" Brennan whined, itty-bitty eyes darkening. "*Freya's* thirty-three! She should've popped one out before her thirtieth if we have any hopes of keeping the Araedians alive."

"Enough, *enough!*" Momma screeched, waving her arms wildly. "Can we stop crowding the hall? It's getting stuffy in here. Momma, come help me in the kitchen. Come see what our sweet Freya baked."

My mother loved putting emphasis on my name. *Freya.* She was quite proud of it—of its origins—and she was keen on reminding me of what power it held since the moment I could speak.

Freyja—the Norse goddess of love, beauty, fertility, sex, war . . .

The real Freyja would be embarrassed to share her name with me, for I was none of those things.

"That reminds me," Brennan suddenly said, curling his fingers around my wrist and yanking me towards the living room adjacent to the hallway. "I learned something new with my energy, it's pretty fucking cool. Raiden, come see, too!"

Reluctantly, Raiden and I followed the monster of a man into the living room, where he busied himself with the disorganized desk in the corner of the room, an assortment of items and paperwork haphazardly overlaid along the surface. Although our father had an entire office for his belongings, most of his forgotten documents piled up in this room. It drove my mother mad, but he kept it *somewhat* orderly, ensuring that the papers remained stacked, the pencils and pens shoved into dated movie theater cups.

Brennan waved us over to the coffee table, the only flat surface that was wholly visible in the entire house. My brother placed a piece of printer paper onto the table, bony fingers spread out along the empty page. A pair of wild eyes met mine before shifting sharply to view Raiden's puzzled stare.

"I've been really focusing my energy on this," Brennan began, stepping backwards towards the desk. He snatched a blue ball-point pen from a *Jurassic Park* cup, nearly tipping the entire thing over as his trembling palms steadied the object.

"Brennan, what–"

"Just *watch,* Freya!" Brennan hissed, lengthy arms thrusting upwards in exasperation. He looked terribly tense, and I wondered what in the world he could've possibly taught himself to do.

With a weighty exhale, Brennan placed the pen parallel to the empty page, eyelids gently fluttering closed as he lowered himself onto the cushion of the couch. His forearms met the rugged material of his dark wash jeans, left hand curling inward to cradle his knee. Blindly, Brennan raised both the index and middle finger of his right hand, clammy digits quivering.

I could've sworn that I felt the tips of Raiden's fingers dance along my elbow, but I was saddened to see my surmise debunked. Raiden, in fact, was nowhere near my elbow—instead, he was timidly itching his own. I ripped my gaze away before he could question my gawking glare, and that familiar sense of overall unease began to blossom within my core yet again.

When my muddled mind cleared and I was able to focus on the scene at hand once more, the pen was floating—*writing.* Only, Brennan hadn't moved an inch; he was still seated on the sofa, both eyes sealed shut, two fingers faintly raised. It appeared as if the inanimate object had a mind of its own, and although the apparent ghost's penmanship was sloppy and sloven just like its proprietor, I couldn't help but chuckle.

"No *fucking* fair!" I exclaimed, ogling the shaky "H" scrawled across the page. The pen busied itself with the latter letter of the word as Raiden released an amused exhale.

"Shit, Bren. That's awesome."

Once the statement was complete—a simplistic "HI" etched along the paper—Brennan opened his eyes, a sour scowl crawling along his mouth at the sight of the sloppy scrawl.

"Jeez, it looks like a kindergartener wrote it." Brennan scoffed, snatching his handiwork up from the table to closely inspect it.

"Dude, you wrote that with your *mind.* Who cares what it looks like?" Raiden mused, approaching my dispirited brother. His palm met Brennan's shoulder, slender fingers softly squeezing as the pair exchanged soft smiles.

"It sounds weird when you say it like that," my brother said, chuckling slightly before handing the paper over to Raiden. "For you."

Exaggeratedly, Raiden fawned over the gift; knuckles dancing along his forehead as he feigned elation. "Oh, *Bren!* This is the best gift you've ever given me!"

"Freya, can you go get your father? It's almost time to eat!" Momma called from the kitchen, her terse tone somewhat cloaked by the presence of several walls. She caught me mid-eye roll, and before exiting the room, I snatched the loose-leaf paper from Raiden's grasp, folding it up into a tiny triangle and slipping it into my pocket.

"Mine, now," I heartily mocked, sticking my tongue out at the duo. Brennan spat a profusion of obscenities my way, and I overheard Grammy sharply scolding my brother for his foul language. It was comical how she still treated him like a child, regardless of the fact that he was mere days shy of thirty.

Dad's office was adjacent to the staircase, a mediocre space with a whiny, old glass door. I caught a glimpse of the lofty lad through the fingerprint riddled glass, the winding cord of an aging phone looped around his fingers as he mindlessly paced. His ebony locks were unkempt, and I wondered if he'd ever chop it all off. Although he would never admit it aloud, we all knew quite well that he used cheap box dye to keep his hair dark. After all, the prickly stubble that arose upon his pale cheeks was almost always littered with a majority of a salty hue versus his desired pepper color, and I could only imagine that his disorderly mane was as white as snow beneath the artificial dye.

With a shy knock, I entered; earning a stiff smile and an uncomplicated thumbs-up. My father collapsed against the tattered hide of his leather chair, the wheeled object obnoxiously squeaking beneath his weighty frame. His knees were too tall for his cheap, maple desk, a mass of overstuffed moving boxes surrounding the perimeter of the room. The rugged, ruby carpet was barely visible beneath the massive amounts of clutter, and on more than one occasion, I'd witnessed my father trip and fall over his own mess, leaving behind a puddle of blood and bruising his nose.

When I failed to evacuate the office after several moments, my father lowered the phone from his ear, little lips parted in protest. It was an all-too familiar sight.

"Hey, honey. I'll be out soon. Can you make sure the door is completely closed when you leave?"

A peeved frown crept along my lips, and with a nod, I left; ensuring that the door was securely shut before navigating my way towards the kitchen, where Raiden was helping my mother set the table.

I vaguely heard my mother speak, but it wasn't until she called out my name several times that I fully comprehended the situation at hand. I felt hollow—*numb.* It seemed so stereotypical—*the daughter of an emotionally absent father*—but that was all I'd ever known. Our parents constantly worked through most of mine and Brennan's youth, leaving most of my childhood memories in the hands of our babysitter, Blanch. I felt woozy as a surplus of undesirable childhood memories assailed my mind, trembling palms steadying against a nearby chair as a pair of hands met my elbow.

"Frey, is it happening again?" Raiden whispered, his tone waved and warped. I choked down a lump of bile as I shook my head.

"No, I'm fine," I lightly lied, shooting him a faux grin. His brows were arched in curiosity, fingers still threaded around my arm.

"You know, Brennan's been feeling odd, too. He told Grammy about his symptoms, and she brought some old Araedian book with her to see if she could find some answers," Mom explained, caressing my cheek. "Take a seat, Frey. Momma, go fetch that book, will you? We can look it over during supper. Raiden, want to help me get the rest of the stuff out of the oven?"

"Of course, Gaia," Raiden replied, tucking a stray strand of hair behind my ear. "Sit down, Frey. I'll get you some water. Maybe you're dehydrated."

"Maybe," I murmured, obeying orders as I lowered myself into my seat.

"Brennan, fetch me that book, will you? I'm not going up those stairs again until it's time for bed," Grammy grumbled, collapsing against the chair to my immediate left. The old wood shifted and creaked beneath her weight. "Frey, you look a mess. Tell Grammy what exactly has been happening."

I sighed, threading my fingers through my hair as Grammy toyed with several stray strands over my shoulder. Brennan busied himself with locating her book, eager eyes upturned into his skull, eyelids glimmering, index finger elevated. Usually I would tease him about looking possessed, but I seemed to be void of any energy—*numb.* I could feel an intolerable heat generate within my chest before journeying outward, gliding down each upturned arm and coiling around each individual finger. With a wince, I lifted a single palm up towards my face, inspecting the boiling digits one by one. They appeared normal on the outside, but within, it felt as if my blood had been replaced with boiling magma.

"My hands," I croaked, just as Brennan summoned Grammy's ancient book. The hefty tome landed directly on my lap, prompting my legs to inadvertently jerk, sending the object flat onto the floor.

"Shit," Brennan murmured, jumping to his feet to claim the object. Grammy, however, paid no mind to the yellow, curled pages, which were haphazardly fanned out along the tile floor. Instead, she was preoccupied with my burning hands.

"They're generating some sort of burning sensation, aren't they?" Grammy inquired, gliding her thumb along my wonkily shaped index finger. At this point, Momma and Raiden had finished setting the table—an abundance of tasty food strung along the center and ready to be consumed. Per usual, there was a meat entrée and a vegetarian alternative, for Grammy was picky about what animals she consumed, and my mother couldn't stomach any kind of animal fat anymore.

"Yeah," I mumbled, catching Raiden's worrisome glare. He took the final seat on my right side, a friendly palm immediately taking refuge upon my leg.

Grammy dropped my hand, reaching over to snatch the dusty, aged book from Brennan's grip as Momma took her seat beside my brother on the opposite side of the table. With crimped brows, she held out a hand, urging her elderly mother to hand over the book.

"Eat something first, Momma."

"I can do both, Gaia," Grammy snipped, curling her fingers beneath the curve of Momma's fine china. With a grin, she thrust her empty dish in my mother's direction, wordlessly urging her to pile some food onto it. "No meat, as you know. I'll take extra mashed potatoes, though. You make the best there is, *figlia*."

Momma rolled her eyes, and Raiden snatched up my plate, scooping a generous heap of potatoes onto the surface and dressing it with smooth, warm gravy.

"Raiden, I could do that myself," I pressed, resisting the urge to sit on my hands. The sensation was on the brink of excruciating, and I wanted nothing more than to drown the sore skin in a bucket of ice water.

"It's really no big deal," my best friend said, a sly smile slapped across his mouth. If he kept up this friendly façade, Grammy would have our wedding invitations drafted by dessert.

Raiden finished off my plate with ease, gently requesting that both Brennan and Momma pass him the platters that were out of reach.

She made roast beef for those who would eat it, and garlic and herb tofu for those who refused. Being the absolute doll that he was, Raiden took a serving of both the roast and the tofu, earning a scarlet smile from my mother as she heartily handed over the vegetarian dish.

Grammy was busy thumbing through her book, brows piqued in curiosity as she scanned the information on each page. I was unaware that our history was so extensive, and I felt a flicker of sorrow at the thought that the only Araedians left were seated at this very table.

"I can't believe Peter is *still* on that damn conference call," Momma murmured, bitterly shaking her head. "You'd think he'd want to spend some time with his children."

"List off your symptoms," Grammy keenly interrupted, settling upon a specific page in the center of the leather-bound book. My mouth was full of mushy potatoes, and Raiden seemed to read my mind, answering in the place of my audible absence.

"Extreme burning in her hands and arms," he said, trying the tofu. He made sure to acknowledge how good it was halfway through his first bite, a proclamation that made my mother blush. "Fatigue, irritability. She just looks sickly, feverish. I never took her temperature, although I probably should've."

"And you, Brennan? Similar?" Grammy queried, glancing my brother's way. He, too, was busy downing spoonfuls of potatoes.

"Er, yeah," he grumbled. "My veins went all wonky, too. I thought they were going to explode inside of my arms. Scared me half to death."

Grammy released a forceful exhale, bitterly flipping the page. It was evident that the answer was nonexistent in that section.

"Momma's been practicing," Brennan suddenly said, snatching a warm roll from a maroon-stained wicker basket. I nearly choked on my food at his announcement, my eyes widening as my mother merely rolled hers.

"If you can even call it that."

"Practicing what?" Raiden wondered, requesting a roll. Brennan shuffled the basket into his grasp whilst simultaneously scooping another round of potatoes into his mouth.

"Her energy," I revealed, setting down my fork. Suddenly, I didn't feel so hungry. "You're gaining your strength back, Momma?"

"Yes," Momma revealed, a somber smile etched along her mouth. She tucked a spool of faux red hair behind her heavily pierced ear before continuing. "I'm better, Frey. I'm strong enough to use my energies again. I promise I wouldn't use them if it wasn't safe."

"But Momma–"

"I just realized something," Raiden keenly interrupted, brows knit together in curiosity. "I've known you for over twenty years, Gaia, and I have no idea what your energy is. I don't think I've ever seen you use it."

"That's because I've been sick most of the time you've known me, Rai. Besides your youthful years, which is when I used my energy heavily, but you were probably too young to notice or realize," Momma explained, grabbing a roll for herself. "My energy is unlike anything you've ever seen from Brennan and Freya."

"She's a Manipulator," I said, twiddling with a loose thread on the navy fabric napkin. I twisted and twirled the fiber between my fingers, incredibly anxious at the thought of my mother exhausting herself with her energy.

"A Manipulator?" Raiden questioned, tone slightly muffled by the presence of the garlic tofu.

"She can manipulate time," Brennan revealed. "To an extent, at least. What's the furthest you can jump, Ma?"

"Well, I *could* jump as far back as I want to. But, it's not necessarily safe," Momma began. Grammy was still solely fixated on her ancient Araedian book, occasionally grabbing her fork and taking small bites of her meal.

"My personal safe limit is two hours, although I'd gone back as far as six days in the past. I was only a child when I did such a large jump—a few days over nine years of age—and I made a massive mistake."

"What kind of massive mistake?" I wondered.

"Gaia," Grammy warned, bright eyes darkening. "Watch your tongue."

"Momma, *per l'amor del cazzo*, telling a story so old won't hurt anyone," Momma countered. The mere memory blanched her sunken cheeks, and she almost looked as if she'd be sick. "It was partially my fault that the De Mörka learned of our whereabouts. I was in primary school, and I had a friend called Aurora. We still lived in Pietrapertosa at the time—that's in Italy, Raiden—and Aurora died. She was struck by a vehicle while riding her bike. She died, and I was devastated. Distraught. It wasn't fair; we were too young to die. So, I made sure she didn't."

Momma paused, painted bottom lip drawn between trembling teeth. I could tell that she was trying her best to hold back the tears, for they'd wreck her makeup. At this point, Grammy's attention had shifted from the book to meet her dejected daughter, and she even reached out a wrinkled hand to meet Momma's quivering palm. Even Brennan had quit shoveling food into his mouth.

"The whole neighborhood was grieving. Aurora's mother had been hospitalized after the memorial because she tried to kill herself. She couldn't live without her little love. I felt as if it was my duty to bring her back, but I was young . . . *so* young. I didn't know of the consequences, I didn't know how to properly alter the timeline. I didn't know enough. I was able to alter the event. I did it good, I did it well. I went to the spot where she'd died—they'd set up a white wooden cross on the side of the road, accented with the prettiest flowers I'd ever seen. There were wrinkled photographs of Aurora and her friends, trinkets and toys. The sight of it made me angry, so I went back. I stood in that very spot and turned back time, an entire six days. When I finally stumbled upon the scene, I froze it, and I just stared. Stared at little Aurora, sat upon her black bike, a pink helmet on her head. Her ginger hair was pulled into two braids, one over each shoulder. She forgot to look both ways before crossing, and the car was only feet away from her innocent self."

Momma paused once more, a single tear slipping down the slope of her flushed cheek. Weakly, she wiped it away, clearing her throat before continuing. I'd barely noticed the presence of Raiden's hand as it creeped down my leg, warm palm settling upon my knee.

"I was too young to have so much power. I didn't know how much I could really do. I'm able to freeze time around me; alter it. I'm able to have full control. It's more power than anyone should ever have, especially a young child under the age of ten. While my surroundings were frozen, I wheeled Aurora out of the way, ensuring that the car would have absolutely no chance of striking her. And, when I allowed time to resume, she survived. I watched her wheel away completely unscathed."

"Why was that such a bad thing?" Brennan asked, rotating his fork between nimble fingers. "You saved your friend's life. She was too young to die, anyways."

Momma sighed. "If only it were that simple, Bren. I was too young to comprehend what had to be done to properly manipulate the timeline. Although I'd saved Aurora's life, there were . . . *complications.* The original timeline including her death was erased for everyone except her. I don't know how, or why, and I was too young to know what I'd done wrong. She remembered the alternate timeline. She remembered dying."

Grammy took notice of Raiden squeezing my knee, a grin slithering along her lips at the sight. Uneasily, I brushed his touch away, worried what Grammy thought of the innocent action.

We were best friends, nothing more.

"I remember our sleepovers afterwards. She told me about how she'd died, but nobody seemed to remember. She cried about it to her mother, and it made her parents panic. They thought she was suicidal. She ended up getting sent to therapy as a young kid. She was pulled from school because she had panic attacks every time the thought of dying graced her mind. She couldn't comprehend how she was alive. I didn't have the heart to tell her what I'd done. Besides, I couldn't tell her anyway. There are not many people who know of our energies, and those who do are special. Like you, Raiden." Momma breathed, wiping away another tear.

"Aurora died at sixteen. I couldn't save her the second time. It was almost ironic how she went out. She stepped in front of a car on the autostrade. I didn't live in Italy at that point, but I found out through mutual friends who I kept in contact with. Where were we at that time, Momma? Romania?"

"Yes," Grammy confirmed. "Gaia's heroic episode generated an extreme amount of energy. It was almost like a bright, red flare sent up for the De Mörka to see. Two years after Aurora's revival, the De Mörka invaded Milan, the hub for a majority of the Araedian people. The invasion was known as The Great Clash, and it would go on for months, wiping out both the Araedian and De Mörka people. We were lucky, since we didn't reside in Milan, we had a way out. We fled to Finland and went into hiding, riding out the clash and surviving. Come to find out, we were all that remained at the end."

"What about these De Mörka people?" Raiden interrupted, butchering the pronunciation of our enemy clan. "Did they all die, too?"

"That's what we thought," Grammy muttered, returning her attention to the book. "But according to this book, I fear that may not be true. All of Freya and Brennan's symptoms point to one single inevitable outcome: the De Mörka still remain."

Pure, unadulterated chaos immediately enveloped the dining table, startling my father Peter, who was peeling apart a roll and slathering it with butter.

When did he get here?

Raiden visibly flinched, bewildered at the sight of my father opposite him. It appeared as if my mother had used her energy to alter our current timeline, inserting my father in our current conversation as if he were here all along. However, she kept our memory of the original timeline unscathed. To my father, he was here all along. To the rest of us, he'd just appeared out of thin air, as if by magic.

"Peter?" Raiden stammered, blinking several times to steady his vision. "When did you get here?"

My dozy father met Raiden's puzzled stare, thin, bony fingers encircled around a knife as he continued to butter his freshly-baked bread. He looked unenthused about Raiden's inquiry, as if my best friend were nothing but an irritable, little child yanking at his pant leg.

"I've been here the entire time, Raiden. Are you feeling ill or something?" Dad halfheartedly probed, taking a bite out of his buttery bread.

"No, I–" Raiden stammered, suddenly meeting Momma's amused glare. She was unable to stifle a smile, and she burst into joyous laughter at the sight of Raiden's immense perplexion. It was then that he'd realized what she'd done: she used her energy to rewind time and ensure that my father cut his conference call short in order to join us for dinner. He didn't seem too pleased at the fact that his work was interrupted, but then again, my father hardly ever smiled.

Although Raiden was thoroughly captivated with the fact that his timeline was altered, I couldn't quite kick the thought of our mortal enemy still remaining. In fact, I could almost feel the burning sensation begin to bubble within my veins once more. "Can we go back to what Grammy said, about the De Mörka still existing? How is that possible?"

Grammy shuffled the hefty book into my arms, pointing out a particular paragraph that explained exactly why Brennan and I were experiencing such odd symptoms. It was all there: the burning hands, the bulging veins. Nightmares, cold sweats, anxiety, fevers. I read halfway down the page before shoving the dusty book back into her lap, a fearful shiver enveloping my spine. According to the ancient Araedian text, the only reason we'd feel this way is if there is a rising De Mörka nearby—as close as a mile or as near as fifty miles. Either way, fifty miles was too close for comfort for an enemy to be lurking, and with Brennan just shy of his thirtieth birthday, this could only mean one thing: peril.

"My guess is that someone in the De Mörka bloodline did the very same thing that we did. Instead of fighting, they fled. It was frowned upon on our end, and I'm sure it was discouraged for them as well. But in the end, we were the sole survivors. Fleeing was the best option, and in the immediate years during the Clash and shortly thereafter, we bounced around from country to country—Romania, Estonia, Finland, Germany. When we were sure that no De Mörka remained, we went back to Italy, where Gaia met Peter as he was studying abroad. That's what brought her here to Canada, and you two were born," Grammy thoroughly explained, nibbling on her nail. Brennan hadn't touched his food since the mention of the De Mörka, and I swore that his complexion even looked a little green. The only one of us that continued to eat was my father, who'd barely spoken a word since his sudden, magical arrival.

"But you said that a De Mörka has to be within fifty miles for us to feel the way we are," I interjected, knobby knees bouncing. I felt as if I may succumb to a dark, dreadful panic attack at any moment. If the De Mörka *did* still exist, they only served one purpose: exterminate my brother Brennan before his energies solidified the moment of his thirtieth birthday, which was next Sunday.

"Correct," Grammy confirmed with a frown.

"How the hell did they find us here, all the way over in Canada?" Momma weakly wondered. "I was sure that we'd be safe here, we're not even in Europe."

"I was sure, too. I was also sure that they'd all died out during the Clash." My grandmother snapped the big book closed, tossing it onto the floor before releasing a hefty exhale. "As you all know, the De Mörka are not born with their energies like we are. They grow into them according to circumstance. The goal of their entire existence is solely to destroy us."

"So, this remaining De Mörka member is growing into their energies because–" I shakily began, but Brennan cut my statement short.

"Because I'm turning thirty. Once I'm thirty, I'll be more powerful than even the most dynamic De Mörka."

My mother burst into tears, her reddened expression concealed by wide palms as she viciously sobbed. Raiden instantly climbed to his feet, circling the table to comfort my distressed mother. My father lowered his utensils, weakly attempting to soothe her with a pat on the shoulder. It was comical to even see him try.

Momma buried her head into Raiden's chest as he fell to a crouch, slender fingers gently combing through the curls of her red wig. He shot me a sympathetic glance, and I found myself rising from the table, debating whether or not to flee to the nearby restroom to empty what little amount of food sat in my rumbling stomach. Brennan was white as a ghost, wide eyes bloodshot and blurry. It was as if he were visualizing all the ways he would die in less than fourteen days time.

"We need to be on our toes," I began. "Grammy, what do they look like? The De Mörka?"

"Eyes black as coal, soul as dark as the night," Grammy began, her voice barely above a whisper. "You'll know it when you see them. You'll feel it. At least, we used to be able to. I'm not so sure anymore. This new generation of De Mörka may be more powerful than the last."

"How do I defeat it?" Brennan asked, hands balled into fists atop the table. "Can they die?"

"Yes, they can," Grammy confirmed. "The De Mörka are unique. Their power and energy is not embedded within their bones like ours is. Although it is a part of their chemical makeup, it can be banished—*locked away.* It would take a sacrifice, however. A human one. Someone would need to occupy their subconscious and *lock* the negative energy inside. But if you simply want to kill them, slit their throat."

My brows inquisitively raised. "Locked away? Human sacrifice?"

"Yes. It's complicated—extremely so. I'm not even sure I can put it into words. Think of it as a safe, stored away in the subconscious of a De Mörka. Their evil energy can be locked away in that safe, but only if it contains that of a human sacrifice, too. They serve as some sort of seal," Grammy explained, standing to her feet.

"What's the point of banishment? If they're evil, why not just kill them?" I asked, bewildered by the fact that anyone would sacrifice their soul to save a wretched De Mörka.

"Like I said, their energy is not their entire being, like yours and ours. Although their kind evolved to counter ours, they aren't all exactly evil. Not always, at least. Some may be worth the banishment process," Grammy explained. It still didn't fully make sense to me, but I let it be.

A teary-eyed Momma pulled away from Raiden's wrinkled dress shirt, revealing an essence of smeared mascara along the fabric. She gasped at the sight, woefully wiping it away. The makeup only smeared, creating an unattractive black blob across Raiden's left pec.

"It's fine, Gaia. I promise. I'll get myself a washcloth to try and rub it out," Raiden assured, politely stepping away from my miserable mother and approaching the kitchen cabinets in search of the clean towels.

"Momma," I purred, earning her attention just as Raiden unintentionally slammed his finger in the sharp corner of the drawer. The woman watched as I involuntarily mirrored his actions exactly; my reflexes taking over as I hissed in pain. Momma widely watched as our arms jerked upward, fingers sorely clenched in pain. My index finger achingly throbbed, and her jaw literally dropped as she watched both Raiden and I slip the very same tender finger into our mouths.

She knew.

She goddamn *knew* what was happening, and she'd warned me of it a thousand times. I never listened, I always brushed it off.

It isn't possible, Momma.

Don't be ridiculous, Momma.

I could feel Raiden's strongest sensations—his pain, his pleasure, his glee. I'd become one with the man after healing him for so long. By now, there was no turning back. Regardless of where we went from here, I would experience the very same sensations that he would until the end of time.

"Freya," Momma growled, glare darkening significantly. "Can I speak to you in the living room?"

"Later, Momma," I dismissed, tongue still wrapped around my throbbing index finger. Her vexed stare challenged my reply, and with a sigh, I followed the stiff woman out of the room.

I prepared myself for the impending lecture, nodding curtly in Raiden's direction as I trudged towards my inevitable doom.

I was so fucked.

nine

Momma barely glanced my way for the remainder of the evening.

Our conversation was rigid and short, littered with an abundance of *I told you so* and *he has no privacy anymore* and *you're stripping that boy of his identity* and blah, blah, blah. Although she made some fair points, overall, she sounded like an absolute nutcase. However, I made sure not to mention my erotic experience from several nights prior, for the bright red wig atop her head would most definitely burst into flames. The bold, loopy curls already reminded me of Medusa's sinful serpents, and if I'd let the statement slip through my vile lips, they'd surely spring to life and turn me to stone.

By the cusp of dusk, Momma had shed nearly her entire face of makeup, cheeks soiled a sorrowful, scarlet hue. It'd been awhile since I'd seen her cry so much in a single sitting, and although Grammy and Dad both assured Momma that Brennan would be fine, she just couldn't contain her sobs.

Brennan, on the other hand, didn't seem so sure. He'd barely finished his supper, and he refused to touch the vanilla candy brownies I brought. It was unusual for him not to eat, and if his lack of appetite didn't give him away already, his facial expressions did. Unlike Momma's bright-red complexion, his features were pasty and pale. He sat stiff in his seat, droopy eyes fixated on the salt and pepper shakers for nearly an entire hour. He didn't move, he didn't speak. He resembled a statue; stiff as stone. Evidently, he'd succumbed to Momma's snakelike locks.

Brennan had disappeared shortly before Raiden and I left, claiming that he was spent and ready for bed. I knew better. He would lie on his back until dawn, widened, doe-like eyes glued to the rotating ceiling fan. He'd study the way it turned, how if he focused hard enough, he could observe each individual blade as it continuously gyrated. He wouldn't notice his lack of sleep—lack of presence, in fact—until Momma came knocking on his door halfway past noon, discovering the mute boy in a stiff stance on his bed, empty, ebbing eyes meeting her bloodshot orbs. She'd spend the entire night crying, and Dad would probably sleep on the sofa. He was a light sleeper.

"I think I'll go to bed," Raiden spoke, dismissively tossing the car keys onto our kitchen counter. I glanced at the stove, viewing the vibrant, viridescent numbers.

8:09.

"So early?" I teased, yanking open the pantry door. The warped panel whined, and an improperly sealed box of cereal fell to my feet, littering my bare toes with an assortment of multi-hued Cheerios. A trio of impatient animals immediately hounded my legs, clearing the area as if nothing had ever spilled. I sighed, bending down to retrieve the box as I hastily shooed the dogs away, earning a lively lick from a slobbering Kelso.

"Do you need a shower?" Raiden wondered, squeezing past my fickle frame to claim the plastic bin filled to the brim with dog kibble. He filled their bowls before I could seal the cereal box, as if out of impatience.

"I could've done that." The statement emerged as a shy murmur, and Raiden merely smiled. I couldn't help but feel as if it were anything but genuine.

"We have work early tomorrow," he said, stepping aside to allow our dogs access to their bowls. "You should probably shower tonight. I'll lay out a towel for you."

"Raiden," I croaked, but he hadn't heard me. He was already halfway across the house, nimble fingers pulling at the buttons on his shirt. With a sigh, I placed a sealed-lip kiss upon each of the dogs' skulls, bidding them goodnight (even though they'd join us in the bed in less than an hour's time). I cleaned up after my messy roommate, collecting his keys and draping them over the metal keyring, a cheesy trinket that read *love.* Momma gifted it to me on my thirtieth birthday.

By the time I eased into the bedroom, Raiden was already buried beneath the covers, ample eyes fixed on the twinkling television screen. A short smile crawled along my lips at the sight of a *Sabrina the Teenage Witch* rerun, and a chipper, lubberly Kelso nearly knocked me onto my nose as he barreled into the bedroom, Mimosa close on his heel, nipping at his tail.

With a clumsy shout, I steadied my posture; thin digits curling beneath the hem of my shirt as I lifted it from my torso. When I glanced over my shoulder to view Raiden, he hadn't moved; big, doe-like eyes still suctioned to the screen. Frivolously, I unclasped my bra, letting the padded material flutter to my feet. Raiden still paid no mind, innocent expression immersed in all-things Sabrina Spellman. A part of me wished that he would look. Watch. *Stare.*

The other part was thankful that he paid no mind at all. *We aren't a couple. We aren't anything but friends.*

With a scoff, I stumbled into the bathroom, kicking the door closed with my heel. Just as he'd promised, there was a yellow folded towel draped over the counter, along with a petite package of sweet-smelling bath salts. It appeared as if Raiden wanted me to treat myself to a nice, warm bath.

I couldn't help but wonder if he would want to join.

I shook my head, ridding my mind of the incredibly venereal thought before filling the tub. The superb scent of apples and cinnamon invaded my senses, and although I'd yet to ease into the warm water, I felt instantly relaxed; thoughts of the De Mörka disintegrating along with all of my worries. A muffled moan tickled my tongue as I settled into the basin, lively, fragrant waves lapping at my skin.

Beneath my sealed eyelids, our imminent threat appeared; an angry De Mörka, gloomy, ebony eyes piercing through my skin, stripping the skin away, clawing at my muscles and gnawing on my bones. The cryptic being refused to take on a specific shape or identity—for it was neither male nor female— instead, it was just . . . *there.* Dark, looming; *evil.* I could feel the anger—the *hatred*—penetrating my lungs, peeling them apart in search of my heart.

With a gasp, I lurched forward in the tub; the odorous water slopping over the sides, soaking both the feathery purple rug and my clothes. Bubbling within my throat was a scream; hoarse and dry, and I hadn't even realized that I'd fallen asleep until the De Mörka reared its ugly head, invading my dreams as if it were a modern-day Freddy Krueger.

The flesh stretched along my palms was brutally burned, the skin singed a searing scarlet. Fearful tears cloaked the entirety of my cheeks, intermixing with the sweet-smelling bath salts that only briefly cloaked my being. With trembling legs, I drained the tub; wrapping the towel taut around my torso before vacating the bathroom. I felt dizzy and ill—increasingly so—and with a slight stumble, my naked self collapsed atop the bed, where a snoring Raiden lay. Sabrina was still slapped across the television, along with her uproarious black cat Salem.

Mimosa, who was wrapped around Raiden's legs, violently flinched at my sudden presence, a fearful bark cascading over her tongue as my best friend stirred in his sleep. When Mimosa barked once more,

Raiden's heavy eyelids fluttered open, revealing blurred, bloodshot orbs. I nearly jumped out of my skin at the sight of his open eyes, awkwardly aware that I was—in fact—completely nude.

Sloppily slipping beneath the covers, Raiden released a throaty inquiry, a string of words that blended together into an unidentifiable blur.

"What?" I breathed, my tone unsteady.

Raiden pulled himself up on a single elbow, raised brows studying my flushed complexion. "Are you naked?"

"No," I lied, pulling the duvet up to my neck.

"Is something the matter?" he added, curled knuckles rubbing the sleep from his eyes. Once more, I feigned confusion, insisting that nothing was wrong. He seemed unconvinced.

"All right," he murmured. "Come here."

Panic boiled within my chest, and before I could protest, Raiden wriggled his way over to my side of the bed, gentle fingers dancing along my unclothed belly. Instantaneously, his large eyes widened, lips parted in shock as he hurriedly pulled his hand away from my belly.

"Freya!" he exclaimed.

"I'm sorry!" I countered, my tone high-pitched and whiny. "Raiden, I had a nightmare in the bath. I fell asleep and had a dream about the De Mörka. I swear I could feel her . . . him . . . *it* . . . breathing down my neck. And my hands—they're burning, again. I soaked my clothes and I was so dizzy so I just went to lay down but Mimosa barked and you woke up–"

"I've seen you naked before," Raiden interrupted, a slight chuckle present in his voice. "It just caught me off guard. Plus, if I'd put my hand any lower by accident–"

"Okay, *okay,*" I hurriedly interrupted back, tossing my hands airborne. "Close your eyes, I'll get dressed."

"You don't have to," Raiden said, green eyes diverting from mine, as if out of shyness. "I mean, whatever you're comfortable with."

With a slight pause, I contemplated my decision. He was right, he *had* seen me naked before, but this time felt entirely divergent from all of the others. We'd bathed together several times in the past, and admittedly, he'd helped me breathe through a mental breakdown that I'd had mid-shower. Other times, he helped me undress when I was ill. This time, I felt completely conscious, and utterly exposed.

"We don't have to cuddle," he said, shyly severing the silence. "I'm in my boxers, if that makes you feel better."

"Raiden, we don't have to make this weird," I countered, settling against the pillows. Evidently, I'd made up my mind.

"It isn't weird," he defended, mirroring my actions as his head met the pillow, spirited curls encircling his skull. He looked angelic, and I felt the heat rise to my cheeks at the sheer proximity of our minimally clothed bodies.

"I'm scared, Rai," I whispered, creeping closer to the man beneath the blankets. Naturally, our legs enlaced; the heat of his calves generating goosebumps along my legs.

"I know," Raiden replied, threading his fingers through my damp hair. The shifting scenes on the television fervently illuminated only a quarter of his complexion, revealing one single eye, the lengthy slope of his nose, and a half-mooned frown. The volume was low, but I was still able to decipher Salem's quirky quotes, some of which tugged my lips into a smile.

"You'll protect me, won't you? If Brennan can't?" I asked, a sharp breath hitching in my throat as his thumb inadvertently clipped my lower lip.

"Of course I will," he assured, retracting his touch. "That's what best friends are for."

With words unspoken, the pair of us nuzzled into individual pillows, lengthy legs still enlaced like the vines of a Christmas wreath. I could feel his drowsy exhales along the curve of my jaw, evenly-spaced and reeking of mint. I was suddenly aware of the fact that I'd neglected to brush my teeth.

Just as I'd drifted to the void between alert awareness and a profound slumber, I took notice of an icy shock along the arch of my exposed hip—a trio of fingertips, daintily dancing along the surface. Although I wanted to jolt awake in sheer shock, I felt serene—*secure.*

With a gentle groan, my hip shifted upward, welcoming the foreign feel.

Thus, the fingers stirred, kindly waltzing along the rugged flesh of my goosebump riddled abdomen. I didn't dare to breathe, for I was unsure if the slightest movement would deter the lustful act. Rather, I waited; dangling between consciousness and sleep as the roaming palm claimed my opposite hip, flattening against the surface as it sharply tugged.

Breathlessly, I obeyed; rotating my fickle frame sideways and shimmying backwards until the bend of my back was met with Raiden's snug front. The moment our bodies collided, I could've sworn that I overheard him sigh, and with parted, puzzled lips, I laid lax within the man's open arms. I felt him bury his nose in the expanse of my thick, wild mane, and as his hold on me tightened, as if out of fear that I'd somehow escape, I couldn't help but smile. Wide. Large. A grin so massive that it made my cheeks hurt.

I was home.

Luckily, Raiden and I were on opposite ends of the restaurant that following morning.

Our uppity manager, Sierra, assigned Raiden most of the prep work, whereas she asked me for assistance in the dining room. Late last night, our best hostess quit unexpectedly, and none of the remaining hosts or hostesses had answered Sierra's agitated text messages or phone calls. It appeared that they all simply had something better to do than come into work on the morning of their day off, or they were busy with school. Not that I could blame them in the slightest—on Raiden's and my days off, we would screen Sierra's phone calls. It was almost hypocritical of me to even speak illy of my co-workers for doing exactly as I did.

We'd spent the majority of the morning setting up, and she gave me a crash-course in hosting. It seemed simple enough, but the stars never seemed to align just right for me, and by noon, I was up to my eyeballs in stress. I unintentionally dropped a stack full of hefty menus on an elderly woman's foot, tripped over a small child, and mixed up several tables, seating a few parties in sections where a waiter wasn't even assigned.

By the end of my shift, I was reduced to a slobbery ball of snot, persistently wiping my weeping nose on the wrinkled sleeve of my sweaty work shirt. Due to lousy weather, Raiden and I decided to take the short drive to work in hopes of avoiding the melancholy rain storm that had been brewing overnight.

Mighty raindrops rapped against the windshield, the gigantic droplets creating an inimitable tune against the metal roof of the idle vehicle. I sheepishly sobbed in the passenger seat, the engine warily whining as I awaited Raiden, who was finishing up his final task.

When I caught wind of his obscure shape rushing towards the vehicle, I bent over the console, trembling fingers encircling the handle of his door as I shoved the heavy entrance open. He audibly thanked me as he slipped into his seat, sodden, chestnut curls suctioned to the surface of his cheeks. With a sigh, he pulled the wet hair away from his face, tossing it up into a sloven bun at the base of his skull.

"It's raining cats and dogs out there," he breathed, releasing a winded exhale. "How was it, working the floor?"

Containing my composure, I feigned happiness, insisting that it was one of the best shifts I'd ever worked. If Raiden hadn't been fixated on the road, he would've seen right through my pitiful lie. He could read me like an open book.

"Are you sure you need to run to the store?" Raiden grumbled, brows uneasily arched as he studied our hazy surroundings. The violent downpour made it nearly impossible to see more than a car's-length in front of us.

"Yes, we desperately need butter and oat milk," I pressed. "Just run to Foodvio, it's right down the road."

"Foodvio is ridiculously overpriced," Raiden pressed, but nonetheless, the vehicle merged into the left lane as he prepared to turn towards the organic grocery store. "If you *have* to go, grab me some cookies. I'm all out."

"Peanut butter?" I asked, already knowing his reply. He pulled up to the entrance to drop me off, a slew of prim women with pantsuits and soaked umbrellas crowding the entrance.

"The best there is."

With a nod, I avoided his gaze, careful not to let him catch wind of my red-rimmed eyes. I refused to admit my defeat, or even acknowledge how utterly awful my hostess shift was. I clambered from the car, avoiding the icy droplets as they threatened to soak my skin. It was almost May, and there was still a slight winter chill present in the air. It appeared as if spring would be nonexistent this year.

Shoving my way through the pampered swarm, I snatched up a baby blue basket from the rack, immediately making my way towards the very rear of Foodvio. The store's decor was lush and exorbitant, and although I was easily middle-class, even I felt out-of-place in this sumptuous space. The best part, by far, was the lovely scent of baked bread, which wafted towards the entrance from the far left corner. It was said that you could smell the bread from every inch of the establishment, and even the nail salon next door could smell it over the stench of their chemicals.

The open refrigerator from the plant milk section sent a shiver down my spine, enveloping my arms in a series of patchy scales as I reached out to claim a carton of oat milk. Just as the tips of my fingers grazed the cool surface, the burning returned; wrapping around each individual finger like a scalding hot glove. With a hiss, I retracted my touch, uneasily eyeing the unscathed surface of my palm. A middle-aged woman with an obnoxious blonde up-do strolled past me, penciled-in brows arched at the sight of my peculiar behavior. She reached out and grabbed the carton I'd just recently touched, slipping it into her basket before shooting me a bewildered look, as if to wordlessly ask me what my problem was.

Awkwardly, I nodded; massaging the searing skin of my inner palm as the lady finally fled, making a beeline towards the low-fat yogurt. The massive refrigeration system cradling my back whined and groaned, mercilessly cooling the horde of contents. Other shoppers continued to pass by, occasionally glancing my way, their brows raised in curiosity. I felt shaky, anxious, *weak.*

Something was wrong.

Remaining on high-alert, I snatched a carton of oat milk and dropped it into my basket, the fiery sensation creeping up my arms and jabbing at my bony shoulders. It was nearly impossible to hold the basket within my searing flesh, and with a racing heart, I searched the shelves for some butter, eager to exit the establishment as soon as possible. Only, with every passing moment, the pain seemed to intensify tenfold. Once I'd located the boxed sticks of butter, my knees nearly collapsed, the weight of my upper body unbearably heavy. It was a struggle to stand, and as soon as the butter met the base of the basket, my legs gave out, sending my buzzing frame to the floor.

I released a coarse cry, thick, blurry tears invading my vision. It felt as if my entire torso were lit ablaze like a luminous, crackling flame; a fire so raging and hot that it would scorch a fluffy marshmallow in under a minute. I wanted nothing more than to burrow my lengthy nails into my skin, to strip it from my body piece by piece until I was nothing but muscle and bone. Perhaps, at least then, it wouldn't burn.

The pain reached a peak when a towering stranger fell to my level, inky, black eyes studying my quivering limbs. I resisted the urge to scream, and I was genuinely surprised that I wasn't a literal ball of fire at this point.

Was this what it felt like to burn alive?

Wordlessly, the ebony-eyed stranger collected my things, politely stuffing them back into the basket before extending a hand. His skin was smooth—*pale*—unblemished and unmarked. A single silver ring encircled his index finger, an unidentifiable marking carved in the center. His hair was almost as black as his eyes, and when the very tip of his fingers brushed against my knuckles, I unintentionally shrieked.

Dumbfounded, the stranger stood to his feet, tossing his hands airborne as if out of surrender. A woman with kind, ocean-blue eyes and a floral sundress rushed to my aide, helping me stand to my feet. The burning began to fade, replaced by a bitter, buzzing numbness that made me dizzy and nauseous.

"Is this man hurting you?" the woman wondered, angrily eyeing the black-eyed stranger. He muttered something unattainable, and before I could reply, he vanished; both a basket and cart absent, his hands empty. I wondered if he was even here to shop at all.

"Are you okay?" the unnamed lady cooed, retrieving my fallen items before handing over my basket. With a shaky nod, I thanked her, ensuring her that I would be okay to finish my shopping. Warily, she bid me farewell, returning to her cart full of fruit. With a whining wheel, she sped away, shooting me a sympathetic glance before rounding a corner.

When I spilled out of the store an agonizing ten minutes later, I nearly collapsed once more; the flimsy paper grocery bag slipping down the slope of my arm and nearly littering everything onto the flooded pavement. I grabbed Raiden's cookies like I'd promised, and I even picked up a fresh loaf of sourdough. Fresh-baked bread always seemed to bring me comfort in my most anxious moments.

The roaring rain had diminished to a shy drizzle, and I was able to locate our vehicle in a nearby parking spot. With the little amount of strength I had remaining in my weakened legs, I bolted towards the car, stumbling into the passenger seat and unintentionally spilling the contents of my shopping bag all over Raiden's lap. He animatedly jumped, his mobile phone slipping from his grasp and burying itself between the seats.

"Jeez, Frey! What's the rush?" Raiden exclaimed, but the moment he laid eyes on my rigid form, his complexion completely softened. Suddenly, his phone was the least of his worries, for he knew that something unsavory had happened to me inside of Foodvio.

"What happened?" The words gently oozed off of his tongue as his hands found my arms, daintily pulling me close and urging me to crawl over the center console. Stiffly, I obliged; edging over the bulbous object before settling upon his warm lap, his dark wash jeans still damp from the rain.

His pleasant palms met my cheeks—gaunt and gray—and with a simple swipe of his thumbs, he wiped away each individual tear. I felt broken, *numb;* as if I'd met death himself. Perhaps, I had—the sickly, pale skin, eyes as black as coal, unbelievably tall and lanky, an eerie, silver ring around a long, slender finger. He *reeked* of death, just as Grammy had described.

I had met the rising De Mörka in the dairy alternative section of a Foodvio. He'd touched me—laid a *hand* on me—made his presence known.

He was the one who would murder my brother.

"The De Mörka," I breathed, sucking in a sharp breath when Raiden's thumb drifted along my plump lower lip. His eyes, however, were firmly fixated on mine, assuring me that he was listening to every word.

"Are you sure?" Raiden whispered, hands rotating downward toward my bottom. With a wince, he lifted my hips ever-so-slightly, adjusting my weight on his lap. Evidently, I was hurting his legs.

"I can get off," I murmured, preparing myself to move. Raiden, however, refused to let me leave. He roughly claimed my hips, pulling me closer to his somewhat smaller frame. I stumbled, forehead smacking against his long, pointed nose as his hips naturally jut upwards in response.

"Ah, *shit,*" he droned, fingers pinching the bridge of his nose. With a gasp, I inspected the surface, gently peeling his fingers away one-by-one to examine the damage. His hot, labored breaths cascaded over my chin, causing an assortment of prickly goosebumps to arise upon my arms and my chest to flush.

"I'm sorry," I whispered, pleased at the absence of blood. *Not broken.*

"Hard-headed inside and out," Raiden chuckled, massaging his nose once more. "Sorry I pulled you back like that, it's just . . . you can sit here, you know. This is your spot."

My spot? On his lap?

"I'm going to go in with you next time," he added, tucking a strand of hair behind my ear. "I'm going to make sure you're safe. I should've been in there to protect you."

"No, Rai," I countered, shaking my head. "You're mortal. There's nothing you could do. You're powerless against a De Mörka. He could snap your neck without even touching you."

Raiden flatly frowned. "I don't like this feeling."

"What feeling?" I asked, nuzzling into his neck. A pleasant hum cascaded over his lips as I buried my face into his warm skin, trembling arms circling his torso. He leaned forward slightly so I could hug him fully.

"This feeling of helplessness," he whispered against my hair. I felt my anxiety instantly lift the moment his fingers met my back, gently kneading the surface as if he were a kitten and I was a soft, furry blanket.

I wanted to exist in his arms forever.

"I'm so scared, Raiden," I whined, hot tears spilling over my cheeks and showering his skin. He knotted his fingers in my hair, enveloping my shivering frame in a tight bear-hug.

"I won't let you die," he said. "I'd rather die than watch you die."

He held me in silence for what felt like an eternity, the aging engine of our car audibly crying in protest. The rain ceased to exist, and a gloomy glow shrouded the sun, enveloping the sky in a glum, cloudy darkness. Although it was barely four, it felt as if we were easing into nighttime all thanks to the storm.

"The last thing I want to do is move right now, but we have to go. I have plans tonight," Raiden suddenly said, detangling my messy locks with his fingers. Puzzled, I tore my face from his neck, shooting him a bewildered glare.

"Plans? With who?"

The crimson blush that crept up his cheeks confirmed my suspicions, and if it were possible, I was almost certain that my heart plummeted straight to my stomach.

"You know that regular we have at the restaurant? Jordan?"

Jordan. She was probably one of the prettiest women I'd ever laid eyes on, with the most sleek, stunning skin in existence, which was free of any scars or blemishes, as if she were manufactured in a laboratory. Her hair was always different, but nevertheless flawless—my favorite style of hers being the result of tight-knit braids from wet hair the night prior, loose and spiraled, loopy around her shoulders. Her sweet-smelling skin reminded me of a gorgeous autumn day, so warm and cozy, and I found myself envious of how sunkissed and stunning she was naturally, right out of the womb. A perfect blend of each divergently hued parent, so elegantly mixed to create *her.*

She was friends with one of our hostesses—Kira, I think—and she spent more time at the restaurant than anyone ever should. I was shocked that Sierra hadn't offered her a job yet. Now that we were down a hostess, she probably would.

And, Raiden had a date with her.

"You're going on a date?" I croaked, eyes widened to the size of marbles. I wondered if he could sense my discomfort.

"I've been wanting to ask her for a few weeks," Raiden sheepishly revealed. "That's why I took so long to get to the car, today. She caught up with me after my shift. We're going to that macaroni and cheese place, y'know, the one that makes those bagels with mac and cheese and shit? She picked it out, sounds like we already have something in common. Good food."

"I don't want to be alone," I said, my tone choppy and rushed. "Not after what just happened–"

"Maybe you can spend tonight with your mom," Raiden shyly suggested. I half-expected him to cancel his outing with Jordan, but that would be incredibly rude of me to even ask for such a thing. After all, Raiden hadn't gone on a single date in over six months, maybe more. Meanwhile, I was busy having shitty sex with Maxwell McKinnon more times that I'd like to admit.

"Yeah," I mumbled. "Yeah. I'll go to Momma's."

Raiden smiled. "Great. I'm supposed to meet with her in an hour, so we should probably hurry. Plus, I don't want that butter to melt or that milk to go sour."

With a nod, I climbed off of his lap, settling into the seat beside him before stiffly latching my seatbelt. I couldn't kick the thought of Jordan out of my mind—how *dare* she be so beautiful—but then again, Raiden deserved this.

He deserved happiness, even if it wasn't with me.

I held in my tears as we fled the parking lot of Foodvio, and the thoughts of my possible encounter with the rising De Mörka suddenly seemed insignificant.

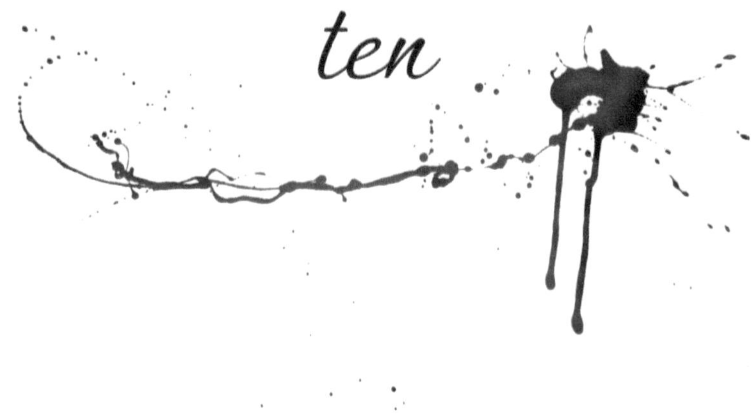

ten

"So," Grammy began, speedily flipping through her magazine seemingly out of annoyance. There was no way that she could read any of the articles that quickly, and I was convinced that she was simply using it as a way to physically express her annoyance.

"You're telling me," she bitterly continued, shaking her head from side to side. "He's on a *date?* And it isn't with *you?*"

"Raiden and I aren't together, Grammy," I countered, picking at my food. Momma ordered an abundance of fried rice and orange chicken, probably enough to feed an entire army. Brennan had yet to come downstairs for supper, and although I didn't ask, I knew that the impending threat of a painful death was weighing heavily on his mind. Meanwhile, I was pouting over my fried rice, over something as silly as a date that I *maybe* wished that I was on.

"You two *live* together," Grammy pressed, requesting an eggroll from my mother, who'd just filed into the room. She was wearing a lime-green wig today, one so long that it tickled the curve of her bottom. Raiden would love it.

Fuck. I need to stop dwelling over Raiden.

"That means nothing," I argued. "We're just best friends. We have been for a very long time."

"Best friends don't sleep in the same bed, Freya," Grammy pointedly explained, thanking my mother for the eggroll.

"Your grandmother has a point," Momma chirped, settling onto the sofa next to me. Dad was busy on a conference call in his office, and Brennan was up in his bedroom, most likely buried beneath an abundance of blankets.

"I don't like Raiden like that," I explained, my voice slightly muffled by a mouthful of rice. I paused, swallowing my food before continuing my speech. "Plus, he hasn't been on a date in awhile. Like, half a year. I've been sort of seeing this guy called Maxwell for a few months now, too. So, it's all good. Really. It's fine."

Although I was persistent, both Grammy and Momma saw right through me, per usual. However, they refused to pry any further, and instead, Momma asked why I was so afraid of being alone tonight. I had to set down my food if I was going to indulge in my eerie experience at Foodvio.

"I need to tell you guys about something that happened a few hours ago," I hastily began, setting down a carton of rice. I went on to describe the entire event in explicit detail, picking apart the stranger's appearance little by little, from the top of his head to the tips of his toes. It was ingrained in my memory, stamped into my subconscious. I'd never forget his face, the oily hook of his nose, the blackness of his eyes.

He was, without a doubt, the man who would murder my brother, and would finish off what remained of the Araedian bloodline.

"What happened when he touched you?" Momma inquired, suctioning her palm to my knee. Her nails were painted an electric blue hue, obnoxiously long and coffin shaped. She was wearing the ring Raiden had gifted her only a few nights prior.

"I just felt this overwhelming urge to jump out of my skin," I revealed, glancing down at my hands. It was a miracle that the flesh still remained, for it truly felt as if my entire being was on fire today. "The worst pain wasn't even when he touched me, though. It was weird. I thought physical contact would somehow make me combust, but nothing happened. It just startled me. Scared me to death. I screamed in the middle of a freaking Foodvio."

"You need to stay indoors," Grammy suddenly said, tossing an unwanted magazine aside. "Brennan, too. Take vacation or sick days from work. The only time you need to be out is at Brennan's birthday party. Once Sunday passes, he'll be a full Araedian, and the De Mörka cannot hurt either of you."

"You said that we're more powerful than they are once we're thirty, right?" I wondered, gaze gravitating towards the staircase. The ripening wood creaked and groaned, and eventually, a pale Brennan stepped into view, eyes as wide as saucers, skin flushed a gauntly green. He looked as if he'd just been sick.

"The De Mörka touched you?" he asked, tone gravelly and thick. He sat suspended on the bottom stair, as if he were afraid to come any closer. As if I harbored the ability to off him myself.

"We don't know if it was the rising De Mörka for sure," Momma chirped, waving my brother over. "To answer your question, Freya, it's not that we are invincible against them after thirty, but we're a hell of a lot stronger. If it's just the one against all of us, they have no chance."

Brennan sauntered over, distraughtly eyeing my stiff frame. I'd never seen him so scared in my life.

"Are you going to stay here, Freya? Until the venue tour and my birthday party?" Brennan lightly inquired, taking a seat on the floor. He didn't bother sitting next to me on the sofa, even though there was an ample amount of room.

"No. I'll be safe at home with Raiden," I said. "You're still going to have the party? Even with this threat?"

"We cannot let fear stop us from enjoying monumental moments in our lives," Grammy interjected, still nipping at her eggroll. She took her time with food, and she was often the last person to finish her meal. "Although this is a terrifying time, all of us will be present at Brennan's birthday party. If the De Mörka dares to show his or her face, it will be easy enough to ward them off. I'm more concerned about them attacking beforehand, because Brennan will have—*hell*—how many people are supposed to be there, Bren?"

"Sixty, I think," Brennan boasted, unable to mask his grin. "Lots of people like me."

I don't think I even knew or liked sixty people.

"The venue tour is on Thursday," Momma began, twirling her faux green hair around a ring-clad finger. "It's up the mountain. This big, beautiful estate. A family friend owns it—Wilhelm Weatherby—and he's more than pleased to let Brennan have his birthday there. Get this, Frey—it's *free of charge!* It's massive; six-thousand square feet, with a pool, a ballroom, and more. He doesn't even live there full-time, it's a goddamn getaway house. *Immaginalo!* Must be nice."

"Yeah," I mumbled. "Must be."

"So, you'll be there?" Brennan pressed, referencing the house tour. "Bring Raiden, too. He should be off work by then."

"Raiden should take time off work, too. To be home with you," Grammy pressed. "To make sure you're safe."

"I'm not going to ask that of him, Grammy. He should be able to save his sick and vacation days. This is my burden to bear, not his."

However, the more that I thought about it, the more I wanted him home with me at all times, just at least until this hell passes.

I despised myself for my inability to function without Raiden Crow breathing down my neck. Maybe Grammy knew more than I gave her credit for. They always say that your parents and grandparents have a second sight for seeing things that we never can. Things that in our eyes, are completely invisible.

"Grammy," I breathed, glancing at the clock. Half past eight. "I think you may be right."

It was a short walk from my parents' homey abode to the townhome Raiden and I shared. Less than twenty minutes on foot, even shorter on wheels. Unluckily for me, I lent Raiden the car for his date, so I was stuck hitchhiking. Brennan offered to drive me, but I already felt as if I were suffocating, and the fresh, crisp air after a violent rainstorm was exactly what I needed to clear my head.

We lived in a pleasant neighborhood, surrounded by a multitude of lively children and a surplus of barking dogs. I passed by a nighttime jogger wearing a pair of pricey headphones, who awkwardly waved in my direction before scurrying past. They looked warm and toasty, whereas I was trembling beneath my thin, weak coat. It was ridiculous how cold it was so close to May. If the temperature dropped any lower, we'd surely be woken by a blanket of snow come sunrise.

Pulling my zip-up jacket closed, I continued onward; quickly crossing the main road and easing into our community. An elderly woman was walking her dog, someone I'd never seen before, but waved to nevertheless. She ignored my greeting, acting as if she hadn't seen me at all. She lacked a coat, dressed in nothing but a homely dress and bright, white sneakers. I wondered if she was even conscious of her whereabouts, and she slightly reminded me of Raiden's adoptive mother, withering away in her bed, forgetting chunks of her identity with each passing day.

A smile stretched along my mouth at the sight of our car parked in its usual space, tires moderately crooked, the left rear window unintentionally cracked. I dug through my purse in search of my keys, and I couldn't quite shake the feeling of immeasurable glee that enveloped my every limb. It was so silly—I was *excited* to see him, although I'd seen him only several hours prior, and I saw him every single day. Admittedly, I'd missed him—missed his laugh, his smile. The way his curls cradled his shoulders, the assorted rings that hugged his fingers. The hair ties threaded around his wrists, multi-colored, mostly pink. He liked the color pink.

I let out a laugh at the ridiculous thoughts—*I mean holy shit, Frey, come on*—and I shook my head. Here I was, *analyzing* my best friend's every feature as if I were some lovesick puppy.

Was I?

The dogs failed to greet me at the door. It wasn't entirely a shock, for Raiden was already home, and around bedtime, they preferred not to move from their comfortable slumbers. They were God-awful guard dogs.

I filed into the foyer, which was solely illuminated by a tiny, yellow night light, which took on the shape of a beautiful butterfly. The wings were once painted purple, but the extensive years of use seemed to strip the wings white, casting a creative, oddly shaped glow along the wall. It highlighted one of my favorite framed photos directly above—one of Raiden and me on a hike in the mountains, aged nearly seven years. I smiled at the sight, and fell to my knees to greet a sneezing Mimosa, tail wagging a million miles a minute.

"Hey, sweetie," I cooed, voice barely above a whisper. "Where's Dada? Is he sleeping?"

I tossed my purse aside on the floor, completely disinterested in the object and the contents within. I didn't care about my phone, nor did I even need or want to see it for the rest of the night. All that I cared about at this very moment was Raiden. I could feel the heat rise up to my cheeks as I crept towards our bedroom on the right of the hall, and I couldn't quite mask my excitement as it bubbled up my chest in the form of a furious blush. I wanted nothing more than to cuddle up to his sleepy frame, brush his hair out of his eyes, nuzzle into his neck . . .

The door was cracked, a gap only wide enough to fit Mimosa. My fingers danced along the wooden surface, a stupid smile slapped across my face as I imagined how innocent—how *beautiful* a barely-clothed Raiden likely looked, snuggled up beneath the blankets–

My thoughts were interrupted by a foreign sound. It startled me at first, made me freeze in fear, but when it finally registered in my brain, I couldn't help but gasp. Lowly, just barely enough even for me to hear. My palm flew up to my parted mouth, shielding my shock as I repositioned myself in front of the parted doorway at just the right angle to slyly view what laid within.

Routinely, the tiny television was on—generating a shy, blue hue along the room. Kelso was curled up in a big ball at the foot of the bed—*my bed*—but in my bed wasn't just Raiden, but also a stranger. *Jordan.* Bundled up beneath my blankets, curled hair fawned over my pillow, loose lips glued to *my Raiden.*

All that was visible was a multitude of hair and a mess of lips, and although I couldn't see beneath the blankets, I knew *damn* well that she was naked on my sheets—on *my side, my bed, my spot . . .*

Although the sight was borderline unbearable to witness, and the tightening sensation in my stomach seemed to intensify with every waking moment, I couldn't quite tear my glare away. I was transfixed, yet horrified; dejectedly gawking at the duo beneath the thick, weighty duvet. I watched as his mouth detached from hers, gliding teasingly along her jaw before dipping down onto her neck. A lustful sigh slipped off of her tainted lips, and I caught wind of a sensual shift underneath my blanket, one which made the blood curdle within my veins, surely shifting to the consistency of syrup. I felt sluggish and sick, and I finally tore my blurry gaze away when Jordan clambered on top of him, a profusion of elegant curls cloaking nearly the entirety of her curved spine. The sight of his hands—the *rings*—trailing along her torso and dipping down the bend of her hips pushed me over the edge. As quietly as I could, I stumbled down the hallway, choking down an immeasurable amount of bile as I filed into the pitch-black kitchen at the rear of the complex. Using my hands as my guide, I found my way towards the sink, thankful not to witness the sight of my dinner as it collided with the bare basin.

Mimosa whined, gently rubbing against my leg as if to comfort me. I couldn't quite nudge the vivid visuals of Jordan straddling Raiden from my mind, and as I gently rinsed the sink clean, the stranger in my bed boldly made her presence known, a staccato of giggles and girlish groans ricocheting off the paper-thin walls.

My palms met my ears, desperately attempting to drown out the sound of Jordan's sensual sounds. Although I'd expelled a majority of my dinner, my stomach still churned, threatening to spew what little remained.

I should've never left my Momma's house.

It was ridiculous—*comical.* Hypocritical, almost. I spent several nights with Maxwell and Raiden never said a word, but the one time—the *one single time* Raiden brings a girl home in over six months, I nearly lose my mind. I wondered now how Raiden felt when I spent the night at Maxwell's, and if he experienced the very same burning feeling deep within his belly at the thought of me in Maxwell's bed.

I retired to the sofa after several moments of pitiful sulking on the kitchen floor, fingers still shoved within the canal of each ear. I nearly tripped over my tiny dog twice, lowly cursing as I navigated the astonishingly dark room, and I made a mental note to order another night light (or four) to brighten the area up in case I found myself in a similar situation. Hopefully, a repeat of tonight would never occur.

Hopefully.

The moment my head hit the decorative throw pillow, Mimosa met my lap; curling up into a dainty ball atop my legs. She lovingly lapped at my fingers, soaking my skin in an abundance of wet kisses. Out of the three of them, she was an absolute guru at reading our emotions. Every time I cried, she was the first at my side.

"Mommy's okay, baby," I whispered, careful not to let my voice travel. Jordan's gratified whimpers met my ears once more, prompting a pained cringe to arise upon my features.

I'd never be able to look her in the eye after this.

Mimosa was unconvinced. She continued her gentle assault on my hands, rubbing the skin raw. Thus, a thought dawned upon me, resurfacing a recent memory. Due to our completely abnormal circumstances and my apparent ability to extract bits and pieces of someone's soul each time I healed them, I could physically feel Raiden's abundant emotions. The fact was proven when I was woken from my slumber to the feeling of invisible fingers gliding along my nether regions, confirming the inevitable: I can, and would probably always feel Raiden's pleasure. Only now, in this very moment, I felt nothing. Naught. Zilch. It was as if . . .

My racing thoughts were interrupted by the presence of a familiar voice—*his*. Gravelly, low. I could barely make out what he was saying—something along the lines of washing up—and as I shifted my stance on the sofa, slightly startling Mimosa, I heard the bathroom door slam.

Were they moving it to the shower?

My breaths thinned as roaring water met tile, mostly muffled by the sealed door. I couldn't quite tame my racing heart, and as Mimosa nipped at my fingers, I nearly gasped, for that dreaded sensation suddenly arose, swallowing me up whole. I weakly attempted to muffle my moans with a clammy palm, back flattening against the cushion as Mimosa jumped off of my lap, as if to give me privacy.

I nearly shrieked when Jordan unexpectedly exited my bedroom, stumbling into her six-inch stilettos, curled hair a mangled mess. I couldn't quite make out her features due to the darkness of the hallway, and I nearly bit down on my palm as an additional wave of pleasure coursed through my core.

Jordan paused in the doorway, fumbling through her purse in search of something specific. She extracted her mobile phone, the bright, white light illuminating her flawless features as she dialed someone's number. I sunk into the cushions, desperately attempting to make myself as invisible as possible as the blinding light disappeared and the phone met her ear.

"Hey, Kira? I'm at Raiden's—yeah, that guy from Tostada's. Could you come pick me up? I don't think I should stay the night."

My ears perked up at her statement.

"Yeah, I'll give you the address. Let me just step outside for a second," Jordan added in a hushed tone. She glanced over her shoulder once more to view our bedroom, where—judging by the sensations invading my entire being—Raiden was still busy with himself in the shower. "He's in the shower, I don't really know if I should say goodbye. Things were nice and hot for a bit, but then got weird really quick. He almost seemed like he was trying to think of someone or something else. He had his eyes closed most of the time, and he couldn't even finish, but he had the courtesy to help me get there. I actually think he may be getting himself off in the shower."

I resisted the urge to gasp. *He couldn't get off?*

"Yeah, yeah. I'm stepping outside. Just a second," Jordan slurred, slender fingers encircling the doorknob as she yanked the unlocked entryway open. The door slammed on her heel, and I could still slightly hear the low tone of her eager voice just outside the window.

I sauntered over towards the window, the shell of my ear suctioning to the cool glass surface as I eavesdropped on Jordan and Kira's conversation.

Poor Raiden, how would he ever be able to face either of them head-on when we returned to work?

My knees suddenly buckled, an overwhelming sensation engrossing my interest as I nearly fell to the floor, eyes rolled—*tipped* back into my skull, a shudder traveling along my limbs. Then—*nothing.* An empty, eerie void. Resentment. *Depression.* He was upset, exceedingly so. I could feel his sorrow, as if it were a tangible thing that I could hold close to my heart.

I flinched at the sound of the bathroom door abruptly opening, and Raiden audibly sighed at the sight of an empty bed. Jordan was still blabbering away outside, talking Kira's ear off. I was in a bitty ball beside the television, completely concealed from Raiden's sight if he were to venture into the hallway. Only, he stayed in the bedroom, a hushed string of obscenities replenishing the stagnant void. I remained inert against the wall, frantic heart fluttering beneath the cavity of my chest. I felt weak—*spent.* My fingers and toes lewdly buzzed, reminding me of the event that had just transpired yet again. Poor Raiden would never be able to touch himself without me knowing, and I hated myself for it. I'd misguidedly absorbed so much of his soul over the years, from something as simple as healing his wounds.

I regretted ever laying a finger on him.

The explicit terms that tickled Raiden's tongue grew louder in intensity, and I flinched when I heard him start stripping the bed. The sound of the bedsheets violently slapping skin made my own crawl, and with trembling legs, I crawled forward, taking a small peek across the hallway to view the damage. A growing pile of soiled sheets enveloped the doorway, along with wrinkled pillowcases and my favorite duvet. I couldn't see the bed itself, but judging the size of the pile, I could conclude that he'd torn every single article of material from the mattress, leaving it stark nude. He was angry—*bitter.* I could feel it creeping up my spine. In turn, it almost made *me* mad, but I reminded myself that the emotions invading my being were his, not my own.

I heard him collapse atop the mattress, a defeated groan easing off of his lips as he laid stagnant on the surface. Then, there was a shift; the coarse creak of the aging box spring, the sound of his phone being disconnected from the charger.

I nearly keeled over dead when my purse began to buzz from the hallway.

"Fuck!" I hissed, heart halting clean in my chest. If he heard the vibration, it was game over. He'd be livid—*furious.* I was a goddamn peeping Tom.

With as much strength as my weak limbs could muster, I dodged the open doorway and filed into the foyer, scooping the pulsating purse up into my arms. By the time I flattened myself up against the front door, the vibration ceased, and Raiden cursed.

"Come *on,* Freya. Answer the damn phone."

I nearly cried when he called again, the vibration within my purse promptly resuming. I wanted to scream—to cry—but instead, I bit my lower lip with such force that I tasted blood. The unpleasant flavor drained down my throat, provoking a disgusted grimace to overcome my features. I was trapped between Raiden and Jordan, and I wasn't sure whether or not to bite the bullet and reveal myself, or to screen his calls and hide out behind the couch until he fell asleep.

I was pleased to no longer hear Jordan's preppy voice beyond the door, and with a short spurt of adrenaline, I eased out of the entrance;

filing into the front lawn. The woman was still pacing in the parking lot, big, bright eyes fixated on her feet as she walked. Her phone remained glued to her ear.

Quivering from head-to-toe, I rounded the townhouse, concealing myself between the buildings before digging my hand into the buzzing purse. I answered on the very last ring, exhaustion evident in my slurred speech.

"Frey?" Raiden began, his tone laced with suspicion. "You okay?"

"Yeah, sorry. Brennan and I are playing those dumbass interactive video games, you know. I need to work out more, I'm winded." I lied straight through my teeth, cringing with every false word. I hated lying to him. "What's up? Is everything okay?"

"Come home." Raiden spoke. It wasn't a question, it was a command.

"What? Why?" I queried, feigning confusion. I still couldn't catch my breath.

"Just . . . come home, Freya. I need you."

I need you.

I could hardly contain my glee. *He needed me.*

"I'll be right there."

eleven

We didn't discuss Raiden's date with Jordan. I didn't ask, and he didn't tell.

Although the bed was still stripped bare when I entered the bedroom, I refused to acknowledge it, and instead, I curled up into his arms. He held me tight and close, heart thickly thumping against my skull as my cheek claimed his chest. We laid like that for hours, gazes glued to the television. Words weren't necessary, for each other's presence was all we really needed.

It was well into the early morning hours when Raiden finally succumbed to a deep sleep, his light, airy snores tickling my forehead. Even in his slumber, he refused to let up on his grip; arms tied taut around my torso, legs intertwined with mine. Shortly after, I followed suit, and when the doorbell rang less than four hours later,

I woke up to a sticky spot of spit, one which suctioned my chin to Raiden's bare belly.

Repulsed by the drool, I swiftly wiped it away, ridding Raiden's skin of the evidence as the irksome bell sounded once more. Raiden's gorgeous, green eyes fluttered open by the third irritable ring, and I was already scooching myself across the mattress, waking both Kelso and Mimosa. Bear was already at the door, a deep bark crawling up his throat.

"I'm coming!" I bitterly exclaimed, hoping that whoever was beyond the door wouldn't ring the damn bell again. I caught wind of Raiden's sleepy groan, and when I glanced over my shoulder, he had turned himself over, burying his pointed nose into the fluffy pillow.

I nearly tripped over the heaping pile of discarded bedsheets on the way to the door, and Bear continued to bark even after I yanked it open to reveal my brother.

"Brennan?" I breathed, a silken pillowcase wrapped around my ankle. "What the hell time is it?"

"Seven," he said, blinking twice. "Can I come in?"

He didn't ask about the mangled mess of bedsheets in the doorway of our bedroom, nor did he acknowledge a slump Raiden sprawled out along the mattress. Instead, he took it upon himself to ease into the living room, casually collapsing upon the sofa. Bear, Kelso, and Mimosa all crowded him, taking turns showering him with affection as he eagerly grinned.

"So, I take it you two have taken off of work?"

My eyes widened. *Shit.*

"Uh, let me call Sierra," I stammered, disappearing from sight. I wasn't prepared for the possible screaming match, but there was no way that Raiden was getting out of bed anytime soon, and it wouldn't be smart of me to go into work alone, especially with the rising De Mörka on the loose. He ran into me at Foodvio, so it wouldn't surprise me if he was the first customer at Tostada's this afternoon. He'd probably occupy the very rear booth, denying food but requesting a tall glass of water, which would remain mostly untouched. Once the glass was slick with condensation, he would surely slip his fingertips along the wet exterior, etching cryptic shapes along the surface. He'd lie in wait, obscure eyes fused to the swinging kitchen doors, just aching for our eyes to meet. He'd smirk when I'd catch wind of his lofty frame from the parted doorway, and my arms would give out, sending an array of shiny, red tomatoes to my feet. A shrill scream would bubble up my throat, and before anyone could question what I'd seen, he would be gone. That was, until the end of my shift, when I was alone at the back of the building, he'd be lurking—*waiting.* Waiting to snap my neck with a simple stare. Waiting to end the Araedian bloodline for good.

I shook Raiden awake before calling our manager Sierra, hands violently trembling against his warm skin. A pair of bloodshot eyes met my widened orbs, and he sensed my distress; immediately sitting up on the mattress and taking my flushed face in his hands.

"Frey, what is it?" The statement slipped off of his plump lips in the form of a coo, and I nearly melted to goo at the sound. His voice was husky and deep, still laced with sleep.

"Grammy told me that you and I need to take off work and stay home in case the De Mörka comes for me," I shakily explained, unable to calm myself down. "Just until after Brennan's birthday party on Sunday, because at midnight Monday morning, he'll be thirty. Then, we'll be safe."

Raiden nodded. "Okay. Have you called Sierra?"

I bit my lip. "I was hoping you could. I'm afraid she'll yell."

Raiden smiled. "I'll take care of it."

I busied myself with my brother in the living room, while Raiden slipped outside to get a better signal. I felt anxious and stiff, nimble fingers lightly kneading the tense flesh of my neck as I took a seat beside Brennan on the sofa. He'd taken the liberty of turning on the television, his glare fixated on an early-morning cartoon. The TV remote dangled in thin-air, partial to the left of his skull, dipping down towards his chin. Absent-mindedly, he spun the hovering object with his index finger, patiently waiting for the sleek, black plastic to complete a full circle before spinning it once more.

"You're up early." I spoke, breaking the silence after what seemed like an eternity. Raiden was still on the phone outside, his calm, comforting tone absent in my time of need. Regardless of how hard I'd tried, I couldn't quite banish the thoughts of him and Jordan from my mind.

"I wanted you and Raiden to come with me to the clinic today," Brennan began, coiling his fingers around the floating remote. He flipped through the channels before eventually settling on an episode of *My Wife and Kids.*

"The clinic?" I questioned, flinching when Mimosa unexpectedly hopped onto my lap. I ran my palm along her fur as she peppered wet, sloppy tongue-kisses along my arm.

"I'm going to have my sperm frozen," my brother revealed in a tense tone, refusing to waver. "You know . . . just in case."

"Nothing's going to happen," I dryly defended, but I wasn't so sure. I felt as if the rising De Mörka was around the corner—lying in wait, preparing to strike. Every day leading up to Brennan's thirtieth birthday felt like it could potentially be the last for both of us.

"We can never be too sure," Brennan mumbled. "If something happens to me before I reach thirty, I need to be sure that our bloodline goes on. I don't think he'll come after you. You're already fully established, you could defeat him if you really tried. I'm still weak. Underdeveloped."

"You aren't weak," I countered, resting a hand atop his knee. His leg impulsively jerked away from my sudden, invasive touch before eventually easing back, as if seeking comfort. "But, I think it's a good idea. We can never be too sure."

"Maybe you should get your eggs frozen, or whatever they'd do," Brennan shyly suggested.

Before I could reply, Raiden reappeared, stuffing his cell into his pajama pant pocket before offering a hand to my brother, who enthusiastically shook it. My roommate went without a shirt, a sight that made my stomach turn, regardless of how many times I'd laid eyes on his naked torso.

Brennan asked about Jordan. The sound of her name prompted both Raiden and I to simultaneously stiffen; as if the mere mention of the girl was enough to send the both of us into a frantic frenzy. Raiden settled into the leather barcalounger, eyes glued to his knotted fingers as he told the tale of his failed date.

"She's nice," he began, avoiding Brennan's curious stare. My brother audibly urged him onward, undoubtedly curious of what had transpired less than twenty-four hours earlier. I wasn't sure whether to flee, or simply endure the torture.

"She calls herself an *aspiring author,* but claims that disgruntled is a better word for her. She writes once in a blue moon, but has dreams of being published. She's had a few publications in the paper, nothing significant, but her mom has all of the clippings framed," Raiden began, purposefully avoiding my downcast stare. Brennan neglected to pick up on the stiff vibe, and instead urged his friend onward, as if the tale of Jordan's life interested him beyond comprehension.

"Jordan's like a literary guru. She started spewing off a bunch of names—Vladimir something, and George Orwell I think was one of them, I've only read a part of that one book of his, 1980? 1984? Something like that. I think Tolkien was another. She kept asking what my favorite novel was and—*shew.* When's the last time I actually read a book cover to cover, Frey?"

I wasn't aware that he'd asked me a question until Brennan tapped my leg, repeating the inquiry. Lowly, I murmured something about not knowing when, and he continued.

"Anyways, the food was okay, but she ate a sandwich with a fork. Have you ever seen someone eat a *sandwich* with a *fork,* Bren?"

My thoughts drifted to that of Jordan's and his date, and I could almost hear the pretty girl droning on and on and *on* about her favorite works of literature, quoting parts of *The Great Gatsby* as if liking the old tale was a personality trait. In my made-up scenario, Raiden was quiet, *awkward.* Poking and prodding at his food, he slowly sipped his carbonated coke, choking down a pesky bubble that threatened to spew in the form of a forced cough. Jordan cutting up her sandwich into cubes, like some rich-bitch prissy pants who was afraid to smear her lipstick or get her hands dirty. She probably wiped her mouth after every individual bite, dotting the surface, barely brushing against the painted skin. Most of Raiden's food remained untouched, his thoughts riddled with jumbled conversation starters, all of which fell through when Jordan changed the topic to something literary related.

How she ended up in our bed at the end of the night was still a mystery in itself.

"So, no second date, then?" Brennan wondered, expression smug. I wanted to slap him clean across the face.

Raiden shrugged. "We just didn't click. It's okay, though. I had a good time. I think she did, too."

I'd say so.

"Hey, Bren?" I began, eager to end the conversation. I'd rather not dwell over Jordan and Raiden and be reminded of what I'd witnessed them doing *in our bed.* I couldn't help but steal a glance at the balled-up sheets in our doorway.

"Oh yeah, what are you doing here so early?" Raiden asked, calling Kelso over. The large, graceless dog skipped over towards his father, eager to climb up into his lap.

"I was just telling Freya that I wanted to run to the clinic and freeze some of my sperm," Brennan said. "Just to be safe."

"Oh," Raiden replied, clearly dumbfounded by my brother's statement. "So, this is pretty serious, huh?"

"Did Sierra say anything? About us taking the rest of the week off?" I keenly interrupted, suddenly sick at the thought of my brother perishing right before his birthday.

"She's pissed," Raiden muttered, scratching behind Kelso's ears. "But, she said she'll get it covered. We owe her big time, she says."

"Can we get to the clinic? I don't want to be out too much. I'm nervous as hell about this De Mörka fucker that Frey ran into at the Foodvio. I feel like he's lurking around every corner, and I just want to get this done and over with to cover my ass," Brennan blurted, standing to his feet. "Do either of you need to shower? I know I woke you both."

"Um, no," I muttered, eyeing Raiden as he climbed to his feet. "I mean, it can just wait until tonight."

"Great," Brennan purred. "Let's get this shit over with, so we can hunker down and avoid any encounters with this De Mörka bitch. The less time we spend out and about, the better."

The last place I wanted to be at half-past eight on a midweek morning was in a fertility clinic, surrounded by several squirming strangers and an elderly nurse behind the reception desk. She looked either asleep or dead—I couldn't quite tell—and I felt awkward and alone. Brennan had already gone back to a room, and Raiden excused himself to go outside for a smoke.

Although he claimed he'd quit this week, he still hadn't, which wasn't much of a surprise. Just as anyone and everyone who relied on the cancer sticks to tame their anxiety, Raiden used them as a crutch, especially now, when at any given moment, he could lose both of his best friends to some deranged psychopath. He referred to the little, poisonous tubes as a circular safety blanket—the warm nicotine instantly calming his nerves and keeping him grounded.

I was lucky that I didn't feel the cravings, and I almost wondered if they even existed at all. I'd always learned that the urge to smoke was almost overbearing, but if that were so, I'd feel the urge creep up my spine like a chill—tyrannical and cold, enveloping my lungs and squeezing until every last puff of air escaped, and I was left gasping—*suffocating.*

Instead, I felt nothing at all. No urge, no desire. It was evident that Raiden wasn't as addicted to cigarettes as I'd originally thought, and perhaps, he only smoked them simply because he wanted to, and not because he *needed* to. The fact almost pissed me off more, especially knowing how dangerous smoking can be. It was a well known fact that it could absolutely obliterate his lungs—give him cancer, even—and knowing that he could easily quit, he could pretend as if he'd never laid hands on them, had upset me beyond comprehension. The fact of the matter was: he simply did not want to.

I suddenly recalled his comparison to quitting with that of me weaning off of my antidepressants. The comparison was comical, all things considered. I took the medication because I *needed* to, and I stopped because I *wanted* to. Raiden smoked because he *wanted* to, not because he *needed* to. There were little similarities at all, and he knew how hard it was for me to stop taking my medication. It wouldn't be nearly as hard for him to stop such a silly habit, something he was barely even dependent on.

The clinic was downtown, and Brennan had offered to drive us. He was a reckless driver and played his music a tad-bit too loud, but I was thankful that he didn't ask to take our car. The aging vehicle was—quite frankly—an embarrassment, and I wouldn't be shocked if it decided not to start the next time we needed to use it.

A thick, lemon scent clung to the air, one which reminded me of cheap cleaning chemicals. The chairs were warm and worn, the bland, brown checkered fabric slightly stained and torn. Mindless magazines littered each side table, laboredly stacked, several pages curled. A celebrity that I did not recognize laid plastered along the front cover of the magazine that laid across my lap, bright, bold letters scrawled along the surface, displaying the pretty woman's name and a statement about sex. That's all anyone ever cared about anymore: *sex.* Sex, drugs, technology. I felt a headache blossoming in the rump of my skull before I'd even peeled the paper book open to reveal its nettlesome contents.

Raiden returned moments later, collapsing into the chair beside me with an exaggerated exhale. I could smell the smoke on him, clinging to the loopy curls of his hair like a sweet-smelling perfume. It didn't bother me much—the smell. Most complained that it reeked—*what a foul, filthy scent*—but I paired it with happiness, with *him.* It just reminded me of Raiden.

We didn't speak. Instead, we just sat in our separate seats, his ring-clad hands folded atop his lap, mine tangled within the straps of my purse. A loopy, auburn lock tickled the bone of his jaw, dancing along with the infrequent bursts of air that emerged from the vent directly above.

I knew that Jordan was on his mind, stuck to his thoughts like glue. He had a bad habit of replaying foul memories over and over and *over,* fixating his mind on every single event, *wondering*, thinking how he could've done things differently, worrying that he'd said or done the wrong thing. I knew he regretted sleeping with her, that much was evident by his outburst. He'd stripped the bed bare, utterly repulsed by what had transpired atop the sheets only minutes prior. I wasn't sure if he'd ever admit what happened upon them, but perhaps, he assumed that I already knew. His mind was a tangled web of emotion, and although I couldn't quite read his thoughts, I learned over time how to read him, as if he were a book that I'd read over and over. I'd memorized every page, every sentence, so much so that I could recite it line by line, word for word.

Suddenly, I became achingly aware of the surplus of suggestive posters, pamphlets, and decor that cluttered the room. He must've noticed too, for he visibly tensed beside me, his grip tightening around oily fingers. The sexually-charged energy that bounced between was undeniable—so thick and weighty that it made my cheeks grow hot. I almost didn't want to look him in the face, for I knew what naughty thoughts presumably plagued his mind—he was a man, after all—and although we'd discussed the ins and outs of sex countless times since our teenage days, something about this moment felt different. Suddenly, it seemed as if the man beside me was no longer just my *best friend*—no, right now, it felt as if I were seated beside someone I'd been undeniably infatuated with for an ungodly amount of time.

But *no*—it couldn't be possible. Raiden was my *friend.* My *best* friend. He had been for nearly ninety-percent of my lifetime. There was nothing between us besides two entire decades of memories.

We'd slept in the same bed for *years,* unintentionally touched one another in *forbidden places,* seen what laid beneath our clothes. And . . . *nothing.* It was never more than just—*this.* Companionship. Best friends. *Only* friends.

Or were we?

The sudden shift was impossible to ignore. The fact of the matter was, something *had* shifted. Significantly so. For the first time in existence, I felt nervous—*awkward*—around him. The thought of sex and intimacy and nakedness made my cheeks flush a fire-engine red. Suddenly, the sheer *nearness* of him—the feeling of his clothed elbow brushing mine—was enough to send me into a buzzing frenzy.

As much as I wanted to acknowledge his presence, I refused to. Instead, I studied our surroundings, desperately avoiding even the smallest amount of physical and verbal contact with the man. I could smell the smoke on his shirt—pictured the way his curly hair framed his face—and immediately, my heart began to race.

We weren't alone in the waiting room. I craned my neck to scan the stuffy area, and I caught wind of a newcomer's arrival: a woman, twenty at most, with sleek, shiny black hair and eyes as dark as coal. Her skin was white—translucent, almost—and she reminded me of one of the ghosts you'd see on a crappy Lifetime movie.

Although there were an endless amount of empty seats, she chose the one directly opposite of mine, and I couldn't help but stiffly stare as she settled into the chair. The cushion released a dramatic puff of air at the presence of her tiny, stick-like frame, and something was . . . *wrong.* Very, very wrong.

The flushed surface of her flesh was free of any markings; not a single blemish. No scars, pimples, lumps, bumps, or beauty marks. Nothing at all. A blank, clean slate. She was dressed in the most peculiar outfit I'd ever seen—a flimsy, floral blouse and cropped, checker-patterned pants that certainly did not match, a small rip across the knee, exposing the pasty, translucent skin beneath. As much as I wanted to pick apart every inch of her outfit, I couldn't help but meet her stare—ice cold, dark, *black.* Irises absent, nothing but a giant, gaping pupil, fixated *directly* on me. Unblinking, unwavering; completely and wholly glued to my squirming self.

That's when the burning began.

Gradually, then all at once. Beginning at the tips of my fingers and gravitating upwards, creeping up my forearm in a winding, snakelike motion. It felt hot, *deep.* Buried beneath the veins, submerging into the very marrow of my bones. With every agonizing moment, she stared; empty eyes rotating towards my fiery arms, as if she *knew*, as if she could feel it, too.

As if she were causing it.

Panicked, I latched my fingers around Raiden's wrist, warm tears beading up at the corners of my eyes as the fingers on his opposite hand danced along my hot flesh.

"Frey? What is it?" he cooed, gliding his thumb along a particularly peppery part.

"It's her," I hissed, unable to tear my glare away from the woman. She was stiff—*still.* She still hadn't blinked. She appeared to be staring at everything, yet nothing at all. Empty and cold, like a lifeless body perched up in a chair.

Before Raiden could reply, I was on my feet, breaking the bond and refusing to let her in—*the De Mörka, undoubtedly*—and I audibly begged for him to climb to his feet, too.

"We need to go," I rushed, refusing to look back at the woman—*girl*—whatever the hell she was. She was still staring, I could feel it. Like a hole burning into my back.

"Brennan's still back there–"

"We need to go *get* him!" I exclaimed, unraveling my fingers from his arm. The receptionist was still consciously absent; lazy eyelids gradually fluttering. She appeared to be in between sleep, and she hadn't even noticed my sudden outburst. The few others in the waiting room did, though, and my face felt almost as hot as my arms at the realization.

"Can we even go back there?" Raiden wondered, but I was already tumbling through the double doors, a trio of yellow signs suctioned to the surface—*Patient Access Only/Do Not Enter/Emergency Entrance*

Only. This was a goddamn *emergency,* and it didn't matter if I failed to obtain permission, because the fucking De Mörka was seated in the waiting room, and my innocent, unknowing brother was somewhere deep in the clinic without a single clue.

Raiden tumbled through the doors after me, calling out a series of requests that barely graced my ears. All that mattered right now was finding Brennan—*protecting* Brennan—and god*damn* my arms hurt so unbelievably bad. Even if I sliced the skin clean off, I was convinced that they would *still* burn, because the sensation was so deep in my bones that it almost physically didn't exist at all.

The rear of the clinic looked like a blended blur of white—all of the doors looked exactly the same, differentiated only by a single, numerical symbol. I had no idea which room Brennan was in, but nevertheless, I knocked and tugged at every occupied room, shouting a plethora of pleas mostly muffled by my tears. Raiden's arms laced around my waist, an abundance of sweet nothings tickling the shell of my ear as he attempted to calm me, whilst gently reminding me of what the patients were actually doing behind each of these doors.

"He's safe in the room," Raiden pressed, burying his nose in my neck.

A nearby nurse approached, concern etched across her features as she demanded to know why we were back there without permission.

"I'm trying to find my brother," I breathed, crawling out of Raiden's constricting hold. "Brennan Gallo. I need to see him. It's an extreme emergency."

The nurse dressed in nothing but bright blue polka-dots raised a suspicious brow before waving us over to the end of the hallway, which led to a foyer containing a circular desk and other nurses. Just as the little blonde woman picked up her lime green clipboard, a male nurse rounded the corner, slightly out of breath and shaken.

"Nicole," he croaked, catching the attention of our nurse—evidently called Nicole. "There's an em-emergency in room eleven."

My heart stopped. *Brennan.*

I broke into a sprint, shoving past a puzzled Nicole and a breathless male nurse, who'd claimed his knees with wide, open palms in order to catch his breath. The eleventh room on the opposite side of the rooms we'd already passed, and by the time I reached the door, I heard it: the sobs.

With palms as hot as a wicked, warped flame, I stumbled into the room, where my younger brother was curled up into a ball on the floor, nails roughly brushing against his forearm, drawing beads of blood. A steady strand of the vivid liquid seeped from each of his nostrils, dipping down onto his jeans and soaking the fabric through and through.

"Bren!" I shrieked, falling to my knees beside him. He was worse off than I was, and I nearly burst into tears when his bright, bloodshot orbs met mine.

"It's here," he croaked. "The De Mörka. It's here to kill me."

Raiden finally joined us, a horrified gasp easing off of his lips at the sight. He, too, fell to Brennan's aide; coiling his fingers around my brother's wrist as he yanked his nails away from his skin.

"Stop that, you're ruining your arm," Raiden scolded, big, bug-like eyes meeting mine. "Frey, heal him."

I obeyed orders, releasing a staggered, shaky breath before gyrating my thumb against the miniature, self-inflicted wounds on Brennan's inner arm. Instantly, they sealed, and the only evidence of their presence that remained was the bright, red blood smeared along his arm.

"Thanks, Frey," Brennan whispered. Raiden snatched a few tissues from the nearby counter, balling them up and suctioning them to Brennan's bleeding nose. He held them there tenderly, the opposite hand claiming the rear of my brother's skull to hold him in place.

"It's okay, Brennan. You two are both safe in this room," Raiden assured, discarding the soiled tissues before grabbing more.

A trio of nurses tumbled into the room—*quite the delay*—and as soon as they did, they requested that both Raiden and I step away from their bleeding patient. We watched from the corner of the room as the three women thoroughly inspected my brother, asking him what had happened and if he needed an ambulance.

"No, I'm okay," Brennan assured, slightly shaken. "I need to go home. I need to go. Can I please? I have to go."

"Were you able to like—*do it?*" I wondered aloud, feeling a bit awkward about the entire thing. Wordlessly, Brennan nodded; clearly exhausted and annoyed by the nurses' presence. They were busy taking his vitals, now, and all I could think about was that little ghostly bitch in the waiting room who was just itching to end our lives.

How would we avoid her on the way out?

"I really think he's okay," Raiden pressed, abruptly grabbing my hand. "Can we go? Please?"

"Just a second," one of the nurses replied, bitterly eyeing both Raiden and I. They had no idea of what fate awaited my brother and I in the waiting room.

"Is there a back door?" I rushed, pulling my hand from Raiden's. He seemed frazzled by my sudden action, but even the smallest touch—the tiniest feel—made my skin crawl. I felt jittery and anxious, and the burning in my arms seemed to intensify with every moment. At this point, I wouldn't have been surprised if the De Mörka was waiting just outside the door.

"Back door?" a red-headed nurse queried, informing my brother that his blood pressure was a little on the high side. "What's wrong with using the front entrance?"

Before I could reply, Raiden interjected; politely approaching the slightly smaller lady and spilling a completely absurd excuse. "Look, ma'am . . . it's my ex. She's extremely irritable, and absolutely *loathes* my girlfriend—this pretty lady right here."

He paused briefly to acknowledge my shaking self, delivering a sultry wink in my direction before returning his attention to the disinterested nurse. Suddenly, I found it difficult to breathe.

Raiden just called me his *girlfriend?*

"Things could get ugly *really* quickly if we pass her, and we don't have time to stick around until she leaves. She might've already gone back for her own appointment, but it's just not worth it to risk—after all, this girl is *psychotic.* And, I don't say that lightly. She tried to claw my eyes out, once. I had scratches along my cheeks for *weeks,* I tell you. My skin was sore, all cracked and crusty, I thought I was going to lose my eyeballs. That wasn't even the worst of it, and she did it all in public, too. I wouldn't put it past her to try and physically assault my new girl in your waiting room. So, we need to slip out without a sound. Quickly. *Easily.* Does that make sense?" Raiden finally finished, seemingly in one single breath.

"Yeah, there's a back entrance for the employees." The nurse opposite the gentle ginger spoke, fingers wrapped around a bright blue stethoscope. "If she's as agile as you say, it really wouldn't hurt to let the three of you leave that way. The last thing we need is another altercation in our waiting room."

Raiden smiled—big and bright—before snatching up my hand and pulling it to his mouth, lovely lips colliding with my knuckles as he pressed an audible, animated kiss to the surface.

Girlfriend.

"Fantastic," he beamed. "If Brennan's good to go, I'd appreciate it if you could show us the door."

twelve

"I thought you crossed paths with the De Mörka in Foodvio?" Momma wondered, running her fingers through my brother's mangled locks. She had on a purple wig today—short, shiny, and stick-straight—just barely kissing her collarbones.

Brennan was curled up beneath a blanket on the sofa, resembling that of a sickly, small child. He looked tiny and pitiful, and although I felt just as awful as he did, (perhaps worse, considering I stared straight into the cold, careless eyes of death itself), I couldn't bring myself to act so defeated. Perhaps, he just wanted to be babied. *Coddled.*

Save me from my premature death, Mommy.

"I thought so too," I muttered, dismissively tossing my purse aside. It missed the coffee table barely by an inch, droopily dropping to the floor in a depressed lump. If the zipper had been undone, all of the contents within would've surely spilled out onto the carpet.

Raiden was pacing, his right thumb pinched between gnawing teeth as he did circles around the couch where both my brother and mother lay. He hadn't said a word since our arrival—instead, he'd only offered both my mother and Grammy a short smile and their own individual hugs. He was deep in thought; forehead wrinkled, brows knit together in concentration. I wanted nothing more than to lace my arms around his shoulders—to let all of our worries vaporize into thin air, *vanish.* Only, it would never be so simple. Not until after Brennan's birthday on Sunday.

Five more days.

It would feel like an eternity.

"When are we supposed to tour the venue for Brennan's party?" I asked, desperately trying to ward off the thoughts of the De Mörka. I wondered if she'd followed us home—followed us *here.* I felt a chill creep down my spine.

We should be dead.

"Thursday," Momma said, brushing a particularly pesky strand of hair from Brennan's slow-blinking eyes. "We'll all be there—Grammy, Brennan, myself. Even your father's coming for extra protection. His mortal self couldn't do much, but you know how men can be. He thinks he can ward off an entire army."

My mother snorted at the thought of Dad trying to defeat the De Mörka, and admittedly, the visual *was* quite comical—until he'd be brutally murdered, that is.

"Would the De Mörka kill others? Mortals?" I wondered, settling into a sitting position on the floor opposite the sofa, the small of my back uncomfortably balanced against the television stand. Raiden was still silently pacing behind the furniture, and Grammy had entered the room—wide, gentle eyes fixated on my best friend as she wordlessly attempted to calm him down. Perhaps, he felt my anxiety, too; the way I absorbed his emotions. Like a tether, binding us together—two bodies, one soul.

I couldn't stop the shiver as it enveloped my spine.

"They have in the past," Momma revealed, a gentle grin cascading over her complexion when Brennan began to shift several objects into the air. The remote, my bag, an unlit candle. At least he still had his humor.

"The De Mörka are unpredictable," Grammy chimed in, wrinkled arms threaded through Raiden's. She snatched his hand away from his mouth, shortly scolding him for chewing on his nails before continuing her speech. "Years ago—and when I say years, I mean *years* ago—a rising De Mörka wiped out an entire town of mortals in Sweden. Absolutely zero affiliation with the Araedia. Completely innocent beings—aged newborn all the way up to ninety-nine. Three-thousand of them, I've heard. All dead within a day—just like that. Today, it's one of Sweden's greatest mysteries: the mass death of an entire town. There was no bloodshed—no blood at all. It was as if they'd all just stopped breathing at once. Many speculated a massive poisoning, others thought it was a curse. But the Araedians knew better . . . We'd seen such cruelty, such *destruction* many times before."

"Do you think there's more than one, Grammy? Well, I *know* there is—I've seen two of them," I began, but my grandmother merely shook her head. She promptly abandoned Raiden's side, little legs scurrying around the sofa as her soft palms met my wrists.

"There's only one, love," she said with a squeeze. "This I know for certain. Don't ask me how, but I do. This is the last of their kind—it's been lying dormant for so long, aching—*waiting* to rise. Waiting for the opportune moment. *This* opportune moment. Bren's thirtieth birthday. For Sunday night, your brother will be at his weakest, for hours leading up until the solidification of his energies."

I felt my eyebrows creep together in uncertainty, and although Grammy confirmed that there was—in fact—only *one* De Mörka, *(shouldn't I feel relieved about this?)* I didn't believe her. *Couldn't* believe her. For I'd seen *both* of them with my own two eyes, felt the sting of their presence seep into my veins, smelled the rot—the *decay* of their entire existence. I saw the blackness of their eyes, just as Grammy described. An iris without any color. A darkness so absolute that it made the whites of their eyes pop.

"Which one do you really think that it was, Frey? The man from Foodvio, or the woman in the waiting room?" Momma questioned from the couch, mindlessly toying with the objects suspended midair, all thanks to my stark silent brother curled up beside her, still buried beneath his blanket.

"I-I don't know," I stammered, unable to decipher the difference. I felt threatened—*terrified* at the hand of the man in Foodvio, but the woman I'd encountered less than two hours prior seemed to make more of an impact. It's almost as if she radiated terror, like a tangible thing that I could peel right off of her skin. The sheer sight of her cold, sinister stare was enough to prompt an unwavering amount of trepidation. I felt uneasy since the moment she'd walked in the door.

"The girl," I revealed, swallowing thickly. Grammy still held onto my forearms, her grip unyielding. "I felt worse around her."

"Maybe she was at Foodvio too," Momma muttered, attempting to piece together the peculiar clues. "Or close. Within a few miles."

"I have a question," Brennan interrupted, pulling himself into a sitting position. Raiden was still pacing behind the furniture, seemingly deep in thought, his thumbnail back between his front teeth.

Before any of us could reply, my brother continued with his inquiry. "If there's a rising De Mörka, or a De Mörka in general, why do only Freya and I feel it? Or, *her,* I guess. Why don't either of you have the burning, or the nightmares, or the overall sense of dread?"

There was a pause. He had a point—a great one, at that. Both Momma and Grammy were Araedian as well, and neither of them exhibited the same symptoms as Brennan and I.

"Truthfully? I have no idea," Grammy replied.

"None of this makes any sense," Momma added, shaking her head. "I don't know how the De Mörka survived. I don't understand where they've been hiding all this time, or how they found us. Did you recognize her at all, Freya? Is she someone that grew up around here? Did she go to school with you?"

I shook my head. "No. I've never seen her before in my life."

Peter, my father, made a rare appearance immediately after, equally stunning both Raiden and I. What was even more appalling was the fact that his bluetooth headset was absent, and he didn't even have a cell phone in tow. It was just—*him.* My dad. Dressed in a pair of khaki pants—slightly wrinkled—a black polo, and some off-brand boat shoes that hardly matched. He looked like some average, middle-aged father, and the sight made me somewhat uncomfortable. I couldn't even recall the last time I'd seen him dressed this way, especially without a headpiece crammed into his ear.

"Hey Frey," he greeted, breathless from his descent down the stairs. He nodded in Raiden's direction before greeting him as well.

"Does Dad know about everything?" I wondered aloud, awkwardly avoiding the man as he hastily approached me. I flinched when his stubbled chin met my cheek, a shy, closed-lipped kiss grazing the skin. The odd act of affection generated an uneasy thought, and I couldn't help but frown.

He thinks we're going to die.

"Yes, I do. Your mom caught me up last night before bed. You both know I'll protect you until my last breath, right?" His statement felt forced, and I struggled to come up with a reply as he glanced between Brennan and I.

"You're ordinary, Dad," Brennan breathed, refusing to look our father in the eye. "There's not much you could even do."

Peter scoffed, shaking his head before strolling towards the nearby desk and mindlessly thumbing through a stack of paperwork. "Well, I doubt some little lady will be *that* strong. I've never hit a girl, but if she's trying to kill my kids, I may make an exception."

"Don't be daft, Peter!" Grammy exclaimed. "If that girl from the fertility clinic really is the rising De Mörka, she could snap your body in two without even touching you. You wouldn't stand a chance."

My father opened his mouth to reply, but when words failed him, he collapsed onto the desk chair. The worn leather discharged a stale burst of air, and with every slight rock of his limbs, the springs whined and groaned. His fingers met his lips, nubby nails slipping between gnawing teeth as he anxiously chewed.

There was the Dad I knew.

"I've been practicing," Momma said, unable to stifle her smile. "I'm growing stronger everyday. It's like my energy knows—it can *feel* the threat. Peter broke one of my favorite plates last night, and I corrected it before he could even notice that it had hit the floor."

Dad raised a brow. "I broke a plate?"

"In an alternate timeline, yes. You fucking brat," Momma slyly replied, earning a chuckle from each and every one of us—except Raiden, who was still pacing in the background.

His raging anxiety bubbled up within my belly, and once more, I wished that I could not feel what he felt. I had enough worry—enough fear and anger and anxiety of my own, and to carry the burden of his emotions too was almost too much to bear.

I wondered if Grammy's big book of Araedian knowledge would perhaps know of a way to sever our unbidden bond.

thirteen

Sierra, our boss, was quite bitter about us missing the next several days of work. She even threatened to have us both replaced, the thought of which almost made me chuckle a bit. After all, why would I risk my life for some mediocre job at a Tex-Mex restaurant?

To make matters worse, Raiden refused to let me leave the house. He was stern—*strict*—and I felt like a rabid dog; a sturdy, silver chain encircling my neck, my little limbs cramped up in my crate. Although it was for my own good—*my safety*—I felt claustrophobic, *trapped.* I was itching to leave the house, and oftentimes, when he left to grab food or essentials, I'd sneak outside for some fresh air. The sun felt warm and welcoming against my flesh, and I basked in its beauty; inhaling the fresh scent of the outdoors with glee.

It was evident that I'd never survive being bedridden, or anything of the sorts. A lack of fresh air and Vitamin D was enough to send me into an anxious frenzy, and although I was always cuddled up to my best friend—my protector—I still felt crowded, *cramped.* The walls were closing in, suctioning to my skin, flattening me against the furniture. The air from the vents felt atrociously artificial, almost suffocatingly so. I almost found myself dramatically gasping for air after two days indoors.

When Thursday came around, I had difficulty stifling my delight. Raiden took notice of the substantial shift of my mood, and he teased me nearly the entire way to Wilhelm Weatherby's estate—the gorgeous grounds that would host Brennan's birthday bash.

He held my hand the entire way there, and although nothing had physically changed in the two days we'd spent together at home, (forty-eight hours of just Raiden and I, nothing to do but cuddle and eat) I felt the bond between us alter. For the first time in two decades, I felt different around Raiden, nervous almost. *Bashful.* I was careful not to walk in front of him wearing nothing but a towel or my undergarments, even though I'd done it a thousand times over. I was increasingly aware of my appearance, and would often wake up moments before he did to cover up my dark circles and dab some concealer on my blemishes. It was incredibly bizarre how I was acting around him—like a little schoolgirl with a crush—and that left a looming realization over my head that I had casually ignored up until now: *did I have a crush on Raiden?*

As promised, Momma, Brennan, and Dad were all at Weatherby's estate when we'd arrived several minutes late. I was eager to tear my hand from Raiden's before he turned into the driveway, for I could already feel the heat rising to my cheeks at the thought of my parents or brother sensing my newly found feelings for the long-haired lad.

It came in waves: the burning. The anxiety. The worry.

I thought about her constantly; the De Mörka. I had nightmares of her—the sharp curve of her jaw, the coarseness of her skeletal, sunken features. Lips as red as blood, oozing, *dripping.* Eyes as black as the night, sharp, unwavering. Piercing into my soul, peeling apart my flesh section by section, unkempt fingernails digging—*squelching*—bone, muscle, mass shifting around each digit, staining the ghostly flesh a striking, scarlet hue.

I usually woke up screaming. *Inconsolable.*

He'd hold me—rock me like a baby, dainty fingers threaded through my matted locks, plump lips grazing the surface of my forehead. Sweet nothings gently caressed the skin, a series of indistinguishable phrases that were mostly muffled by my cries. Around my legs laid Kelso, whilst Bear nudged at my side. Mimosa kept to herself, for any loud noises left her a shaking, startled mess.

Last night, I broke another vase. This time, it was a cheap one—full of half-dead daisies that Grammy got me days prior. She believed that flowers generated joy, *light.* She figured they'd bring me peace during such a dark time, especially since I wasn't under the same roof as her. She offered to stop by on multiple occasions, but I denied her requests, and instead insisted that she, too, stay indoors.

None of us were safe.

"This place is fucking ridiculous," Raiden exclaimed, ripping the keys from the ignition.

"Yeah," I murmured, curling my fingers around the door handle, vision glued to the dusty dashboard. I wasn't sure where my mind currently resided—on Saturn, Raiden would probably say—but all I knew was that this all felt wrong.

We shouldn't be here.

The two of us clambered out of the car, which was crookedly parked at the very edge of the wide, circular driveway, the right front tire just barely hovering the border between pearly white gravel and cold concrete. I took notice of the gravel almost instantly, and how it shifted and groaned beneath the soles of my worn-out sneakers. When I glanced down to view the source of the sound, I was unexpectedly greeted by an overwhelming abundance of teeth. Most were in good condition—intact, for the most part. A round, molded crown, dipping down into a sharp edge. Others, however, weren't so pretty. Cracked. Chipped.

Rotten.

Panicked, I stumbled backwards, the curve of my bottom colliding with the car as I lost my footing. The profusion of teeth beneath my feet audibly shifted, and when my palms met the uneven mounds, I couldn't help but cry out.

"Freya?" Raiden exclaimed, his tone masked with bewilderment. He rushed to my side, wide hands slipping beneath my armpits as he hoisted me up to my feet.

"T-teeth," I stammered, eyes widened to the size of marbles. "The pebbles are *teeth,* Raiden."

Raiden glanced down at the decorative pebbles, a puzzled expression slapped across his features as he shot me a worried, wide-eyed glance. "Teeth?"

I blinked, blurred vision steadying once more on what I thought was a massive pile of teeth. Instead, I was met by nothing but a surplus of decorative, white rocks.

"I think you're just under a lot of stress, Frey," Raiden sweetly said, brushing a stray strand of dark hair away from my clammy chin. "With the De Mörka nightmares, and the lack of sleep, and the anxiety—it's a lot to handle. I get it. You're afraid to be out in the open right now, and I think your mind is being cruel. It's playing tricks on you."

"Oh," I muttered, nodding curtly. "Yeah. Right. You're right."

I brushed Raiden's unwanted touch away, an ineffable amount of energy coursing through my veins as I took in the sight before us. What I currently felt wasn't actually anxiety—in fact, it was a sensation that I couldn't quite identify at all. It felt as if my body was no longer mine. A foreign entity stuck in the skin of a stranger. I felt uneasy, *sick.* I wanted to rip myself in half and flee—whether it be from this place, or from *myself,* I couldn't quite identify. Either way, I felt absolutely *atrocious.*

The building before us, property of Wilhelm Weatherby (evidently some kind of family friend who I'd never had the pleasure to cross paths with) was undeniably stunning. The structure was elegantly adorned with smoky, gray brick, ranging between three divergent hues, all of which complemented the others perfectly to create a work of art. The stunning brickwork, however, was undoubtedly upstaged by the grand circular entryway, jutting outwards and scaling three stories. At the lower level stood a set of deep ebony double doors with sleek, silver, vertical handles. Hovering above the main access point was a trio of tall windows, engrossing the upper two stories and allowing an influx of natural light to bleed into what I assumed was the front foyer. I could already imagine the exorbitant chandelier that certainly sat beyond the grand entrance, illuminating the area when sunlight was absent.

The driveway looped around the right side of the building, leading down to what I assumed was a set of garages. For a house this large, there had to be enough space for six or more vehicles. It wouldn't shock me in the slightest if a fleet of pricey cars lay beyond the sealed doors.

Gorgeous greenery accented the ashen brick, blossoming buds of varying hues—the rarest of reds, lively yellows, boasting blues. Even a dash of lilac, a bundle of thriving flowers that hovered above the front door, recently watered and dripping with dew. I'd never seen such animated foliage, and I almost pitied the plants that barely thrived in their pots in our home. They were lucky if we remembered to water them on time, and the soil in which they grew was some cheap bag of fertilized dirt from the convenience store.

If the house itself wasn't elegant enough, the Weatherby estate defied the norm of having a swimming pool in the backyard. Instead, the accessory claimed the left side of the front yard, a little yellow-brick-road connecting the concrete driveway and the showy, artificial lagoon. To no surprise, a grandiose rock waterfall cradled the opposite side, a rush of white, foaming water tumbling over the rocks and easing into the basin beneath. It almost seemed as if Weatherby wanted to create some sort of tropical haven, as a series of miscellaneous flowers and trees lined the lengthy rectangular pool. It looked expensive and tacky, and I hated people like Weatherby, because they used their wealth for silly things like building some front-yard pool that was probably never used and cost upwards of hundreds of thousands of dollars to both build and consistently maintain, when instead he could use his wealth for something virtuous, like building free housing for the homeless, or supplying food to food banks that were barely scraping by and could hardly feed the starving mouths that always stopped in . . .

"How the hell do you know this guy?" Raiden croaked, clearly charmed by the estate.

"I don't," I replied, eyeing the parked car that belonged to my parents. They must already be inside.

"I feel like I don't belong here because of how broke I am," Raiden added, warm digits skimming the tips of my fingers. He was aching to hold my hand, but the uninvited amount of butterflies that swarmed my belly prevented me from taking it. Instead, I stuffed them into the sorry excuse for pockets at the front of my jeans.

"It would probably be awkward if we just walked in the front door," I said, glancing towards the pool. "Maybe we could just put our feet in the heated pool and wait until they come out. We'll be back on Sunday anyways, we'll see the rest of it then."

Raiden audibly agreed, starting towards the pool on the opposite end of the driveway. I found myself occasionally glancing over my shoulder to view the ivory pebbles beside our crookedly parked car, as if one more glance would confirm whether or not an array of loose teeth actually coated the ground.

Alas, it was nothing more than a bundle of decorative rocks, just as it always had been.

Halfway to our destination, I could hear Raiden's cell vibrate against his upper thigh. My gaze gravitated towards the lanky lad, whose fingers were already knuckle deep in the denim pocket, wrinkled digits desperately attempting to yank the device from its cozy cove.

"Who is it?" I wondered, achingly aware of the silent phone stuffed up in my back pocket.

I could count the amount of friends that I had on one single hand. If they were even friends at all, actually. And Maxwell McKinnon didn't count, even if he sent me several messages at *least* once a week, all usually back to back. He was never a genuine friend, and he only ever wanted one thing from me—and me, pitiful as I am, lonely, little Freya Gallo, always gave it to him. It sickened me how easy I was.

Raiden's brows furrowed at the sight of the message, and before I could repeat the question, he replied with a single, short statement: "It's just Jordan."

My chest flushed as her name tumbled off his lips. *Just Jordan.* I adjusted the loose neck of my blouse with a trembling finger, careful not to let Raiden get a peek at my distressed flesh. I could feel the radiating heat from the surface of my skin against my knuckles, and I hoped that the foundation slapped along my cheeks would be thick enough to mask the bashful blush that crept up to the surface.

"Oh. You two are friends?"

Raiden shrugged, thumbs dancing across the screen as he speedily replied. "Yeah, I'd say so. She's pretty cool. I think you two would get along really well, actually. Hell, you could use a girl friend. It's been a long time since you've hung out with a girl, hasn't it?"

"I don't need friends," I grumbled, barely loud enough for him to hear. "I have you."

Raiden's lips twisted into a wild grin, and before I could question his reaction, he did a cute, little caper right towards me, like a toddler running towards his mother. His arms coiled around my waist like lengthy vines, fingertips jabbing at my sides in the form of an aggressive tickle—which he *damn* well knew that I absolutely *hated.*

I released a choppy cry, unable to contain my pleas as he continued his playful assault on my sides. My stomach hurt from uncontrollable and uncomfortable laughter, and my sides blissfully burned from the presence of his touch. For a split second, my shirt had gravitated slightly upwards, revealing a prickly patch of flushed flesh. The shy stroke of his fingers against my skin was enough to make me melt into a bashful heap.

"Sorry," Raiden coyly cooed, although he wasn't sorry at all—that much was evident by the boyish grin stretched across his mouth. I studied his smile, admiring the way his canines dipped down below the surrounding teeth, slightly jutting outwards and somewhat crooked. Growing up, I jokingly referred to them as his *vampire teeth,* but as he aged, the stick-straight fangs began to shift, somewhat overlapping their neighbors and providing him with the cutest, most crooked smirk I'd ever seen.

I adored every piece of him.

Suddenly, his expression faltered. "Is there something wrong?"

"No!" I exclaimed, reaching out to claim his hand. I couldn't quite deny the ardent sparks that consumed my spine the second our fingers met—a rapturous whisper, just barely there, but nevertheless present. If he continued to hold me, I was sure that the electrified pressure at the bottom of my spine would gravitate upwards, consuming me fully and reducing me to nothing but a buzzing, butterfly-ridden mess—*all over my best fucking friend!*

"You're right about this place. It gives off negative vibes," Raiden said, dropping my hand before the sensation could fully intensify. A pang of disappointment pulled at my belly as the two of us climbed evenly placed rocks leading up to the massive pool and its adjoining jacuzzi.

"Maybe it's haunted," I suggested, admiring the gorgeous chlorine reservoir laid out before us. The perimeter of both the rectangular pool and its neighboring hot tub were meticulously lined with perfectly placed amber-hued bricks. Littered atop the surface of the tranquil water were a multitude of dissimilar leaves, courtesy of the blooming trees that hung over the area like a parasol, shielding the water from the sharp rays of the sun.

"Oh, it's *definitely* haunted," Raiden confirmed, chuckling slightly. "Hey, doesn't the border of bricks around the pool kind of remind you of the plastic playground borders we used to walk on as kids? Remember? We'd pretend they were tightropes and race each other around the perimeter."

"Yeah," I muttered, a young, cheerful, round Raiden flooding my mind. He hardly resembled his youthful self—not that it was a bad thing. No, he'd blossomed into a healthy, handsome man. *Matured.*

"These bricks are even raised a little bit too, they're exactly like those playground borders! Oh, come on, Frey. We gotta do it!" Raiden exclaimed, steadying the sole of his left shoe on the border.

"Do what, Raiden?"

"What we did as kids," he confirmed, arms extended outwards, resembling wings. *Raiden Crow, preparing for flight.* "Race each other around the border and shit. Come on, it'll be fun."

"I don't know, Rai," I countered, uneasily glancing over my shoulder to view the entrance to the estate. My family was nowhere in sight, which probably meant that they were buried deeply within.

Never to return.

"Don't be such a priss, Frey." Raiden taunted me, walking the raised, brick perimeter as if it were a taut tightrope. After a few steps, he froze; digging his heel into the surface of the stone before twisting around to view me, a sly smile stretched from ear to ear.

"Come *oooon,* baby," he purred, both palms colliding with his forehead as he slicked back his wild, awry hair. He looked so lean—*fit*—messy, mangled locks dipping down past his collarbones, curly and cute, in desperate need of a trim. A pesky pimple claimed his chin, reddened from irritation, cystic and bulbous. It embarrassed him, and he even asked for a bit of concealer to cover it up before we left the house. By now, his oily fingers had rubbed most of it away, revealing the angry mountain beneath. So ordinary. So *human.*

An assortment of rings adorned his lengthy digits, claiming all but one on his left hand—his wedding finger left bare. *Empty.* Waiting to be marked—*claimed.*

He took another step—backwards, this time—and I'd noticed that his right sneaker was almost untied, a rather new pair of name-brand Vans, a bold burgundy.

Your favorite color, Frey.

"Come *play* with me, baby," Raiden mused, unable to contain his giggles. Everytime the pet name fell off his lips, a burst of butterflies consumed my core. "Don't be *chicken.* Don't make me get on my knees and *beg.*"

My bag met my feet, a piteous pile of mangled fabric, and to his pleasure, I joined him—skipping along the brash border of the pool. We lustily laughed, carelessly chasing one another around the perimeter. I felt young—*free.* Like a child discovering the world bit by bit, piece by piece.

Occasionally, Raiden would spin around on his heel, changing course solely to chase me. He almost caught me—*almost*—but I was stealthy; *quick.* Like an antelope escaping its prey. Only, I wasn't so sure that I wanted to escape his doting touch. He was warm, he was cozy.

He was home.

Admittedly, I craved him. His presence alone could calm even the roughest of seas. The way his lovely, lean arms encircled me, grounded me. Brought me back down to earth. I craved his scent—a sweet, shy hint of cologne, an underlying layer of smoke. He was particularly good about keeping the cigarette smell to a bare minimum, and although I constantly begged him to quit his filthy habit for his health, I almost feared the day that his natural scent would shift. I didn't want it to change. I didn't want anything about him to change. I wanted to wrap him up—cocoon him. Halt time. Right here, right now. To live in this moment for an eternity. Never age, never die. Just . . . *exist.*

Halfway around the rear bend of the pool, the burning began.

It started at my wrists, raging rings spiraling around the skin, squeezing, *suffocating.* My vision blurred, and I stumbled; nearly falling into the chlorinated water below. It felt as if there were chains latched around each of my wrists, tightening with every waking second. It was pure torture. I felt the blood struggle to reach my palms, my veins swelling and weeping within my wrists. My fingers tingled, a whisper of a rumor dancing from ear to ear. I felt lightheaded, *weak,* and just as I caught wind of a dainty group of individuals emerging from around the back bend of the house, it all went quiet. *Dark.* Numb. Nothing but my pounding heart, the organ racing, struggling to pump blood to my dying, purple palms.

It had arrived. That dreaded, familiar, nasty noise. A whisper, a gasp. A sound that only arose a split-second before trouble. Before something disastrous occurred. Before . . . *before* . . .

I saw Brennan toss a hand airborne—a wave, a smile—before he broke into a jog, heading over towards the pool. Everything felt foggy, slow. *Muddled.* I felt drunk, or drugged. A blur between the two. A feeling I couldn't quite identify—but nevertheless, I witnessed something that I wished I'd never seen. The slip of a step, a startled gasp, a garish *crack.*

A surplus of scarlet claimed the chlorinated water, easing *up up up* towards the surface. Spreading, *pooling.* Painting the walls red, staining them with the mark of death.

Then, there was pain. Harrowing, profane pain.

It felt as if my skull was on fire, a sensation so vast that it devoured my every atom. Spine set ablaze, a roaring flame lapping at my insides, tearing my head apart inch by inch—nimble, nubby fingers clawing, *cranking.* It felt as if a pair of claws had sunken into my brain, ripping it apart piece by piece, chunk by chunk. Tossing the unwanted mounds aside, going back in for seconds. Thirds. *Fourths.*

I could barely hear Brennan over the agony. It was yelling, *screaming.* Shouting so loudly in my head that I saw nothing but stars.

Stars and blood.

"Freya, *now!*" Brennan shouted, threading his fingers around my elbow. I struggled to steady my vision, and before I could attempt to reply, I'd heard a splash, and my brother had left my side. Someone was screaming in the distance—my mother, I think. I wanted her to stop. I wanted *it* to stop. The hurt, the pain. Maybe, I would just die. Let it kill me.

The actualization of the event at hand struck me like a chord, and with difficulty, I pulled myself out of my distressed state.

It isn't real. This pain isn't yours to feel.

My vision steadied just barely enough to study the scene. By now, the amount of blood seemed to triple, encircling both my brother and my best friend's skull like a morbid, liquid halo. Perched up by

Brennan was a limp Raiden; unconscious, unresponsive, and bleeding at the head.

Dying.

"Get the fuck in here!" Brennan screamed, an order directed towards my statuette self.

I didn't hesitate.

Using the little strength that I had, I rounded the remaining corner of the pool, trembling knees bending as my palm met the dirt-riddled bricks. Icy waves lapped at my legs, soaking my skin and chilling me down to the very marrow of my bones. Only, none of that mattered—what mattered now, in this moment, was that I had to use the miniscule amount of energy that remained in my fickle frame to prevent Raiden from dying in Brennan's arms.

"Raiden!" I cried, quivering from head to toe as I took his limp skull in my clutch. Brennan supported his weight for me, propping his upper half up and out of the water. By now, both of my parents had made their presence known; cradling the side of the pool, horrified cries easing out of Momma's mouth.

Raiden's lengthy, brunette locks were matted and wet, drenched with fresh, oozing blood. My left hand cradled his sweet, sullen cheek, whereas the other traveled outward, encircling his scalp to locate the source of the bleeding. My index finger found it first—the wound. I felt his blood spill over the surface of my skin, seeping out like a leaky faucet, his life dwindling away within my palm.

"I got you, Rai," I wheezed, flattening the center of my palm against the vulgar wound.

"Hurry up, Freya," Brennan begged, fearful tears coating the apples of his flushed cheeks. "He's dying."

"You're not dying on me, Rai," I whispered, the curve of my thumb dancing along his snowy lower lip. "Not today."

Only, he was dying. I could feel it. It was as if we were bound by a rope—*connected.* Tethered together, molded into one. With every passing moment, with every blob of blood that slipped through my fingers, I could feel it fade. Pull and fray, as if it were easing undone. I felt his life—his light—slowly slip through the cracks of my fingers. I felt the figurative rope of our adjoined souls ease out of my hands, quickly, so sudden that it left burns behind.

My forehead met his, eyelids fluttering closed as I focused solely on the healing. I'd done it so many times before, but right then, it felt different. *Off.* As if I couldn't even save him anymore. As if he were too far gone.

Too close to death.

"Come on, Raiden," I muttered, tightening my hold on his weeping scalp. "Don't leave me."

As Raiden withered away within my hold, I felt as if my life—my *existence*—was slowly dwindling. Disappearing. *Drowning.* I felt my heart slow to a sluggish speed, the blood in my veins turning to lazy, muddled jelly. My hot tears danced along Raiden's swollen skin, dribbling down his forehead and joining the mangled mess of varying liquids within the pool.

"Come on, Raiden," Brennan hissed, tightening his hold on my best friend's body.

I felt Raiden slightly shift within my hold, and with the minimal amount of strength that remained within my frail frame, I sealed his gaping, lethal wound.

I pulled back to view his pale features, a vicious tremble exhausting my every limb. I could barely hold myself up in the water, and I felt the sweet pull of a dark, peaceful oblivion beckoning me in.

My vision waned, a confining blur oozing into my line of sight as I struggled to keep consciousness. Through the haze, I was able to identify a pair of forest green eyes—wide and bloodshot—staring back up at me, pulling me back down to reality.

Then, it was just us—Raiden and I. Skipping through the trees, dancing barefoot along the verdant forest path. Warm, yellow stripes decorated the way, the welcoming rays of the sun peeking through the gaps in the trees. The spirited thumps of his heart radiated through his perspiring palm, which was securely suctioned to mine. He refused to let go, even when I threatened to outrun him, and I outwardly yelped when my toes met a protruding log, one which sent me tumbling into a pile of crunchy leaves.

Raiden lost his footing, stumbling forward as my back met the forest floor. Unintentionally, he landed atop me; a series of giggles cascading over our lips as he lifted his weight from my lower half.

"Shit," he mused, unable to stifle a smile. He looked healthy. *Alive.*

"Rai," I cooed, craning my neck to view him. He was hovering my waist, propping himself up on his elbows. "Come up here."

"Yes ma'am," Raiden replied, a deep, guttural sound that almost resembled a growl. He propelled himself upwards, his pointed nose tickling the apple of my cheek. I outwardly sighed as he settled between my legs, slender digits waltzing along my upper thigh as he coaxed my legs around his waist.

"Hey, Rai?" I breathed, cupping his face with my hands. He'd never been so close to me—not like this, anyways—but somehow, it felt natural. As if this was where I was meant to be for an eternity.

"Hmm?" Raiden hummed, plump, eager lips dipping down to meet the shy skin of my neck. The foreign feel made me flinch, eyes rolling—*tipping*—back into my skull, fingers knotting into his hair. His long, soft locks; dainty curls hovering his ears.

"Are we dead?" I asked, fearing the inevitable. Perhaps, death was the only way we'd truly be together. *Finally* together.

One.

Puzzled, Raiden pulled away from my neck, gaze glued to my trembling lower lip. I felt as if I was on the edge of tears, which almost humored me, because what on earth could possibly be upsetting about this scenario? I was with Raiden, the only man who's ever loved and appreciated me for me. Who has remained by my side through the past two decades of my life. Who made me feel whole. Happy. *Complete.*

The one for me has been right in front of my face for over twenty years, and until now, I was too blind to even realize it.

"Do you feel dead?" Raiden replied, brushing a pesky strand of hair out of my eyes.

"I don't know," I admitted, tracing his chin with my thumb. "But I do know that this feels like Heaven."

"Maybe it is," Raiden whispered, eyelids fluttering closed as he sealed the torturous gap between us, lips just barely brushing against mine—a whisper of a kiss. A taunting touch. *Torture.*

I slipped into a bitter blackness before I could taste him for the first time.

"You should probably check her vitals again. She should be up by now."

"Stop worrying, Brennan. I've been monitoring her closely. We'd know if there was an issue."

"What about Raiden?"

Raiden.

The mere mention of his name revived me, yanking me from the dreamless oblivion in which I lay entrapped. It was suffocating—*dark*—nothing but an endless, empty space, occupied by only myself. I couldn't speak, I couldn't move. All I could do was stare at the blackness, desperately attempting to see a sliver of color—an inkling of life—beyond the black abyss. Only, there wasn't any color, or light, or life. There was just . . . *nothing.* Nothing but myself, frozen in time and space, left to my grueling, suffocating thoughts. All I could do was think. Dwell. *Worry.* Worry about Raiden, who laid dying in my arms before my apparent banishment to an eternal sleep.

Worry about Brennan, who was the sole target of the rising De Mörka. Worry about my mother, a cancer survivor. A woman whose life revolved around her children. Just an endless loop of worry. That's all that I am, now.

Or, *was,* rather. Evidently, the entrapment was only temporary, for I felt myself resurfacing. *Awakening.*

The uncomfortability of drifting from a state of a subconscious, statuette-like being was jarring, despite the brush of the clean, soft sheets underneath. My gritty eyes blinked up at the popcorn-textured ceiling, and I closed them again, wondering if it was actually real.

I should be dead.

"She's waking up," an unfamiliar voice exclaimed. It was low and husky, audible evidence of a feeble cigarette addiction.

Cigarettes. Nicotine. *Raiden.*

"Raiden?" I croaked, his name emerging choppy and hoarse from my dry, cracked lips. My eyelids eased open once more, revealing a moderately blurred version of our bedroom. By my side was someone I'd never met a day before in my life, and at the sight of them, I immediately felt panicked.

That was, until my brother stepped into view, a series of comforting coos dancing along his tongue. He took my hand in his, his thumb gently caressing the curve of my knuckles as I vigorously blinked, desperate to rid my vision of the nettlesome blur.

"You're okay, Freya," Brennan confirmed. "You're alive, and Raiden is alive. He's next to you."

My heart leapt into my throat. *Raiden's alive.*

With as much strength as I could muster, I rotated my head to view the rest of the bed. Just as Brennan had promised, Raiden was next to me. My vision finally cleared, and I was overjoyed to see Raiden—*my boy*—alive and breathing beside me, eyelids securely shut, bare chest rising and falling with every evenly spaced breath. His lovely, lengthy locks were stiff with dried blood, physical evidence of the dreadful event.

Beside the bed was an IV pole, complemented with a boasting bag of bright, red blood. My curious gaze followed the scarlet tube to its endpoint, snuggled right in the crook of his inner elbow.

"Raiden," I whispered, maneuvering myself across the bed. My limbs felt achy and stiff as I awkwardly eased across the mushy connected mattresses. I hoisted myself up over the dramatic dip, which wasn't there prior, but somehow the beds must've been pulled slightly apart when we were brought back. Nevertheless, I pressed on; a trembling arm extending as my eager fingers grazed the surface of Raiden's chin. His lips were parted; hot, even breaths cascading over his swollen lower lip and eventually reaching my frigid fingers.

"He should wake up soon," the stranger said, rounding the bed. They poked and prodded at the half-full bag of blood before tampering with an assortment of items laid upon one of our collapsible tray tables from the living room.

"Their name is Vole," Brennan chirped, as if he could read my mind. *By now, he probably could.*

My palm cupped Raiden's cheek, lanky legs draped along his lower half as I craned my neck to view my brother. He was on his feet, trudging towards the stranger called Vole, who was busy inspecting the surplus of medical supplies on the tiny table.

Vole was incredibly short—a maximum of five feet tall—with sleek, ebony hair that tickled the rump of their bottom. Flecks of sunlight from the open curtains danced along the inky, stick-straight locks; creating a constellation of orbs along the shiny surface. Their heavily freckled flesh was an ochre hue—stunning, mellow brown—complemented by a series of dissimilar tattoos, completely coating the entirety of their left arm and just barely claiming parts of the right.

Vole didn't look like a doctor—not like any of the doctors I'd seen before, anyways—for they were relatively young, twenty-five max, and both of their nostrils were accented with a pair of bright gold hoops, four in total.

"Who exactly is she?" I queried, holding an unconscious Raiden close. I could feel his heart drumming against my arm—*thump thump thump*—a steady tune that could put me to sleep.

"Vole's an RN, and they're non-binary," Brennan politely corrected, only to be interrupted by a grinning Vole, their palm flattened to my brother's chest.

"I can speak for myself, Brennan, but thank you," Vole lightly scolded. They pulled a chair to the side of the bed, taking a seat before toying with Raiden's IV.

"Like your brother said, I'm a registered nurse, but I actually care for my patients in-home. I had some leftover supplies, like the fluids I gave both you and Raiden, but I needed to snag some blood for him. Don't worry, it's our secret," Vole assured with a wink. I felt uneasy.

Did they know what we were?

Once again, as if he could read my mind, Brennan answered my inquiry.

"Vole knows," he said. "About us. The energy."

"What?" I nearly jumped out of my skin, unintentionally adding a certainly uncomfortable amount of pressure and weight to Raiden's belly. He didn't seem to notice. I was worried that he may be in a coma.

"*Relax,* Freya," Vole cooed, urging me to lay back down. "You're still weak, and it's unwise to move right now, especially with an empty stomach. You were asleep for more than fifteen hours."

"Fifteen hours?" I guffawed, refusing to lay back down. "Is it fucking Friday?"

"Yes, it is. But, it's fine. Once Raiden wakes, he'll be good as new, and so are you. You'll both be fine to attend my party on Sunday," Brennan assured me whilst nibbling on the skin of his thumb. "Plus, you really can't get mad about Vole knowing. Raiden knows."

"Raiden's been my best friend for *two decades,*" I hissed. "Vole's just some fucking stranger! I mean, no offense, but you are."

Vole tossed their hands airborne, a chuckle cascading over their lips. "None taken. Brennan didn't actually tell me, I figured it out. You know, Italy isn't the only breeding ground of peculiar energies. You guys may be the last of your particular kind, but that doesn't mean that similar energy doesn't exist elsewhere."

"Wait, are you for real?"

I pulled myself into a sitting position, fingers anxiously pulling at the fabric of my jeans as a whirlwind of possibilities flooded my mind. *We weren't alone.*

"I'm not sure when the Araedian energies evolved, but to my best knowledge, the oldest and wisest of the hyperpoweristic people actually began in Japan. They call us *Kyōryokuna* (強力な). Our energy isn't as vast as yours, nor as unique. Brennan can influence objects, you can mend the injured. I believe your mother can manipulate time, if I recall right."

"Yes, she can. She's damn good at it, too," Brennan confirmed, twirling a piece of Vole's inky, black hair around his finger.

"The Kyōryokuna have a very small range of abilities, but instead of each of us having our own unique energy, we all share the very same set. Occasionally—although rarely—there is a deviation, but it doesn't happen often. I don't know of any Kyōryokuna currently living with a deviation."

"Where were you guys when the Araedian bloodline almost went extinct?" I didn't mean to interrupt Vole's speech, but if the Araedians weren't the only group with supernatural abilities, they must've known . . .

"The Araedians were very reclusive," Vole revealed, their smile fading. "I wasn't around during the downfall—for I'm younger than both you and Brennan—but from what my parents have said, they refused help. We knew of the Swedish De Mörka, of their imminent threat to the Araedians, but they would not let us assist in their fight. We were unaware of their defeat until weeks following, when a messenger delivered the news."

"I don't know if you know much about our counter—the De Mörka—but do you guys have anything like that? I mean, this group literally evolved solely to *kill us.* How fucked up is that?" I pressed, shoving aside the vivid visuals of the woman in the waiting room.

Icy, black eyes, pasty, white skin. An overall essence that reeked of death.

"Yes, a counterpart also existed for us. However, they went extinct sometime in the 1700's. Truthfully, we all believed that you were all extinct too, the De Mörka as well."

"We thought they were, too," Brennan mumbled. "Somehow, one of them survived. Only one. And by some cruel act of God, she's here in Canada, in our town, probably right down the street."

"What type of energy do you yield?" I interrupted, earning a side-eyed glare from my brother. He continued to toy with Vole's hair.

"I can communicate with the dead," they revealed. "I can cross into alternate dimensions, visit a deceased individual's permanent paradise. It's not how they say it is, you know. One giant Heaven or Hell. It's more complicated than that."

"Marvelous," I breathed, completely stunned by Vole's explanation. Suddenly, I felt envious of them. I always thought it was neat to heal others, but to be able to contact the deceased was an entirely different ballgame. "Now, you mentioned an alternate universe . . ?"

"We don't know how many there are," Vole said with a sigh. "Twenty-six, at least. It's dangerous for us to jump through them. It's common for a Kyōryokuna to actually get trapped within an alternate dimension, and it happens more often than we'd like. I personally haven't tried it, but I lost my sister to it a few years ago. She's never returned."

Raiden shifted beside me, an achy groan tumbling over his lips.

"I'm really sorry," I murmured. "I just can't believe we aren't alone. It's refreshing to hear that others have such unique abilities like us."

"I was relieved to learn of your existence as well. My parents and grandparents were also pleased. We were all sure that your lineage had perished on that fateful day. I am saddened, however, to hear of the De Mörka threat. I've made Brennan promise me that he'll be safe, but having a birthday party while being the target of a manhunt is rather unwise," Vole stated, shrugging my brother off of them. They seemed upset at the thought of losing Brennan.

"It's tradition to celebrate our thirtieth in an exaggerated fashion," Brennan pressed. "Between me, Freya, Grammy, and Momma—we'll be okay. It's four against one. That De Mörka bitch can't be *that* powerful. Plus, I'm not afraid to hit a girl."

"He's waking up," Vole said, ignoring my brother's banter. My heart fluttered within my chest like a frivolous hummingbird, bare toes dancing along the warmth of Raiden's thigh as my wide, doe-like eyes met his hazy, emerald stare.

"Freya," he breathed, voice hoarse and thick. He reached out to me, and I claimed his cold fingers, curling my warm palms around his ring-riddled hand. I pulled him close, holding our conjoined palms to my chest as I buried my nose into the crook of his neck, the tears freely flowing, soaking his skin.

"I'm so sorry," I sobbed. I wasn't quite sure what I was apologizing for, but it felt necessary. It felt right.

"Hey, *hey,*" he lowly cooed, twirling tendrils of my oily hair around his free fingers. He tore his hand from mine, slender digits tickling my chin as he lifted my chin away from his neck. "Look at me right now, Freya Dagmar Gallo."

My stomach fluttered at the sound of my full given name, and I did as I was told; removing my snotty nose from the dip of Raiden's collar to meet his sleepy gaze. Through my peripheral vision, I witnessed both Vole and Brennan silently exiting our bedroom, gently closing the door behind them, as if they were never there at all.

"You saved me, Freya," Raiden revealed, pink tongue darting out to wet his lips. "I was dying, and you saved me. You breathed life back into me with everything you had. I felt it—the passion, the urgency. It felt as if you'd ripped your own heart out of your chest and stuffed it into the cage where mine once beat."

I'm yours, Raiden Archimedes Crow.

In the place of a verbal reply, I simply smiled; blinking back tears before reaching up to meet Raiden's matted hair. Blood caked the loopy locks, binding them together in bulbous chunks. My fingertips danced along the surface of his skull in search of a wound, only to find nothing. Not even a scar.

It was as if it never happened at all.

"Let's get all of this blood out of your hair," I whispered, lightly pulling out of his embrace. "Let me get Vole, they'll take out your IV so you can get cleaned up."

"Who's Vole?" Raiden croaked, uncomfortably eyeing the needle in his arm. My gaze followed his fingers, which traveled across his chest, dipping down towards the IV. I saw him visibly cringe when his forefinger collided with the bruised skin.

"They're one of Brennan's friends," I replied, unsteady on my feet. I felt wobbly and faint, and suddenly craved the mouthwatering essence of a cold glass of water. "I'll be back, don't mess with that IV."

Before Raiden could reply, I was out the door; stumbling through a hoard of giddy dogs as they nearly trampled me to the ground. Dismissively, I patted each of their heads, trembling legs easing in the direction of the living room in search of my brother and his friend.

I found them on the sofa at an arm's-length apart, speaking lowly to one another. A chipper Mimosa gave away my presence, emitting a shrill bark which caught Brennan's attention.

"Everything all right?" he queried, brows raised.

"Uh, Raiden wants a shower," I stammered, avoiding Vole's gentle gaze. I felt awkward with them here, especially now, when I felt so dazed and dizzy. It was as if I were a stranger in my own body.

"That's fine." Vole smiled, standing to their feet. "I'll take out the IV for now. When you both are done washing up, I'll pump some more fluids into you and finish off his transfusion if need be. It should be almost finished, anywhats."

"Are you and Brennan staying here?"

"We did last night," my brother confirmed, smiling weakly. I took notice of the bunched-up blankets strewn across the floor, and I'd wondered how I missed them before. "We'll head out in the morning. Vole just needs to be sure that you're both completely stable before leaving, and since you're a little weak, I wanted to stay here to protect you from the evil lurking outside."

"It's not me who needs protection," I countered, but Brennan acted as if he hadn't heard me. Vole brushed past my arm, slipping into the bedroom and out of sight.

"Ideally, it would be best if you stayed at Mom's with me, but I know how stubborn you can be. At least we'll all be together on Sunday. My big day." Brennan grinned, running his fingers through his hair. The dark locks were oily and awry, and I wondered just how awful I looked myself—greasy hair, pasty skin. Blood stained palms, spattered arms. I looked as if I'd been elbow-deep in the gory guts of a human body.

"I want to stay here with Raiden." The words emerged as a whisper, and although Brennan preferred otherwise, he did not counter my statement.

"He's all unhooked," Vole announced, sneaking up behind me. Their sudden presence made me jump, pulse erratically fluttering beneath my chest.

How was I supposed to fight off the De Mörka like this?

"Oh," I murmured, the tips of my toes digging into the wiry carpet. "Thanks, Vole. You guys can help yourselves to anything in the kitchen, I guess. I'm going to help Raiden get un-bloodied and I'll clean myself up, too."

"We'll probably order some takeout, so let me know what you two are feeling," Brennan said, slender arm wedged within the crevice of the couch. He was nearly elbow-deep, bushy brows knit together in concentration as he searched for the presumably lost remote control. I could almost feel the filth beneath the cushions, a profusion of crumbs, lint, dog hair, and dust tickling the surface of his palm as he rummaged around for the plastic object.

"Make yourself at home, I guess," I dryly murmured, unamused as my brother yanked the remote from its hiding place. Usually, I didn't mind the company, but right now I would prefer to be alone with Raiden. "I'll let you know what we want to eat. Just feed the dogs and let them out, please."

Brennan beckoned the dogs over, freeing me from my temporary trap as I escaped to the bedroom once more, slamming the door closed behind me with such force that it rattled the walls.

Raiden was on his feet beside the bed, tempestuously touching the bruised flesh on the inside of his elbow. He was obsessive about certain things—wounds especially. Marks. Scars. He toyed with them, examined them. Scabs barely lasted, for he'd itch them right off almost as quickly as they'd formed. Pimples and blemishes never stood a chance—he'd squeeze and poke and prod until they bled and oozed and eventually disappeared for good.

"Stop that," I pressed, stepping forward to meet his still frame. His stare met mine, and I felt as if I'd dove into a lively, verdant forest, a series of trees encircling my frail body, bright, green leaves fluttering in the wind. He had the most gorgeous eyes; a color so sharp, so striking that it caught you off guard every single time.

"Sorry," he mumbled, sheepishly tearing his hand away. "I feel disgusting. Help me wash all of this blood out of my hair."

It felt like a command instead of a question, but nevertheless, I obliged; leading the way to our en-suite bathroom. The tile felt frigid against the soles of my feet, and I couldn't help but shiver, fingertips tickling the goose bump riddled flesh of my arms. Raiden was close on my heel—*too close*—and I could practically feel him breathing down my neck as I cranked the faucet sideways, eliciting a vicious, noisy, sputtering stream. When I'd spun around to grab a towel from the linen cabinet, I outwardly gasped; for Raiden was naked before me, clothes awkwardly discarded in a pile at his feet. His eyes visibly widened at my clearly uncomfortable reaction.

"What?" he slurred, suddenly bashful about his nakedness. Uneasily, he glanced down at his pale form, most of it peppered with bright blotches of dry blood.

"Nothing," I dryly dismissed, refusing to even glance in his direction. I could already feel the heat radiating beneath my cheeks, an intense sensation that I'd never once experienced in regards to Raiden's nakedness. Hell, I'd seen him naked an abundance of times, and just recently, he'd held my nude frame as I slept. Only this time, something had changed. *Shifted.* The thought of Raiden standing before me in his full glory generated a tantalizing tingle within my belly.

Lost in my own thoughts, I tore a towel from the warped stack, squeaky, wooden door easing closed as I caught a glimpse of Raiden's rear side as he stepped into the warm, cozy cubicle. The jet-black curtain remained open, however, and as my lips parted in preparation to speak, Raiden requested my presence.

In the shower.

With him.

"Is that really necessary, Rai?" I whined, slightly panicked. The curtain was still ajar, and I felt the color drain from my face as Raiden stepped into view once more, completely confident and unashamed of his current state.

"I don't know what's gotten into you the last few days, Frey, but if I repulse you *that* much, just tell me," Raiden said, his tiny voice almost entirely masked by the roaring water.

"No, *no* . . ." I slurred, shaking my head from side to side. He looked so small—so *fragile* in our blue-tiled shower, and I wanted nothing more than to step into the amiable abyss and wrap him up in my arms.

Without a second thought, I crawled into the shadowy cubicle along with him. The plastic tub audibly groaned beneath our combined weight, and my hands were shaking so violently that I could hardly pull the curtain closed. The shower was poorly lit, the only light source being that of the bright bulbs which hovered over the sink. The obnoxious lights cast a flimsy glow that barely penetrated the small space, and Raiden's features were mostly masked as he studied me up and down.

"Freya," he started, left brow cocked.

I followed his gaze, shamefully viewing the soaked jeans that were slowly suctioning to the prickly surface of my legs. I was so flustered that I'd managed to step into the shower completely clothed.

"If you're uncomfortable being naked, that's okay. But, at least get down to your bra and panties and help me get all of this blood off, please. I still feel really weak and sore," Raiden politely requested, a small smile stretched across his cheeks. I knew the question burned on his tongue—*why now? Why have things changed?*—but he refused to let it spill. This wasn't the first time we'd stuffed ourselves up in the outdated shower, the tile walls cracked and worn. In fact, the amount of times we'd innocently bathed together exceeded the amount of fingers I had—fingers that couldn't stop shaking as I struggled to unbutton my jeans.

Luckily, Raiden failed to notice my struggle, for he'd dunked his head beneath the steady stream, eyelids sealed, head tipped, chin jutting outwards, plump lips partially parted . . .

He looked elegant—*regal*—like a young prince. Royalty. The water gently caressed his scarlet skin, dripping down his curls and soaking his scalp.

My drenched jeans met my feet in a weighty lump as Raiden's fingers drifted down to his neck. I rid my lanky limbs of the wet clothing—everything but my undergarments, at least—as I admired the man standing before me, head lolled off to the side, a muted moan tumbling off of his lips as he kneaded the sore flesh.

"Does your neck hurt?" I asked, dismissively discarding the sopping bundle out of the shower. The wet clothes met the tile floor with a dignified *smack,* prompting Raiden to reemerge from his pleasant trance. He seemed displeased at the sight of my undergarments, but he didn't dare breathe a word of it. Instead, he requested the bottle of shampoo, which was buried behind my frozen frame.

"I can wash your hair," I offered, snatching the half-empty bottle from the metal rack.

"That'd be nice," Raiden said, spinning around to face the water. His hair was matted and messy, blotches of blood binding the curly locks together in unsightly heaps.

I squeezed a substantial amount of soap into my palm, lathering the smooth liquid between my hands as Raiden softly spoke. His tiny tone was mostly muffled by the roaring waves, so I had to ask him to repeat himself.

"Have I done something?"

My quivering fingers met his scalp, tenderly kneading the clumpy locks as I stripped the blood from his hair. I felt awful—*guilty.* He probably thought that I hated him.

"No, Rai," I whispered, working extra hard on a particularly pesky clump of gore. "Things are just . . . weird. For me. It's nothing you've done."

"Were you there?" Raiden wondered, his fingertips warily waltzing along the shiny shower wall. "In the in-between. The limbo. Was that really you, or did I just imagine that it was?"

My limbs stiffened, vivid visuals of our incredibly realistic trek through the woods invading my mind. The giggles, the tumble, the near-kiss. My legs around his waist, his lips tickling my neck.

"In the forest?" I croaked, studying the abundance of clotted blood falling to our feet.

"No," Raiden murmured, glancing over his shoulder to view me. "At my childhood home. It was you and Mom. Only, Mom was better. Healthy. She was baking cookies, wearing some silly apron with lips printed all along the front. I was lounging in the lawn chair, and you were chasing butterflies in the garden. You don't remember it?"

"I wasn't there," I revealed, slightly saddened by the fact. It appeared as if the Raiden in my individual oblivion was nothing more than a falsified fabrication. I should've known it wasn't really him, for the Raiden standing before me would never reciprocate the libidinous emotions that plagued my every atom. Every part of me screamed for him—*begged* to be his. The man I'd grown up with, shared countless memories with, and even become *one* with, had stolen my heart. He'd torn each rib apart one by one, yanking and pulling, peeling them open, mangling the cage beyond repair. He'd hollowed me out, swallowed me whole. Claimed every piece of me like I was some sort of timeless trinket in an antique store, one with multiple pieces, all piecing together to form something unique. Special.

With every mend, I'd unintentionally inherited a diminutive chunk of his soul. Only, what I hadn't realized before was that the missing fragment was actually replaced by a slice of my own. Molding us into one.

"Something's shifted," Raiden spoke, fingers creeping up towards my jaw. "I can feel it, Freya. I can feel you."

I wanted to tell him that I loved him, but he never gave me the chance.

Eyes welling up with tears, I began to spill my innermost thoughts, barely uttering a single word before being silenced with the presence of his soft, warm lips.

A gasp, a shiver, a moan. His mouth was warm—*welcoming.* Wet. Fingertips easing along my arms, leaving prickly, pleasant bumps in their wake. The walls came tumbling down, crumbling apart, showering my feet. Leaving me bare. Open. *Breathless.*

He stripped the barrier away using nothing but his tongue, tapping against the seal of my lips. Once. Thrice. Demanding entry. His palms cradled my cheeks, thumbs etching wide, warm circles into the flushed flesh. I allowed him in, mouth parting as a generous moan tumbled onto my tongue.

I didn't have to speak those three words aloud, for he could undoubtedly taste them on my tongue.

IloveyouIloveyouIloveyou

I slipped my fingers between his drenched locks, now free of blood, and tautly pulled; eliciting a low growl from the lustful man. I'd been kissed plenty of times—recently by a super sloppy Maxwell McKinnon—but none of them even compared to this. No, this wasn't *just* a kiss. It was a proclamation. An admittance of adoration. *Of love.*

I nearly whined when he pulled away, the absence of his lips irritating me to no avail. He'd barely pulled away—wide, doe-like eyes fixated on my features—when I wrapped my arms around his neck, tugging him back down to meet my mouth.

After all, we had two decades of kisses to make up for.

Our noses numbingly collided, exposed teeth clattering as Raiden's reddened lips curled into a wild grin against my mouth. A deep chuckle arose from the depths of his chest, and although I wanted to kiss and kiss and *kiss,* he pulled away, a cheery smirk stretched along his swollen lips as he met my pouty, puppy-dog stare.

Raiden held my face in his hands, unable to stifle his smile as I shied away from his merry glare. His thumb caught my chin, tenderly turning my face to meet his emerald orbs.

"Hey, look at me," he purred, his tongue swiping against his lower lip. I felt emotions—one that mirrored my own. The tether that bound both our spirits and bodies was knotted—*tight*—and I could feel the miniature, feathered creatures frolicking about in his belly, signalling that he, too, felt just as content with this scenario as I did.

I can feel your lust.

"I've been wanting to do that for nearly ten years," Raiden revealed. "I love you, Freya. I have for a very long time."

A sigh slipped through my lips. *Relief.*

"I love you, Raiden."

To my complete delight, he dove back in for more; lively giggles dancing along our tongues. Beside my own batch of butterflies, another entity existed—burrowing deep within the marrow of my bones, igniting the ivory, setting my insides ablaze. The pure passion that resonated within Raiden's being had fully consumed mine, making us one.

Whole.

Complete.

You have to tell him.

But *how?* How could I possibly put into words the sensations that I experienced? How could I spill the secret I kept hidden—*buried*—to the man who had just confessed his love for me? If he knew what I felt, what I'd *done,* he'd be embarrassed. Horrified. *Repulsed.* I'd unintentionally shared his intimate, physical moments; moments that I had no business being a part of. His every emotion—anger, joy, sorrow—they were all open to me, spread apart, available. I wasn't sure if I could even turn it off, for I wasn't sure what exactly it was.

Stealing bits of his soul.

Raiden's warm, wide palm cupped my rear-end, still clothed with a pair of cute cotton panties. A torturous tingle consumed my core—

whether it be evidence of Raiden's arousal or my own, I couldn't quite tell—and my wide, wary eyes met his shining, ardent stare.

"Are you okay?" The inquiry emerged as a hushed whisper, and I merely nodded, suddenly at a loss for words.

"Brennan and Vole are in the living room," I breathed, slightly shaken from our lustful affair. The warmth of the water made me dizzy—*weak*—and if I stood in this shower a single second longer, I may faint.

"You look like you're going to pass out," Raiden observed, cupping my flushed cheeks. Gently, he pulled my face to his; lips softly sliding along the surface of my forehead. "Let's get out. Is all the blood out of my hair?"

Weakly, I nodded, running my fingers through the saturated tendrils. "Can we just lay in bed? Vole said we probably both need another round of fluids."

"Of course, Frey," Raiden replied, delivering a short-lived peck to my sealed lips before killing the scalding stream. His skin was blotchy and red from the warm water, and I couldn't help but take notice of the way the muscles beneath his back shifted as he bent over. I felt feverish and frail, and the thought of Raiden standing naked before me after what just happened—*what we'd done*—made my vision slightly fade. My temples ached and throbbed, sight shifting to black as I slightly stumbled, toying the border of consciousness.

"Jesus, Freya," Raiden hissed, coiling his arms around my midsection. "Come on, let's get you back to bed. You definitely need more fluids. You must've used a lot of energy to save me yesterday, babe."

"I love you," I mumbled, burying my nose in the crook of his neck. The rapid pulse beneath the shy skin of his throat put me right to sleep, and I welcomed the blackness like an old friend.

fifteen

Pain.

It devoured me, swallowed me whole. Ate me up. Gnawing, grating, *tearing.* Severing the sweltering skin, bleeding me dry. Stealing every ounce of my being with every bite, every rip. Stripping me of my purpose, my identity.

I tried to move—to scream—but all I could do was wiggle my toes. What remained of them, that is. Raw, chunky flesh. Clotting blood. Detached muscle. The bones were surprisingly still intact, but not for much longer, I feared.

How I was still alive, I wasn't quite sure. Most of my midsection was ravaged, torn apart. Mutilated. Skin sliced open, flayed. Opening me up like a brand new novel, one that reeked of polished paper and print. The forgotten flabs laid on either side of my frail frame, wrinkled and ruined, exposing the obliterated cage that once guarded my heart. My ribs were cracked—*snapped.* Bent and broken. It appeared as if a wild animal had quite literally clawed its way out of my chest, bending the boned bars of the cage as if they were made of cheap plastic. Inside, my heart still beat—a determined little organ, hurriedly pumping blood throughout my core. Most of it spilled through my open wounds—coated the floor—only to be replaced by a batch of fresh, bright blood, which met the same fate.

With the slight strength that remained, I curved my neck, desperately attempting to view my apparent attacker. I could hear them feasting to my right, several feet back. Although my heart still occupied my chest, each of my lungs were missing. Vacant. *Gone.* I tried to breathe—*inhale*—but the task proved impossible, and my lips remained zipped. Glued. *Sealed.*

Gradually, I rotated my skull, my eyes widening significantly as they met my attacker, seated a mere two yards from my current location, a crushed, bulbous lung pinched between their fingers.

Sleek, black hair. Translucent skin. Eyes as dark as the night.

Her.

My mind told me to scream, run, *hide*—but it was too late. She'd had her way with me already, dipped her razor-sharp nails beneath my soft, silken skin. Torn away my flesh. Stripped me of my organs, all but my heart.

The remainder of my internal organs hugged her hip, a bloody, foul mound of rotting meat. Her ebony eyes studied me with each and every bite, pointy teeth penetrating the fatty flesh of my lung as she heartily fed. A combination of blood and drool dribbled down her chin, puddling between her parted legs, painting the concrete floor with a multitude of dissimilar shapes.

I hardly noticed what laid at her feet until then.

A body, wounds almost identical to mine. Dark, scruffy hair. Pronounced aquiline nose. Legs too long for his torso. Hands the size of baseball mitts.

My brother.

Brennan.

I needed to scream—*cry*—but my jaw refused to budge. Unlike me, his heart was missing; torn from its cavity, consumed by the enemy. I could see her stomach throbbing. *Pulsing.* A steady staccato of beats. Like a growing fetus pawing at the wall of her uterus, begging for release.

Thump thump thump.

She'd swallowed his heart whole.

Thump thump thump.

My vision flushed a pale white, momentarily blinded by the excruciating pain in my body, my nerve endings frayed and clipped like old wires.

When my shaky vision steadied once more, I saw them all: the bare, empty bodies of my loved ones. Momma. Dad. Grammy.

Raiden.

They too were denuded. *Stripped.* Chests torn open, limbs mangled, organs removed. What remained unscathed were their faces—unmarred, untouched. They looked peaceful, as if in a deep sleep.

Momma's red wig was lopsided, a single strand suctioned to her chapped lower lip. Stunning, ebony eyeliner claimed her eyelids, drawn upwards in dramatic wings that nearly kissed the tails of her brows. She looked beautiful. Healthy. *Dead.*

Most of Dad and Grammy's features were invisible, heads turned slightly sideways, robbing me of their presence. I hoped that they looked just as pleasant as Momma, delightful dreams dancing behind their sealed lids.

For a while, I refused to look at Raiden. I couldn't bear to look him in the face, to know that his fate was my doing—my fault.

My fault my fault my fault.

When I finally viewed him, he looked calm. Tranquil. His gorgeous, brunette locks framed his face like a halo, and a small section gently tickled the apple of his cheek, as if a continuous flow of air was suspended above his skull. He looked so handsome—*whole*—and I'd do anything to rip my heart out of my chest and shove it into his. Force it to beat. Bring him back to life.

Was this hell?

Before I could truly process my family's deaths—*my death*—the De Mörka dropped my meaty lung and cocked her head, eyeing me up and down before crawling on all fours towards my still frame.

The last thing I saw was the blacks of her eyes and the pointed tips of her teeth.

sixteen

Breathe.

I awoke with a start, clawing at my heaving chest as staggered sobs danced along my tongue. I was relieved to find everything exactly where it should be—sealed skin, lungs filled with air, a beating heart.

"Hey, it's okay. You're okay," my favorite voice cooed, warm fingers tickling my thigh. Raiden was seated beside me on the bed, whereas Vole's knees cradled the curve of the mattress, gentle fingertips pawing at my flushed flesh. Their fingers were wrapped around my arm, swiftly securing the IV that I'd unintentionally yanked out of my inner elbow.

"Jesus, what the *fuck,*" I gasped, massaging my sore throat. "I think I was just in hell."

I met my brother's soft glare from the doorway, lengthy arms crossed over his chest as he gnawed on his lower lip. Although he stood before me completely alive—all of his organs in their rightful places—I couldn't quite kick the intrusive thoughts of his dead body from my mind. The image plagued my thoughts like a vengeful virus, along with *her*—the rising De Mörka from the fertility clinic. Everytime I blinked, I saw her face. The blackness of her eyes. The sharp edges of her teeth. The blood dribbling down her chin, pooling around her bare feet.

"Well, if you were, you're back now," Raiden dryly teased, earning a harsh glare from my shaken self. He immediately apologized, coiling his arms around my shoulders before burying his forehead into the crook of my neck.

"How long was I out for?" I wondered, inaudibly thanking Vole for the IV.

"About six minutes," Brennan confirmed, stepping aside to let Vole exit the room. "Just enough time for Vole to get an IV in both of you. Where do you go, Frey? When you pass out like that?"

I swallowed hard, resting my chin atop Raiden's head as I avoided Brennan's stare. He was always curious about us two and our peculiar relationship, but I wasn't ready to indulge him with what happened just before my episode.

You kissed Raiden.

Butterflies waltzed around within my belly, a small smirk tugging at my lips as I answered Brennan's inquiry. "Last time, I think I briefly visited Heaven. But only for a short time. After that, it was just . . . nothing. Blackness. Oblivion. I couldn't see anything, hear anything. Nothing except my own voice, my own breaths. It was torture. But, not as torturous as this time. This time, I think I was sent down to hell."

"What did you see this time?" Brennan warily wondered. I couldn't look him in the face. Every time I did, I saw him dead.

"Death," I murmured, unable to stifle the shake that crept up my spine. I pulled Raiden closer to me. "So much death. And *her*. Black eyes, sharp teeth. Blood. I was dead, drained of my blood and organs, but my heart kept beating, and I could see, but I couldn't scream. All I could do was watch. Watch as she feasted upon my flesh. Watch all of you rot away, chests ripped open. Empty."

"Shit," Raiden muttered, removing his pointy nose from my neck. His eyes met mine—an array of emerald stars penetrating my soul. I couldn't help myself—I kissed him. Right in front of my brother.

Although my eyelids fluttered closed, I could clearly picture Brennan's widening significantly, realization etched along his features as Raiden and I softly smooched for what seemed like less than a second. Painfully short. I craved his taste almost as soon as he'd pulled away, and I had to remind myself of the presence of my nosy brother, who would surely give me hell for what I'd just done.

"No way," Brennan breathed, unraveling his arms. "How long . . ?"

"Just now, actually," Raiden revealed, his cheeks ripening like a pair of bright red apples.

"Don't tell me you just had your first kiss after twenty-some years in front of *me,*" Brennan gawked, shaking his head. "Please tell me you've kissed before. Please."

"Before I passed out," I whispered, giggling slightly at the sight of my twitchy brother. "But, if you don't like seeing it, you may want to close the door. We have decades of kissing to make up for."

"Yuck," Brennan animatedly spat, flashing me a reassuring smile before lacing his fingers around the doorknob. "Holler if you need anything, and when your saline runs out. Vole and I are going to go ahead and order takeout."

"Just be sure to knock when our food gets here," Raiden called, delivering a wink in Brennan's direction. My brother playfully gagged, swinging the door shut behind him as Raiden and I erupted into joyous laughter.

"You're a sick little shit, Raiden Archimedes Crow."

Raiden raised a brow. "Oh, we're using full names from now on? Game on, Freya Dagmar Gallo."

He caught me mid-giggle, tackling me onto my back as his IV pole warily whined from being pulled too tight. He grumbled, extending his arm outward and adjusting the tube as I occupied myself with his neck, trailing wet, hot kisses along the blushing surface.

I felt him shudder beneath my mouth, a hushed groan cascading up the length of his throat. I watched his eyelids slip closed, pretty, pink lips parted, head rolled—*tipped* back, Adam's apple bobbing beneath the tip of my tongue. I buried my fingers within his wet, lengthy curls, forcing his face down to meet mine as I stole another kiss.

"It's weird how *normal* this feels," Raiden cooed, flattened palms glued to the pillow on either side of my skull, his weight suspended above my weakened frame. "Like it's something we've been doing for an eternity."

My fingertips caressed the curve of his jaw. "Maybe we have."

"I forgot you believe in that kind of stuff," Raiden dryly teased, dipping down to capture my lips in a swift kiss. He pulled away abruptly, leaving me hungry for more.

"There's too many coincidences in life for past lives to not exist, Rai," I weakly defended, toying with the collar of his plain, white tee. "You act like unexplainable things can't exist when your girlfriend is a literal magical being."

Raiden raised a brow. "Girlfriend?"

Shit.

"Well, I'm pretty sure we've just completely soiled our platonic friendship, don't you think?" I timidly teased, eyeing him up and down. "There's really no going back from this."

"We've only kissed, Frey," Raiden purred, rotating onto his side. He collapsed against the mushy mattress, an open palm suctioned to his cheek as he admired my wary glare. "You act like we've done some kind of sensual blood ritual."

"Don't give me any ideas . . ."

Raiden playfully slapped my arm, grinning lips colliding with mine once more. I melted into his embrace, tiny moans tickling my tongue as I resisted the urge to flatten him into his back and ravage his neck with violent kisses.

Take it slow, Freya. You have all the time in the world.

Unless the De Mörka kills you and your entire family on Sunday.

"What is it?" Raiden whispered against my mouth, his palm cradling my cheek. It was as if he could read my thoughts.

"Nothing," I fibbed, shaking my head as if to rid my mind of the treacherous thoughts. "Let's just enjoy this moment. Brennan's bound to barge in soon with our food, and I have plenty of kisses with your name on them."

"That was incredibly lame," Raiden chuckled. He took hold of my hips, and before I could protest, he'd yanked me on top of him; a leg on each side of his hips, fingers knotted within my hair, emerald eyes darkened with lust.

"Never let me go." The words emerged in the form of a pitiful plea, and he reassured my worries with a deep, open-mouthed kiss.

Never.

seventeen

Rays of lovely, yellow light eased along my eyelids, generating a welcoming warmth that gently danced down the length of my torso. I felt the weight of all three dogs along my legs, curled into my lithe frame like a warm blanket.

I reached down to meet one of their faces—Kelso's, I think—and I heard a low, contentful groan resonate deeply within his throat as I scratched behind his ears.

A prickle of pain stroked the base of my skull, a taunting reminder of the harrowing event that transpired less than forty-eight hours earlier. With eyelids still firmly sealed, I gently kneaded my fingers against the sore skin, knotted tendrils tangling around my overgrown nails.

Pleasant memories of the previous night replayed within my mind—visuals of a blushing, grinning Raiden, his lips red and swollen. He held me as I slept, a slumber that was constantly interrupted by bouts of panic. With each attack, he comforted me; a whisper of sweet nothings tickling the shell of my ear, roaming hands squeezing, stroking, petting. He held me close, lips gently pressed against my forehead as I'd drifted back off into a dreamless slumber, only to wake less than ninety minutes later drenched to the bone in slick sweat.

My arms outstretched towards Raiden's warmth, only to be met with a cold bundle of blankets. Dissatisfied by my findings, my eyes flew open, revealing a mangled mess of sheets where he should be.

The static-riddled television displayed an unidentifiable show, something from well before the days of colored television. With a gentle coo, I brushed the animals off as I climbed out of bed.

Last night's Chinese food sat heavy in my belly, an overwhelming wave of nausea coming over me as I stood to my feet. My vision wavered, and I nearly fell onto my face as I blinked away a series of black, blotchy spots.

Mimosa jumped down to meet my unsteady frame, tiny, pink tongue lapping at the salty skin across my foot. I didn't dare bend down to pet her, for the action alone would probably prompt me to lose consciousness. Instead, I continued on; rounding the mattress with shaking legs.

I wasn't one to rely on others to care for me—I was usually quite independent—but the thought of Raiden not being within arms reach of me was enough to prompt a panic attack. My forearms lit ablaze like the scorching sun, which had barely graced the horizon. Trembling fingers pulled at my flesh, desperately attempting to rid them of the stinging sensation.

I felt worse than I ever had before—an unbearable burning encircling my limbs as if they were physically on fire. I bit back tears, and blinked away the persistent, spotty dots that occasionally littered my vision.

Somehow, I managed to find my way to the kitchen, where Raiden was busy washing the dishes. Bright yellow rubber gloves claimed his hands—silly Raiden, so afraid of touching wet food—and just as my lips parted in preparation to call out his name, I felt the world begin to slip away from me.

A glass plate clattered to the base of the sink, startling me back into consciousness as Raiden's arms hooked around my center, steadying my dead weight.

"Frey," he breathed, helping me to my feet. "Just take your time, okay? You probably need some water and protein."

"How are you completely fine, whereas I can barely stay awake? You almost died, Raiden," I muttered, barely loud enough for him to hear. He ripped the soaked gloves from his hands, dismissively tossing them atop the counter before pulling me close.

"Freya, I think you accidentally breathed a little *too* much life into me, baby."

Baby.

I felt the heat rise to my cheeks, a soft gasp tickling my tongue as his mouth met mine. Blindly, he twisted the both of us around, flattening the soft curve of my back against the edge of the counter. He pulled away slightly, a broad, toothy grin smeared along his lips as his lively, green eyes met mine.

"Let me breathe some of this life back into you."

I felt weightless in his arms. *Free.* His tongue tasted like wine and suddenly I was tipsy—*no, drunk*—completely intoxicated, head swimming with satisfaction. The pain in my arms ceased; the flames extinguished.

Out.

Safe.

Raiden gently pried my lips back, nibbling on the plump, lower lip as I giggled into his mouth. It felt surreal—kissing him. Kissing Raiden. For a moment, back in our teen years, I thought that maybe we'd end up this way. I'd dismissed the feelings almost instantly—paired them with that of puberty—but now, years later, wrapped up in his arms, I realize that those innocent thoughts were a vision. A sign.

Meant to be.

Raiden's fingertips teased the hem of my shirt, and I bit back the obnoxious moan that crawled up my throat. His touch felt like ice against my hips, forefinger nestled in the bend of my protruding hip bone. He replaced it with a thumb, applying the perfect amount of pressure to the surface, sending sparks up my spine.

His touch was interrupted by the shrill ring of his phone, nestled deep within his pajama pant pocket. I couldn't quite stifle the irritable sigh that slipped from my lips, and with a broad grin and a small laugh, he pressed one last kiss to my mouth before answering the line.

I couldn't help but watch Raiden as he stepped aside, his ebony-hued phone glued to his ear as he lowly spoke. His opposite hand was in his hair—per usual—delicately toying with the unruly strands as he paced the puny kitchen. His cherry-red pajama pants were snug around his hips, and I openly frowned at the sight of the faded black v-neck suctioned to his upper half. My mind drifted to the lewd thoughts buried at the very rear, thoughts of his back, the muscles beneath. The way they'd ripple and shift with even the smallest of movements.

Raiden winked in my direction, the tip of his tongue darting out to teasingly wet his lips. I felt my chest tighten at the sight, and I felt like a middle-school girl with a pitiful crush. Not even Maxwell McKinnon made my heart race like this, or any of the men I'd unfortunately encountered before. My longest relationship lasted six months, a guy named Levi, and he was so disgustingly jealous of Raiden that I eventually dumped him over a thirty-second voicemail.

Most of the men that I'd "dated" had something negative to say about Raiden, which is possibly why none of the relationships blossomed.

It was always him.

"I've got bad news," Raiden murmured, stuffing the phone back into his pocket. "That was Sierra. The opener flaked and Sierra's sister is in labor, so she can't come in either. There's no one else to open, and she even threatened to fire me if I didn't come in for her."

"Are you serious?" I spat. *Fucking Sierra.* "Today's our second to last day off. Tomorrow's Brennan's birthday and then it's back to work for us Monday. She couldn't find anyone else?"

"I'm sorry, Frey. It's just two hours. The restaurant is going to open an hour later to give me more time to set it all up. Kira comes in at eleven for her shift and I'm free to leave then," Raiden said. He tucked a stray strand of hair behind my ear, curved thumb caressing my cheek as he sweetly smiled. "Come with me. Just hang out in a booth or something. Sierra said most of the prep is finished, I won't have much to do. Then, we'll have the rest of the day. Just us."

I frowned, glancing down at the thumb that cradled my chin. I pressed a kiss to the surface before nodding in agreement.

"Keep the doors locked. Just in case the De Mörka finds me," I whispered.

"She won't," Raiden assured, nodding towards the bedroom. "Are you sure you'll be strong enough to attend Brennan's birthday tomorrow?"

"I have to be," I replied, wincing as I walked. "It'll be a celebration that I simply can't miss."

I set up camp in a back booth, a bundle of blankets wrapped around my torso as I thumbed through a creepy psychological thriller that I found on our bookshelf. Raiden had some kind of classic rock radio station playing throughout the restaurant, and I could hear him rummaging around back in the kitchen. A stack of boxes kept the kitchen door propped open, and I found myself wanting to playfully crawl through the entrance and catch Raiden off guard.

I felt guilty about lying in the booth, completely useless, but he insisted that I needed rest.

You need your strength for tomorrow.

The only *rest* that I wanted was in our bed, tangled up with him. Touching. Kissing. *Loving.*

Thanks a lot, Sierra.

I skimmed past a part about some serial killer slicing off the fingers of his victims when a noisy crash startled me, followed by an aching pain in my left foot.

"Raiden?" I concernedly called, dropping the book onto my lap.

"I'm okay!" he exclaimed, my foot still throbbing. "I dropped one of those heavy mixing bowls on my foot."

Blood turned to ice within my veins, and I was suddenly reminded of the simple fact that I still hadn't told Raiden about our . . . *special connection.* He had absolutely no clue that I could feel the very same sensation in my own foot—a dull throb, a second heartbeat beneath the skin. Uneasily, I massaged the sore area, brushing the thoughts to the back of my mind.

Maybe later.

I returned to my story, shuffling through the fanned-out pages in search of where I'd left off.

Something about fingers and knives and blood . . .

I only made it through half of a page before I was interrupted by a sharp, noisy knock at the front glass door. I dog-eared the page before sinking lower in my booth, avoiding the early guest. I didn't want to be the one to tell them that the restaurant would be opening an hour later than usual.

Sheer, mahogany curtains cloaked the surrounding windows, effectively keeping out the harsh warmth, as well as shielding my shy frame from view. I studied the dark silhouette of the stranger just outside, and even caught a glimpse of beautiful, braided hair in the doorway, a pair of wide, curious eyes peeking in.

The knock came again, and out stumbled Raiden; wild curls pulled back into a bun. He was wiping his wet hands on a dish towel; lengthy, ring-clad digits slipping between the fabric.

I watched him toss the towel aside, draping it across the dark wood of the hostess stand. He greeted the stranger outside with a smile, and instead of pointing out the CLOSED sign in the window, he unlocked the door, slid it open, and vacated the restaurant.

Utterly perplexed by his peculiar actions, I sat up in the booth, the worn leather releasing an exaggerated burst of air as I wriggled my bottom across the surface. I could clearly hear Raiden's voice beyond the curtain-clad glass—he spoke loudly around people he knew—and I felt my heart beat irregularly within my chest.

As quietly as I could, I tip-toed towards the entrance, careful not to let the duo get a glimpse of me through the exposed front door.

Who the hell was he with?

I crept over to the very corner, thin, warm breaths caressing the curve of my lower lip as I hooked three fingers behind the curtain, gradually peeling it back to reveal Raiden's *friend.*

Beautiful, brown skin glimmered beneath the morning sun, as if an array of teeny-tiny reflective diamonds claimed the surface. Neatly threaded black braids grazed strong, sturdy shoulders; cascading down the fabric of a dainty, floral sundress. Cherry red nails that mimicked the shape of coffins danced along the conflictingly pale skin of Raiden's forearm, a pearly white smile slapped across the woman's features as she audibly laughed.

Jordan.

I let the curtain fall back into place, a bundle of bile creeping up my esophagus as I recalled her and Raiden's date less than a week prior. Once again, my blood turned to ice, and before I could reason with my conscience, I was storming out of the door.

"Oh," Jordan chirped, bewildered by my sudden presence. "Hi . . . Uh, Freya, right?"

A faux, exaggerated grin pulled at my lips as I offered her my hand. "Yup. Jordan, is it?"

Her palm met mine, freezing fingers nearly shocking my warm touch as she shook my hand. I could see Raiden awkwardly shift beside me in my peripheral vision, hands buried within his front pant pockets.

"It's nice to meet you, Freya. I thought Kira was coming in earlier; I was going to have some breakfast. Raiden just told me that the opener called out, though."

I hated the way his name slipped so easily off of her tongue, as if she'd said it a million times before. Moaned it, even.

I was making myself sick.

"Yeah," I muttered, avoiding Raiden's piercing glare. An overwhelming essence of discomfort danced along my bones, and I immediately knew that it was Raiden's emotions invading my body, for I didn't feel uncomfortable in the slightest. Instead, I felt irritable. *Rage.*

Don't be such a psychopath.

"Kira won't be in for over an hour, and you don't work here, so we can't really let you in," I added, shooting Raiden a stiff stare. He visibly frowned at the sight of my annoyance.

"Right. Raiden told me that as well," Jordan replied, fidgeting in place. "I'll probably run down the street for some coffee to waste time. I can bring you guys back some at eleven, if you want?"

I was about to decline the offer when Raiden immediately answered. "That'd be great, actually. We could both use the caffeine. I'll text you our orders, if that's okay?"

Jordan sweetly smiled, bright eyes solely fixated on Raiden. *My Raiden.* As if I didn't even exist.

"That'd be great. I'll see you both at eleven."

She gave Raiden a cute little wave before trodding off, glancing once over her shoulder to view the stiff man beside me.

I bit back tears as I slipped back into the restaurant, indirectly allowing the door to slam right in Raiden's face. I heard him shuffle in the doorway with a sigh, the lock audibly latching as I made my way back towards the cozy booth. I didn't dare glance over my shoulder to view him, and all I could think about was him and Jordan. Jordan and Raiden. Bundled up beneath the blankets, her hair sprawled out around her skull in diverse directions on my pillow. *My pillow.* Raiden's lips assaulting her neck, nipping, *sucking.*

I buried myself beneath the blanket, wrapping my trembling frame up into a tight cocoon. I heard the paperback novel tumble to the floor, and my foot unintentionally nicked the table, prompting the wooden legs to garishly screech.

I felt like a small child throwing a temper tantrum. It was immature of me to act in such a rash way, my advanced age considered. I wouldn't be surprised if Raiden were to reconsider his feelings for me after witnessing my juvenile fit.

"Freya," Raiden hummed, pulling at the weighty blanket. I pulled the fabric closer to my shaking self, refusing to acknowledge his gentle coos as he delicately unraveled my protective cloak. He peeled the suffocating layer from my face, revealing a set of flushed cheeks.

"There's my girl," he murmured, unable to stifle his smile. His knees cradled the curve of the booth cushion, and although I felt a bitter resentment towards him, I wouldn't have minded if he'd crawled atop me.

"Leave me alone," I hissed, attempting to pull the blanket back over my face, but to no avail. Raiden tightened his hold on the quilt, yanking it clean off and revealing my balled-up body.

"Never," he lowly teased, extending a hand in my direction. "Sit up and talk to me."

With a huff, I obliged; maneuvering my bottom towards the edge of the cushion. I propelled myself a bit too far, the tip of my nose mistakenly colliding with the metal clasp of his belt. I could feel the heat blossom within my cheeks as I diverted my stare upwards to meet his, where I was greeted with a cheeky chuckle.

"I don't mind this view," he said, and my jaw dropped. Before I could conjure up some sly reply, he'd claimed my wrists, tugging me upwards in a standing position. The sudden shift made the room spin and my head throb, and my parted, puzzled lips were met by the warm caress of his mouth.

"I saw how jealous you were out there," he purred between eager, sealed-lip pecks, his tone lustful and low. He backed me up to the table, the choppy edge sharp and uncomfortable against my spine. With a whine, I knotted my fingers in the collar of his Tostada's uniform shirt, teeth clattering upon impact as we unashamedly smooched.

He was right, I *was* jealous. And, for good reason. However, Raiden was unaware of my impolite eavesdropping on his date, and I was certain that he'd be beyond embarrassed if I'd confessed my knowledge of that night to him. How he seemed entirely disinterested in Jordan, the way he excused himself to the shower to finish the job that she failed to accomplish.

How he thought of me.

And, the time before, when the sensation of his pleasure had felt so tied up within myself that I had craved his release as if it were my own. The memory of how I had exposed myself on the bed, as if yearning for his discovery in those moments sent a warm wash of desire throughout my being.

The subtle parts in my eyelids registered the windows, as if for the very first time, finding their presence to be a nuisance due to the exposure they offered. Something dark and naughty whispered *let them watch,* but Raiden was already moving me, impatient and shamelessly uncaring that he was dragging us onto the floor. I claimed my spot on his lap, but not without stumbling. Raiden stifled a giggle, big, moony eyes filled with longing and a dash of mischief.

"Don't ever make me jealous again," I warned, teasing him with a light buck of my hips. I was denying him the friction I *felt* him yearning for, and I was denying it of myself. I suppressed a moan when I felt him twitch, my fingers shaking as I fumbled with his belt.

In my frustration, I crouched, slinking my jeans down to my knees. My conscience kept screaming at me, indubitably reminding me that the man beneath my nearly bare hips wasn't Maxwell McKinnon, or just some random guy. No—it was Raiden.

The very same Raiden that I'd grown up with. The same Raiden that couldn't ride a bike until fourteen, and still had trouble keeping himself steady to this very day. The same Raiden who called me half-past one in the morning when he'd kissed his first girl—Ella was her name. Ella Greene. I wondered if Ella even remembered him, that geeky, stout boy with a head full of curly hair and the brightest eyes I'd ever encountered.

A kiss, a sigh; roaming hands and racing hearts. Sweet whispers grazing the arch of my jaw, greedy fingers unlooping a belt, tossing it aside. I found it difficult to breathe, and Raiden took notice, a tiny coo coiling around my tongue as he suctioned his mouth to mine.

Breathless whimpers, tiny touches. Warm, wet skin. He touched me, and I gasped; fingers knotting within his hair, index finger curling around the hair tie, snapping it in half. Handsome, brunette tresses framed his face like a halo—*angelic*—and with every small shift of his friendly fingers, I whined, proclaiming my love for him with every shy breath.

"Is this okay?" Raiden wondered, a hint of innocence present in his husky tone. He'd barely touched me, but between the overwhelming sensations bubbling within my own belly and the company of his as well, I began to worry that I may completely combust before we even reached any kind of peak.

Tell him.

"Yes," I breathed, ignoring my conscience. There was a time and a place to reveal our bond—*the tether*—but now was not the time.

"This is kinda weird," Raiden said, laughing lowly as I nipped at his neck. He freed himself from his constraints, and with great impatience, I settled onto him, earning a baffled—yet contentful—groan from a doe-eyed Raiden.

"Just shut up and fuck me," I countered, rocking against him. I wasn't quite sure where the sudden burst of confidence came from, but instead of questioning it, I simply rolled with it; taking control of the situation and asserting my dominance.

Raiden squirmed beneath me, and with every stroke, I felt his pleasure mixed within my own, stacking atop each other like a twisted tower, inching up my throat and emerging as a mangled moan.

He told me he loved me more times than I could count, lazy, hooded eyes penetrating my soul. His skull collided with the freckled wood of the booth's backside, faint moans cascading off of his tongue as he unconsciously rocked himself against me.

My palm flattened against the wood parallel to his head, steadying my shaking self as my eyelids fluttered closed. The gratifying entanglement of our mixed emotions generated a weighty warmth within my lower belly, and as I increased my speed, the dreaded, loathsome burning returned. Only this time, it didn't only exist in my forearms.

No—it spread. Rapidly.

I tried to ignore it, but it seemed almost impossible. It was blinding—*harsh.* Nausea bubbled up within my belly, and I nearly cried when Raiden's fingers met my hips, squeezing so hard that bruises were sure to form in the morning. He was getting close—I could feel it—but with every second that slipped by, the pain intensified.

Raiden whimpered my name, and when my eyelids fluttered open, I was met by the black, twisted tongue of the De Mörka herself; pointed teeth bared, blood dripping down her chin. The hold tightened on my hips, and with a cry, I pulled away; a strangled scream slipping between my lips as my palms collided with my cheeks, shielding my eyes from the murderous maiden that had replaced my Raiden.

As soon as I'd hit the ground, my core energetically pulsated, electric sparks consuming my spine as I let out a cry. Above my shielded eyes, burning bulbs blew—showering the pair of us in sparks as every light in the establishment simultaneously combusted, cloaking the entirety of the restaurant in darkness, the only light being that of the sun's rays that barely peeked beyond the curtains.

"Frey?" A breathless voice inquired, the squeaking shuffle of boots bringing me back to reality. With a tremble, I uncovered my eyes, anxious to face the demon that sat beneath me only moments prior. Instead, I was met with Raiden's worrisome stare, white ribbons etched along the lower half of his shirt.

"R-Raiden–" I whimpered, observing the blown-out lights above us. "What the hell happened?"

"Did you do this?" Raiden asked, glancing up at the broken lamps. He struggled to buckle his jeans, cringing at the sight of the mess he'd made on his shirt.

"The De Mörka—she's here," I murmured, struggling to pull my jeans back up to my hips. "She–She somehow appeared in the form of you . . . Or, something. I don't know. I *saw* her, and then the lights blew, and my whole body was on fire. I don't know where she is, or how she managed to implant herself into my mind and trick me into thinking that she was *you,* but she's *here,* Raiden. You have to save me. You have to get me out of here."

"Okay, give me a second–" Raiden stammered, snatching several napkins from a nearby table. He weakly wiped at his shirt, audibly cursing when the fluid did nothing but smear.

"Now, Raiden! This is life or death!" I screeched, glancing over my shoulder to view the nearby windows. I peeled back the curtain, widened eyes observing the empty parking lot.

"Let me call Sierra–"

"Fuck Sierra!" I screamed, snatching the soiled napkins from his clutch and tossing them aside. Raiden cringed at the sight, brushing past my shoulder to collect the tainted recycled paper.

"Go to the front door. Let me just make sure the heat elements are all off so the place doesn't burn to the damn ground," Raiden snipped, stuffing the napkins into a trash can before disappearing beyond the swaying kitchen doors.

With every passing moment, the unbelievable essence of overall unease intensified within my chest, bubbling up into my throat in the form of sporadic, vulgar retches. I feared that I may lose my breakfast all over the nearby booth, and I couldn't help but continuously peek beyond the curtains, widened eyes observing our surroundings.

Tostada's was located on a shopping strip, parked between a vibrant, girlish boutique and an ordinary insurance office. The business strip was separated from the parking lot by a semi-busy two-lane road, an occasional vehicle passing by. From the distance, I could see that the parking lot was mostly empty; all besides a small cluster of cars parked directly across from the boutique. The insurance office next door claimed the very edge of the strip, which curved an entire ninety-degrees before continuing onward down the other road. It was on that side where Jordan ran to grab us coffee at a quaint (but ever-busy) café. For such a seemingly small town, the strip gave off big-city vibes.

"Ready?" Raiden purred, fingertips dancing along the small of my back. "Let me make sure the front door is locked so we can sneak out back to the car."

"I feel so sick," I confessed, blinking back tears as Raiden tugged on the front door. My arms were on fire, throbbing and aching, and I couldn't help but scratch at the surface, as if my fingertips could magically ease the pain.

As they should.

"I can't heal it." The words emerged rushed—*panicked*—and Raiden took my hand in his as we vacated the restaurant. "I can't heal myself. I can't make the pain go away."

"Maybe it's an illusion," Raiden suggested, seemingly disinterested. He was probably thinking about how we would both no longer have jobs come afternoon. "Like a hallucination. Brought on by the De Mörka. Because physically, your arms look fine."

Did he even care?

"Are you angry?" I queried, easing out of the back door. He quickly locked up before leading me towards the parked car. I couldn't help but continuously glance over each shoulder, eyes torturously peeled for any sight of the villainous De Mörka. I feared that if I let my guard down for even a second, she'd appear out of thin air—claws extended, fangs bared—beady, black eyes bright and wide as her nails dipped into the slick flesh of my neck, fraying the skin, slicing me open . . .

"I'm not mad, Frey. Let's just get you home," Raiden weakly assured, ushering me into the vehicle. "Are you sure you don't want to be with Brennan and Momma?"

"No," I murmured, shaking my head from side to side as I settled into the passenger seat. I was still on high alert, the tip of my nose tickling the icy window as I glared out at our immediate surroundings.

Without another word, Raiden eased into the car, a soft sigh cascading over his lips as he shoved the key into the ignition. I knew damn well that neither of us would have a job come noon, but that seemed so insignificant . . . so *juvenile* compared to the sheer possibility that my entire family could be eliminated sometime within the next twenty-four hours.

You don't need a job if you're dead.

"Hey," Raiden cooed, a warm palm claiming my thigh. I flinched upon impact. "It's okay. I'm here."

"Just drive," I ordered, and he obeyed; shooting me a worrisome glance as he peeled our aging vehicle from its temporary home.

In order to head in the direction of home, we had to round the corner of the strip and ease past the coffee shop. For a split second—as I anxiously tapped my leg and gnawed on my fingernails—I thought of Jordan, and how we'd surely see her seated outside, sipping her coffee before running back in to grab Raiden his order. I didn't want to see her—not even for a second—because the sight of her pretty self alone would most definitely send me into a raging panic attack, one which I was teetering right on the edge of.

"Breathe, Frey. I've got you," Raiden lowly assured, fingertips dancing along my thigh. Even the tiniest of touches augmented my anxiety, and with a cluster of apologies, I lightly shoved him away. I couldn't stand to be touched when I felt this uneasy, and the last thing I wanted to do to an already distressed Raiden was to irrationally erupt.

With a sigh, Raiden hugged the curb, easing out of the back lot of Tostada's and heading towards home. Almost instantly, he was pumping the brakes; courtesy of a couple cars rowed at the stoplight.

To my complete dismay, we were stationary in front of the *exact* location that I did *not* want to see—*Carly's Coffee.* God, even the name made me queasy. Overpriced drinks with overrated edible treats and the snottiest customers and—

—her.

Promptly, the air exited my lungs, adorning the conflictingly cold window with a blotchy, blurry haze. I felt weak—*sick*—and suddenly, my surroundings felt sluggish, as if someone switched the dial on my reality to that of extra slow motion. The blood in my veins struggled to flow, switching to syrup beneath my skin. My heart feebly pumped, watering gaze failing to focus on the sight before me as my weakened fingers wiped the window clean.

There she sat, like a phantom—*a ghost*—perfectly still on a bench in front of Carly's. Palms glued to knobby knees, stringy, long hair framing her cratered cheeks.

The world seemed to proceed around her, whereas she remained perfectly still; *rooted.* Her eyes remained unblinking, gaze boring so deeply into mine that I could feel the ice that pumped through her veins in the place of regular, red blood.

I studied those ebony eyes long and hard before being welcomed into an identically hued abyss, the sound of Raiden calling my name soothing my soul as I departed.

There was nothing for me on the other side again.

Nothing but blackness. A bleak, empty space.

Oblivion.

It ate me up, swallowed me whole; made sure I knew that I was—in fact—alone. Just me, myself, and my subconscious.

I no longer had a body. Not a finger, nor a toe. Nary a single limb or slab of skin.

Nothing but a thought.

A soul.

I felt claustrophobic, *trapped.* As if I were crammed into an itty bitty box, my eyes ripped from my skull, the blood in my veins drained dry. I wanted to look down—see my hands—but there was nothing to see, nor could I look.

There was nothing left of me but my psyche.

With every fleeting moment, I became more agile; *panicked.* The obscureness of my surroundings was horrifying, and I found myself wishing for an ending after this one—an ending without an eternal darkness.

A place where I'd simply cease to exist.

Any place would be better than this. This twisted eternal rest. This pure fucking emptiness. A demented, permanent version of sleep paralysis—an episode where my eyes would never even open, no matter how hard I tried to wake up.

To wake up.

To wake.

wake

wake

wake . . .

"I don't think death is really like that," Raiden whispered, bringing a cool, damp towel to my sweaty forehead. "I'd like to think that it's more than just blackness for an eternity."

"It was the worst thing I've ever experienced," I muttered, biting back fresh tears.

I'd had enough of these near-death episodes. Next time, it better be fucking final.

"Your forehead is hot enough to roast marshmallows on," Raiden murmured. "I should probably get you something for a fever. I don't know if you'll be well for Brennan's birthday tomorrow, Frey."

I shoved Raiden's hand away, a miniscule burst of panic easing up my throat as I shook my head. "I can't miss that party, Raiden. I need to be there to protect him, in case she shows up. She hasn't done a damn thing yet, and I have this sinking feeling that she'll show her ugly mug at the event."

"You were unconscious for almost three hours, Freya. You're in rough shape. Do you really think you could take on a rising De Mörka? Won't she be at the height of her power on the eve of Brennan's birthday?" Raiden asked, dismissively discarding the rag atop my bedside table. He unintentionally knocked over several empty water bottles, rigid fingers greedily grabbing at the softened plastic as he weakly attempted to straighten them.

As I awkwardly watched him fumble around with my bedside garbage, I wondered if Sierra had called our cells and formally fired us yet. It was only a matter of time if she hadn't already.

I'd ruined our lives.

"I think so," I whispered, wincing at the slight searing sensation in my arms. At this rate, I'd probably completely combust the second the De Mörka laid a single finger on me.

"This party is the dumbest thing your family has ever done. No offense," Raiden said, letting out a sigh as he stood to his feet. He looked utterly exhausted—shy bags cradling his eyes as he offered me a small smile.

"It's tradition to throw a large celebration on the eve of an Araedian's thirtieth birthday. It's the day our energies solidify forever. But Brennan's special—he's the very last Araedian male. He'll become an omnipotent," I replied, snatching up one of my empty bottles from the table. I turned the freckled plastic over in my hand, intently eyeing the soft curves of the pliable body. I squeezed it once, crushing the shape between my fingers, molding it into something nearly unrecognizable.

"He'll be fucking unstoppable," Raiden whispered, a whimsical sense of admiration present in his tone. "Pretty badass, ain't it?"

I returned the smile, tossing the garbage aside without a second thought. "Sure is. Do you want to take a bath?"

Raiden raised a teasing brow, a sly smirk dancing along his pretty, pink lips as he eased onto the bed. I tried to stifle a giggle—but ultimately failed as he crawled on all fours towards my blushing frame. His forehead gingerly grazed mine, the cold tip of his pointed nose tickling my cheek as he let out a low chuckle.

"You want to take a *bath?*" he toyed. I could feel his tongue tickle my top lip as he lightly lapped at his. "With *me?*"

I coiled my arms around his neck, chin jutting forward to capture his mouth in a quick, sealed-lip kiss before pulling away to reply. "I mean, I could always just bathe with Kelso. He loves baths. Or even Mimosa."

"Ouch," Raiden slurred, knees directly positioned on either side of my thighs. We probably looked so comical in such a position—so stereotypically backwards. His weight suspended above me, as if he were sitting on my lap. I couldn't help but giggle when I envisioned it.

"What?" I cooed, clammy palms cradling his face. His mouth met mine once more in the place of words—hot breath tickling my lips as his mouth gently pried mine open. His tongue tasted of berries and boy oh *boy* did I have quite the sweet tooth—and as I dove in hungry for more—*more more more*—I felt a sudden weight compile near my ankles, a tiny, animalistic whine, an audible beg for the bathroom.

I pulled away from Raiden's hungry mouth, emitting a garish groan as my gaze rotated to that of an impatient Mimosa at my feet, desperate to use the toilet.

"I'll let them out," Raiden politely offered, placing a petite kiss atop my nose. I detangled my fingers from his lengthy locks—a brunette mess of too-long curly hair—and he was gone; a trio of dogs on his tail.

I settled into the pillows, the hushed hum of the television filling the void as my eyelids fluttered closed. Some vampire show was playing—one I barely cared for or paid attention to—but it made for some good background noise, one that nearly put my feverish self to sleep as Raiden took an eternity with the dogs.

I thought about him—*Raiden*—the way everything seemed to fall so easily into place, at the very same time that my life was actually falling apart. The episodes, the burning, the impending doom.

My inevitable death.

I'd been blinded by false loves over the years—ignorant to the fact that I lived under the very same roof—*slept in the same damn bed* as my actual soulmate. And now, as I'd finally realized the feelings that existed all along, I'd spend mere days with the one I truly love before inevitably perishing in some hellish form by the hand of the De Mörka. I couldn't even handle seeing her, nor being within several feet of the evil individual. Imagine how doomed I'd be if she chose to act upon her wicked, brewing energy . . .

My fatalistic ponderings were interrupted by the presence of a warm, welcoming mouth, which had found its way beneath the sheets in order to attack my inner thighs. With a squeal, my eyes shot open; trembling fingers yanking the blanket upwards to reveal a grinning Raiden positioned between my legs.

"What are you doing?" I breathlessly exclaimed, suddenly aware of the frigid fingers dancing along my skin. He was dangerously close to the bunched-up fabric of my pajama shorts, and I felt my pulse thumping in my throat.

"Is this not okay?" Raiden wondered, expression faltering. He looked so pitiful and small, and I just wanted to eat him up.

He was all mine.

"Yeah, it's okay. Sorry. I'm just—it's different, y'know? This . . . *us.*" I weakly replied, caressing his lower lip with my thumb. It was so plump—so round. I wanted to bite down. *Hard.*

"It is," he admitted, his tone light and airy. "It feels right. *Natural.* I love it."

I smiled. "Me too."

In the place of a verbal reply, he resumed his actions; peppering gentle, open-mouthed kisses along the surface of my skin, inching *up up up* towards the hem of my shorts. He took a section of skin between his teeth—a mere nibble—one which evoked a startled gasp to bubble up my throat. The blanket fluttered from my fingers, encapsulating the handsome man in a cozy dome between my thighs, but he didn't seem to mind, for he'd slipped his jeweled fingers between the fabric in search of a particular warmth.

Tell him.

The tether—like a fucking iron fetter shackled around his ankle.

Knowing about it fucking tortured me. About how I'd stolen bits of his soul, taken on such a private, intimate chunk of the man. What would he think, if he knew? How would he feel knowing I'd violated him in such a way—not only once, nor twice, but indefinitely. I would feel every ache of his—all of his pain, his *pleasure*—until the moment he exhaled his very last breath.

Nausea crept up my throat at the sheer thought of him knowing—of what he'd even *say*—but I found myself struggling to concentrate on what he'd do, for his fingers had found my center, and *oh fucking hell . . .*

I wanted to scream—to tell him to stop—because how could I let him continue, knowing what I know? How could I betray him in such a way, lead him on as if everything is so ordinary—so *normal*—when nothing about me has ever been normal. I'm anything but average.

A freak.

A danger to society, some would say.

Witch.

A finger.

Two.

His tongue.

"Raiden," I panted, knotting my hands in his hair. Such dainty, pretty ringlets. Soft. *Cozy.* I twisted the curls around my fingers, studying the texture, the feel. The way the tresses drifted across my skin with ease, not a single knot or tangle in sight.

A gasp.

A sigh.

I beckoned him upwards—*closer*—and he obliged; breathless, blushy. His lips met mine, so swollen and wet, and I hated myself even more with every aching silent second that passed between us. The statement drummed against my teeth—*tap tap tap*—hurriedly knocking, *aching* to spill out.

I have a secret

let me share my secret.

Wandering fingers were accompanied by low moans, and although my teeth physically ached and my stomach threatened to spew; I helped him with his belt, the faux leather slipping between my fingers like butter, so silky and warm.

"Is this okay?" Raiden whispered, guiding my legs around his waist. We were both still mostly clothed; unrobed just enough to allow access. It seemed rushed—*careless*—but that seemed to be the norm for situations such as this. Most of the time, in the past, Maxwell McKinnon had barely shrugged his slacks down past his hips.

Before I could encourage him, Raiden paused; a lost look twinkling within his emerald orbs as his thumb tediously traced circles against my cheek.

"This isn't right," he breathed. "You deserve better from me than some rushed, sloppy fuck."

"Oh, Raiden," I murmured, pressing a soft, shy kiss to his mouth. "You're too good to me."

But you're awful to him.

"You deserve the world and more," he said, pulling himself upwards to remove his shirt. His muscles flexed and rippled beneath his pale skin, and I found myself biting back a groan. "Let me give you the world."

God, I hate myself.

With every article of clothing that fluttered to the floor, my guilt grew; expanding past my belly and erupting into my throat. His tongue felt warm and snug against my ice-cold lies, and I nearly choked on my thoughts as his naked frame met mine.

"Raiden," I whispered, eyelids squeezing shut to hold back my guilty tears. His lips met my neck—biting, *sucking*—and I couldn't hold it in any longer. "Raiden, stop."

Breathlessly, he obliged; vast, doe-like eyes meeting mine. Instantly, his entire demeanor shifted—a worrisome expression plastered across his features as he cradled my cheek.

"Honey, what is it? Did I hurt you?"

"No, of course not," I muttered, unable to look him in the eye. He took note of my aloofness, kind fingers gently rotating my head to look him in the face.

"What is it, Freya?"

"I have to tell you something," I said, my tone barely audible above the television. "I don't want to ruin this moment—this beautiful, wonderful moment—but it's killing me to hold it in. Literally killing me. I feel like I can't even breathe."

Raiden rolled off of me, settling beside my stiff shape as he wordlessly encouraged me to continue. I remained flat on my back, fatigued glare fixated on the popcorn-textured ceiling above our bed. I could feel his stare—vexed and wide—and I couldn't quite ignore the tender touch above my left hip, a trio of fingers elegantly gliding along the surface.

"You can tell me anything. You know that," he softly said, invisibly engraving a heart shape into my skin with his forefinger.

"I didn't mean to do it, Rai. I didn't mean to steal something so intimate from you." I started, a soft sob wracking through my chest. My palms met my face, shielding my reddened eyes from the man beside me as the tears freely flowed. "I'm so sorry. I'm so sorry."

"Sorry for what? What did you steal?" Raiden pressed, delicately drawing my hands from my face. With a curved thumb, he cleared my tears; smooth lips meeting my flushed cheeks as he kissed them away.

"Freya, calm down and tell me. I swear I won't be angry. What's mine is yours. Nothing you could've taken would be an issue," he whispered, placing a kiss upon my trembling lips.

"It's not a *physical* thing that I've taken, Raiden. It isn't so simple," I argued, slightly pushing him off. "I didn't know I was capable of such a thing, but it started from the first time I healed you. It isn't just you, either. It happens to everyone that I mend. But I've fixed you so many times . . ."

"Keep going, Frey," Raiden urged, a hint of impatience present in his voice. Nevertheless, his touch idled, softly circling my shoulder.

"We have this . . . this *bond.* It's from the healing. Apparently, everytime I heal, in return, I'm awarded a minuscule chunk of someone's soul. But when I repeatedly heal over time, the pieces add up, and I'm left with this—this *link*—like a rope tying our souls together." I finally revealed my secret, unable to look him in the eye. "I've established this invasive attachment with you, and I'm not sure if I can even sever it. I think it's permanent."

"I'm confused," Raiden confessed, shaking his head from side to side as he repositioned his weight. I felt the mattress delicately drop beneath my left hip, and in one swift motion, he managed to rotate me onto my side, forcing me to look him directly in the face.

"Tell me exactly what this bond does, Frey. Does this mean that you aren't actually in love with me?"

"Oh my gosh, *no,* Rai," I quickly countered, heartbroken by his expression. "It's more . . . *complex* than that. It's a physical bond, one where I can feel everything that-*uh,* you . . . do. Well, not *everything,* but the more intense things, I suppose."

Raiden's brows instantly raised, a mischievous smirk slithering along his lips as he swiveled onto his back. "Is that right?"

Puzzled, I nodded. "Yeah. I told you that it's really weird. In a way, I can also feel your emotions, but it's the tangible stuff that trumps it all. Like when you dropped something on your foot earlier at work? My foot ached like it happened to me, too. But if you just grabbed a cup and held it, I couldn't feel that."

"Interesting," Raiden articulated, pulling an arm up behind his head. The other arm, however, seemed to travel south, dipping down to the part of him I'd hardly seen, but was now on full display . . .

"So, you can feel *intense* physical sensations that I experience? Is that what you're saying?" he teased, grabbing hold of the most intimate part of himself.

"Raiden–" I warned, desperately trying not to stare down . . . *there.* "This isn't a joke."

"I never said that it was," he throatily teased, forest green eyes considerably darkening. "I'm just . . . *experimenting.*"

"Oh–*oh*–" I gasped, eyes unintentionally rotating to the back of my skull as the sensation finally arose. I felt my cheeks grow hot in shame, hips jutting upwards with every electrifying touch.

"Holy shit," Raiden breathed, slightly increasing his pace. "You weren't kidding. I don't even have to touch you to get you off."

"H-hey," I pressed, biting back a chuckle as I fisted the sheets. "That doesn't mean you can get away with never touching me again."

Suddenly, the sensation ceased, and he was on top of me; fingers interlaced, lips parted, panting breaths. Within moments, we were properly entwined, a lustful sigh spilling over my lips as he ravished my neck. A series of sweet nothings met my slick skin, and I nearly yelped at the feel of his cold rings against my hot flesh.

He told me he loved me more times than I could count, and it almost felt bizarre, for up until just recently, I would've never fathomed kissing Raiden, let alone having sex with him. It all felt so surreal—like a dream that I couldn't wake from—and momentarily, I worried that maybe I'd perished from the De Mörka already, and this was my peaceful purgatory.

"This is where we're meant to be," Raiden panted, kissing me softly. "I love you, Freya."

"I love you, too." I gleamed, unable to stifle my smile as I roped my arms around his neck, pulling him in close. He milked both of our climaxes, keenly watching my every expression with a cheeky grin on his face. He was loving this—more than I ever expected him to—and he reveled in both the sight and sound of my splendid peak, one so strong that my sight temporarily evaded me.

"So beautiful," Raiden murmured, showering my face in kisses. He refused to break the bond even after we'd both finished, an affectionate gleam in his eye as he periodically thrust. "How are you mine?"

"I have been since the day we met," I replied, legs encircling his waist, drawing him in deeper. "It just took us forever to figure it out."

Forever too late . . .

Whilst I remained wrapped up in the bliss of Raiden and me, the nettlesome thoughts of tomorrow's event bombarded my brain. The mere thought of the De Mörka was enough to make my arms burn, and regardless of how hard I tried to shove them away, they repeatedly arose; reminding me of my inevitable demise.

The most I could do in this moment was enjoy this—*him.* Raiden Crow. Enjoy his presence, his mouth, his touch, his love. Savor every second of it until it was too late. For it already was

too late.

nineteen

"Have you seen my favorite purple shirt?" a topless Raiden called, shuffling through his disorderly drawers. Heaps of clothing laid at his feet, courtesy of his panicked evasion.

I choked back a giggle as I rounded the doorway, clad in nothing but a skimpy pair of panties and Raiden's beloved button-up, the very same one that he'd been rummaging around for.

"Is this the one?" I tauntingly called, knowing quite well that it was. My elbow cradled the doorframe, balancing my weight as I bit back giggles. I knew damn well that I wasn't as sexy right now as I intended to be, but the grin that erupted upon Raiden's face suggested otherwise.

"You little *thief,*" he purred, crossing the room in three abnormally large steps. His arms coiled around my waist and I animatedly screeched; a loud laugh tumbling off of my tongue as he lifted me up into his arms.

My back met the wall, lengthy legs naturally looping around his jean-clad hips as I clung to him for dear life. His mouth met mine—warm and wet—and I found it hard to breathe, hard to think; for Raiden was mine—*mine mine mine*—and I wanted to soak up every single second and make it last for an eternity.

His fingers tore at the buttons, prying them open one by one to reveal my bare chest. The skin on my fingers tempestuously buzzed, a lasting heat frolicking along my forearms as Raiden's lips peppered kisses down my neck, teeth occasionally nipping at the flushed skin. I knotted my hands in his hair, hoping for a bit of relief from the burning, but nevertheless, it persisted; rudely reminding me of the forthcoming terrors of the day.

Your entire family could perish before nightfall.

"Are you feeling better today?" Raiden rasped, continuing his gentle assault on my flesh. He finally tore the shirt completely open, revealing my naked torso. He ogled me like I was some kind of goddess, and I felt my cheeks grow hot from his stare alone.

He busied himself with my breasts, a glorified groan crawling up my throat as I struggled to form a sentence. I didn't want to tell him about the burning, but I had a feeling that he already knew. After all, mere moments after we'd woken, I somehow managed to fry the television, a puff of smoke oozing from the cords.

"I need to take a shower, we can't be late," I rasped, the words emerging in the form of a pant. Raiden was already unbuckling his belt, greedy lips leaving behind a constellation of ecchymoses across my collarbones.

Those will be a bitch to cover.

"Don't worry, we'll be quick," he assured me, pulling my lips to his as he fumbled with his zipper.

Our amatory event was impolitely interrupted by the shrill ring of my cell, a sound which prompted Raiden to bitterly grunt. He, however, refused to cease his movements, and instead ignored the noise as if it were nothing but a slight inconvenience.

"Rai," I cooed, pressing a kiss to his earlobe. "I need to get it."

"It can *wait,*" he pressed, but I wasn't having it. With a wiggle of my hips, I escaped his lascivious grasp; wobbling out of the room on weak, trembling legs. I felt Raiden rush up behind me, delivering a smack to my backside that made me yelp.

"Quit!" I chastised him, jogging towards the living room sofa, where my phone needily rang, displaying my baby brother's name.

"Hello?" I answered, balancing the phone between my ear and shoulder, nubby fingers struggling to button back up Raiden's shirt. He'd disappeared into the kitchen, a triad of dogs following suit.

"I need you to look at the photo of this girl and tell me if she looks familiar to you," Brennan said, not even bothering to greet me.

"Well hello to you too, Bren," I countered, collapsing onto the couch. "What's with the urgency? Who is she?"

"Her name is Gunora Falk, and Freya . . . I think she's the De Mörka. She's in all of these articles and she looks exactly how you've described. Just put me on speaker phone and look at the link I sent you and confirm or deny, please. My anxiety is through the goddamn roof today as it is, and I just need to know how to plan for tonight," he replied, his tone slightly clipped and rushed. I could hear the urgency in his voice, and I did exactly as I was told—I put him on speaker phone, and opened the link he'd sent over.

The link took far too long to open, and I could already feel bulbous beads of sweat blooming along my palms with anticipation. My knee restlessly bounced, and as the article finally launched, I was gobsmacked.

There she was.

Glossy, black hair and pasty, white skin. Gaze as dark as a clouded night. It was a poor photo of her—slightly blurred and crooked—and she had a mopey, miserable look to her, as if she'd just learned of the death of her beloved pet.

The headline made my jaw drop.

GUNORA FALK, DAUGHTER OF COUNCILLOR OSTEN FALK, DEAD BY STABBING, AGED 20

"Is it her?" Brennan pressed, anxious by my silence.

"Yeah. Holy shit," I breathed, nearly dropping my phone. "The De Mörka is dead. She was *murdered.*"

"She was Councillor Osten Falk's daughter, too. I talked to Momma and she said they're Nordic. The De Mörka are *Swedish.* It all adds up, Frey. I always got bad vibes from that Falk guy. The community has been trying to get him out of office for years. Go figure—his daughter was the last living De Mörka to top it all off," Brennan explained. He shifted the phone, generating a noisy shuffle that made my ears throb.

"Who killed her? Does it say?" I asked, scrolling through the article. By now, Raiden had made an appearance; crashing onto the couch beside me. He peeked over my shoulder, a puzzled stare meeting my widened eyes.

"Who is it?" he wondered, stuffing a veggie straw into his mouth.

"Brennan. The De Mörka is dead."

"What?" Raiden gawked, jaw dropping to mirror my own initial reaction. "How do you know?"

"Hi Raiden!" Brennan called as I slipped my cell into Raiden's grasp. It was easier for me to show him rather than to tell, and he was quite a quick reader, anyways.

"She was stabbed in an alleyway less than an hour after we left work," Raiden revealed, handing me back my phone. "They don't know who did it, but she was confirmed dead at the hospital. She's gone."

"We're safe, Freya," Brennan said, unable to mask his glee. "We're safe. And free. We don't have to worry."

"Yeah," I whispered, nuzzling into Raiden's chest. "Where's the laptop? I just want to look into it a little more."

"I thought you had to shower," Raiden teased, showering the top of my oily hair with an abundance of kisses. "We don't want to be late to Brennan's party. They wanted us to come early."

"We won't be late. I just need to look into this more. I promise; I won't waste too much time," I countered, pulling out of his loving embrace. "Where is it?"

With a sigh, he revealed the computer's location. "The kitchen counter."

I nearly tripped over a drowsy Mimosa on the way to the kitchen, a vexed growl easing off of her tongue as I ushered the animal a series of apologies. Just as Raiden promised, the laptop was on the kitchen counter, surrounded by a bounty of bills. Bitterly, I brushed them aside, yanking open the laptop to reveal my favorite photo of Kelso, Bear, Mimosa, Raiden, and I on the screen.

We looked like such a happy little family.

Brushing the thought aside, I browsed the internet, misspelling Gunora's name several times before the search engine suggested the correct spelling. Thus, I was granted access to every bit of information that I could ever want—her date of birth, hometown (Östersund, Sweden), siblings' names, information about her father, our *councillor*, and the nitty, gritty details of her death.

She wasn't just stabbed. Her throat was *slit.*

If you simply want to kill them, slit their throat.

A horrified gasp tickled my throat, a clammy palm suctioned to my parted lips as I read the statement several times over. *Slit.*

"Frey?" A tiny voice tickled my ear, and I nearly screamed; instinctively slamming the laptop closed before twisting on my heel to view a bewildered Raiden, still shirtless and sleepy.

His brows raised at my reaction, arms tossed middair in surrender as he audibly questioned my rigid stance.

"S-Sorry," I stammered, a tremble cascading up my spine as Grammy's statement bombarded my mind over and over and *over* . . .

If you simply want to kill them, slit their throat.

"Rai," his name emerged as a pant, a profusion of scenarios flooding my mind as the De Mörka's lifeless eyes plagued my mind. Beads of blood trickling up towards her ears, a shocked, open-mouthed expression permanently plastered to her pasty face . . .

"Freya, what's going on? There's no reason to be so on edge, the threat is gone. *She* is gone."

She is gone.

"Raiden . . . she died an hour after we saw her. An hour after I lost consciousness in the car after my episode," I stammered, unable to stifle the violent shake that consumed my core. He went to grab my arms, but I pulled away; unwanted visuals of him . . . doing . . . *doing . . .*

"Freya, you don't think–"

"Where were you, Raiden?" The statement was sour as I spat it out, dewy hands tugging at my flushed cheeks as I gradually backed away from him. Suddenly, I was fearful of him.

"I was with *you,* Freya. You don't actually think that I went to hunt that girl down while you were unconscious in the passenger seat, do you? Left you in the car while I cornered her in an alleyway and slit her throat?"

He looked offended—*hurt*—that I would even accuse him of such a thing. Truthfully, it was difficult to envision Raiden hurting anyone or anything, but when it came to a life and death scenario, to what lengths would he go to ensure the safety of my family and me?

"You were there, Rai. When Grammy said how to kill a De Mörka. If you don't have a human sacrifice to lock away their curse and free them of it, you have to slit their throat–"

"You're accusing me of *murdering* someone, Freya. Do you even hear yourself? When have I ever hurt a living thing? I don't even kill bugs!" Raiden dryly defended, tears pricking the corner of his eyes. I felt incredibly guilty accusing him of such a thing, but if he didn't do it, and obviously Brennan didn't do it, who did?

"You just said you'd protect me and she would never hurt me. I'm sorry, I'm not thinking straight. I'm not accusing you of anything. I would never call you a murderer or a monster, especially not for protecting the person and family that you love and adore," I spilled, allowing my tears to freely flow.

It didn't feel real for the threat to suddenly be gone. I didn't want to believe it until I saw her dead and drained with my own eyes.

"I know you're under a lot of stress, Freya, but I'd tell you if it was me. It wasn't. I was here, with you, the entire time. Cross my heart, hope to die," Raiden whispered, a single, pitiful tear slipping down his cheek. "Now please, let me hold you."

I eased into Raiden's open embrace, burying my nose in the curve of his collarbone. His arms encircled my shoulders, a gentle squeeze drawing me as close to him as we could physically be.

"I love you," he whispered, and for a split second, it seemed as if all was well.

Perhaps, it was.

"Figlia!" Momma called, arms outstretched in preparation for a hug. She looked effortlessly stunning—an abundance of jewels adorning her fingers and wrists, all of which flawlessly matched her red, sequined dress.

She skipped along the concrete, leaving the front door of Weatherby's estate wide open as she rushed towards Raiden and I in the driveway. We were the first to arrive, and naturally, we snagged a spot closest to the door.

"Hey, Momma," I cooed, a faux smile slapped across my mouth as I pulled her close. She felt so tiny and frail in my arms, courtesy of her ghastly health battles, but nevertheless, I held her tight; nearly squeezing the air out of her lungs as I did so.

Raiden's fingertips danced along my lower back, and I almost anxiously shoved him away—that was, until my Grammy spoke up.

Shit.

"Dio mio!" my grandmother exclaimed, startling my miniscule mother, who openly flinched in my arms. She strutted a head full of jet-black curls today, loopy and large, dancing along the arch of her shoulders.

As if on cue, Raiden yanked his arm away; a scarlet blush creeping up his neck as he met my fixed glare.

"Lo sapevo! I damn well *knew it!"* Grammy added, little legs swiftly shuffling towards the both of us, a wrinkled finger wagging back and forth as if to scold us. "How long?"

"What?" I replied, feigning confusion. Momma's dark, drawn-on brows were elevated, her curiosity piqued as she rotated her stare between Raiden and I.

Suddenly, it dawned upon her—dark eyes widening to the size of saucers as her palm met her gaping mouth. To make matters worse, both my father and Brennan had joined us; pulling the big, broad doors closed behind them as we all gathered before the luxurious estate.

"You're looking rather peachy, sis," Brennan teased, adjusting his mahogany tie. He looked incredibly dapper in his birthday outfit, a handsome, custom-tailored suit adorning his limbs. "Long night?"

"I don't care if it's your birthday, I swear I'll still beat your ass," I hissed, taking a single threatening step forward, fists clenched. Brennan tossed his hands up in surrender, a lively laugh easing off of his tongue as he took several steps back. He knew damn well that I'd deliver the punch, regardless of it being his *special day.*

"What's the matter?" my father queried, curling his arm around my mother's shoulders. "Gaia?"

My giddy grandmother approached the two of us, a silly smirk painted along her cherry red lips as she pulled both Raiden and I into a tight squeeze. She muttered a staccato of congratulatory statements before turning her focus to me. I nearly keeled over when her palm met my belly, applying a slight amount of pressure.

"Absolutely fucking not," I hissed, stern stare meeting my Grammy's giggly frame. Hesitantly, she pulled her hand away, a gleeful grin permanently engraved upon her face as she swung her arms around Raiden's neck.

"Would anyone care to enlighten me on the situation?" my father pressed, clearly agitated by the lack of information. He kept eyeing my stomach, and I swore that the vein in his forehead would burst at any moment. "Freya, is there something . . . *in there?"*

"Oh my God, *no!*" I shrieked, slightly repulsed by the thought. "Why must you all be so damn *weird* about it all? Jesus."

"Her and Raiden are together," Brennan revealed. "Finally."

"Oh," my dad said, a small sigh escaping his thin lips. The bulging vein receded, and he pulled Momma to his chest. "I thought Freya got pregnant from that Maxwell dude or something."

"Please never say *pregnant* and *Maxwell* in the same sentence ever again," I snipped, choking back a gag.

"Oh, *sweetie!*" Momma exclaimed, tears staining the apples of her cheeks. "I'm so happy for you. You two are meant for one another, I've known that forever. I was just waiting for you both to realize it."

"We all knew that it was going to happen," Brennan said, delivering a pat to Raiden's back. Grammy still had him in a near chokehold, a profusion of lipstick kisses staining his cheek as she welcomed him to the family. "It was just a matter of when. And Jesus, it took you two *forever* to figure it out."

"I can't believe she's dead," I said, shifting the topic to that of the recently deceased De Mörka. For a split second, I swore that I felt a phantom of heat coil around my forearms. I unconsciously danced my fingers along the surface, wondering if the burning would ever return. If *they* would ever return.

"It's almost ironic how she died. A slit throat," Brennan chirped, shifting his weight from side to side. "The only way to kill one of them. Besides freeing their curse with a sacrifice, or whatever the hell it is."

"It's *too* ironic, Bren. Are you sure . . ." I glanced over each shoulder, ensuring that no one besides my immediate family was around to overhear my inquiry. "Are you sure you didn't do it?"

"How could I have killed the bitch if I had to call and ask you if it was even her?" Brennan countered. "I'm a bit disappointed, really, that it wasn't me. I wanted to have the honors of making the De Mörka extinct."

"Enough of all this," Momma suddenly snipped, squeezing my palm. "Let's go inside. Everyone is anxious and on edge, and such a thing shouldn't be discussed outdoors. Hell, we're talking about the murder of Counsillor Falk's *daughter.*"

Brennan merely shrugged, patting our father on the shoulder before beckoning him inside. After a moment of hesitation, the rest of us followed—an oddly silent Grammy walking beside Raiden.

"Brennan has someone special he'd like to introduce you both to," Momma announced, unable to mask her toothy grin.

I raised a brow, following closely on my mother's heel as we approached the elegant entryway of Weatherby's estate.

God, I loathed the rich.

"What? Who is it?"

Raiden's fingertips grazed mine, desperately pleading to be held. My heart fluttered, and I took his hand; glancing over my shoulder to see his smile. It all happened so quickly—he and I—but just as my family had stated: *it was only a matter of time.*

"You don't think your brother's been single all this time, do you?" Grammy throatily teased, hovering by Raiden's side. *He really was her favorite.*

"Well if he hasn't, he's sure kept it a secret," I snipped, stepping over the threshold and entering Weatherby's home. Just as I'd expected, the foyer was stately, an ostentatious chandelier hovering over our heads and illuminating the area. The light fixture was adorned with authentic jewels, an array of colors that generated a kaleidoscopic glow along the white, marble staircase, positioned dead-center. It was so gorgeous that I nearly gagged.

"He's always been hush-hush about his love life, even after coming out," Momma added, adjusting the thin straps of her flashy gown.

"He could at least tell his sister. Hell, he was the first to find out about Raiden and I." The words were bitter on my tongue, and I felt Raiden squeeze my hand, his polite way of asking me to *cut it out.*

"The event will be held in the ballroom just off to the left. There's an absolutely grandiose butler's pantry off the room, almost as large as our kitchen. It looks more like a kitchen than anything, but once you see the kitchen, you'll realize just how small it actually is in comparison." My mother carried on about our distant family friend and his tiny slice of heaven, gloating over the sleek shine of the wood floors beneath our feet. It all just looked like a bunch of wasted fortune to me—plain, white walls, a sprinkle of overpriced artwork here and there. I felt slightly suffocated by the way Weatherby embraced his opulence, and I wondered if he'd ever struggled, or if he'd been born into wealth.

Lost in thought, I nearly collided with a stranger, who seemed to appear out of thin air. Raiden gently scolded me, and as a series of apologies graced my tongue, I was met with a pair of deep, ebony eyes and impeccably smooth, porcelain skin.

He extended an arm, the sleeve of his baby blue dress shirt cockily rolled, and my gaze immediately gravitated towards a profusion of black and gray ink, scattered and sectioned along the skin.

"Elden Moure," he said, offering to shake my hand. I warily took it, giving it a weak shake as I awkwardly studied the art on his arms.

"Freya Gallo. You're a bit early to the party, aren't you?" I said, stepping aside as Raiden shook Elden's hand.

"Shouldn't the birthday boy's boyfriend show up before the other ordinary guests?" Elden cheekily countered, clicking his tongue. His gaze met Raiden. "This must be Raiden, right? Bren's told me lots about you two."

"Wait, *wait,*" I pressed, tossing my hands airborne. *There's no way.* "You're Brennan's boyfriend? *You?"*

"God, Frey," Brennan scoffed, slinging his arm around Elden's shoulders, his fingers mindlessly toying with Elden's ashen brown hair. "You act as if I'm this hideous, undesirable buffoon."

"You know I didn't mean it like that," I bit back, scrambling for proper reasoning to defend my inappropriate comment. "Elden's just . . . he has a lot of tattoos."

"I'm a tattoo artist," Elden revealed, jet-black painted nails gravitating towards the buttons of his silky shirt. "I've done a few on my legs myself—I'll have to show you them another time—but I'm really proud and passionate of my art. I'm pretty picky about who inks me."

Before I could utter a single sound, Elden's shirt was open, and my brother had taken the liberty of navigating the abundance of black and gray hued ink littered along his lover's pale skin. I felt as if I were intruding upon an intimate moment of theirs, and I felt my skin slightly crawl.

"This one's my favorite," Brennan announced, etching the outline of the artwork with his index finger. It was an entire scene—a simple story told upon his flesh. A shoddy shipwreck, an angry kraken, weeping waves. It was extraordinary, unlike anything I'd ever seen before. I've never been fond of tattoos—never even desired one—but Elden's artwork made me begin to reconsider.

"Wow," Raiden gawked, palm flattening against the curve of my lower back. "That's really excellent work, Elden. How long have you been tattooing?"

"Five years. I started on my eighteenth birthday," Elden revealed, playfully swatting my brother's greedy fingers away from his inked belly. I averted my gaze as he rebuttoned his shirt, making small talk with my boyfriend as I drifted off into my own thoughts.

My boyfriend.

Raiden was my boyfriend, now. How utterly . . . *odd.*

"You guys want some wine?" Brennan asked, placing a kiss upon Elden's temple. Admittedly, they were a charming pair, and it was evident that they were wild for one another. From the tiny twinkle in my brother's eye to the goosebumps that arose upon Elden's stomach when Brennan's touch met the surface—they were truly, doubtlessly, madly in love.

Raiden denied Brennan's offer, and before I could question his peculiar reply, he'd abruptly excused himself in search of a toilet. Something was off about him. He seemed fidgety; *anxious.* I made a mental note to ask him why when he returned.

"With a wave of my palm and a wiggle of my nose, I present to you a stunning glass of *Pinot Noir,*" Brennan sang, dramatically waving his arm as if to magically conjure up our order. With a bent elbow and tenderly spread fingers, he summoned our drinks.

Within days, his energies had strengthened tenfold. Now, he had the ability to blindly choose a bottle of wine from out of sight, pop the cork, gently pour the liquid into even portions within each glass without spilling a single drop, and transport the drinks across several rooms all while barely lifting a single finger. It was extraordinary to observe—and comical, too—a small giggle slipping off of my tongue as a trio of wine glasses softly sailed through the air, the ruby liquid slightly sloshing within its windowed walls.

I outstretched a hand, gleefully welcoming the alcohol as it nuzzled into my warm palm. Graciously, I drew the glass to my lips, taking a generous swig as Brennan stole a kiss from a grinning Elden.

Elden.

I nearly spat out my drink in realization, eyes bugging out of my skull as I thrust an accusatory finger in my younger brother's direction.

"He knows!" I exclaimed, the words emerging as a statement rather than an inquiry. Elden bit back a chuckle as he, too, took a large sip from Brennan's magical wine.

"Of course he knows, just like your boyfriend does," Brennan pressed, delivering a wink in my direction. "If you'll excuse us, El and I have some business to tend to before the guests arrive. You should go check on Raiden, he's been gone awhile."

"Shit," I murmured, dismissively discarding my unwanted wine glass on a nearby decorative table, a cheesy guest book stamped with Brennan's photo in the center. A dozen inky, black pens littered the surface, as well as a profusion of faux white and purple flowers.

My fingertips danced along the artificial garden, index finger hovering over one with a slightly bent petal. "Where's the bathroom at?"

"Through the banquet hall right behind us. There's two of them, right by the butler's pantry," Elden replied, lacing his fingers within Brennan's. "I have Tums if Raiden needs them."

"Thanks." The word emerged clipped and coarse, and I ignored Brennan's bitter glare as I began my search for an obviously ill Raiden.

The banquet hall was buried behind a pair of unbelievably fulsome double doors, a deep mahogany wood littered with an abundance of various carvings, mostly floral. I nearly gagged at the sight—how fucking *haughty*—as I shoved them open, revealing a space so ritzy that it made my head spin. Ceilings extending beyond reach, a majority of the surface substituted by tempered panes of glass. *A gateway to the stars.*

Ordinary windows were obsolete within these walls, and instead, they were adorned with stunning stained glass, sublime pieces of art engraved within, each individual pane telling a tale. An alluring angel claimed the closest to me, whereas a handsome devil occupied another further down. Their robust story chilled me to the core, and once more I wondered how the *hell* my family knew the man who owned this opulent estate.

True to Momma's celebratory fashion, the sturdy, wooden floors were lined with decorative furniture—snowy white oval tables complimented by dreamy, golden chairs. Lengthy serving tables dressed in white gowns, filled to the brim with edible eatery and surrounded by the very same phony flowers from the tiny table holding Brennan's guest book. It appeared as if the budget went dry, and real flowers had been out of the question. Nevertheless, my mother completely blew it out of the water, and although it was uncommon for me to feel jealous over materialistic things, I suddenly felt my chest grow hot.

My thirtieth celebration was nothing of the sort.

Per Elden's instructions, I weaved through the grandiose hall, arriving upon a hallway which led to what was evidently a butler's pantry, but well surpassed my own kitchen in size. On either side of the short passageway was a door, and Raiden was behind one of them.

Like a contestant on *Let's Make a Deal,* I chose a door, knuckles lightly rapping against the surface as I softly called out Raiden's name. When I went without an answer, I crossed the hall and tried the second, only to be met with a staggering silence. Perplexed, I turned the handle, revealing an empty washroom twice the size of our bedroom. With raised brows, I mimicked my actions, trying the first door once more. Once again, I was greeted by an empty area.

I immediately felt panicked as I abandoned the area. The banquet hall was empty besides myself, and I felt as if the figures in the windows were mocking me with every hurried step. A rippled smirk from the handsome devil, broad wings fluttering in the wind. A side-eye from the angel, hands folded over her heart. Curious, poorly-dressed peasants glancing over their shoulders—whispering, *watching.*

My pulse quickened with every aching step, trembling fingers encircling the ice-cold handles of the hall doors as I ripped them open, revealing several puzzled family members on the opposite side.

"Freya?" Momma questioned, lively expression shifting to that of grave concern. "What is it? What's wrong?"

"I can't find Raiden." The statement emerged rushed and choppy, heart thickly thumping in my throat as my tiny Grammy stepped forward, arms outstretched to offer me a hug.

"There's no reason for you to be on edge anymore, darling. Your biggest threat is dead."

Your biggest threat is dead.

But *how?*

"He went out front. He's fine." My grandmother finished, pressing a sealed-lip kiss to my cheek before stepping away. She beckoned Momma into the banquet hall, abandoning my trembling self in the foyer as if there wasn't a worry in the world.

Desperate to locate Raiden, I fled the estate; nearly tripping over my chic, beaded sandals in the process. For the occasion, I seemed to be slightly underdressed in comparison to my relatives. Sporting a dark-washed pair of jeans torn at the knees and a flowy, black blouse, I was comfortable, yet merely in common clothes. Even Raiden wore a dashing dress shirt along with a pair of clean-cut, black jeans and his favorite Doc Martens.

Milky white pebbles shifted beneath my feet, their likeness to clean, pearly teeth uncomfortable and uncanny. Just like last time, I found myself stealing a second glance, knees slightly bending to view the decorative rocks that lined the perimeter of the driveway.

Just plain, ordinary rocks.

With a sigh, I continued onward; nearly trampling a flower bed full of half-dead posies. Unsurprisingly, Raiden was exactly where I'd imagined him to be—hovering right at the edge of Weatherby's unorthodox front yard natatorium.

His back was to me, shoulders stiff and square, a singular strand of smoke orbiting his shaggy scalp. His gaze was cast downward, ogling the clean, glimmering water, gaily sparkling beneath the sunlight.

My palm met his exposed elbow, the sleeves of his shirt carelessly furled beyond the pointy joints. He took a long drag off of his cigarette before acknowledging me with a simple kiss.

"I thought you were going to quit those," I dryly teased, resting my chin atop his shoulder.

"I haven't quite found another coping mechanism to replace them yet," he sheepishly admitted, twirling the stick between his ring-clad fingers. He flexed the center digit, admiring the bulky jewelry that claimed his finger. It was his favorite piece—he never left the house without it. A silver band, intensified by the elaborate depiction of a daunting woman, one which sported a head full of obedient serpents.

I reached out to claim his hand, daintily drawing the cigarette out of his clasp as I eased it into my own mouth. Gently, I clamped the object between my teeth, cheeks hollowing out as I free handedly mimicked Raiden's long drag. All the while, I took hold of his hand, the curve of my thumb delicately caressing the curve of Medusa's small jaw.

"I almost died here," Raiden suddenly said, slipping his fingers between mine.

I tossed the undesired cigarette aside, my hold tightening on Raiden's hand as he reminisced on his near-death experience only days prior. Momma wasted no time in cleaning up the crime scene, and she even went to the extent of hiring a professional pool cleaner. Today, the water and tile were both so miraculously clean that I found myself wondering if the event had even occurred at all.

"This place makes me anxious," he added, squeezing my palm. "I get heavy vibes here. I don't know if it was the fast food we ate earlier or my anxiety, but I threw up in the bathroom, and my stomach is in constant knots."

"Oh, honey," I cooed, cradling his face with my palm. He felt clammy and cold beneath my amiable touch, and I wanted nothing more than to wrap him up in my arms like a cocoon. Admittedly, he did look somewhat off. His usually bright, lively eyes were dull and dark, red-rimmed as if he'd been crying. I could tell that he wasn't quite himself, and I swore that I could feel his heart racing beneath the flesh of his face.

"You know I love you, right?" he muttered as his droopy gaze settled upon my mouth.

"Yes, of course. Come here."

He instantly obeyed, fingers detaching from my own as he cupped my cheeks, urgently pulling me close. Our lips combined in a rushed embrace—sloppy and wet—a pleased groan tickling my tongue as he deepened the kiss. It felt final, like a passionate, needy goodbye kiss, and I couldn't quite ward off the panicked feeling arising within my chest at the thought.

"Rai, baby," I murmured against his mouth. He politely ignored my plea, curled thumbs etching invisible shapes into my skin.

Breathlessly, I pulled away; worried stare colliding with wide, loving eyes. He looked so small and sad, as if he'd just received the worst news.

"Can we go inside? I want to talk to Momma and Grammy a little before the guests arrive," Raiden wondered. I was completely puzzled by how swiftly he shifted the subject, and before I could reply, he was already leading me back to the front door.

We found Grammy, Momma, and my father in the banquet hall, where they were finishing up some last minute preparations for the party. Guests were due to arrive in less than thirty minutes, and they were scrambling to set out the remainder of the food. Brennan requested a nacho bar, and my parents even went to the extent of renting a towering fondue fountain, one which consistently recirculated warm, white, liquid cheese.

Raiden placed a kiss upon my forehead before abandoning me, and as soon as our hands disconnected, I felt uneasy. *Cold.* With a slight shiver, I stepped towards my mother, whereas Raiden took comfort in the arms of my elderly grandmother on the opposite end of the room.

"Momma?" I murmured, snaking my arm through the curve of her elbow. She'd just stuffed a cheesy tortilla chip into her mouth, wild, playful eyes settling upon my rigid frame as she chewed.

"What is it, baby?"

"Raiden's being weird," I whispered, casually glancing over my shoulder to view my boyfriend across the room. He seemed so tiny on the other end, and I wondered just how large this house really was if this one room alone could comfortably fit over seventy people.

Momma nonchalantly glanced over her shoulder as well to view Raiden, who was busy being babied by my grandmother. She'd poured him some kind of drink, and was urging him to take a seat in one of the gold-plated chairs. It was difficult to decipher from the distance, but I could've sworn a tear had dripped down his cheek.

"What's going on?" she asked, offering me a chip. I politely declined, for it felt as if a crowd of cords had tangled themselves into a painful, billowing knot within my stomach.

"He said he threw up in the bathroom and he feels really anxious. But Momma, I just . . . I have this feeling that I can't quite kick, and everything just adds up and–"

"He didn't kill that girl."

Puzzled, I paused; an empty gaze meeting Momma's somber stare as she chewed on another chip. She seemed so dismissive—so *sure*—and suddenly, I felt as if everyone were in on one big secret, and I was some measly, nosy outsider.

"But how do you know for sure? I was unconscious, he *saw her* right there at the coffee shop, and she ends up dead not far from there while I was in some comatose state–"

"It wasn't *him,* Freya," Momma spat, her lips formed into a thin, straight line. Her expression hardened as she glanced in Raiden and Grammy's direction, frigid fingers claiming my wrist as she pulled me achingly close.

Her lips tickled the shell of my ear, and when her dainty, soft voice revealed the truth, I could barely believe it.

She released my arm and returned to the queso fountain as if nothing had even happened, whereas I stood utterly perplexed beside her. I felt frozen; *numb.*

Grammy did it.

"M-Momma," I choked, chest growing hot in realization.

My grandmother killed someone.

"Listen, if we're going to discuss this, you need to come to the bathroom with me. We cannot be overheard. Do you understand?" Momma said, nodding towards the butler's pantry at the rear of the banquet hall.

Wordlessly, I followed her trail, a bitter blob of bile inching up my throat as I envisioned my frail, elderly grandmother wielding the blade that severed a young woman's throat.

Not just any young woman, but the girl who was born and bred to murder you and your loved ones.

Momma locked the door behind me, urging me to take a seat upon a dreamy, floral, velvet chair. I wondered what on earth such a luxurious item of furniture was doing in a bathroom—so close to a *toilet*—and suddenly my head was spinning and I felt hot and dizzy and I wondered if perhaps I might *need* said toilet . . .

"*Scopata.* You're pale as a ghost," my mother acknowledged, routinely flattening her knuckles against my forehead as if to check for a fever.

"Tell me how," I croaked, lightly brushing her touch away. I felt claustrophobic at the thought of being held. All I wanted was to break out of this bathroom—to run until my legs gave out. To collapse in the grass and bask in the sunlight and just . . . let go. *Exist.* Embrace the numbness.

"Let me get this straight, Frey. You thought that Raiden, your best friend of over twenty years and most recently your boyfriend, *murdered* our biggest danger and threat, and you were considerably calm—hell, *literally* calm—but the thought of your grandmother actually doing it is enough to thrust you into some type of frenzy? Am I comprehending this all correctly?"

"There's just no way my Grammy could kill someone," I dryly defended. *But Raiden could . . ?*

"Oh, but Raiden could?" Momma countered, mimicking my thoughts. "You obviously don't know your grandmother well enough if you think she's all innocent. She'd do anything to protect her family."

"Raiden too." The counter emerged as a throaty whine, and I could barely look my cross-armed mother in the eye. Frankly, I was still in disbelief.

"I'll answer every question that you have about this entire incident *after* your brother's birthday party. We have a long night ahead of us, and the story is just far too long. Plus, I'm sure Grammy would want to tell it herself. It was unfair for me to say anything, even if I was involved."

"You were involved?" I exclaimed, eyes nearly bugging out of my skull.

I came from a family of killers.

My mother threw her arms up in surrender, an exasperated slur of Italian obscenities slipping off of her tongue. "Listen, Freya. I know this is a lot for you to take in right now, but we will discuss all of this with you and Brennan in the days to come. *Lo prometto.* Just, *please* try and relax tonight. It is a big day for your baby brother. My sweet boy is becoming an Araedian omnipotent. We've done what needed to be done. We eradicated the threat. She's *gone,* baby. You can finally breathe. We all can."

You can finally breathe. We all can.

With a sigh, my mother placed a kiss atop my head. She told me that she loved me, and then she was gone; abandoning me to my scrambled thoughts. Admittedly, she was right. Tonight was a big night for Brennan, and even if I felt lost, helpless, and completely confused, I had to put on a happy face and be there for him.

I had to.

twenty

I glared down into the depths of my glass, empty, ebbing eyes silently studying the ruby red liquid within. Red wine.

Red like the devil.

Red like blood.

I felt on edge. *Uneasy.* As if a scare actor at a haunted house was bound to leap out from around the corner, stunning me silly and causing me to shake in my boots. Only, there were no scare actors here, or any type of actors at all that I knew of.

No—I was surrounded by a surplus of mostly strangers. Brennan's friends. The fact that he even *had* this many friends was astounding all in itself, and as I awkwardly shuffled between the masses of finely dressed folk—head hung low as I muttered a series of apologies—I wondered if Brennan even knew all of these people at all. It wouldn't surprise me if most of them were acquaintances. *Friend of a friend.*

People who piggy-backed off of one of Brennan's *real* friends in order to get a ticket to one of the most high-class parties in town.

It wasn't a secret that our parents harbored a bit of untouched wealth, Grammy especially, and to top things off, hosting a birthday party in some upscale mansion owned by some faceless family friend . . .

Yeah. This was the party to be at.

I scowled at the sight of my drink, stomach turbulently twisting at the sheer thought of the evidently deceased De Mörka: eyes dark as coal, pale, sunken cheeks. Hollowed out. *Empty.* Like she was sucking on a lollipop, inner cheeks suctioned to her presumably razor-sharp teeth. I had never *actually* seen her teeth, so I couldn't confirm if they had mimicked the shape and severity of a great white shark's. Perhaps, she had multiple rows of them, huddled together in her pretty little mouth—rutted in deep. *Stacked.* Ready to sever the flesh straight from my bones.

She's dead, Freya.

Stop worrying so much, Freya.

I knew maybe a handful of people—some folks from high school, mostly. Brennan was a social butterfly in school, whereas I was practically invisible and achingly average. I had a small group of friends, enough to count on one hand. Three of the girls were happily married with several children, and another had been dead six years now. Although we were all relatively close in school, and even a few years after graduation, I lost contact with all of them, resorting to nothing but meaningless interactions on social media. A congratulations on their pregnancies, a nice message to commemorate their weddings, none of which I'd received an invitation to. They all drifted. All besides Raiden, of course.

He was the only one who ever stayed.

I ran into a chipper Vole at the buffet table, dressed to the nines in a dapper, green suit. I'd shoved my way through some strangers just so I could thank them for nursing me back to health just days prior. I considerably liked Vole, and truthfully, I'd assumed that Brennan had a bit of a thing with them. However, I was beyond mistaken, for even in a room full of people, I caught wind of my brother with his tongue down Elden's throat several times.

Raiden stayed close for the first few hours. I could tell that he was feeling relatively unwell, and at one point, I even offered to drive him home. As expected, he refused, claiming that he was completely fine. Perhaps he was, for I failed to feel even a twinge of extreme emotion from him. I kept reminding myself that if something were gravely wrong with him, I would be able to feel it from a mile away.

I nudged Raiden in the rib, calling out a question over the obscene volume of Brennan's favorite music. Lately, he was really into nineties alternative, and he kept blasting Soundgarden over the boxy rental speakers. The guests didn't seem to mind, and most of them busied themselves with food, alcohol, and suggestive dancing.

"Do you want me to make you up a plate of nachos?"

A slightly pale Raiden simply shook his head, fingers tightly clasped around a plastic cup full of room temperature water. He was nursing the tasteless drink as if it were a bitter alcohol that he barely liked.

"You need to try and eat something," I urged, desperately attempting to study his unreadable expression. The sun had nestled itself beneath the horizon, leaving behind a shy, blue glow that barely bled through the stylish stained glass windows. The lighting inside the ballroom was muted and low, making it difficult to decipher the guests' facial features. The classy party had shifted to that of an upscale club scene, and admittedly, I didn't entirely despise it.

"I'm not hungry," Raiden clipped, anxiously eyeing the crowd. An abundance of attendees began to gather in the center, unintentionally spilling their drinks on one another as a single chair was passed overhead.

"Jesus Christ," I groaned, snaking my arm through his. "I feel like I'm in a club. They've even got a damn *chair* in there."

"Stop complaining. Brennan's having fun, that's all that matters," Raiden countered, taking an impossibly small sip from his cup. Sure enough, my brother—obnoxiously crowned like some sort of king with a paper trophy on his scalp—wormed his way into the center, earning a thrilled cheer from the surrounding swarm. A tipsy Elden clung to his arm, easing alongside him and disappearing into the mass. I swore I could see him on my brother's lap already, and the thought transported me right back to my senior prom. Brennan was a sophomore at the time, but some girl in my grade insisted on bringing him along. Similar to tonight, I stumbled upon my brother seated on a chair in the center of the dancefloor, his date sloppily seated upon his lap as several onlookers gleefully encouraged them.

I wanted to drag Raiden away, but just as my hand slipped into his, my gaze settled upon a familiar face.

Jordan.

"What the hell is she doing here?" I spat, tightening my grip on Raiden's arm. He visibly winced when the curve of my nails nearly penetrated his supple skin, a whisper of crescent moon imprints left behind in their wake.

"Fuck, Frey. You nearly drew blood," Raiden whined, prying my fingers away from his reddened flesh one by one. "Who are you talking about?"

"Your little friend." The words oozed off of my tongue like hot venom, slitted stare welded to Jordan's merry expression. She looked beautiful as ever, heavenly brunette tendrils framing her face like a halo. She was truly the human embodiment of an earthside angel, and being as average as I am, I envied her. Mostly for the fact that my boyfriend had been buried inside of her somewhat recently.

When Raiden finally spotted her, he sighed; delicate digits dancing along my jaw. He cocked my head sideways to meet his somber stare, gorgeous, green eyes colliding with dark, angry slits.

"You have no reason to feel jealous of her. I'm yours."

"She's gorgeous," I thickly countered. "Super smart, too. She has a hell of a personality and so much dimension. Meanwhile, I'm as flat and bland as they come."

"But she isn't you," Raiden said, tracing circles along my chin. "She could never be you. None of them were you. That's why none of my past relationships ever went anywhere. I spent over a decade searching for someone that I had all along."

"Oh, Rai." Tears welled up within my eyes at his loving declaration.

I didn't deserve him.

"I mean it," he whispered. "Every word. I love you."

I sealed our moment with a quick kiss, one which was fairly short lived due to Raiden's rumbling belly. Once more, he looked pale—*weak*—beads of sweat peppered along his forehead. Grammy always carried some magic medicine for nausea, and he made it his mission to hunt her down and find it, wherever the little old lady may be.

Meanwhile, I escaped the cheerful chaos in the center of the dance floor, desperate for some space and perhaps a bit of light.

I figured that I'd maybe find my mother or father in the butler's pantry—which was literally *twice* the size of our dinky kitchen back home—but alas, they were nowhere to be found. I figured that perhaps they'd excused themselves from the banquet hall entirely and escaped to somewhere less . . . *loud.* I wouldn't be surprised if my mother had her nose stuffed up in a book in some exquisite library a few doors down, one stacked sky-high with first edition books. My father, on the other hand, probably scoured the estate for an office, desperate for a computer that he could feast his eyes upon. Even when he wasn't working, he was working. I'd never met anyone so utterly addicted to their job, and truthfully, I blamed him for my dead-end jobs. A real career like his terrified me. I could never fathom being so immersed in my work—so *lost*—that the days trickled away and eventually, I'd missed out on every important event in my children's lives.

The small of my back met the rounded counter as I parked myself against a row of cabinets. A variety of spices lined a wooden rack, ranging from the staple household seasonings to rather unusual flavorings that I'd never heard of.

Unfortunately, I was not alone in Weatherby's eccentric kitchenette. People bobbed in and out, slipping in to fill up on their drinks, exchanging a few laughs, then leaving—all except a select few.

A gentleman with sleek, blond hair and an abundance of freckles hovered the beverage cooler, pudgy fingers wrapped around a perspiring bottle of beer. The drink looked relatively untouched, and I wondered if he just held it in his hand to appear socially acceptable. It was pitiful how much people did to simply *fit in.*

Beside him was a considerably shorter man, with a red, round face and bright, blue eyes. They were deep in conversation, and both politely nodded my way when I entered the room.

I busied myself with a bowl of lemons, my forefinger graciously grazing the blemished flesh. I thought of my brother—sweet Brennan—and the fact that he'd become this almighty God come midnight—*less than six hours away*—and then I chuckled at the thought of comparing my baby brother to such a deity. We didn't believe in God—not the one most around here believed in, anyways. Instead, we considered the possibility of a divine entity, a faceless, nameless being that was responsible for our creation. Similar to the Christian bible, we also acknowledged a wickedness, a force powerful enough to generate our villainous counterpart, which as of yesterday, was officially extinct.

By my grandmother's hand, no less.

With a shiver, I clutched my wine glass; drawing it up towards my mouth before taking a hefty swig. There wasn't enough wine in this glass to make me forget her face.

"That's a lot of lemons."

Gracelessly, I dropped one of them; watching with wide eyes as the fruit tumbled over the edge and fell to my feet. I'd never seen the woman opposite me before, and it truly baffled me how many friends Brennan actually had—friends that I'd never seen a day in my life.

Her round cheeks reddened, a shy smirk slapped across her mouth as she bent over to retrieve the fallen citrus. In her hand was a drink identical to mine, a wine so red that it nearly matched her blush.

"Sorry," she said, dropping the lemon back into the bowl. It snugly slipped alongside its friends, appearing as if it had never even left. "I didn't mean to startle you. I just needed some water. Plus, I'm not a huge Nirvana fan, and Brennan's switched the soundtrack over to them."

Not a big Nirvana fan?

"How do you know Brennan?" I asked, realizing then how bizarre that must've sounded. I didn't even know the girl's name, and I was already bombarding her with a heap of questions.

"We worked together at the news station before they went broke," she revealed, unbothered by my inquiry. "Gosh, that was what—three years ago, now? He told me he's back with his parents because he hasn't found a stable job since. I guess we have that in common. I've been back with my Mama for almost a year."

"How long were you guys coworkers at the station? He never introduced us. Did you guys hang out at all outside of work?"

The stranger raised a brow at my extensive examination, a slight smirk tugging at her thin lips as she giggled. "You're his sister, aren't you?"

I felt my cheeks grow hot. "Is it that obvious?"

"Plain as day," she teased. "I've never had someone ask me so many invasive questions in a single breath. I'm Scarlet, by the way. Brennan and I hung out a few times outside of work, mostly in groups. We maybe got drinks together once or twice. He didn't speak much of his romantic life at work, but I could tell that he was generally disinterested in girls. Hell, he was the only guy at the station to not ogle our weather woman, Helen. The woman had breasts bigger than my head."

A genuine chuckle tickled my tongue at Scarlet's statement. I fairly liked the woman, and I was slightly peeved that my brother had failed to ever introduce us before tonight.

I had a feeling that Scarlet and I would be good friends.

"We need to talk about your disdain for Nirvana. Quite frankly, it's a bit unnerving," I teased, unable to mask my smile as Scarlet and I burst into identical giggles.

I was halfway through a gracious sip of wine when I felt it.

The burning.

Oddly, it originated in my skull; a tight, searing sensation. Then it drifted, dipping down my neck, slicing through the veins like white-hot knives. My body stiffened, a surge of panic easing up my throat as I desperately attempted to mask my extreme discomfort. Scarlet didn't seem to notice at first, but when the pain hit my chest, I outwardly gasped.

"Freya?"

She inched towards me, a worrisome expression stamped across her features as I exploded with a pain so severe that it knocked the wind right from my lungs.

My ears grievously buzzed, the sweet sonance of Kurt Cobain's vocals fading to black as I heard nothing but a dull, aching ring. The ringing lasted maybe half a second before it was swiftly replaced with that of a labored gasp—an exaggerated intake of air—and then, there was blood.

Within my feeble grasp, the wine glass combusted, sending sharp shards of glimmering glass flying. As if by magic, the fragments flew forward, joining the mass of floating pieces lingering over Scarlet's palm. The inanimate pieces gathered like a group of old friends, bundled up in a lustrous mass. No sooner than they'd conjoined, the shards met skin—sweet, smooth skin, once untainted, now soiled by a cruel, unusual punishment.

Scarlet's fingers gravitated up towards her gory complexion, a weighted gasp wedging against a particularly vast piece that severed her windpipe. She collapsed to my feet, and I was on the ground in a matter of seconds—bulbous, blinding tears muffling my sight as the woman struggled to breathe beneath me.

Virtually every inch of her face was maimed by a scrap of glass, bubbling blood oozing out of the wounds. She desperately clawed at her neck, weakly attempting to rid her throat of the large shard, but to no avail.

Her blood coated my fingers, a harsh cry wracking through my chest as I attempted to heal the dying woman beneath my hips.

The two men mere feet away were in complete shock; eyes widened and jaws dropped as they watched Scarlet whine and wheeze. I begged for their help, but they refused to budge. All they could do was watch. Listen. *Stare.*

Scarlet's bloodshot gaze refused to stray from mine; lips graciously parted as her lungs neglected to intake air. I audibly begged for her to keep trying—*keep breathing goddammit*—and although I knew it would do no good—*no good at all NO GOOD*—I took a deep breath, censored my scream, and plunged my fingers into the mushy, mangled flesh of her throat.

Suddenly, I was transported back to a happy, familiar place.

My limbo.

My heaven.

Skipping through the trees with Raiden, leaves crunching beneath our bare feet as we skipped along the wooded path. Warm waves of sunlight dancing along his features, a shimmering smile pulling at his lips. His pulse drummed against my palm, and I was safe.

I was home.

Only, I wasn't home. I was in hell. A hell where my fingers were drowning in a surplus of warm, wet blood. I could feel the razor-sharp shard against the tip of my pinky, planted perfectly in the center of Scarlet's windpipe.

And then, she was gone. Empty eyes glazed over, cold stare eternally glued upon my troubled features. She was dead, and my fingers were still buried in her throat; hoping, waiting, *praying* for some kind of miracle. I retracted my intrusive touch, soiled palms flattening over the gaping hole in her neck as I attempted to seal the wound—*close it up*—but it only seemed to widen, *broaden,* as if to mock me. *Laugh* at me.

You couldn't save her.

Then, the fury. The disdain.

The anger.

"Why didn't either of you try to help me?" I seethed, standing to my feet to face the cowardly men opposite me. Beyond the kitchenette, the party remained unphased; Bush's *Glycerine* bouncing between the speakers.

There was a dead woman on the floor.

"Do you have anything to say for yourselves? You're *men* for Christ's sake!" The statements emerged like venom, and I couldn't quite ignore the abundance of blood smeared along my hands and arms. I felt woozy—*weak*—and I wanted nothing more than to wake up—*wake up wake up wake up*—wake up from this nightmare, this *terror,* and roll over in bed to see Raiden sweetly snoozing beside me, his innocent features reminding me that all was well.

The freckled blond opened his mouth to speak, but instead, his words were masked with a groan. I watched as the untouched beer tumbled from his grasp, shattering at his feet and showering the tile with foamy liquid. His pale eyes were boggled and bulging, blue veins swelling within his forehead as his knees buckled, sending his stiffened frame to the floor in a seizing heap.

"What the–" I gasped, rushing to his aide. He violently shook in my arms, white, bubbling foam dripping down the curve of his lower lip as he struggled to breathe, just as Scarlet did.

I shifted my woeful stare to the second man, who had side-stepped towards the counter to retrieve a sleek, silver object. I could barely utter a shout when he brought the blade to his neck, round fingers securely fastened around the handle. The rushing blood surging up the slope of his throat sprayed outwards like a wonky fountain, showering his feet with an aching array of bold, red hues.

He'd just slit his own throat with a butcher knife.

The seizing blond tumbled from my arms as I crawled backwards in horror; a horrified sob wracking through my chest as three complete strangers dropped dead around me within the span of several minutes. It felt surreal—*horrifying*—and I kept squeezing my eyes shut, forcing myself to blink hard several times until blinding stars frolicked along my inner eyelids.

This wasn't a dream.

It was real.

I solemnly studied the man with the slit throat, hollow blue eyes boring into mine. Their colorful vibrancy dwindled as his life slowly seeped from the wound in his neck, a crimson pool circling his head like a thin pillow, one that he'd rest upon for an eternity.

Tears threatened to spill from the rims of my eyes, but I couldn't quite cry—I couldn't do much of anything, really, except breathe. *Exist.*

Time slowed around me, the little hand on the clock sluggishly shifting—*tick tick tick*—a whiny, garish ring replacing the noise as I drifted into an unsought limbo. My extremities felt weighty—*weak*—and with every gradual blink, the scene around me shifted.

Round, white pebbles—the very same from Weatherby's driveway—crowded my legs, pouring into the room like a rumbling wave. They tumbled over one another, resembling a rush of eager animals in search of their prey. Only, their prey was *me,* and they weren't pebbles at all, but teeth. Teeth that varied in size, shape, and color; all completely diverse and unique.

With frozen limbs, I watched them crowd my body; overlapping my legs, piling over my knees. I felt a pinch at my ankle, a bite, a tear. Warm, wet blood cascaded over the bone, slipping from the vein, painting the teeth red.

They were eating me alive.

I squeezed my eyes shut—desperately attempting to drown out the incessant roar of the piling teeth—and I opened my mouth wide and screamed.

The floor beneath my bottom rumbled and shook, and suddenly, the biting and tearing and ripping was gone. *Vanished.* Disappeared the second I opened my mouth. But even when the screaming from my lungs ceased, it seemed to linger—*echo*—like an audio recording stuck on an endless loop. Reluctantly, I opened my eyes; leery gaze settling upon the three dead bodies before me. The teeth were gone, as if they'd never existed at all. As if I'd simply dreamt them up.

Imagined it all.

The ground vibrated beneath my stiff frame once more, my echoing screams replaced by a band Brennan frequented back in the early 2000s when he went through his doom metal phase. I knew the name like the back of my hand, for he'd listened to this particular song so many times that it had simply stamped itself into the deepest pits of my memory—Burning Witch's *Communion.*

On every off-beat, the floor beneath my feet shook. The empty wine glasses atop the granite counter shivered and shook, tumbling from the ledge like a hiker on a slippery slope. They plummeted over the edge, meeting the costly tile with a shy kiss before exploding into a surplus of shards.

The bloody halo around the unnamed man's head trembled with every boisterous boom, like a glass of water atop a rattling speaker, threatening to topple over and fry the equipment. At this point, I wouldn't even be shocked if the blood erupted into flames, eradicating the evidence of his sudden suicide.

An inkling of strength returned to my arms, and with as much energy as I could muster, I rotated myself forward, unintentionally losing my balance. The curve of my nose collided with the floor, blinding stars littering my eyelids as I outwardly groaned. I felt partially paralyzed, both legs completely numb as I wriggled myself across the tile. My vision was blurred—*weak*—and my palms were slick with sweat, stained red by Scarlet's blood. I smeared the red liquid along the pearly, white floor, quivering fingers painting uneven crimson lines along the surface.

The lights above my skull flickered and groaned, a choir of cries tickling the shell of my ear. I'd barely made it three feet—maybe four—before I defeatedly collapsed, rolling onto my back with a staggered sob.

I had no clue what transpired beyond the hall. It seemed impossible for no one to have heard a thing—not a shout, nor a cry—and although I felt sickly and spent, I had to get out of there. I had to find my family.

I had to find Brennan.

The thought of my loved ones made my blood run cold, and I swallowed hard; trying not to waste any more energy on shaking sobs. I cocked my head, muddled glare settling upon the stranger with the slit throat.

I choked back a shout, urgently attempting to cower away, for his face had been replaced with one I'd seen one too many times in my nightmares. *Her face.*

Gunora Falk. The De Mörka. The evidently *dead* De Mörka.

Only, she wasn't dead—she *couldn't* be dead—for the events that had transpired within Weatherby's butler's pantry were that of an unearthly force, an energy that only a unique individual could utilize.

Striking ebony eyes met mine, a dark, sinister smile pulling at the mouth that once belonged to the boy with the round face. A flood of baleful giggles eased off of her lips, which were doused in black blood, oozing, *dripping.* A spiked tongue emerged from the black abyss, lewdly lapping at the liquid, wiping it clean. She bared her teeth—sleek, sharpened spikes—and with a torturous trill, she whispered their names over and over and *over.* A taunting melody, a racing thought.

She yanked herself up into a sitting position, my brother's name slipping off of her tongue in the form of a chant. Gory fingers traveled upwards to meet the seeping slash along her throat, a delighted chuckle emerging from bared teeth as she hooked her index finger within the frayed flesh and pulled. Pulled until her fingers met the edge—finished, *fatigued.* Empty eyes tipped back into her skull as both hands met the gash, burying deep beneath the flesh, widening, *warping.* I squeezed my eyes shut in hopes of drowning it out, but I could hear every tiny tear of flesh, every cackle that flowed from her tongue.

"Just kill me," I begged, refusing to witness her rage. I felt weak—*spineless*—but the thought of continuing on after so much trauma, so much *terror,* seemed simply impossible. "Please, I can't take the torture anymore. Just end it. *Please.*"

Just kill me

kill me

kill me

kill

A giggle, a gasp, and then—*silence.*

Buzzing, aching silence.

Nothing.

I worried for a second that perhaps she had succeeded—maybe I *was* dead—but I was almost disappointed to discover that I was, in fact, very much alive; a racing pulse drumming against my throat as I opened my eyes.

At first, I was met with darkness, and then, a fleeting flash of light—a periodic flicker. Most of the bulbs above my skull had burnt out—*spontaneously combusted*—but the few that remained were enough to paint a proper picture.

Hesitantly, I cocked my head to the side, preparing to face the evil I'd just witnessed once more. Only, she was gone; replaced by the boy with the sliced throat, still face-down in a pool of blood.

No barbed teeth. No black eyes. No pointy tongue. Just a stranger, one I'd never seen before tonight, dead by what seemed like his own accord. But, I knew better. He didn't want to die. Not tonight, not here, not like this.

I reached out towards a nearby cabinet, and with weakened knees, I clambered to my feet; pulling myself up with the tapering strength of my upper body.

"Raiden!" I screamed, haunted by the agonizing silence. My voice seemed to echo for miles, reverberating off of the walls and bouncing back to me in the form of a pitiful cry.

I stumbled forward, smearing Scarlet's blood along the counter as I held on for dear life. I wasn't sure how I would be able to walk on my own once the island ended, but I had to find them, and if I had to crawl through every inch of Weatherby's estate to do so, I would.

I glanced down once more at Scarlet's glassy complexion, an aghast apology slipping off of my lips.

No matter what I did, I couldn't mend her. I couldn't patch her wounds. Seal them up. Erase the scar.

Not all wounds can be mended.

I apologized to the deceased trio in the obnoxiously-sized kitchenette once more before abandoning the area, my legs regaining their strength with every small stride. The lights within the hall were completely blown, a bitter blackness enveloping the space as I struggled to walk. With arms outstretched, I trailed my fingertips along the walls, feeling my way back towards the banquet hall.

What I didn't know was that the corridor was a winding portal to the valley of death.

twenty-one

A desolate, blue glow cloaked the banquet hall, the mighty moon's rays trickling through the cracked panes of the stained glass windows. Some of the decorative sheets of glass remained unsullied, whereas others weren't so lucky—busted, broken, weeping. Half of the angel's face was missing, a mournful, bloody tear dribbling down the apple of her remaining rounded cheek.

The devil was entirely unblemished. *Pure.* Not a single nick nor crack present upon his colossal frame. He was unable to stifle his smirk—big and bold—as if the entire event amused him.

I stood frozen within the walkway, deadened gaze transfixed on the corpse closest to me.

The once animated space had succumbed to silence—*despair*—and all that remained of Brennan's birthday was the stinging stench of death. I almost missed the music—the booming bass that jump started my heart—for the sound had been replaced by a bitter silence. *Oblivion.*

Eerily, I could hear the low hum of traffic from the road, for Weatherby's estate resided right off of an active avenue.

If only the passersby had an inkling of knowledge of what laid beyond those prodigious walls.

Tables were overturned, forgotten food splayed along the floorboards. Cracked chips drizzled with bright blood, the tipped queso fountain frantically whirring, attempting to pump out a continuous strand of hot cheese. Instead, the molten gold was contaminated—*soiled*—littered with a barbaric blend of liquid life. The wine within my stomach bubbled and churned, and I found myself stumbling across the floor, the toe of my sandal mistakenly striking the bruised temple of a woman I did not know.

I ushered an apology her way, widened eyes glued to the empty orbs that claimed her skull. They were a beautiful, bright blue.

"What happened to you?" I whispered, weakly falling to my knees beside her. She was one of many—perhaps twenty or more—and the thought of others running rampant within Weatherby's walls, *alive,* made my chest arduously ache.

The sheer silence of the estate suggested otherwise, but I refused to believe that every guest had grimly perished while I horrifically hallucinated in the other room.

They're all dead all dead all dead all–

A distraught shout eased up my throat, burning tears blinding my vision as I flattened a palm across the stranger's stiff chest. She looked tranquil—*content*—as if she were simply asleep. I figured her lack of wounds made for a swift, soundless death, and for a split second, I pondered over the thought of bringing her back.

Perhaps, I could.

"I'm going to try, okay?" I whispered, blinking back tears. She remained reticent beneath my touch, complexion a guttural, gray hue, skin sweet with rot. It was difficult to explain the scent of fresh death—for any average individual usually would not experience such an atrocity—but I was never average, not even remotely close. I was shocked that I'd made it this far in life without stumbling upon life's cruel joke.

Shards of glass audibly shifted beneath my rounded knees as I leaned forward, the shell of my ear meeting the stranger's rock-hard chest as I listened for the faint hint of a beat. When my ears were met with nothing but silence, I whined; fingers curling around the silken material of her blouse. With a sliver of strength, I attempted to heal her from the inside out—firmly focusing on the arctic heart within her chest. I summoned life into her lungs, lengthy nails digging against the rubbered texture of her chest as I forced every ounce of healing energy that remained within my bones into her cold core.

With a riled shout, I pressed each palm against her chest, fingers heartily separated as I continuously compressed her stationary bosom.

"Wake *up!*" The statement emerged, rushed through a fit of stinging tears, as I clumsily pumped her chest; applying an abundance of pressure to her upper half. Halfway through what seemed like my seventeenth compression, a shrewd *snap* struck me from my trance, my bulging glare shakily meeting her unvaried expression as several of her ribs cracked beneath my weight.

There was no use.

Dead was dead.

Defeated, I fell to the floor; head buried within the cavern of my palms as I weakly whined. I felt depleted—*spent*—as if I'd used up every inch of my energy in my failed attempt to bring a stranger back from the dead.

Thirty-three years of magical mending experience, and I couldn't even breathe life back into the deceased.

I glanced down at my feet, pale toes besmirched with blood. I gawked at the sight, shifting my feet sideways to view them better in the moonlight. Sure enough, my left foot was spotted with bright red blood, fresh and chunky, as if it originated from a glass of snowy, white milk that had sat out in the sun too long.

"Momma," I murmured, unable to stifle the aching sob that tore through my chest. My knuckles brushed against the soiled skin of my foot, smearing blood between the crevices of my fingerprints.

Bloody prints.

I hooked my index finger between the scabbed skin of my heel and the sandal strap, swiftly shifting it downwards before tearing the sorry excuse for a shoe from my foot. I kicked its twin to the side, the clammy soles of my feet kissing the defiled wood floors as I eyed the stranger's sneakers.

Pretty pink Chuck Taylors claimed her feet, bright white laces double knotted, and I found myself pulling at the tongue of one, extending it outwards to view the size. They were half a size too large for my rather tiny feet, but nevertheless, I disentangled the laces, tearing the shoes from her firm feet with difficulty. I lost my balance with the second one, bony elbow nicking a splinter of glass propped upright by her legs. With a howl, I examined the wound, index finger slithering down the bend of my arm.

A sparkling chip from one of the shattered windows was wedged between folded flaps of skin, glossy and sharp, and I nearly lost consciousness at the sight of it.

"F-fuck," I stammered, politely poking the blunt edge of the glass. Blood drops in the shape of beaded pearls formed around the foreign object before dripping down the back of my arm in the shape of a wonky, inverted cross. In a somewhat demented fashion, it reminded me of a rosary, and the longer I stared at it, the more I desired its absence.

"I'm sorry about your shoes," I whispered towards the deceased partygoer, blood daintily leaking from my fresh wound. "And your ribs."

Careful not to disturb the injury, I slipped my sweaty feet into the too-big sneakers, sloppily knotting up the laces before returning my attention to the glass in my elbow.

As I poked and prodded at the lesion, I longed for Raiden. He was here somewhere—if he was dead, I would certainly feel it—and I was confident that wherever he was, he was safe and sound with my family, too. Brennan included.

But if they were alive, that meant that the De Mörka must be, too. After all, I'd seen her with my own two eyes—in the form of a hallucination—but I still saw her. *She was here.* She was wreaking havoc, murdering the innocent.

Avenging her evidently failed assassination.

I wished that Raiden was here with me, cradling me on the floor, peppering kisses along my jaw and assuring me that everything would end up okay. He'd surely faint at the sight of my wound—*blood makes him queasy*—but he'd attempt to help with it until his stomach went sour and bulbous, black spots raided his sight.

Shaking fingers curled around the glass fragment, bottom lip quivering with every timid movement. I had half a mind to tear the damn thing out, but something deep within my mind convinced me to keep it in—just until I could find my family, that is.

Grammy would know what to do.

With wobbling knees, I climbed to my feet; glancing down one last time at the barefoot lady who perished well before her time. Upon one final visual inspection, she truly seemed relatively unscathed, and I hoped that her death was swift and painless. She deserved that much.

Thus, I pressed on, arm bent at an incredibly awkward angle to ease the pressure off of my pierced elbow. It almost appeared as if I were wearing an invisible cast, and I wondered if I'd need one in the days to come (if those days ever actually arrived, that is).

It appeared as if the owner of my new shoes was one of the few who expired painlessly. I tried to avoid some of them, but most were hard to miss, especially the middle-aged man without his left arm. I briefly paused in front of him, jaw agape in shock as I studied his peculiar pose.

While the left arm was completely absent, the right remained; bent at the elbow, twisted above his skull, undoubtedly broken. His jaw lay slack, bruised lips parted in a dramatic O-shape, eyes widening as if he'd seen a ghost. Perhaps he'd caught a glimpse of his own apparition as it departed his wrecked remains, making a beeline for the netherworlds, never looking back.

A full-body tremble consumed my core, and with a skittish cry, I called for my mother, only to be met with the low, haunting hum of a nearby speaker.

I stepped over the single-armed lad, mumbling a series of empty apologies his way before continuing onward. It was evident that none of my family members were present within these four walls, and if I wanted to find them before the De Mörka did, I needed to pick up some speed and explore the rest of Weatherby's grand estate.

I tried not to stare too long at the queso fountain as it rapidly pumped a mixture of warm, white cheese and bright, bubbly blood, a headless body positioned a single step east, nubby fingers coated with the liquid mixture. I wasn't exactly sure of the whereabouts of their head, but if I did enough searching, I was certain that I'd locate it, and truthfully, finding a severed head was the very last thing that I wanted to do.

I wondered if Brennan's head would be placed upon a silver platter when I finally found him.

She'd be balancing the plate upon clawed fingertips, a toothy grin slapped across her deathlike features, black blood dribbling down her chin and smeared across her pointed fangs like paint. One leg hiked up, the sole of her bare foot suctioned to the opposite leg, steadying her weight. The platter would rock and shake, an impish snicker cascading over her lengthy, snakelike tongue as she admired Brennan's detached head.

He's a beaut', ain't he?

I shook the thought from my mind, a bitter twinge of pain radiating up my arm as the glass seemingly wedged itself deeper into my muscle. I feebly navigated the banquet hall, using the white, spotty patches of light from the moon as a pathway. Glass shifted and crunched beneath my sneaker-clad feet, and I dodged bodies like they were nothing but trifling obstacles in my way. The thought alone made me feel an immeasurable sense of guilt, and I craned my neck, apologizing to each and every one in my way.

So far, I recognized none of them. No Jordan, no Vole, no Elden. Just a bunch of unfamiliar faces, friends of friends, people who probably barely knew my brother, but lost their lives celebrating him.

If Brennan made it out of this alive, he would live the rest of his days in infinite regret. Hell, I might just be in the same shape as he, probably even worse for what I've seen. Scarlet's glassy complexion still plagued my thoughts, a crystal honeycomb permanently engraved within her once lovely features.

"Raiden?" I called, stepping over two equally mangled corpses. I carelessly clipped the side of someone's skull, stumbling sideways into a table. The rush of cars from beyond the residence made my head spin, and I contemplated bursting through one of the empty window panes—trudging towards the road, waving my arms around like a bat out of hell, begging for someone to stop, someone to *help . . .*

Only, there was no stopping such a thing. Ordinary folk were defenseless against something as powerful as the De Mörka. The only people who could defeat such an evil were their counterpart, and all that remained of that was my brother, my mother, my grandmother, and me.

We were the last living hope.

"None of you died in vain," I called, nursing my gaping wound. The room remained reticent, a macabre hush that could only be associated with putrid death. Although they could not respond, I felt as if they understood—they *forgave.* They were freed from the bonds of an unforgiving world—out of malice, maybe—but nonetheless, they were all free. None of them would have to suffer with the thought of loss, the memories of *death.*

Meanwhile, I would spend the rest of my days trying to rid my nostrils of the heinous stench of demise.

I took one last glance at the banquet hall, a room that was bright and full of life only two hours prior, perhaps less. Warped images of the spirited celebration wafted in and out, like a busted film reel, shifting between the height of the party to the depth of its aftermath.

I twisted on my heel, a solemn sigh slipping off of my tongue as I gradually fled the crime scene. Although the banquet hall was mostly black besides the low glow of the moon, the remaining areas seemed to have some power—a staccato of flickering bulbs, a low hum, a jerky click as they periodically blinked.

Brennan's guest book was still propped up on the table right before the banquet hall, faux flowers drizzled with glossy, crimson blood, like frosting on a cake. I extended my good arm outward and took one of the purple flowers between my fingers. It expanded upon my palm, like a kitty cat stretching its stiff limbs after a long nap, and I could see the blood begin to transform—*shift.* The once red substance had altered into an obscure hue—colorless, almost. It dripped down the curve of the plastic petals, coating my palm, burning it. Instinctively, I dropped the flower, a startled shout bubbling up my throat as I inspected my weeping palm. The sensation ceased almost immediately, and I watched with wide, doe-like eyes as the flower shuddered and shrunk, purple petals blackened, chafing away, *disappearing.*

"What the hell–" I murmured, eyeing the tiny pile of black soot at my feet. The walls of Weatherby's manor rattled and groaned, like a ship sinking to the darkest depths of the sea. Brennan's guest book lay open, the corners curled, pages worn. The written words from his friends were altered—*vandalized.* Scribbled over with a sloppy penmanship, written by a red hand.

I'll kill them all kill them all kill them all kill them

My stomach unpleasantly lurched once more, tears brimming in the creases of my eyes as I took hold of the book.

"You won't win." The statement emerged like venom, hot tears cascading down the slope of my cheeks as I dropped the book to my feet. My injured elbow warily whined, a second pulse finding refuge at the source as I bit back a shout.

"You *won't win!*"

With the toe of my stolen shoe, I tore the sabotaged sheets from the book, revealing several more inscriptions, all just a bit more gruesome than the last. Bitterly, I kicked the book aside; nearly losing my balance in the process as the overhead lamps rapidly flashed, mimicking a strobe light.

I'm wasting my fucking time.

With a defeated shout, I abandoned the defaced guest book, weak, wobbly knees jutting forward as I continued on my mission. Although it was rather silly to harbor any hope at all, I still searched for a sign of life besides my own. It would make no sense for the De Mörka to murder everyone, including my family and my brother, and leave me (mostly) unscathed. It just made no fucking *sense.*

Thus, I strolled onward, desperately searching for a familiar face, and hoping that face still had a heartbeat.

The front foyer was mostly vacant, all besides a single corpse positioned on the floor directly beneath the chandelier. It was a woman—easily less than thirty—with wicked, red hair and glistening, green stilettos. Her dress was torn at the abdomen, exposing a plethora of mangled intestines. Large beads of blood took refuge upon her forehead, slipping into her unblinking eyes and staining them red.

With a sharp intake of breath, I followed the shy stream, *up up up* to the glittering jewels suspended above her skull. I watched another ruby pearl slip from the surface—*drip drip drip*—plummeting down to the earth, splattering her skin, making its mark.

The chandelier was saturated with blood.

I was uncertain of its source, but I wouldn't stick around long enough to discover it. Instead, I avoided the area entirely, disappearing beyond the grand staircase and making a beeline towards the back of the room.

Near the rear of the foyer, I stumbled over a particularly grotesque corpse, one which lacked half of its skull. Their limbs were mangled, moist, drenched with seeping, scarlet blood. Once more, I did not recognize them. Just another nameless face.

The weak light from the overhead lamps flickered as my frail frame rounded a corner. The absence of light—both natural and artificial—had cloaked the long, slender hallway in a bitter, black fog; one which made my heart skip a beat. Something shifted the second I rounded the corner, and I found myself wanting to turn back—*run away, run far away*—but I knew that I couldn't. My family was depending on me. I couldn't leave without knowing what had happened to them.

I placed one foot forward, sucking in a sharp breath as I prepared to navigate the inky black hallway. Just as my heel met the carpet, an artificial, unknown light source illuminated the area. My lungs neglected to intake any air, and I nearly fell to my knees; sucking in a sharp gasp as the haunting whisper I'd come to know cascaded over my ears—an unidentifiable sonance, an unknown tune, but nevertheless unique. One I'd readily identify, even in my sleep. It resembled something like a gasp, a sharp intake of breath, and then an abhorrent ringing.

I knew that sound.

The lights flickered once more, and I was met with a shape—a tall, lanky figure, one which stood still at the very end of the hallway. Their back was to me, feet spread evenly apart, soles suctioned to the rug. Arms slack at their sides, lengthy curls seemingly unswayed. *Perfect.*

The lights extinguished, and once more, they were gone—but only for a split second, if even that. Blindly, I took a single step forward, shallow breaths tickling my tongue as I cradled my injured elbow.

When the light returned, they'd cocked their head; neck slightly craned to view me over their shoulder. I audibly whimpered at the sight, conflicting emotions boiling within my stomach as I gradually approached them—gradually approached *him.*

"Raiden?"

His gaze swiftly met mine, and my blood turned to ice. My feet came to a screeching halt, heart thickly thumping within my chest as his cold, unwavering stare bored into my soul.

I couldn't quite miss the blackness of his eyes, regardless of how hard I'd tried.

Ice cold, dark, *black.* Irises absent, nothing but a giant, gaping pupil in the place of the forest green orbs I'd grown to love. The whites of his eyes had disappeared completely—*vanished*—replaced by a striking ebony hue.

It appeared as if there were gaping black holes where his eyes once were, only I knew better, for their kind had eyes, just unlike any I'd ever seen before. Pure darkness. *Empty.*

I pondered over the thought once more—*their kind*—before realizing the inevitable: *it was him.*

"No no no no *no*–"

My knees warily wobbled, my good arm jutting outward to meet the wall as I attempted to steady my weight. There wasn't really a point in standing anymore—there wasn't a point in anything, anymore. Simply existing right now felt burdensome. *Purposeless.*

The one who sought to murder my entire family had been sleeping in my bed for more years than I could count.

"It's you?"

Raiden kept his composure, unfaltering eyes glued upon my rigid frame. He hadn't blinked once—not even for a shy second—and although the hallway lights continuously waned, I could steadily see his expression. Distant. *Cold.* Unlike anything I'd ever seen from him.

I think I'd rather die than discover the truth.

"Honey, please tell me this isn't what I think it is. Please, Rai. This isn't real. It's another hallucination, isn't it? An illusion brought on by the real De Mörka? She's trying to trick me, trying to turn me against you, trying to–"

"*Help!* God, help me please!"

Greedy fingers claimed my shirt, almond-shaped nails pinching the fabric, a stunning, pearly white, freckled with dried specks of blood.

Unfamiliar eyes met mine, a trail of bloody spittle glued to the curve of the stranger's chin, as she clung to my good arm for dear life. She was sobbing profusely, auburn eyes red rimmed and worn, and she begged me to help her—*so many are dead, don't let me die*—and I just stood there. Frozen. *Numb.*

She tightened her hold on my elbow, yanking me close, and I felt my angry arm explode in pain. I went to shove her off—*get away please he's here*—but I was met with the sound of a garish *crack,* one which made my skin achingly crawl.

The stranger's neck twisted completely sideways—almost in an animated fashion—before straightening out once more. Deadened eyes were cast downward, silently studying my gaping wound as the woman fell to my feet in defeat.

An unvexed Raiden rotated his blackened gaze to the dead woman at my feet, head cocked slightly sideways in curiosity. A horrified whimper tickled my tongue as I slowly stepped away, avoiding the limp woman sprawled out along the hallway floor. She'd been alive mere moments prior—warm, *breathing*—begging me to help her.

Save her.

I couldn't heal her.

I couldn't heal any of them.

Raiden clicked his tongue, the leather soles of his boots vocally crying out against the wood. His vacant stare was on me once more, and I felt as if my entire world had come crashing down in a fiery fiasco.

"Please tell me this isn't real," I whispered, my voice emerging as a squeak. I knew better than that, but on the surface, I was simply unable to accept the reality of the situation. The reality of *him.*

Raiden took a step towards me, empty, soulless stare fixated on my wounded elbow. His arm outstretched towards the source of my immense discomfort, slender, ring-clad fingers curled inward towards his palm. He moved with such grace—such *elegance*—that it reminded me of a gentle ballerina, movements carefully coordinated.

I sucked in a sharp breath when his icy touch met my throbbing skin, gaping wound accompanied by a sharp shard of glass. He was incredibly close—*too close*—and for the first time, I felt drastically uncomfortable by our close proximity. I wanted to run away, hide, *cry*. Shout into the void, beg for a clear answer.

It just wasn't possible.

"Open your eyes," Raiden whispered, his forefinger softly circling the swollen skin of my elbow. "What do you see?"

I gulped. "I see you. I see a version of you that I don't know."

Raiden's palm met my cheek, frozen flesh stinging against my contrastingly hot face. He was so cold, like a body that's been dead for days and stuffed up in the corner of a refrigerator, limbs folded inward on each other. I felt my rosy, red cheeks flush, the color completely draining from my complexion as his thumb traced my quivering lower lip.

"Open them wider," he spoke, and before I could question what he meant, I was hurtling through a twisted timewarp, a kaleidoscope of colors raiding my vision as I tumbled down down *down* into the unrecognizable abyss.

I was continuously falling, and I wondered if I'd ever reach the ground. There was nothing below me besides a never-ending swirl of hues, and when I finally took the time to study them, I realized that they were much more than just randomized colors scattered around. No—they were moments. *Memories.* Captured in time, like a film, wrapped three hundred and sixty degrees around my falling frame.

I recognized one of the scenes immediately—it was of Raiden and me at work. He'd just sliced open his finger, and I'd stitched up the wound with nothing but a simple touch. Behind us, the knives had tumbled from the magnetic block, and I noticed a prickly patch of goosebumps rise upon Raiden's skin a sheer second before it had occurred.

I thought I'd done that.

I whipped my head around to view the others—countless visuals of every incident. The exploding flower vase, the blown lights at Tostada's, the fried television.

It was all him.

I kept falling, a cry bubbling up within my throat as the footage flickered around me. They began to transform—*turn.* Suddenly, I was spectating our first kiss. Then, our second. Our third.

A tingling sensation tickled my wounded elbow as I viewed our first time through a blurred, tearful gaze; and although he wasn't speaking the words aloud, I could just feel it. *I knew.*

He had no idea what he was.

A single dense tear eased down the slope of my cheek, my weightless arm curling upwards to meet the bizarre sensation. The tip of my forefinger gently slithered along the skin, gathering a dainty drop of the fluid. When I raised my arm up towards my face to examine the tear, I was met with blood.

Bloody tears on a bloody Sunday.

The warm, wet surface of my wounded elbow ached and throbbed, and as I reached around to feel it, I was met with a cold, collective touch. Fingers circled with rings.

He applied pressure to the wound, and I was still stuck in the winding vortex of reminiscence. I felt him against my elbow, a touch so shy, so *gentle* that I wondered if it were nothing but a hallucination. An illusion.

I wondered if it all was.

And then, it was gone. The pressure, the colors. His touch. Vanished into thin air, a whisper of a memory, a lingering presence. The imagery around me faded to black, and I was no longer dropping. Instead, I was stationary—*frozen*—and all I could smell, all I could *taste* was him. The sweet, berried taste of his tongue, the warmth of the nicotine that stuck to his skin. I wanted to revel in it—*bathe* in it. I wanted to completely backtrack—*turn back time*—exist only in a place when Raiden hadn't fully evolved into his final form just yet. When everything seemed slightly okay. *Normal.*

Only, nothing ever was, nor was it meant to be.

I blinked once, and I was back in the flickering hallway of Weatherby's mansion. The stench of fresh death crept into my nostrils, singing the itty-bitty hairs within my nose.

Raiden was gone.

My injured elbow vaguely tingled, curious fingers creeping towards the open wound as I took several short steps sideways, collapsing against the wall in order to steady my weight. My forefinger slid across smooth, sweaty skin, the absence of the glass shard instantaneously alarming me. I glanced down at my arm, fully expecting to see a massive chunk of glass wedged between slit bunches of flesh. Instead, I was met with a completely unmarred elbow, free of any trauma. All that remained was a small smear of blood, a poignant confirmation of the event.

It didn't seem possible—not in the slightest—but I knew what had happened. In my daze, Raiden healed me.

The man who was born of hatred and wickedness, who had evolved solely to slay my entire family, had *saved me.* I was weak, unaware and halfway unconscious. It would've been so easy, he could've ended me without a second thought. Snapped my neck in two, like I was a plastic doll. Torn apart my limbs, severed them with his teeth.

Only, he did none of those things. He had his opportunity, his moment to fulfill his destiny, and he didn't take it.

Instead, he did the opposite.

He saved me.

There was a whisper. A sound.

Shy, soft. Subtle and faint, and I found myself following it. I was careful to avoid the dead woman at my feet, pulling my knees up high enough to avoid her maimed frame.

At least I hadn't stolen her shoes.

With a noisy gulp, I navigated the area, keenly following the recognizable sound. It was difficult to determine its origin, but nevertheless, I continued on; desperate to discover what laid beyond the whisper.

I knew it was guiding me, but I wasn't quite sure where it would lead me.

My mind teetered back and forth between reality and remembrance—visuals of a black-eyed Raiden flooding my vision. Although I was temporarily blinded by the thought, my legs continued to move, as if the house had a hold on my limbs. Imperceptible strings circled my wrists and ankles, tugging, *pulling*—yanking me along step by step, like an inanimate puppet.

When the hallucinations stopped, I found myself before a door.

It was buried behind another staircase, one that was incredibly dark and seemingly led to nowhere. I had a hunch that there was something up there—*people alive, people hidden*—but I feared if I went to explore, I'd expose their hiding spot and they'd end up dead. Dead just like the others. Dead just like the girl whose neck was magically snapped right in front of my face.

Some evidently lived, and I wanted to keep it that way. So, I pressed on, lacing my clammy, trembling fingers around the warm brass handle of the door as I swiftly twisted.

I was met with an overly large garage, one that could easily fit nearly ten large SUVs. There were three grand garage doors, and my sight immediately settled on the center of the trio, which was peeled wide open. The muffled drone of racing cars from the neighboring road brought a chill down my spine, for what was once my favorite sound would now be paired with a dreadful memory, one which was riddled with a profusion of death and despair.

I'd finally found my family.

Huddled near a shiny, silver Porsche were both my mother and grandmother, arms latched around one another as their widened eyes remained fixated on a scene I had yet to see. My mother noticed my presence almost immediately, eyes widening as she ushered me over with the wave of her hand. Instead, I remained motionless on the top of the tri-step stairs, heart thickly thumping within my throat as my forearms painfully prickled.

Within a split second, Brennan had arrived; barreling airborne into the garage at an alarming speed, limbs sprawled outward in a weak attempt to soften the impending blow. A stifled shout oozed off of my lips as I watched my brother's back collide with a haphazard stack of moving boxes, some overflowing with an excess of dissimilar, unidentifiable items.

I watched as his frozen frame disappeared into the cardboard abyss, the lighter boxes toppling over his shrunken figure and swallowing him whole.

I felt compelled to check on my brother, but instead, I remained stationary atop the concrete steps, regardless of how obnoxiously my mother pleaded for my presence.

Just as Brennan began to crawl his way through the mound of fallen boxes, a corrupt Raiden appeared, his thin frame emerging from the cryptic fog that enveloped the whole exterior of the estate. His long, loopy curls were chaotic and knotted, bushy brows pulled together, ebony eyes fixated on my scrambling brother.

"Get *up,* Brennan!" Raiden seethed, the statement emerging as an unfamiliar, deep drawl. "Fight like a fucking man!"

With wobbling legs, Brennan stood to his feet; a gnarly, seeping cut stretched along his eyebrow. Blood dribbled down into his left eye, partially obstructing his sight as he struggled to catch his breath.

"I don't want to hurt you, Raiden. I know this isn't who you are. You can't control it," my brother breathed, momentarily glancing over his shoulder to view my frozen frame. His good eye considerably widened at my presence, and he took a single step in my direction before begging me to leave.

"Get *out* of here, Freya!" Brennan exclaimed, his tone scratchy and hoarse. "You don't need to see this."

"Freya stays," Raiden countered, extending an arm in my direction. My legs involuntarily moved, dragging my weak, shaken body down the steps. The invisible strings around my ankles were back, and I was Raiden's little puppet.

It was him who drew me to the garage.

It was him who planted the hallucinations in my head.

It was him who *wanted me here.*

He wanted me to be with him. He wanted me to *see.*

"Raiden, *stop!"* I shrieked, desperately digging my heels into the ground. I could feel the passion in his pull, but out of fear, I rejected it. *Shunned* it.

He obeyed immediately, loosening his sorcerous hold on my legs. I felt violated—*used*—until I reminded myself of how much I'd violated him by snatching bits and pieces of his soul. I could feel his emotions, his pain, his glee.

There was nothing quite as violating as that. Not even a physical hold on me could compare to what I'd taken from him.

His own privacy.

Brennan took another step forward, and Raiden recklessly reacted; sending a baby blue bicycle hurtling towards my brother's head.

I observed in awe as my younger brother deflected the flying object with ease, countering it with an exhausted wave of his arm. The pair continued to toss randomized objects at one another, and as I crept towards a stiff Raiden with balled-up fists, my mother latched her fingers around the soft skin of my arms, aggressively yanking me back against her.

"Don't you *dare* get in the middle," she hissed, attempting to pull me towards her and Grammy's hiding spot. "They can't control what flies around. You'll get struck and end up dead."

"We'll all probably be dead within the hour," I weakly wheezed, struggling against her surprisingly strong hold. "Let go of me, Momma. Raiden needs me."

"*Raiden* is not himself," she countered, refusing to let up her hold. Her fingernails were digging into my skin, leaving behind angry, red indents. "He's in there somewhere, but he's unpredictable. He'll kill you without a second thought. Look at all of the people he's already murdered, Freya. Look at how many are dead. He won't hesitate to end you, too."

"He won't," I dryly defended. "He had the chance, and he didn't do it. He spared me. He *saved* me. I had a chunk of glass in my elbow. I was bleeding and woozy. He took it out, he healed me like I've done for him all these years. He did the opposite of killing me."

"Freya–" Momma began, but I wouldn't let her finish.

"Where's Dad?" I suddenly spoke, glancing around the garage in search of my father. A hammer clipped Brennan's left elbow, earning a staggered shout from my fatigued brother. Raiden remained unphased, unblinking eyes fixated on his target as he continually thrusted objects Brennan's way. He was relentless, and like Momma said, it was only a matter of time.

The De Mörka solely evolved to extinguish the flame set alight by the Araedian people. To snuff it out, suffocate it, eradicate us.

Raiden was made to kill us.

"He's hidden upstairs with some other survivors," Momma whispered, her hot breath generating beads of sweat along the shell of my ear.

"Is Elden alive?" I questioned, refusing to tear my glare from Brennan and Raiden. I noticed Raiden's expression slightly shifting, an agitated look slithering along his face. He was growing impatient with Brennan's counter strikes, and it appeared as if he was nearing the end of his rope.

Rope.

I barely heard Momma's reply about Elden's fate over my own garish gasp. The frayed, rugged cord of an aged, red rope had coiled itself around Brennan's flushed, heaving neck. Reddened, swollen fingers desperately pulled and pried at the coarse material, but to no avail. With every gasping breath, the rope tightened, circling his neck like a vicious, venomous snake.

Mere yards away, Raiden animatedly grinned; pearly-white teeth bared as he gradually rotated his wrist, empty palm facing upwards, fingers sharply curled.

The tail of the rope wriggled and thrashed about like an eager, bloody serpent; tediously tightening itself around my brother's neck as he repugnantly wheezed. The flesh of his face began to mimic the hue of the rope, and as both my grandmother and mother began to loudly wail, Brennan's feet left the ground.

"Is this your omnipotent?" Raiden roared, a sadistic smirk spread across his lips. All the while, his unblinking stare never left his opponent.

Brennan's legs frantically kicked as he steadily rose several feet above the ground, fingers hopelessly wedged beneath the clamping rope.

"Not so powerful, is he?" Raiden lowly added, fingers playfully curling as if to beckon Brennan to him.

Come hither.

"Stop it, Raiden! You're killing him!" I screamed, prying Momma's fingers away from my arm one by one. She resorted to wrapping them both around my chest, suctioning my back to her front.

At my statement, Raiden visibly blinked; extended arm collapsing to his side. The ruby rope promptly unraveled from Brennan's throat, plummeting to the floor with a showy *smack.* The cord appeared to shrivel up and die, withering away into nothingness at Raiden's feet, evaporating up into an ashen cloud of dust.

Brennan's knees sorely smacked the ground, trembling palms urgently rubbing at his contused neck. The skin was an angry shade of red with a hint of purple, a hideous bruise blossoming to the surface, visual evidence of Raiden's supernatural assault.

"That's the *point,* Freya," Raiden replied, cocking his head to the side to observe my panicked stance. "That's what I was *bred* for, wasn't it? To eradicate the Araedian bloodline for good?"

"You aren't the De Mörka," I countered, unable to stifle the salty, angry tears as they dripped down my cheeks. "It isn't who you are. It's just a very small part of you, but it doesn't define you. You don't have to do this. You don't have to follow in your ancestors' footsteps."

Raiden snickered, the tip of his tongue lapping out to trace the smooth surface of his top front teeth. I couldn't quite get past the sight of his eyes—the cold, black abyss—but I knew that somewhere deep, deep down, those forest green eyes I'd always loved were still there. *He* was still there.

"You're just a fucking coward," Brennan said, his voice hoarse and weak. He continually rubbed at his neck, bloodshot glare glued to a cocky Raiden, who was taking large, mocking steps in his direction.

"Is that what I am, Brennan?" Raiden cooed, a sarcastic chuckle evident in his tone. He crouched before my brother, the lengthy laces of his untied boots scraping against the dirt-riddled concrete.

Raiden's curled thumb derisively stroked Brennan's brow, smearing the bubbling blood down my brother's cheek. The thick, red substance mixed with his slippery sweat, and Raiden merrily painted a sweaty, bloody painting on Brennan's cheek.

Branding him for death.

"Am I just a little coward?" Raiden jeered, brows knit together in concentration. "Would a coward kill you with his bare hands?"

Before my brother could protest, Raiden was at his throat.

Momma shouted beside my ear, a deafening ring consuming my thoughts as I watched the entire scene play out in slow motion. Brennan went from his knees to his back, frail, powerless frame trapped between the cold concrete and Raiden's hips. Although Raiden was visibly thinner than my brother, he appeared to overpower him by an immeasurable amount; for Brennan kneed and kicked and Raiden's weight barely wavered.

Raiden sat suspended over my brother, greasy, brunette curls dangling within his sight as his ring-clad fingers tightened their hold on Brennan's marred neck. I could barely make out the scene over my mother's abhorrent sobs, and I wanted nothing more than to pry my way out of her arms and yank the two men apart.

Raiden wasn't a killer. I needed to stop this. I needed to save him from succumbing to his outdated destiny.

It was time for the war to end.

I stepped out of Momma's arms with an exasperated shout, shaky legs inching towards the two men as Raiden choked Brennan within an inch of his life.

Brennan's arm dropped to his side, buzzing fingers curling inwards towards his palm as if to summon something his way. My breath hitched in my throat as the dreaded sonance arose—a weighty gasp, a brisk intake of breath, and then the ringing.

I saw the silver glimmer of a rusted chef knife for nothing more than a brief second, and then, pain.

It originated in the center of my lower back, *deep,* and I'd lost all feeling in my lower body, a buzzing numbness replacing the areas that once held my frame afloat.

I dropped to my knees, a throaty sob slipping up my throat as the pain temporarily raided my vision with a sequence of stars. I couldn't think—I couldn't move—not about anything but the pain, that was.

Until I realized that it wasn't my pain to feel.

Raiden.

Terrified, I tore my droopy eyelids open to reveal my absolute worst nightmare. Raiden had completely collapsed atop my brother, lips drooped in a dramatic o-shape, sprawled, shaking fingers reaching around to meet the broad blade wedged within the lumbar vertebrae of his spine.

Brennan wriggled around Raiden's weighty frame, a quivering arm looping around his waist to retrieve the knife. With his bottom lip pinched between his teeth in determination, he tore the old, rusted, bloody blade from Raiden's back.

With a sharp jut of his knee, Brennan maneuvered a stunned Raiden off of him, sending the curly-haired lad flat onto his side.

That was when his eyes met mine.

A glimmering emerald dipped in dew, like the morning leaves of a towering tree. The hollow black bulbs had disappeared—*vanished*—leaving their real identity in its wake.

"Raiden," I croaked, paralyzed by the pain. He was so far—easily several yards—and I needed to get to him. I needed to hold him.

I needed to heal him.

I lost sight of what my brother was doing—probably tending to my mother or our frightened, elderly grandmother, but none of that mattered, anymore. Raiden was wounded. Hurt.

Dying.

"Come to me," I muttered, just loud enough for Raiden to hear. He obeyed, dreary eyes the size of saucers as he attempted to pull himself up by his elbows. The simplistic action earned a pained shout, but nevertheless, he fought through it; gently pulling himself along the concrete with nothing but his arms.

In a desperate attempt to meet him in the middle, I did the very same, ignoring the blistering, crippling pain in my back and the numbness in my lower extremities as I quite literally dragged myself across the floor. The only thing missing was an actual wound on my body.

All the while, I refused to take my eyes off of Raiden's. He was sobbing—nearly profusely—either out of pain or fear or regret, but whatever it was, it had broken him. Immensely. I could see him struggling to move, small spasms consuming his legs as he crawled like a child towards his lover. Towards his forever.

Towards *me.*

"I'm coming," I audibly assured him, forcing a smile across my lips as I mimicked his movements. I wanted to just hop to my feet and run, but my legs refused to comply. It was as if they'd been chopped off entirely, for I could barely feel them at all.

I was getting closer to him—*so close, not much further*—and I swore that I could already feel the coolness of his rings against my skin, the soft, pillowy brush of his hair along my cheek. I wanted to nuzzle in his chest and give him every ounce of life that I had left within me.

I hadn't noticed Brennan's presence before it was too late.

The slippery, red blade punctured Raiden's back a second time, directly beside the first wound. Raiden instantaneously cried out, a lonesome tear dripping down the tip of his nose as he reached out to me, but I couldn't reach him—he was still too far. A single yard or two at most, but completely out of my reach.

The pain radiated up my spine once more, sending blood up the slope of my esophagus as I spat it up. My actions directly mirrored Raiden's, for he too had fresh, bright blood dribbling down his chin, intermixing with his fearful tears.

"Brennan, *stop!*" I weakly begged, but the rage within my brother's eyes was undeniable.

He wouldn't stop until the deed was done.

"I have–I have to *heal–*"

Another blow to the back.

My elbows collapsed, sending my jaw to the floor with a painful *crack.* I bit back a moan as Brennan tore blade from flesh, sending specks of blood splattering across the floor like the start of a cryptic painting.

I craned my neck, desperate to see if Raiden was all right. He was saying my name, but I could barely hear it, for the ringing in my ears had intensified, and I was seconds away from vomiting up a mixture of alcohol and blood.

I whispered his name through tears in the form of a plea—*please, baby, come to me, just a little bit further*—but he never got the chance.

Brennan's swollen fingers knotted within Raiden's scalp, gathering a considerable bunch of curls as he aggressively yanked the bloodied man's head upright. I watched in utter silence as my brother positioned himself on Raiden's maimed backside, his hold tightening on Raiden's hair as my mother called out Brennan's name.

In that moment, time seemed to stop entirely. It was just Raiden and I, watery eyes locked on one another's, blood dribbling down our chins in a matching fashion. I swore that I could see his anxious, racing heart drumming against the pale flesh of his neck—a neck that I'd peppered kisses along just this morning. He told me that he loved me with nothing but a stare, and as I opened my mouth to whisper the words back, Brennan brought the blade down to Raiden's unmarred throat.

no

Blood spilled from Raiden's neck like a faucet, saturating the skin of his fingers as he feebly attempted to cease the bleeding.

no no no

I opened my mouth to speak—to *beg*—but I choked on my own breath. I felt lightheaded—*woozy*—and all I could think about, all I could *see* was him.

With one hand, I massaged my aching throat, whereas the other reached out towards Raiden, desperate to hold him, desperate to feel him.

With the little strength that he could muster, his bloody fingers reached out towards me, his favored Medusa ring saturated with ruby red blood. The ring animatedly sparkled beneath the weeping artificial lights as he inaudibly begged to hold my hand.

I love you.

Our fingers barely brushed in a final act of affection, and I felt my eyes definitively roll up into my skull.

FIVE MONTHS LATER

It smelled like him.

With lazy, unblinking eyes, I stared at the burning cigarette pinched between my fingers. It was the same brand he always smoked—Newport. I refused to buy any other kind, for they simply weren't the same.

I let the ash collect along the length of the unsmoked cigarette, just as I always had. Sometimes I took an empty hit or two to keep it going—*keep it burning*—but today, it seemed to start all on its own, as if the fire in my soul had ignited the tobacco within.

It was a hot, muggy day, and I could already feel the beads of sweat accumulating on the rear of my neck. I pulled the cigarette closer to my nose—inhaled its toxic fumes—and loudly exhaled in a sigh of relief, for the warm, familiar scent was enough to bring me home.

"Get your damn feet off the table," Zoey slurred, shoving my legs sideways and off of the rusted, rickety metal table. The abrupt movement prompted the ash to spill over, showering my lap in a profusion of miniature burnt embers and cloudy dust.

With a bitter huff, I dug the soles of my stolen shoes into the dirt, gaze cast downward in a weak attempt to avoid my coworker's nosy stare. She always had something to say about my *peculiar habits.* On more than one occasion, she'd accused me of wasting cigarettes and even snatched them from my fingers in order to finish them off herself.

She collapsed against the mangled metal back of the chair opposite me, pale cheeks flushed and pink. "Wasting another cigarette?"

Yup.

"Cheltsey's been asking about you. Another article was posted about that night, it's all over social media again. Talk of the town," Zoey added, scrolling through her phone. I refused to look her in the face. Instead, I studied the old, dried blood caked along the side of my pink Chuck Taylors, the very same I stole off of a dead girl.

I liked to wear them. They reminded me that it was all real.

"Birthday blaze claims 46," Zoey announced, bottom lip pulled between her brace-riddled teeth. "I know you don't like to talk about it, but I always wonder what happened that night. No one really knows. The other survivors won't speak. It's like this big, huge secret."

"Peter! Come carry Freya, she keeps going in and out of consciousness," Momma called, audibly struggling to drag my rigid frame along the floor.

I blinked several times, desperately attempting to rid my sight of the large, blotchy spots. The sensation in my lower body had returned, and the pain had seemingly ceased—as well as the feeling of Raiden entirely.

"I can't feel him," I mumbled, panic bubbling up within my chest. I felt my father lift me up bridal style, my neck lolled sideways as I lay in a defeated heap within his arms. He'd whispered a series of affirmations in my ear, a

salty tear colliding with my cheek as Brennan loudly wailed from somewhere nearby. He kept calling Grammy's name, and as badly as I wanted to wriggle out of my father's arms—to jump up and move—*I felt weighted down.*

Heavy.

Numb.

"Brennan, are the rest of the survivors out?" Momma pressed. I saw several blurred shapes rush past my sight, and then the fuzzy outline of Weatherby's estate.

Dad must've moved us to the front lawn.

"Everyone's here and accounted for," a voice replied, one that I paired with Brennan's boyfriend, Elden.

So, he had survived.

"I need you to set fire to the house, Bren."

"Freya?" Zoey called, snapping her fingers in front of my face. I resisted the urge to smack her intrusive hand away, and with a slow blink, I bent over and put out my cigarette on the sidewalk. The aged, creaky chair wobbled and whined, and I tossed the cigarette aside without a second thought. It landed somewhere in the mass of overgrown weeds, joining the growing pile of garbage and filth mere feet before the dumpster.

"I don't understand why we can't smoke out front. It smells like a sewer out here," I hissed, pulling my hair into a bun.

"You know how Cheltsey is ever since she inherited the hotel." Zoey shrugged, mindlessly scrolling through her cell phone. She took note of my antisocial attitude and resisted the urge to stare me in the face. *"No smoking, no pets, no drugs, no orgies."*

"I'm pretty sure the guests do all of those things just to spite her," I muttered, running the pad of my thumb along the shiny, silver chain strung around my neck. Buried beneath my shirt was its charm—Raiden's recognizable Medusa ring, buffed and polished and rid of all the blood. It looked brand new, but I almost wish that it hadn't.

I should've worn his blood around my neck.

"I guess I'll get back to work." The statement emerged as a sigh, and Zoey merely nodded, waving in my direction as I kicked the back door of building six open.

Sunflower Inn was as cringy as the name suggested, and even though a thirty-three year old named Cheltsey Fox had tried her best to turn things around in the past two months since her father's demise, not much had changed. It was still a low-rate motel, sixty bucks a night, and it attracted all sorts of individuals, locals and travelers alike. Cheltsey's entire first week as acting manager and owner was spent ridding the older rooms of the freeloaders, most of which were high or drunk. She even found the start of a meth lab in building four.

I was going on month four of employment here at the Sunflower. It wasn't much, but the pay was decent, and I didn't have to deal with the direct public. Most of the guests were absent when I did my rounds, and I had quite a bit of freedom to take as much time as I needed. I usually stuck my earbuds in and just cleaned.

I enjoyed cleaning. I felt as if I were washing away the sins of my past. I felt normal doing it, like a real human being.

Lately, that's all I was.

After that dreadful night—*that scarlet Sunday*—I vowed never to heal another person. So far, five months in, I'd kept true to that vow. Not only for myself, but for Raiden, and Grammy, and all of the others who died that night.

"We need to wake up Freya, she needs to go back in there and heal Grammy!" Brennan cried, distressed hands buried in his hair. I lifted my head slightly at the sound of my name, and my father outwardly cooed, ensuring me that it was all going to be okay.

"Just rest, baby. It'll be all over soon."

I caught a glimpse of my mother taking hold of a weeping Brennan, a stern expression plastered across her features as she repeated her orders.

"I k-killed Raiden," my brother wept. "I can't kill Grammy, too."

"You need to listen to me, Brennan. This is something you need to do. Do you hear me?" Momma countered, trying her absolute best to contain her composure. "Set the fucking house on fire."

The carpet in building six was the oldest of the bunch. Buildings one through three were newly renovated, the musty maroon carpets ripped up and replaced with light gray laminate flooring in both the hallways and suites. By building six, the flooring budget had dried up, leaving the old, outdated floors and furniture completely untouched. Six was only used in the event of a full house, and most of the time, Sunflower Inn never booked past the fourth building.

Unbeknownst to a preppy Cheltsey, Zoey was living at the very back of the forgotten building. The carpet in her room reeked of piss and cigarettes, and the mattress box spring held several gaping holes. She didn't seem to mind, for it was better than crashing on a coworker's couch.

On multiple occasions, I debated letting her stay with me, but ever since Raiden's untimely departure, our townhome was considerably sad. Dishes piled up in the sink for so long that the water within the tiny reservoirs began to sprout mold. I tossed most of those dishes out once they grew fuzzy, for the sight of mold alone was enough to turn my stomach sour, but the effort it took to clean them made my motivation nearly nonexistent after I got home from work.

Brennan offered me his second bedroom, but with the dogs, it would be just too much. Instead, I stayed in my personal hell—surrounded by countless memories of my sweetheart, a consistent string of hurt that slapped me in the face every time I walked through the front door.

Last month, Momma began stopping by during my work day to clean up around the place. I hated that she went out of her way to clean up my messes, but deep down, I appreciated her for it. She knew I was mourning—*grieving*—and she even offered to help pay for my rent, so I could stay home instead of work. I'd politely declined on multiple occasions, for spending too much time in those lonesome four walls would propel me into utter madness.

When I located my cleaning cart in building four, I was met with three missed calls from my brother. It had been weeks since he'd tried contacting me, for all of his past attempts had resulted in failure.

I simply could not bring myself to speak to him. Every time his face flashed before my eyes, I saw that rabid, angry look in his eyes—the blood dripping down the knife, the spatter smeared across his cheeks, the walls engulfed in flames.

The wheels on my cart were creaky and old, and one of them constantly spun in infinite circles. I was low on glass cleaner and Hohen forgot to wash my rags this morning, so I was making do with what I had, which was barely anything at all. Hohen was our laundry guy, and when he wasn't chain smoking behind the washers, he was arguing with his wife on the phone. Although it wasn't one of my assigned duties, I debated doing my own laundry to ensure that it was all done on time.

I learned pretty quickly that you could only count on yourself here at Sunflower.

Momma called while I was scraping a wad of strawberry red bubblegum off the underside of 403's desk, a peeved groan slipping off of my lips as I balanced the phone between my shoulder and my ear.

"Yeah, Momma?"

"Did I catch you at a bad time?" Momma's tiny tone was barely discernible over the significant gap between my shoulder and my ear, and with a huff, I fell to my bottom, steadying the cell against my ear.

"Just scraping some gum off a desk. Better than stepping on a used condom. What do you need?"

With a curved wrist, I wiped the sweat from my brow, the glob of gum staring me straight in the face. Teasing me. Mocking me.

You'll never catch me.

"Brennan's been trying to contact you. I know you probably aren't ready to talk to him, but he has some big news," Momma revealed. I could hear Kelso whining in the background, probably at the sound of my voice.

"I'm not having the best day," I murmured. It wasn't entirely a lie, but then again, I'd been having bad days every day for almost half a year now. "Could we talk about it another time? I'm sure it can wait."

"Brennan and Elden are having a baby."

My stomach fluttered at her words.

My brother is having a baby.

"They're arranging for a surrogate mother?" I questioned, giving up on the gum. I felt each and every bone in my leg blatantly crack as I stood to my feet, and I wondered if I still had a bottle of Tylenol stored somewhere on my cart.

"Not just arranging for one, they've got her, and she's tested positive! She's nine weeks, Frey! You're going to be an Auntie. Brennan's chosen to keep the Araedian legacy alive, regardless of his sexuality. It's amazing, isn't it?" I could practically see my mother gleaming through the phone, a broad, toothy grin etched along her mouth as she kept my dogs company while I was away for the day.

"It's amazing news," I admitted, eyes glossing over with tears. "The best news I've heard in months, actually. Do they have some names picked out? Or am I getting ahead of myself?"

"That's the thing, actually," Momma replied, giggling slightly. "Brennan and Elden have agreed that they want *you* to name the baby."

I felt my heart leap up into my throat.

"He's just doing this so I forgive him for killing Raiden," I muttered, barely audible enough for my mother to hear. Unfortunately, she caught every single word.

"You know that isn't true. He wants you to name his child because you're his *sister,* and he loves you. It's nothing about forgiveness. He knows that's something you'll never forgive him for. He's accepted that."

A single, weighty tear dropped down the curve of my cheek. I thought about Raiden—the terrified, torturous look in his eye as my brother's fingers clamped around his curls, yanking, *pulling* his head up, revealing his smooth, silken throat, slicing it open with an aged, rusted blade.

I swallowed a mouthful of bile as my mother called out my name, and I resisted the urge to completely come undone in the middle of an empty hotel room.

"I have to go, Momma," I croaked, exiting the room and returning to my cart in the hall. "I'll see you later, if you're still at my place."

Before she could reply, I'd abruptly ended the call; a grief-stricken sob spilling off of my lips as my palm suctioned to my mouth, silencing the sound almost instantly. I glanced around at my surroundings—an empty hallway—and breathed a sigh of relief. The last thing I wanted today was to make awkward eye contact with an unexpecting guest, who would probably report my bizarre actions to the front desk.

A weeping housekeeper in building four has disrupted my joyful mood!

I buried my phone beneath a stack of cherry red towels, resisting the urge to toss it onto the floor and stomp it into a million pieces. I didn't want anyone to call—I didn't want anyone to speak.

Maybe, I just no longer wanted to exist.

I pulled 403's door closed and moved on. I glanced upwards just in time to view the shape of a person emerging from 404, awkwardly stuffing their keycard into the torn denim pocket of their jeans. My heart dropped when the woman twisted around on her heel, a staggering array of glass claiming her face.

Scarlet.

My knees nearly buckled as I blankly stared, watering eyes fixated on the beads of blood dripping from her lacerated features. She nodded my way, completely expressionless as she put one foot forward and nonchalantly strode past, not even bothering to glance over her shoulder when I cocked my head to watch her pass.

I blinked twice, and she was gone.

She was nothing but a phantom. A figment of my imagination. A harsh reminder of the atrocity I'd witnessed half a year prior.

Swallowing a mouthful of bile, I pressed on—passing by 405, 406, and 407. All of them had the *Do Not Disturb* tag looped around the door handle, and I could've sworn that I heard the constant creak of old bed springs behind door number 405.

At noon on a Tuesday?

With a scoff, I continued onward; parking my cart in front of 408. I couldn't quite shake the thought of Scarlet's ghost from my mind as I dipped my hand into the slack front pocket of my vest, retrieving my universal key card before forcing open the door. Although cluttered and slightly messy, the room appeared unoccupied.

Thank the heavens.

I breathed a sigh of relief and propped open the door with an old wooden stopper. My Bluetooth earbuds were buried beneath a new set of pillowcases, and after some peeved searching, I eventually located both buds. I put on some tranquil, ambient tunes. Raiden used to love listening to instrumental melodies. They inspired him, but also made him comfortable and cozy. He particularly favored the genre during times where he felt vastly stressed, and the tunes always seemed to calm his spirits.

My forefinger coiled around the silver chain draped along my neck, and with a slight tug, the unique pendant appeared from the cavern of my shirt. I ran my fingertips along the grooves of Raiden's old ring, quivering lips pulled into a frown as I brought the stunning silver object to my mouth. I planted a tiny kiss along the surface before concealing the memorabilia once more, hiding it from view as if to keep it all to myself.

It was the inability to feel Raiden's emotions that made me feel nearly lifeless. Without his soul tethered to mine, I felt like a hollow, meaningless shell.

Barren.

The king-sized bed was a miserable mess, snowy white sheets crinkled and clustered in the lower left corner. Two out of five pillows were forgotten on the floor, a multitude of curious dust bunnies frolicking about the faux wooden surfaces as I swayed my feet from side to side. They must've taken refuge under the bed, only to resurface when the housekeeper arrived for another cleaning.

"You pesky little demons," I grumbled, dismissively kicking the balls of dust beneath the bed. "You're someone else's problem."

I mindlessly did my duties, replacing the worn sheets and pillowcases, fluffing them up, making them appear brand new. The tiny trash can was filled to the brim with to-go cartons, and to my pure, utter luck, a half-drunk bottle of dark soda toppled from the can as I emptied it, spilling onto my shoes and soaking into my socks.

A low curse eased off of my lips, and with a bitter groan, I fell to my knees, desperately attempting to rid the cloth of the sticky liquid.

Just my luck.

The en-suite bathrooms were inconveniently placed at the rear of the rooms, and I usually saved them for last. Typically the guests treated the restrooms the worst, leaving piss stains on the seats, balls of toilet paper on the floor, and empty toiletries used up and forgotten at the base of the shower. Judging by the state of the room, I figured I would be met with a similar state of messiness in the lavatory.

I caught wind of a scribbly note on the surface of the sticky desk as I wiped it clean. It was uncommon for a guest to use the hotel notepads, and even more peculiar for them to tear off a used sheet, fold it up, and place it in the center of the table, as if it were aching to be found. Beside it was a bible, old leather cover worn and torn, the very one found beside each and every bed throughout the establishment.

With raised brows, I eyed the single sheet. OPEN ME was scrawled along the center, the penmanship muddled and messy, as if rushed. I brushed the bible aside, my curious focus glued upon the note. Nosily, I pried the paper open, dropping the used, blue rag atop the surface of the desk beside the book of God.

sorry for the mess

A tiny chuckle tickled my tongue as I turned the paper over, inquisitively searching for another note. Alas, there was none—and I was left moderately amused.

"It's fine. I've seen worse," I announced. I placed it back where I found it—opened up to reveal its contents—before finishing off the desk and returning to my cart for my bathroom supplies.

I grabbed hold of a trio of unwrapped toiletries—a single shampoo, body wash, and bar soap—along with a pearly, white towel snug beneath my armpit. The bathroom door was closed—which wasn't unusual, most guests preferred it that way when they were away—but the moment my fingertips danced along the doorknob, I felt it. A miniature flame boiling beneath the skin, waltzing across the flesh of my fingers. With a hiss, I pulled my hand away, eyes widening as I observed my warm, tingling hand.

Something was wrong.

The towel and toiletries tumbled to my feet, the bottle of shampoo rolling off to the side and disappearing beneath the desk. My pulse immediately quickened, violently pounding against my ribcage. I felt sluggish and slow, head sorely spinning as I snatched the door handle and twisted it open.

What I witnessed within was unlike anything I'd ever seen inside Sunflower Inn's old, outdated walls. The blood instantly pummeled me back five months—transporting my warped, miserable mind back to the very day that my entire life changed forever. I could still smell the blood, the death, the *rot.* I caught whiffs of it when I was laying in bed, desperately attempting to sleep, but ultimately turning to the assistance of over-the-counter sleep medication.

I could see the stranger called Scarlet, a galaxy of glass permanently placed within her face. Although I hadn't witnessed it myself, I could clearly visualize the mighty, blue flames that frolicked along the crystal; the roaring image in her empty eyes as the fire reduced her to nothing but ash and dust.

My eyes cautiously followed the trail of bloody, balled-up tissues, which led a winding path to a woman I'd never seen before. She appeared to be thirty at most, with stunning, shiny brown skin and the brightest, most beautiful auburn eyes. They met mine with a mixture of guilt and fear, her swollen, chapped bottom lip quivering as my stare dropped down to meet her wrists.

A duo of dissimilar gashes marred her wrists, weeping with blood, crying big, bulbous tears. Her bottom and legs were sodden—*soaked*—as if she'd taken a dip in a ruby red pool. The puddle gradually grew, and I stumbled into the bathroom as she spewed a series of apologies my way, her head shaking back and forth as if to banish my unwanted presence.

"I didn't mean for you to see this," she sobbed. "It's taking too long."

I dropped to my knees beside her, the lopsided tiles throwing my balance off as I blinked back furious tears. I'd encountered enough death to last a lifetime, and here I was, less than half a year later, living through it once more.

"I said I wouldn't do it," I muttered, winding my fingers around her weeping wrist. "I promised myself I'd never heal another fucking person."

The stranger swallowed her sobs, perplexed tears trickling down the apples of her cheeks as she questioned my statement. She delicately attempted to pull away, but I tightened my hold on her arm, causing her to cry out in pain.

"Look at me," I demanded, softening my tone. I didn't want to overwhelm her.

Timidly, she met my glare, bloodshot orbs fixated on my determined gaze as I forced my lips into a smile.

"Tell me your name."

"Sarah," she said, unable to control the spasms that wracked through her arm. Her lips parted in preparation to speak once more, but I watched as her words eluded her, and she teetered the edge of consciousness. The careless cuts convinced me that even she was unsure of what she wanted—life or death. Ultimately, it seems, after trying to hinder the flow with balled-up toilet paper (and unfortunately failing), she'd given up and accepted her inevitable fate.

Only, fate wasn't always so certain.

"I couldn't heal them," I began, referencing the nearly fifty lives lost on the eve of Brennan's birthday. "But I can heal you. I can *save* you."

Defying my oath, I claimed each of her wrists in open palms, eyelids easing shut as I focused my energy on nothing but her. *Sarah.* The stranger who reminded me of who I am, of what I'm capable of.

Of what I was born to do.

The ruffled skin against my palms promptly sealed, smooth and fresh, as if it were the flesh of an infant. Sarah let out a tiny whine, and when I finally opened my eyes, I was met with a stunned stare.

With a nod, I dropped her wrists, silently watching as she studied the enclosed surface. The blood was still present—smeared along her arms and puddled around her like a liquid rug. It was the only confirmation that the event had even occurred at all.

She took one look at me before drifting into unconsciousness, presumably from a mixture of blood loss and shock.

I wasted no time in guaranteeing her life and safety. Crimson shoe prints followed me all the way to the corded hotel phone, smears of scarlet saturating the buttons, dripping into the cracks, solidifying their presence for an eternity.

Cheltsey was there in minutes, a horror-stricken shout cascading up her throat as she observed the blood smudged all along my hands and clothes. She had yet to see her unconscious guest in the shower, but I prepared myself for the obnoxious sound that would emerge when she did. Her reaction would catch the attention of the entire building, and nosy neighbors would surely snoop, desperate for a single glance at the scene.

"Jesus *Christ,* Freya! What happened?" Cheltsey demanded, a shaking palm hovering her heart. As expected, she imitated a pitiful teenage girl in a horror film, and I couldn't help but walk right out of the room when she'd disappeared into the bathroom.

I'd dealt with enough for a single day. Cheltsey could puzzle the pieces together on her own.

Only, how could anyone explain what I'd just done?

As calmly and coolly as I could, I shuffled through my rags in search of my cell, dialing my mother's number as quickly as my trembling fingers could type, and I told her the news.

"You can't tell the police what actually happened," Momma pressed. "Lie. Come up with something, anything. Say you don't remember."

"She knows I healed her, Momma. There's a ton of blood and no wounds," I whispered. Cheltsey rounded the corner once more in search of me, and I nearly dropped the phone at the sight of her. "Gotta go."

"Freya! There's so much blood, and she's conscious and alive and I can't find the source of the bleeding. She's all jumbled, can barely speak! The ambulance needs to hurry the hell up! This stuff doesn't happen at Sunflower . . . it just doesn't . . ."

Didn't a homeless man die from a heroin overdose in building five last year?

I bit my tongue, snatching a red rag from my cart as I awkwardly attempted to erase the evidence from my skin. My hands burned at the thought of what I'd done, and although I could've possibly blown my cover, I felt happy. *Relieved.*

I'd done for one woman what I wished I could've done on that night. I was robbed of the chance of healing anyone that day, but today, nothing stood in my way. I didn't stumble upon this woman by chance. We crossed paths for a reason.

A purpose.

I openly scoffed at my racing thoughts, for they reminded me of the pep talks my mother used to give me as a teenager. *Everything happens for a reason, figlia. You have a purpose in this world.*

"Cheltsey, is it alright if I go home? Considering what I survived this year already, I'm a bit traumatized that I stumbled upon this today. All of the blood triggers me," I said. It wasn't completely a lie, but the thought of giving a statement to the police was enough to make my skin crawl. After all, what could I possibly say to them without raising suspicion?

"Oh, *no,* Freya. You have to give a statement to the police! We have to do paperwork! Someone almost *died* in my hotel, Freya! This is serious, there's so much to do . . ." Cheltsey slurred, shaking her head from side to side as she paced the hallway. Curious guests began to trickle in, and I was suddenly *very* aware of the blood caked along my clothing.

"Cheltsey, go sit in there with her. Her name is Sarah. Make sure she's okay. Give her some water, keep her company. I'll get rid of the nosy guests," I fibbed, gently urging my boss back into the room. With a sigh, she agreed, pleading that I say as little as possible to the other visitors, at least until the authorities arrived.

They wouldn't even know that I was there.

Grabbing a fresh folded sheet from my cart, I looped it around my front, carefully concealing the drying blood that stained my clothes. I managed to sneak past most onlookers, their inquisitive stares meeting my downcast glare for only a moment as I hurried by.

I carried the linens with me all the way to my car, which was parked parallel to the dumpster in the rear of building six. It was around the same spot where I sat with my cigarettes, and although I was somewhat used to the foul scent of the trash, I felt my stomach overturn as I helplessly gagged beside my passenger door, the sheet slipping from my fingers and exposing the evidence.

Zoey, who was unfortunately still on her break, witnessed my momentary lapse in strength, and with big, boggling eyes, she kicked the chair out from under her and took several steps in my direction.

"Shit." The curse slipped off my tongue in the form of a hiss; a tedious tremor overcoming my arms as I swiftly gathered the soiled linens.

"Freya? Is that blood?" Zoey called, rapidly approaching my sinful frame. I felt the bile steadily rise in my throat with every lengthy step she took.

"No, it's just paint," I boldly lied, tearing open the driver's side door. "I spilled some-*uh,* paint."

"We don't have red paint, Freya. That's fucking *blood,*" my coworker countered, brows furrowed together in terror. She brought her cell to her ear, presumably phoning the police. I choked down the overbearing lump of bile as my elderly vehicle roared to life.

I was out of the parking lot before Zoey could even report what she'd seen.

Halfway home, I recalled the fact that Cheltsey had my address on file, and I pulled over to empty the contents of my stomach along a concrete curb.

Momma was waiting for me at the door, a bubblegum pink bob framing her face. She seemed entirely too calm, all things considered, and I couldn't help but shout directly in her face.

"The cops are probably on their way to arrest me, *how* are you this calm?" I seethed, tearing the gory clothing from my slick skin until I was left in nothing but a bra and panties within my front foyer. The dogs were all over my outfit, curious noses poking and prodding at each and every inch.

"Freya, relax. *Fottuto inferno,*" Momma mewed, collecting my clothes from the floor without a second thought. "Have you forgotten what I can do?"

I stilled, realization slowly settling in.

Duh.

"Jesus, Momma. You should've told me the second I called you that you would take care of it. I'm so traumatized and triggered that my mind is completely warped. I genuinely thought I'd spend tonight in a cell, I thought of every possible way to explain how I did what I did." I rambled, unable to suppress the tears that snuck past my lids.

"Sweetheart, I'm sorry," my mother murmured, bundling my clothing into a taut ball within her arms. "Let me toss these in the wash and we can talk a little more. I'll make some quesadillas, if you want."

"I was supposed to go to Lakeview after work," I muttered, scratching Kelso's head. "To see Raiden's parents."

"I won't keep you long," Momma assured, disappearing down the hall towards the laundry closet. "But you need a little time to calm down and get something in your belly."

Momma was sure not to dodge any details when it came to her retelling of today's events. Before she even covered the basics, she told me how proud she was of me, smothering me in an abundance of kisses until I was red in the face. She knew of the personal oath I'd taken after Raiden and Grammy's death, and although I worked as hard as I could to stick to that promise, I knew in my heart that the stranger had to be saved.

"You can tell she was unsure of her choice," Momma said, snatching a cheesy triangle from my plate. A begging Mimosa nearly stole the food right from her fingers, and earned herself a flick on her wet, black nose. "The cuts weren't necessarily shallow, but they weren't deep enough. Grammy would've been proud of you, today."

"I know we don't believe in the traditional Heaven or Hell, but do you think Raiden and Grammy are together somewhere?" I weakly wondered, swallowing thickly at the thought of my loved ones. I still wasn't exactly sure why Grammy died, but my family made it known that what she did was heroic. She saved the others, ultimately injured herself in the process, and that was that. It didn't seem right in the slightest, but nothing about the night was right. Nothing about it made sense.

I was met with a pearly-white grin as Momma nodded, reassuring me that the two people I loved and missed most were at peace with one another.

"Your Grammy loved Raiden dearly, you know. She thought of him as one of her own. She'd always hoped the two of you would end up together, and she nearly burst into tears at Brennan's party when she and I talked about it. She would do anything for that boy, you know. *Anything.*"

"I know," I whispered, poking my forefinger into the golden brown surface of the tortilla. "Do you ever feel guilty about helping her kill an innocent girl?"

Momma's face fell at my mention of her.

Gunora Falk.

We were all completely convinced that Gunora was the De Mörka. So much so that my own Grandmother orchestrated an entire assassination, only to realize in the end that the real enemy was the one sleeping in my bed.

Grammy wasn't the one to personally slice Gunora's throat wide open, but made sure the job got done right. He was some kind of hitman—I only thought they existed in the movies, but I was proven otherwise—and my grandmother had been working closely with him ever since the day I crossed paths with the odd, pasty-skinned girl at the fertility clinic. The assassin tried to back out after discovering Gunora's family tree, but my family promised to pay him extra, only to wipe his memory clean the second he slit her throat, all thanks to my talented mother and her exquisite manipulation of time.

Nevertheless, our little executioner still got his pay—a hefty stack of bills in his mailbox, a return address absent. Criminals like him wouldn't question it, and he probably slipped the envelope into his coat the second his forefinger slid along the curve of the bills.

"I don't want to discuss Gunora," my mother muttered, picking at the loose skin around her lively yellow nails. She was due for a fill. "I've done everything I can to clear my conscience. You know it's not easy erasing death. It almost always ends in tragedy once again. You remember the story of my childhood friend, right? Death does not like to be cheated."

"Yes, I remember."

She stole another piece of my food. I ended up handing the entire plate over to her, insisting that I was finished. She tried to argue that I needed to eat more—*a full belly is a happy belly*—and I simply chuckled, reminding her of my age. I could be in my sixties and she'd still treat and talk to me like I'm a child at times.

Although I wanted to continue our conversation about Gunora's unfortunate end, I bit my tongue, knowing all too well that upsetting my mother would earn me some angry phone calls from both Dad and Brennan.

"I'm going to get ready for Lakeview," I announced, pressing a quick kiss to each of my dog's heads. The three of them were overjoyed by my presence, and I felt slightly guilty about leaving them for a second time today.

Just as I excused myself to the hallway in search of my purse and keys, my gaze landed upon something I'd once locked away—and for good reason.

Raiden's twinkly-eyed stare met mine through a pane of glass; his big, broad smile smacking me clean across the face.

I tore the framed photograph off of the wall before I could even process its presence, a violent, sorrowful shake enclosing my spine. I rabidly shook, resisting the urge to smash the frame into a million pieces as my mother's full name rolled off of my tongue.

She found the photo pinched between reddened fingers, a stupefied stare slapped along her features. She feigned confusion, demanding to know what was wrong, and I could barely spit the words out without lacing them in vicious, spiteful venom.

"Stay out of my shit," I said, enunciating each word individually. I tossed the memory of Raiden and I into the drawer, taking one last look at the pleasant smiles etched along all of our faces. Even the dogs looked absolutely delighted to be alive at that time.

"Freya, I just thought it would be nice to have it out again. You don't need to erase his existence. This house doesn't even look like it belonged to him, anymore," Momma politely pressed, edging towards the drawer.

"Momma, I swear to God, if I come home and see that picture on the wall one more time, I'll leave it on your doorstep in a million pieces."

Utterly appalled, my mother tossed her hands up in defeat, backing herself up flat against the wall as I collected my things. I bid her farewell with a mouth full of spite, and I barely caught the tail-end of her proclamation of love as I stormed out of the door.

With Raiden's jolly, lively face fresh in my mind, I began my journey towards the one place I dreaded most.

twenty-three

The girl at the front desk was new.

I could tell just by the empty void behind her eyes. She was completely clueless, and she could barely work the computer. She had no idea who Ethel even was, and when I asked about the old receptionist called Baylor, she only shook her head, insisting that she'd never heard that name before.

I was almost relieved to see my saving grace—the little old lady called Nettie—who had rolled up to the desk, the wheels of her chair irksomely squeaking.

"I know, the damn things need to be greased," Nettie said with a wave of her hand, as if she could hear my thoughts. She craned her neck to view the tense lady behind the desk, the loose, wrinkled flesh of her throat visibly vibrating with every word. "New kid, I know this lovely lady. She's here to see Ethel, though you probably don't have a damn inkling of who that is. I'll take it from here, you just sit pretty and pretend to know what you're doing."

I choked back a chuckle as the new employee noticeably paled, shaking fingers struggling to peel a GUEST sticker from the paper. She handed it over to me with a shy grin, and I bid her a good day, because Lord knows she needed it.

"Thanks, Nettie." I smiled, making a beeline for room 403B. I walked away before she could bring up Raiden, because everyone *always* brought him up.

—Oh, Raiden was such a lovely boy—

—such a good man—

—a beautiful, kind spirit—

—he's with you always—

—I'm praying for you—

I nearly gagged at the thought of the exhausting well wishes that I was bound to encounter. My knees went weak as the grief washed over me, and for a split second, I wondered if I even had the strength to look at his parents in the face. To see the people who unknowingly raised an ancient, mythical being created solely to destroy myself and my lineage. My fingers looped through the silver chain wrapped around my neck, the pad of my thumb tracing circles around the unique curves of Raiden's Medusa ring.

I hadn't even realized that I was idling in Ethel's doorway until an achingly familiar tone jerked me out of my temporary trance.

"We can go in together, if you want."

My bottom lip trembled as I met the charming blue gaze of Stephen Crow. His thick-rimmed glasses magnified his watery eyes to nearly twice their normal size, and he had crow's feet so deep and prominent that they surely held nests full of eggs just waiting to hatch.

He looked worn and haggard, bloated fingers curled around a chestnut cane. Smoking aged him profusely within the past ten years, and although he was sure to succumb to some form of lung cancer within the next half decade, he seemed shockingly chipper and full of life.

"It's so good to see you, Mr. Crow." I couldn't quite hide the silly smile that snaked across my mouth, and he instantly matched my expression, pulling me in for a single arm hug.

"Likewise, Freya. You know you can call me Stephen now, right? You're not a little kid anymore."

"I have to admit, it's just a bit too weird. Should we go and see Ethel?" I wondered, trailing my clammy palms along the surface of my jeans. I couldn't help but dread the simple mention of his name, but I knew that it was inevitable, especially around his own parents.

"I have yet to see her today. The nurses have told me that she's having a good memory day, so I'm really looking forward to seeing what she says and possibly remembers." Stephen gleamed, clearly excited to spend time with his wife. I had always adored their relationship, but at the moment, the long-lived romance made my stomach twist into aching knots.

Raiden and I would never have that.

Ethel was seated on her sofa, slowly sipping some kind of vegetable soup. She was dressed in a stunning, floral, floor-length dress, one which completely covered the tips of her toes. I could immediately tell that she was having a good day, for she was up and out of bed, which was a *huge* accomplishment for the woman. Most days, she could hardly crawl off of her mattress.

"My sweetest Ethel," Stephen cheered, the tedious *tick tick tick* of his cane generating a sequence of anxious goosebumps to arise upon my flesh. I felt like running—*hiding*—burying myself in the dirt, disappearing for an eternity.

Ethel's features brightened at the sight of our presence, and to my complete surprise, she recognized me almost instantaneously.

"Freya?"

The walls came tumbling down.

I felt the dams burst, releasing an overbearing amount of emotion that I'd recently locked away. Hot tears stained my skin, blinding my vision as I stumbled towards the sofa and melted like butter in Ethel's arms.

I buried my nose in her chest and wept, soft, sweet coos cascading over my ears as the elderly woman held me close. Stephen leaned over to comfort me as well, rubbing haphazard circles against my upper back, as I trembled from head to toe.

I wasn't sure what I expected today, but Ethel recognizing me and calling me by my name was not even a possibility in my mind. But oh, what a wonderful woman she was, and she always had a bag of tricks up her sleeve. When you doubted her most, she surprised you in the absolute best way.

I loved her like she was a second mother to me.

With words unspoken, the three of us enjoyed one another's company, exchanging occasional rounds of laughter at the unnamed show on the television. Ethel held me close the entire time, refusing to lessen her hold, as if I would simply wither away without her loving embrace.

Raiden's ring slipped out of my shirt, tickling the soft, wrinkled skin of Ethel's forearm. With piqued curiosity, she reached down to view the object, claiming it with weak fingers.

"This is Raiden's, isn't it?" she asked, holding it up for Stephen to view.

"I'm sure it is, Eth. You know he was always a fan of eccentrics. Remember when he used to sneak into your jewelry box and wear your rings?" Stephen said, a small smile curling along his thin lips. "He was always so nicely dressed, even when he had those secondhand rags because it was all we could afford at the time. He tried so hard to dress them up, to look nice."

"He took pride in his appearance," I chimed in, watching Ethel closely as she turned the ring over in her palm. I felt protective of it—*give it back*—but instead of snatching the object away, I let her observe.

After all, it had belonged to her son.

"He used to keep a hair brush in his school backpack," Ethel added, slipping the ring into my palm. She curled my fingers around the jewelry, entrapping it in a warm, welcoming cocoon.

"I miss him," I whispered, burying the necklace back beneath my shirt. The ring settled just above my heart.

Ethel released a curious gasp, arms unraveling from my lithe frame as she stood to her feet. She wobbled slightly, and Stephen extended an arm, steadying his wife's weight.

"What is it, Eth?"

Ethel avoided his question, a series of inaudible statements slipping off of her lips as she limped towards her bed. She was a woman on a mission, and as Stephen and I exchanged bewildered glances, she continued onward, the tips of her fingers trailing along the foot of her mattress for support. She arrived at her bedside table, the very one that held a framed photograph from Raiden's high school graduation. If I closed my eyes, I could still see his itty bitty frame swallowed up by the baggy gown, the cap crooked atop his curls.

"Come here, Freya. My legs don't work like they used to," Ethel announced, leaning her weight against the curve of the bed. When I met her side, I was met with a shiny silver urn, a big, bold **R** engraved on the face of the vase in a classy, loopy print.

"Oh, God," I gasped, palm flattening against my parted mouth. I knew my mother had Raiden cremated, but I'd never once asked about his ashes. It only made sense that she would bring them here.

"I want you to have him," Ethel spoke, a single, sparkling tear claiming her red, rounded cheek. "All I do is forget. He deserves to be with someone who remembers. He deserves to be with the woman he loves."

"Oh, Eth," Stephen uttered, his emotions masked by a tight frown. "That is so kind of you to do."

Ethel eased the urn into my shaking hands with a reassuring nod. She brought two fingers to her lips, a shy kiss dancing along the surface as she grazed them along Raiden's first initial.

"You'll watch after him, yes?"

"With my life," I whimpered, holding him against my chest. The peace I felt with him in my arms was immeasurable. It granted me a sense of closure, but also reminded me that he was never truly far away. Wherever I was, he would be right there with me.

Always.

I remained with Ethel and Stephen until the woman faded back into her standard hollow nature, vacant stare studying my white, ghost-like features as she called me by a name I'd never heard before. I kissed her forehead, told her that I loved her, and left; holding Raiden close to my heart as I finished my visit. Stephen was sure to thank me several times over for my presence, and he even told Raiden that he loved him before I exited the building. It was rare to see the man so raw, so vulnerable, but it was evident that the death of his adopted son had stripped him of his entire reason to be.

Once Ethel perished, Stephen would soon follow. I was sure of that. At one point, he held on for Raiden and her. Now, it was just for her. After all, she was all he had left.

The sun had dipped beneath the horizon, casting a stunning orange glow over the clouds. I held Raiden in my lap the entire drive home, an arm tightly cradling the vase. I was in awe of the sunset, how it painted such a pretty picture along the sky, and I wondered for a split second if it were the work of my Raiden. Nestled somewhere within the clouds, a paintbrush pinched between ring-clad fingers, a palette of paint on his knee. A snicker, a dip, a smear. Crooked lines, odd mixtures of bright colors in peculiar places. Nevertheless, he continued on until it was perfect.

He painted the sky just for me.

Admittedly, I was slightly disappointed to find the framed photo of my family still buried within the drawer when I arrived home. I half expected my mother to hang it back up, but I didn't blame her for leaving it untouched. My outburst must've rattled her, and the thought of stepping on glass shards on her way to grab the morning paper was enough to keep her prying hands out of my things.

I greeted each dog individually, announcing that I'd brought their father home with me. The three of them perked up at his name, and I nearly burst into tears for what seemed like the millionth time in a single day.

When I nestled into bed that night, the photo was back on the wall. All three dogs curled around my tiny frame, and in my arms laid the remains of the only man I'd ever loved.

twenty-four

Sunflower Inn was all over the news the following morning.

It made my stomach turn to even imagine what the headlines would've said if I'd held true to my word. A part of me wishes that I had. For a while, I was somewhat normal.

Human.

Sarah's near-death experience reminded me that I was nothing but. I was born to heal. Mend. *Save.*

I read an abundance of articles several times over, most of them displaying the very same title.

ATTEMPTED SUICIDE AT THE SUNFLOWER INN

The event replayed on a loop in my head like a busted vinyl, circling back to the very moment I'd found her. Ruby red tissues, crumpled and curled, a trail of torment leading up to her weakened frame. I could still feel her skin—slick with sweat—and the way her blood left a lasting impression along the prints of my fingers. I swore that when I studied the surface for long enough, I could still see it. Her blood. Scarlet's blood.

Raiden's blood.

I was curled up next to a sleepy Mimosa on the sofa when my guest finally arrived. There was some murder mystery documentary on the television—one I barely paid any mind to—and I swiftly switched it off before answering the door.

As if death would even bother them at all, all things considered.

A sweet smile curled along Vole's lips at the sight of me, bubblegum pink nails curled around the left strap of their black backpack. I hadn't seen Vole since that night, and the sight of their living, breathing self was enough to bring tears to my eyes.

"Don't cry, Freya. You'll just make me cry," they said, fingers fiddling with the strap of their bag. They glanced downward at my dogs, a joyful grin smeared along their lips. "Can I come in?"

"Of course," I murmured, scolding the dogs as they attempted to jump up on Vole. Kelso was nearly twice the size of Vole when he stood on his hind legs, and the last thing I wanted was for my dog to knock my guest down flat on their ass.

"Do you need me to put them up?" I asked, tearing a curious Bear away from Vole's scuffed shoes.

"Not at all! I have four dogs myself. They're just excited to see me again," Vole smiled, placing a kiss atop Kelso's head. "I haven't forgotten you, Kelso. I swear. You're still my best boy."

"You can come into the living room," I began, brushing past the trio of dogs as I slid my socks along the carpet. I barely had enough energy to take a full step. "Sorry for the plates and stuff, I need to put them in the sink. I just haven't had much energy."

"I get it," Vole kindly replied, settling within the center of the living room. I stiffly watched as they crossed their legs, shrugging the backpack from their shoulders. Mimosa lapped at Vole's face several times, earning a joyful giggle from them as they rifled through the contents of their bag.

"Jesus, Mimosa. Quit that," I hissed, redirecting my dogs into the other room. By the time I'd returned, Vole had laid out a series of objects on the carpet, perfectly placed into the shape of a square.

"This may look strange, but they're what I need to safely travel through the veil," Vole explained. "Come, Freya. Sit on the floor across from me. I would love to include you in this."

"Okay," I breathed. I was rather reluctant to move, but my feet carried me forward, edging around the profusion of dissimilar crystals and other objects that I had trouble identifying. They almost reminded me of miniature statues, taking on shapes that held no true meaning to the innocent eye.

I took my place on the carpet completely opposite of Vole, careful not to touch any of their artifacts. Admittedly, I was terrified. I had absolutely no idea what to expect of this meeting, and I wasn't entirely sure if I was ready to experience what laid beyond the veil.

"There's no need to be scared," Vole assured me. "I won't physically leave this room. The most frightening thing will be my eyes, they'll appear completely white. That lets you know that I've traveled beyond the veil. I will be able to vocally communicate with you during my travels, and I will explain what I am seeing and hearing. Are you ready for this, Freya?"

A painful gulp hindered my response. I nodded slightly, chapped bottom lip pulled between my teeth. Within seconds, I tasted blood.

"I'll find him, Frey," Vole whispered, nodding curtly. Without another word, they embarked on their journey, eyes sluggishly rotating upwards into their skull. As promised, what remained was nothing but a chalky white. Empty. Cold.

They almost reminded me of Raiden's pitch black gaze, and I couldn't quite tame the tremble that surrounded my spine. My chest painfully heaved as I teetered on the edge of a panic attack.

Was I ready to talk to him?

"I'm almost through," Vole declared, alert eyes emptily fixated on my shaking frame. I couldn't help it—the trembling. It consumed me like a dark cloud, overriding my senses, taking hold of my limbs.

My heart frantically fluttered, beads of sweat forming along my brow as I succumbed to the sensation.

There was no stopping it.

"It's like a puzzle," Vole added, seemingly unaware of my frantic state. "I've done it plenty of times, but it still can be a challenge. I have just a few pieces left, and I'll be able to cross."

"Is it scary? Crossing over?" I asked, the violent shakes present in my tone.

"Calm down, Freya. I can hear in your voice just how anxious you are. There's nothing to be scared of," Vole assured. They were stiff as stone. "No, it is not scary anymore. It was when I was a child. The dead can be conniving, especially with a young Kyōryokuna. I've learned their tricks and know how to outsmart those with wicked intentions. Plus, my ornaments will protect me."

I wasn't quite sure how the assortment of diverse items on the floor would protect Vole from the dead, but I trusted them. They knew more about the afterlife than I ever would.

"I'm in," Vole announced.

My pulse considerably quickened, palms slick with sweat as Vole set out on their search for Raiden. I wondered what they would encounter when they found him—bitterness? Anger? Betrayal?

"Is there Heaven and Hell, like the mortals believe?" I knew the question was borderline preposterous, for Araedians never believed in such a thing. After all, we harvested our energies from the earth, not from a God.

"Not exactly," Vole confirmed. "It's more complicated than that. There is no Holy Spirit, no place among the clouds. There are, however, certain deities that exist, especially beyond the veil. Most are pleasant, others not so much. If I'm correct in my assumptions, Raiden will be with a rather obnoxious deity, one that usually claims the souls of the unfavorable."

"Like the Christian version of Satan?"

"Precisely," Vole replied, clearing their throat. "They don't take on a gender, nor a shape. They just—*exist.* Like a feeling. A hunch. It's painful and rotten, and it can be torturous to those trapped within their wrath."

My chest ached at the thought of Raiden being tortured in the afterlife. Vivid visuals wracked my mind—images of my sweet, curly-headed boy chained up like a rabid animal, the iron shackles tied too tight. Flesh separated from muscle, frayed and rough, bulbous beads of blood dripping down the links of the chain, painting them red.

"There's someone here," Vole muttered, brows furrowed together in concentration. "I don't think it's Raiden, but it feels like him. They have his blood."

"His *blood?"* I gasped.

What on earth could that mean?

Vole sucked in a sharp breath before announcing: "I found his birth mother."

The world came to a screeching halt.

The shakes immediately ceased, leaving my body in a peculiar state of numbness. A raucous ring infiltrated my ears, an uncomfortable whine slipping off of my tongue as I palmed the shell of my ear. My forefinger slid along something wet, and when I retracted my touch, I was met with the startling sight of blood.

"Freya, are you with me?" Vole called.

"Y-Yes," I stammered, suddenly woozy at the sight of the bright red substance. I would never get used to it. "It's his birth mom? Are you sure?"

"Positive," Vole confirmed. "I'm speaking with her. She seems calm. Her demeanor is shockingly kind. She has this angelic aura about her, but I don't trust her as far as I can throw her."

"She's evil, Vole. She existed only to kill us," I countered. My words tasted of venom, and I wanted nothing more than to deter Vole from speaking to that woman.

She wasn't Raiden's mother.

She was nothing.

"Raiden isn't here," Vole added, stunning me to my core. I blinked twice, shaking my head from side to side in bewilderment.

"Like, he isn't with that deity, or something? That's good, right? Maybe he's with a more positive one. One that takes good care of him, like he deserves."

"No, Freya," Vole countered. "He isn't here *at all.* He doesn't exist beyond the veil. I'm so sorry."

My palm met my parted lips, horrified sobs wracking through my chest as I struggled to process Vole's statement.

Raiden was not only dead, he simply ceased to exist. I'd stolen so much of his soul that there was nothing left to cross. Nothing left to survive. He had dissolved into the void, disintegrated into nothingness.

Gone.

"I know there's nothing I can say in this moment to ease your pain, but I'm sure you have questions for his biological mother, as do I. I'm going to give you several moments of space as I speak with her," Vole informed. The bright blue bead in the square began to glow, casting a frosty shadow along the snowy carpet.

"No, Vole," I choked. "Don't talk to her. Don't."

"Don't you want to know why?" Vole quickly countered. The miniature, glowing globule began to float, hovering several inches above the rug. I wasn't sure what the object symbolized, but I was too preoccupied to ask. My thoughts raced with that of Raiden, the way he simply failed to exist.

It wasn't his fault. He couldn't control his destiny. It was his birthright to kill me, and Vole was right. I needed to know why. I needed to know how.

"Freya, quickly," Vole called, their voice hoarse. "Take my hand. Let me show you."

I hesitated, a choppy statement catching in my throat. My name slipped off of Vole's lips once more—more strained this time—and I quickly crawled around their assortment of articles. I was careful not to topple over any of the objects, for doing so would probably be catastrophic for Vole's travels.

"How can you show–" I began, stumbling over my words. I failed to finish my sentence as my clammy hands slipped into Vole's warm hold, and I was hurled through a spiraling swirl of raging, red hues. I was falling face first, hands ostensibly laced behind my back, preventing me from dampening my fall. Only, I wasn't sure where I was, or where I'd end up.

I arrived at my destination abruptly, a sharp breath hitching in my throat as my feet magically met the ground. I felt severely unstable, my head woozy and weak as I struggled to focus on the scene around me. That was, until a hand slipped into mine, and I nearly shrieked in surprise.

Beside me stood Vole, the hollow whites of their eyes piercing into mine. Admittedly, they looked terrifying, and I almost took a step back in search of safety, only to be pulled closer by their firm grip.

"Stay by my side," Vole pressed, unblinking gaze detaching from my petrified glare. "It is unwise and unsafe for you to venture off on your own."

"What is this?" I whispered, finally taking in my surroundings. We were surrounded by a field of fire, burning rubble buried beneath the soles of my bare feet. The skin under my feet should've been scorched, but instead, I felt nothing at all.

"We call it *kioku*," Vole revealed, their tone gravelly and low. "You're in a memory, Freya."

"Whose memory?" I stammered. My question was answered the moment I laid eyes on her—*his mother.*

"Her name is Anneli," Vole disclosed, squeezing my hand. "As you can see, she was very young during the Great Clash. Barely twelve. She managed to survive by hiding out in her neighbor's basement."

I watched as Raiden's birth mother, evidently named Anneli, navigated the burning abyss, forest green eyes blinded by tears. She was unbelievably small for her age, thin as a rail with sunken cheeks and chapped lips, and for a split second, I almost felt sorry for her.

After all, she'd just lost everything and everyone.

I watched her stumble upon an empty-eyed woman, limbs curiously folded and bent, a single stream of black blood caked along the curve of her chin. A painful gulp claimed my throat as I watched a young

Anneli completely unravel, innocent gaze widening as she let out an emotive shriek, one that would stick with me for the rest of my days.

She fell to her knees beside the dead woman—presumably her mother—and in a tongue I did not recognize nor understand, she audibly cried.

"She shouldn't have lived," Vole murmured, tightening their hold on my hand. "Your family as well. Your mother and her parents were considerably lucky to survive together. Anneli did not have such luxury."

"How did she find them here? How did she know where to go?" I questioned, turning away from a youthful Anneli, snowy-white face flushed red with grief.

Vole's jaw clenched, their bushy brows pulled together in concentration. I tried not to stare too long at their eyes—endless, milky white orbs—for the sight of them was enough to trigger memories of Raiden's conflictingly cold, black glare. Memories I tried so hard to bury.

"She's reluctant," Vole revealed. "She won't give up certain things. She refuses to show me anything right now."

"Does she know who I am? Does she know that I'm here with you?" I questioned, a sharp breath hitching in my throat. Anneli was definitely dead, but admittedly, I still feared her. It was doubtful that she harvested such a kind heart like her kin, and although Raiden would've wanted his evil energy eternally banished, she would have not. In fact, I had a hunch that she embraced the wickedness. Reveled in it.

She wanted us all dead, just as her ancestors had. The malevolent forces were not just a small part of her—no—they were *all* of her. She was a true De Mörka, through and through.

"You need to leave," Vole said suddenly, fingers unraveling from mine. "Go. *Now!*"

"Vole!" Their name emerged as a strangled shout, fearful tears slightly blinding my sight as I frantically shook my head. "I don't know how to leave! I don't even know how I got here!"

And then, they were gone; abandoning me within Anneli's tragic memory. I could barely study the bodies around me, for it reminded me of Brennan's birthday party.

I'd witnessed far too much death.

Reluctantly, I returned my stare to a young, weeping Anneli; her red-rimmed eyes solely fixated on the deceased parent by her feet. She consistently tugged at the collar of the adult woman's shirt, audibly begging for her to draw in a breath—to show even the smallest sign of life.

Just as my lips parted in preparation to speak, Anneli's eyes met mine, and everything shifted.

She could see me.

The child's once innocent glare wickedly warped, her eyes transforming into thin, black slits. She gradually rose to her feet, head slightly cocked, hung loosely on her shoulders. Her expression seemed to cloud over—void of emotion, empty tears easing down the reddened surface of her skin, rounding her chin, slipping from the flesh before disappearing indefinitely. She sucked in a sharp breath, holding it shortly, and releasing it with a wheeze.

Something was wrong.

Bile burrowed within my throat, trembling fingers mindlessly toying with the frayed sleeve of my sweater as I took a small step backward. "Your name is Anneli, right?"

Anneli's thin lips parted, but what emerged wasn't entirely an answer. Instead, it was an incoherent strand of sounds—a mumbled melody—shoulders clenching, *twitching,* as she spoke. What she said wasn't English, nor was it her foreign tongue. It was just . . . *nothingness.* Babbles as you would hear from a baby. Only it seemed deeper—*darker.*

I took another step back.

Anneli's shoulders slightly seized, the left mound hiking up towards her ear. Her head lay lazily draped along her shoulder for an elongated moment, oil-drop eyes suctioned to my terrified frame. I didn't dare move, and I even forgot to breathe. I nearly succumbed to a raspy cough that threatened to spew.

Don't you dare make a sound.

"Vole," I whispered, blinking back terrified tears. "Please come get me. Please."

Anneli's shoulders suddenly softened, neck straightening with a shocking *snap.* It sounded as if the tiny bones had quite literally cracked, and with a horrified gasp, I stumbled backwards, nearly tripping over the weeping skull of a corpse.

"I know who you are," Anneli drawled, abandoning her native tongue to address me. Her voice was coarse and low, resembling that of a middle-aged man instead of a preteen girl.

"You can come back now, Vole!" I wept, gradually backing away from a rigid Anneli. She was significantly smaller than me, but I had very little faith in my own individual abilities when it came to facing a purebred De Mörka.

Dead or not, I was fully convinced that she could still kill me.

A glistening, black tongue oozed out of the child's mouth, spilling a profusion of dark, inky liquid. It bubbled and brewed, slopping over the hump of her chin, saturating both her feet and the asphalt below. Her knees simultaneously bent inward—undoubtedly broken—head lolling unnaturally to the side, resting upon her shoulder. Her spine bent and tore, busting at the seams, slicing its way through her porcelain skin.

A panicked scream exited my mouth before I could stop it—widened, unblinking eyes studying the broken girl before me as she continued to writhe. Her limbs contorted, folding inward on themselves, bones continuously cracking. I felt dizzy and sick, and all I could do was stand there and stare.

This wasn't real it wasn't real it wasn't real it wasn't–

Anneli suddenly stilled, a thin, steady stream of inky black spittle seeping through the corner of her lip. If she weren't still standing, I would've assumed that she'd perished; for she was so silent, so still, it almost seemed impossible.

"It *is* real," she hissed, and then she was at my throat.

Pointy, inhuman claws claimed the surface of my neck, sharp tips promptly puncturing the skin. Within seconds, she'd managed to double in height, towering over my frozen, quivering frame with ease. I wasn't even sure how she'd approached me so fast—for she'd done it within a second, in less time than it took for me to fully blink.

My fingers weakly tore at her wrists, but the more I flailed, the deeper her claws sank. I nearly choked on my own blood as it tickled the base of my tongue, slowly creeping up my throat with every small squeeze of her hand. Her blackened gaze pierced my soul, and my vision waned; eyes glossing over as she dug into my throat. The feeble heart within my chest struggled to beat, unintentionally pumping an excess of blood into my windpipe, which simultaneously crept up into my mouth and showered Anneli's fingers.

"You *ruined* him," she spat. The mysterious, black liquid spurted through her teeth, showering my cheeks in a wonky, dripping constellation. "You're the reason he failed. You're the reason he died. It was supposed to be *you*."

"I'd do anything to take it back," I countered, choking on my own words. The clotted blood curdled within my mouth, and I struggled to spit it out. Her claws only sunk deeper, and I was certain that her entire fingers were buried within my throat at this point.

"It's too late."

Too late too late too late.

My back jarringly met the rocky asphalt, a whirlwind of shapes clouding my vision as a deep, throbbing pain enveloped my spine. Matted locks tickled my cheeks, and suddenly, I was suspended; the ground absent beneath my rigid body.

"Open your eyes," Anneli growled, her demonic tone sending shivers down my spine. "Open them up and see."

Like a small child throwing a tantrum, I refused; shaking my head from side to side as I continuously coughed up blood. This only angered Anneli, claws completely disappearing beneath the tattered flesh of my neck. I could've sworn that I could feel the tips of her nails touch within my throat, and I couldn't help but garishly shriek.

I was going to die.

"Open them!"

My gushing blood turned to ice at the sound of her otherworldly growl, weakened fingers laced lax around her itty-bitty wrists. With her free hand, she tore at my eyelids, razor-sharp nails painfully prying them open one by one. Her fingernails felt like white-hot knives against my skin, and although my eyelids remained entirely intact, it felt as if she'd sliced them right off.

The pain and my severe loss of blood had me teetering on the edge of consciousness, and as she forced open my eyes, I finally saw it all.

Warped, discolored scenes depicted the tale of Raiden's becoming, starting from the very beginning. Anneli's journey through oddly loving foster homes, her eventual adoption at age fifteen, her supportive parents feeding her, raising her, loving her until she tore away from them at eighteen, determined to locate the last remaining Araedian family. Her energies failed to fully bloom, and with every weak attempt to trigger them, she grew more irate. *Angry.*

I felt Anneli's fury course through my veins as I watched her life unravel before me in the form of a film, similar to the oddities I'd experienced from her own son. Her flesh and blood.

Raiden.

She found my family by chance. A crazed psychic buried deep within the loins of Sweden veered her in their direction, pointing her towards their refuge. With the minimal cash she harbored, she hopped on the first flight to Canada the following morning. The psychic dropped dead the moment the plane departed, an oddly coincidental occurrence, and I felt Anneli's grip tighten once more on my neck as the tale wound its way to Raiden's evident creation.

The woman spent countless nights in a variety of bars, anxiously awaiting a potential pair. She only needed him briefly, then never again—for once she bore a child, the De Mörka would rise once again. She would need no one but her child, and she would raise them with the full intent of eradicating the Araedian bloodline once and for all, the very act her ancestors had failed to do.

I saw glimpses of Raiden's biological father—stunning verdant eyes, loopy, brown curls, a big white smile. I knew it was him before Anneli even confirmed it. He was young, barely eighteen, and worked at a local theater. Flashes of memories raided my vision—Anneli stumbling in on one of his shows, watching him belt out the lyrics of an unfamiliar tune, rosy red cheeks gleaming as the audience tossed ruby red roses at his feet. She lured him in—whispered the sweetest nothings in his ear—used him up, and never spoke with him again.

A weighty tear dribbled down my cheek at the sight of Raiden's real father. He mirrored his son almost exactly; the resemblance was uncanny. He'd never known his boy, and never would. He was a nameless man, a little pawn in Anneli's game. He was nothing but a sperm donor in her eyes. The final piece to her malevolent puzzle.

Then, I saw my mother. Fresh faced and full of joy, walking hand in hand down the sidewalk with a significantly younger version of my father. On her hip was a baby, a year old at most, fat, little fingers curled around her natural, dark tresses. *Her real hair.*

The baby was me.

I tried to close my eyes—*please let me close them, I don't need to see anymore*—but Anneli pried them back open, earning a distressed cry from my fickle self.

I felt flimsy—*drained*—and I was certain that within moments, I would bleed out around her fingers. A part of me wondered if I'd even have the chance to go so easily. She'd probably rip my throat out before I croaked, making sure it hurt.

A severely swollen Anneli constantly watched us, spied on our every move. I saw flickers of my parents and me at ice cream shops, an outdated Foodvio, even the park. She'd caress her bulbous belly as she sat in plain sight on a bench, pretending to read through a parenting magazine. All the while, she studied us.

It was all red.

It blinded me, made me flinch. Snowy, white sheets drenched with blood, stained scarlet. Quivering thighs parted, scattered screams ricocheting off of the walls.

"She's hemorrhaging," someone said. It might've been a doctor. I was too woozy—too *weak* to fully comprehend the scene. Nonetheless, a

fiendish Anneli kept my eyes peeled, forcing me to witness the birth of my best friend.

She lived just long enough to name him.

Syver.

A grievous gasp tumbled over my lips, and her touch was gone. Greedy claws no longer claimed my neck, nor my lids. The vile stench of rot still lingered in my nostrils, but her physical frame had dissolved, disappearing into the wind, drifting into oblivion.

For a moment, I was encased in black. It was suffocating—*tight*—and I wanted to scream. I wasn't sure who would hear me, if there was anyone even around to listen. The void shifted, and I was falling, falling, *falling . . .*

I resurfaced with a wail, skin slick with sweat as my blurry stare met the uneven popcorn ceiling of my living room. Vole was beside me, pupils severely dilated as they vigorously fanned my clammy flesh with a folded-up magazine.

"Holy shit," Vole croaked, choking back tears. "I wasn't sure if you'd ever resurface. I was afraid I'd lost you to the other side. Strange things happen when we pass over. I should've never brought you, Freya."

My fingers latched around their wrist, chest arduously heaving as I pulled myself up into a sitting position. The room appeared to spin, and I nearly lost my lunch.

"Let me get you some water," Vole offered, but my grip only tightened on their arm.

"No. I need you to stay right now," I clipped, struggling to catch my breath. I could still feel the phantom touch of Anneli's claws in my neck, and with shaking fingers, I lightly massaged the skin.

Vole's glare slightly shifted down to my neck, a tight frown pulled across their lips. "You're bruised. On your neck."

"What?" I gasped, incessantly smoothing my fingers over the evidently injured skin.

Vole wordlessly nodded. They assisted me in standing to my feet, wobbly knees turned inward as I nearly collapsed face-first. My legs felt like jelly, and I was certain that I'd take a violent tumble if Vole's hands hadn't claimed my hips.

They brought me to my en-suite bathroom—which was a cluttered, unclean mess, no less—in order to show me what they'd seen. Sure enough, a quintet of bruises claimed my neck, tangible proof of Anneli's ethereal assault.

My fingertips lightly danced along the discolored surface, lazy gaze completely entranced by the sight. "How is this possible, Vole?"

"The afterlife is extremely complex. It can be a dangerous place, especially for the inexperienced. I really should've never brought you along. I don't know what I was thinking. I'm so very sorry, Freya," Vole mumbled, running their fingers through my knotted locks. I studied their reflection in the toothpaste spattered mirror, a sorrowful frown drawn along their lips as they mindlessly toyed with my hair, as if to calm my spirits.

"Raiden's real name is Syver," I revealed, tearing my touch away from the circular marks. "I wonder if the name meant anything to her."

"She's unhappy," Vole said, greeting a cheery Mimosa as she pranced into the bathroom, her overgrown nails noisily rapping against the tile. "Extremely unhappy. She asked if her son succeeded, and she was confused as to how he failed. She said his energy would've been more than enough to defeat your brother, unless there was a counter. Something pulling him back. Something that made him weak."

"Me," I whispered, running the pad of my thumb against the shiny, silver curve of his ring.

"Yes, you," Vole confirmed. "I told her he'd fallen for the Araedian girl. She was furious, *enraged.* I thought she'd combust into nothing but dust. I left after that, and found you still trapped beyond the veil. I assume that she took out her rage on you, judging by those angry marks. What did she do? Choke you?"

"More than that." I slipped Raiden's ring back into the confines of my shirt, glare downcast upon Mimosa's wriggling self as I struggled to recall the event. "It almost seems like a distant memory, now. I'm afraid that I'll forget it the moment I fall asleep."

"That's probably a good thing. I'm going to get you a drink from the kitchen," Vole said, patting me once on the shoulder before excusing themselves from the bathroom. By now, all three dogs had joined me, anxiously crowding my legs. They could sense that something was amiss, and Mimosa wouldn't stop nipping at my bare toes, a bad habit she'd had since puppyhood.

"Come on, guys. Let's lay in bed with Dad," I softly cooed, gently brushing Mimosa's mouth away with the curve of my heel. For the most part, the animals obeyed, following close on my heel as I navigated the unkempt bedroom.

Most of Raiden's clothes were in the bed, along with his decorative urn, which was perfectly placed in the center of the pillow in which his head once laid upon. The lily white cushion cradled his ashes like a divine halo, and I was regrettably reminded of the fact that his soul ceased to exist. There was no afterlife for him. No blinding, white light at the end of the tunnel.

It was comparable to an infinite oblivion. A jet-black, cramped limbo. Just . . . *nothing.* Just as I'd feared.

"I'm so sorry, Raiden." I could barely hold myself together, and when I collapsed along the colossal pile of clothing (which somehow still smelled of him), I finally fell apart.

Our dogs surrounded me like a comforting crowd, weary whines slipping off of Bear's tongue as he neurotically licked my neck. His long, pink tongue skimmed over the ghastly marks around my throat, as if his saliva would magically heal the supernatural wounds.

"Hey, buddy." The nickname emerged as a murmur as I laced my arm around his weighty neck, pulling his slobbery mouth towards my cheek. He pressed a staccato of kisses along my jaw before nuzzling against my chin, chilly, wet nose suctioned to the arch of Raiden's urn.

"Yeah, that's your Daddy in there," I whispered, placing a kiss atop Bear's nose. Just as we'd both cuddled into the pillow where Raiden laid in his eternal rest, there was a knock on the door.

It was shy and short, barely a whisper of a beat. I wondered if I'd imagined it at first—that was, until it came again, a bit louder this time. Three even thumps—*who is it?*—and I suddenly felt bitter, *annoyed.*

The last thing I wanted at this moment was company.

I called for Vole, but never got a reply. I assumed they might have taken a phone call in the kitchen, or maybe excused themselves outside, only to get locked out. Either way, it was me who had to answer the door, whether I liked it or not.

With a heavy, exasperated sigh, I slunk off of the bed. A curious Mimosa routinely followed on my heel, whereas her brothers remained reticent, too lazy to leave the comfort of the cushions.

The shell of my ear danced along the cool surface of the door, desperately awaiting the sound of Vole's voice. The sight of anyone else—including my mother or brother—would simply annoy me, so I hoped more than anything that my friend was on the other side of the door.

"Hello?" I called, fingertips trailing along the doorknob.

There was no reply.

Restless and vexed, I turned the knob, pulling the door open as wide as it would go. Vole's name slipped off of my lips in a disgruntled tone, but instead of their voice appearing in front of me, it emerged from behind, asking who was at the door.

At first, I was met with the back of their head.

Charming chestnut curls descended down the length of their scalp, caressing the collar of their navy blue button-up. The alluring tresses truly put my messy mop of unwashed hair to shame, and I practically fainted at the sight of them, for it just wasn't possible—*this isn't real this can't be real none of this is REAL*—but then again, if I'd learned one thing in my thirty-three years of life, it was that absolutely *anything* was possible among the supernatural.

A stunned gasp slid off of my tongue, heart erratically thumping against my ribcage as my unexpected guest slowly spun around on their heel, head cocked slightly sideways as they proudly glanced over their shoulder to view my bewildered self.

Stunning emerald eyes met my severely dilated pupils, a crooked, pearly-white grin slithering along their mouth as they faced me fully.

My name fell off of his lips, and I slammed the door right in his face.

Vole's brows raised at the sight of my stiff, panicked reaction; a plate of brownies balanced along their fingers. In the opposite hand was an ice-cold glass of water, poured out just for me.

"Who is it?"

Their smile faltered when I frantically locked the front door, fingers fumbling along the bolt. "Vole, is it possible that you or I might have brought back some sort of demon or deity or something?"

"Okay, hold on. I need to put this stuff down," Vole replied, clearly trying to remain calm. They set the dishes down onto the hallway shelf, nearly knocking over a stack of books and a dainty framed photo of Raiden and Mimosa.

The trio of knocks emerged once more, and this time, both Vole and I visibly flinched, widened stares set on the sealed door.

This time, it was the muffled voice of my mother that emerged.

"Freya, honey? It's Momma. Please open up. I know you're scared and confused, but I promise, there's a logical explanation for what you've just seen."

"What did you see on the other side of that door, Freya?" Vole whispered, curling their fingers around my elbow. It appeared as if Vole was just as anxious as I was.

I swallowed hard, hot tears pricking the corners of my eyes as I shook my head. *It just wasn't possible.*

"I saw Raiden."

Vole's sizeable stare met mine, jaw lax in bewilderment as they struggled to comprehend the scene at hand. To both of our knowledge, the real Raiden was nothing but ash, sealed up in an embellished urn in our bedroom. The imposter on the opposite side of the door was just that . . . *an imposter.*

"Did we accidentally bring some demons over the veil? Could they pretend to be Raiden and my mother?" I queried, cowering against Vole's somewhat smaller frame.

"I would've known," Vole assured, patting the top of my hand. "That's your real mother out there, but if you say you really saw Raiden, too . . . Well, I don't have any logical explanation for that. Besides the fact that I couldn't find him beyond the veil. So it is entirely possible that he's actually–"

"–alive?" I croaked, a violent tremble soaring up my spine. I physically shook within Vole's hold, blinding tears obscuring my vision. They said something about answering the door, but I couldn't think, I couldn't move—not about anything but the possibility of Raiden being alive.

It wasn't possible.

I had watched him die.

Death doesn't like to be cheated.

My mind wandered into a hazy trance, greedy fingers desperately dragging along the rugged surface of the hallway wall. Knobby knees buckled, nearly sending me blindly backwards as I used my arms to steady my weight, palms glued to the vertical partition.

I hardly noticed Vole opening the door.

"Freya, *tesoro,*" Momma exclaimed, enveloping my trembling torso in her arms. She clung to me like the two sizes too-tight jean jacket I used to wear in high school, one that they paid an ungodly amount of money for and it never quite fit me.

"Look at me, baby. You're in a daze," she commanded, lengthy, manicured nails tenderly pulling at my droopy eyelids. My wonky vision eventually focused on her cheery orange bob, synthetic waves tickling the curves of her defined jaw.

"Momma?" I rasped, allowing the tears to freely flow. "What is this?"

"I wanted to tell you sooner, but the process was grueling. You didn't need to see any of it. Brennan, either. He doesn't know yet. Only your father," my mother ambiguously disclosed. She wiped my tears away with the delicate pads of her thumbs, a sympathetic frown painted along her pink lips.

Hidden just beyond the artificial wisps of her orange wig was a lanky shadow, the blurred outline of the man who had defied death. Without even closing my eyes, I could still envision the gaudy gash drawn along his throat, the metallic scent of fresh, bubbling blood that spewed from his severed jugular.

"Frey," he breathed, using that tiny tone I'd grown to love so much. He only ever used his small voice in times of uncertainty, as if to cautiously tread around the den of a savage, sleeping bear.

Don't awaken the beast.

At the simple sound of his familiar tone, all three of our dogs rushed into the hall, a chorus of enthusiastic whimpers reverberating off of the paper-thin walls. Kelso nearly trampled Raiden to the ground, lengthy tongue lapping at his father's grinning features.

It was then that I knew for certain that Raiden was real. Dogs could sense when something was amiss, and if he was an imposter, they would've known from the moment he'd sauntered into the building. Only, he wasn't a fraud at all. He was just . . . Raiden.

Just Raiden, the man who evidently had the power to elude death.

Suddenly, I was reminded of Grammy's lesson during our dinner not too long ago, the lecture of how to defeat the De Mörka.

Their power and energy is not embedded within their bones like ours is. Although it is a part of their chemical makeup, it can be banished—locked away. It would take a sacrifice, however. A human one. Someone would need to occupy their subconscious and lock the negative energy inside. But if you simply want to kill them, slit their throat.

"Oh God," I gasped, running over Grammy's words several times in my head. *Grammy.*

I could hardly look Raiden in the eye, for I'd discovered the truth behind my grandmother's mysterious demise. She hadn't perished in the blaze after all—*no*—she had sacrificed herself.

She gave up her life so Raiden could live.

Painful sobs wracked through my chest, a clammy, shaken palm gravitating up towards my gaping mouth as I let out a broken, unfinished statement. "Grammy–"

"Let me show you," Raiden said, right arm outstretched. His fingers were barren—*empty*—entirely absent of his shining, silver rings. I became painstakingly aware of his trademark jewelry hidden snug beneath my shirt, pressed against the flushed flesh that guarded my heart.

"How?" I croaked, reluctant to take his hand. Although he was the same Raiden I'd spent over two decades with, things just felt different. *Off.*

"Take his hand, Freya," Momma urged. A blurred blend of emotions consumed my being, and I teetered on the edge of sorrow and utmost rage.

Ignoring the latter emotion, I obeyed, stepping forward towards an ostensibly alive Raiden. Although I felt blindsided by his sudden arrival, I felt mostly betrayed. Worst of all, my own mother was heavily involved. She lied to me for half a year. She watched me mourn, casually looking over her shoulder as I completely fell apart before her. She turned a blind eye as I isolated myself completely, ignored calls from friends, neighbors, ex-lovers. I spent three erroneous nights with Maxwell, regretting every visit immediately after returning home the following morning. She saw it all, and she *knew*—she knew all along.

"Why?" I whispered, hastily brushing away a plethora of tears. My cheeks were flushed and warm, red-rimmed eyes swollen with grief as my mother ushered a series of meaningless apologies.

"You'll understand when he shows you, sweetheart. He'll show you everything, there's too much for me to even tell."

"How? How can he *show* me, Mother? *How?"* I spat, refusing to take Raiden's hand. His lips remained sealed—a wide, woeful stare fixed on my shaking frame. He didn't dare speak. He knew better than to do that by now.

"Raiden," Momma urged, her tone barely above a whisper. I wanted to take her by her itty-bitty wrists, to scream in her face until she sobbed.

How could you do this to me? How could you betray the daughter you claim to love?

I opened my mouth—beyond ready to hurt my mother's feelings with statements so harsh that they made me cringe—but I was impolitely interrupted by Raiden's abrupt touch.

He held my face in his hands—such an amiable, comforting touch—and I immediately melted within his embrace, tears peevishly flooding my sight once more as I struggled to hold them back. His forehead met mine, long, pointed nose smushed against the summit of my own as he welcomed me home.

"I can't feel you anymore," I wept, circling my fingers around his bony wrists. "That bond we used to have—it's gone, Raiden. I can't feel anything anymore."

"My death broke the bond," he said. I could almost taste the nicotine that drifted off of his tongue. I wanted to scold him for *still* smoking, but I figured this wasn't the time.

If he could defy death, maybe a cigarette or two wouldn't hurt.

"Show me," I whispered, squeezing his wrists. "Show me how this is possible."

"Close your eyes," he said, "I'll show you everything there is to see."

Anxiously, I complied, eyelids slipping shut as Raiden gently grasped my cheeks, the tips of his thumbs tracing endless circles along the damp skin.

The scene appeared almost immediately, a flickering image drawn across my sealed lids like a film projector on a screen. The projection was hazy at first, and I smelled the scene before I could see it—the raw, smithy scent, one that clung to the edge of my nose everywhere I went.

Blood.

I was back in the lush garage of Weatherby's grand estate, chaos ensuing the scene as I choked back tears. This time, I was merely an overhead spectator—a drone watching over the events. On one end, I could see myself—lips garishly parted as I screamed in Raiden and Brennan's direction. Although everything felt muddled—*slow*—it simultaneously seemed to slip by at an unusual speed, like the sticky button of a DVD player stuck on a slight fast-forward. My eye caught the glimmer of the rusted blade—hurriedly hurtling towards Brennan's grasp—when the unexpected occurred. Instead of settling within his palm, (and eventually sinking into Raiden's back), it encountered an obstacle, one which wasn't there in my memory of the scene.

Grammy.

My weary, old grandmother stood frozen in place, fingers gently creeping towards the weeping wound between her shoulders. I half expected my mother to completely crumble at the sight, but instead, she seemed to ignore her dying mother entirely, instead charging towards a distracted Raiden atop my brother.

What happened next was entirely opposite of what occured in the timeline I recalled, and oddly, it felt as if I were watching the events of some sort of alternate timeline. A completely separate universe.

Only, it wasn't an alternate reality at all. It was the very same one that I existed in at this very moment.

I felt Raiden's palms grow slick with sweat as I viewed his personal memory in third-person, like a ghost hovering over a crowd.

In one swift movement, Brennan had rotated an inky-eyed Raiden onto his back, a single arm outstretched as he beckoned over a trail of shiny, silver chains. I saw a considerably confident version of myself rush towards the men, running side-by-side with my mother as we worked in a team to keep Raiden glued to the ground. I had apparently assisted Brennan in tying Raiden's wrists up so tight that they nearly bled, and Momma took her spot on his hips, pinning his restless frame to the floor. Grammy had waddled over by this point, wrinkled fingers gradually extracting the blade from her back with difficulty. The gaping wound visibly wept, spilling vibrant crimson blood down the fabric of her blouse. She, however, seemed relatively unphased, instead focused on the task at hand.

Blinding flashes peppered my sight—Raiden's tear-stricken cheeks, Momma's palm circling his wrist, Brennan's fingers enclosing around his throat. Grammy took the corroded kitchen knife to her palm, splitting the skin, before handing it over to her daughter. Momma's hands shook as she did the very same to Raiden's right palm, creating an identical wound along the surface.

The picture went fuzzy the moment their bloody palms met, and for a split second, I wasn't entirely sure of where I was. Then, I was relocated to my parents home, buried deep within the bowels of their unfinished basement. There was a weak excuse for a restroom—a cheap lavatory without a door—and inside sat the dated claw-foot tub that once claimed the upstairs bathroom before the remodel. Within the milky white basin was a distressed Raiden, pale skin flushed and red, wild strands of hair glued to his woeful features as my mother continually dunked his head beneath the riotous waves. It appeared as if she were attempting to drown him, and I wanted to shout—to make her stop—but I simply did not exist in this scene. I was nothing but an onlooker, and all I could do was suffer in silence as my mother forced Raiden's skull beneath the water, baby blue sundress soaked through and through.

He spent several nights in my childhood bed, tossing and turning and sweating through the sheets, changing them in the morning just to do it all over again. I could hear my mother's coos as he writhed and screamed in the basement, nails severing the skin of his palms as he struggled with the pain. I overheard some of her statements—*this won't be easy, you're banishing the biggest part of you. it's fighting back—*

and I felt fresh, hot tears emerge from my sealed lids, dipping down my rounded cheeks as Raiden gently wiped them away.

"It's okay," he murmured, pressing a sealed-lip kiss to my forehead. "Keep watching."

I watched him play card games with a stuffed animal as I ate dinner upstairs with my parents, completely oblivious to the fact that my boyfriend was actually alive beneath my feet. He'd glance up at the ceiling with every creak of a floorboard, a soft smile stretching along his lips as he shuffled his cards.

Brennan discovered him on more than one occasion, only to swiftly forget about it the second my mother manipulated the timeline. My father knew of Raiden's presence—it was too much to hide from him—but he did as he was told and kept it a secret.

Just a little bit longer.

Just until he's fully detoxed.

Countless nights of screaming. Sweating. Swearing.

There was a day or two of self destruction—the De Mörka within him fighting back hard—and Momma had to tie him up and watch him for nearly twenty-three hours straight, ensuring that he wouldn't break free from the bonds and strangle himself.

Momma would run into the room most nights—a cool, wet rag pinched between her fingers. She'd pat his forehead, mumble some words of encouragement, and disappear beyond the door until dawn. He endured a week straight of profuse vomiting, keeping down hardly anything but ice chips and crackers. Some nights he'd rock back and forth on my old, creaky mattress, palms suctioned to his ears, eyes sealed shut as he begged the sounds to stop.

Eventually, it did. It all stopped.

My grandmother's selfless sacrifice effectively banished the De Mörka curse, locking it away in the deepest confines of Raiden's soul, melting the key into nothing but golden rubble. I heard another one of Momma's kind speeches, one where she explained that Raiden had inhabited Grammy's energy, and although the wickedness of his evil nature had been expelled from his existence, a sliver of his own energy remained, only enough to slightly entertain him.

I witnessed a myriad of woeful nights, evenings where he'd beg—*plead*—to see me, to tell me what had happened, only to be silenced by my mother, who claimed that it was not time.

She knew he was ready when the scar on his palm glimmered gold beneath the sun on an early weekday morning, and hours later, they wound up on my front porch.

I resurfaced with a gasp, eyelids tearing open as I met Raiden's shy, soft stare. I became increasingly aware of my tense fingers, lengthy nails penetrating the supple skin of his wrists, drawing blood.

"Fuck," I hissed, tearing my intrusive touch away from his reddened flesh. "I'm so sorry, I didn't even–"

Raiden's sturdy arms encircled my neck, drawing me close as his lips met mine. The kiss was greedy and rough and full of want, the evidence of his utter adoration tattooed along his tongue as it dipped into the cavern of my mouth. He whispered a series of sweet nothings along the surface, ending them all with a hearty *I love you* as he refused to let me resurface for air.

I breathed in his love, and every negative emotion nestled within my core instantly dissipated, replaced with nothing but bliss as I melted within his embrace.

"We're still here, you know," Vole announced, ending their statement with a slight chuckle. They stuffed half of a brownie into their mouth, chewing slowly before announcing, "I love magic."

Raiden giggled against my lips before drawing away, wild green gaze fixated on my awestruck expression as he slid his hand into mine.

"Sorry for all the mushy-gushy shit, Vole," Raiden said, brushing his tedious curls away from his eyes. Beside Vole was my mother, silent, joyful tears staining her cheeks with black mascara streaks. She looked pleased with herself, and although I was still slightly angry with her for tricking Brennan and I so well—*and most of the town, too*—I was thankful for her. She didn't need to do what she did, and Grammy never had to die just for Raiden to live.

But, she did. Her actions spoke volumes, and in her eyes, Raiden was worth saving, regardless of his true identity.

Totally typical.

"I always said you were Grammy's favorite," I teased, wiping the tiny beads of blood away from Raiden's wrist. "This just proves it."

Our lips met in a brief kiss once more, and Momma cheered, clapping her hands together in satisfaction as she approached the two of us. She pulled us both into a tight hug, squeezing extra hard when an abundance of thanks spilled out of my lips.

"Certain sacrifices are worth being made for the ones we love," my mother said, pinching Raiden's cheek. "Although, losing my mother and exhausting my energy was almost the end of my sanity. But, it's easier to grieve when I know that a part of her will live on in you, Raiden."

"I just wish you could've turned it all back," Raiden admitted, his cheeks flushed a pasty white hue. "There'll never be a day that goes by that I don't regret murdering those people in cold blood, even if I was overcome by a malevolent force. It was still *me.* I did it, and I can't take it back."

"Oh, Raiden," I cooed, squeezing his hand. "That's the consequence of our existence. Sometimes mortals get caught in the crossfire. Grammy used to tell us about how hundreds of humans died during the Great Clash, and although they fled, the guilt they felt was immeasurable. Sometimes, it's unavoidable."

"Although your roots are sullied with an evil even I still have trouble comprehending, your heart is pure, Raiden. That's why the moment we all discovered your true identity, our choice was clear. Grammy didn't even have to think twice," Momma said, greeting the trio of dogs that surrounded her legs. "Although, things may be a little weird if we stay here. The town is small, and if word gets around that you survived the accident when everyone thought you didn't, things may get a little . . . *difficult.*"

I paused. "Wait, you're saying that we need to move?"

The thought of leaving our quaint, Canadian town was bittersweet—a somber sadness edged into my bones as I imagined saying goodbye to the only place I'd ever known for over three decades. Leaving was never even a possibility in my eyes before that very moment; I'd simply accepted the fact that I would live and die in the very same town I was born in. It didn't bother me before, but now, it seemed ideal to abandon our old lives and start anew.

"Brennan and Elden will be the last to join us, for they need to finish through with their surrogate mother and do a bunch of paperwork to move the baby out of the country. But, we can go anywhere. We've all actually decided to leave it up to you, Freya," Momma revealed, unable to stifle her beaming, pearly-white grin. She seemed overjoyed at the idea of leaving Canada behind, even though she'd moved here to be with Dad, given birth to two children here, and even lost her mother here.

My eyes met Raiden's sparkling gaze, a genuine grin creeping along his pretty, pink lips as he nodded in approval. It all felt so surreal—like a perfect little dream—and I even took a sliver of skin between my fingers, pinching it roughly to remind myself that I was, in fact, awake.

"Let's go back home."

twenty-six

"Say it again."

"Mmm," Raiden breathed, feathering light, open-mouthed kisses along the inside of my thighs. The tips of his loopy, long hair tickled my skin, prompting a breathless gasp to ease off of my lips as he took a tiny portion of skin between his teeth.

"Stop being a tease. Say it again," I cursed, claiming the sheets between clammy, balled-up fists. I felt him giggle against my flesh before biting down hard, eliciting a stunned shriek from my electrified frame.

"I *said* . . ." he teased, nudging the angry flesh of my thigh with the tip of his nose. *"I love you."*

With a soft purr, I beckoned him upwards, fingers tangled within his delicate chestnut curls. He sighed in relief, and our mouths sloppily met; teeth unpleasantly clattering, lips pulling up into amused smirks. My legs coiled around his hips, drawing him in close.

This is where we were meant to be.

"This feels like a dream," I said, openly sighing when his mouth met my jaw, dipping downwards to place a series of smooches along my neck. "I'm still not entirely certain that I'm awake."

Raiden's lips peeled back, exposing his pearly whites as he bit down on my neck, reminding me that I was—in fact—awake.

"Okay, *okay,*" I gasped, a fierce blush creeping up my cheeks as Raiden chuckled against the angry flesh of my neck. There would be marks where his mouth had been come morning, but I couldn't fathom leaving this bed for days to come.

Mimosa nudged my knee, and I outwardly groaned; slightly peeved at the thought of untangling myself from Raiden. We were both dressed in nothing but our undergarments, which were sure to be shed within moments. That was, if our dogs allowed us to do so.

The littlest dog let out a whine, and Raiden sighed, detaching his lips from my neck before placing a simple peck to my mouth.

"I'll let them out," he offered, crawling off of my buzzing body. "I've missed taking care of them. It was agony being apart from my family."

"Oh, Rai," I murmured, blinking back tears for the millionth time in a single night. I was surprised that I could even cry after all the tears I'd shed over the past six months.

Raiden disappeared, a trio of dogs scrambling out of the door after him as I was left to myself in the bedroom, accompanied only by the low blue glow of the television.

Mere moments after his temporary departure, my cell phone buzzed against my arm, an unknown number lighting up the screen. Usually, I'd let such calls go right to voicemail, but something deep within my bones pressured me to answer it, and before I could brush the sensation aside, I'd taken the call.

"Good evening, this is Nettie Caddel from Lakeview Senior Center. May I please speak with Freya Gallo?"

Nettie.

"This is she," I gulped, my bulging glare fixated on the bedroom door. Any second now, Raiden would return, bombarding me with a series of questions—*who's on the phone at this hour*—and I nearly lost my dinner at the fact that Lakeview simply *never* called, unless . . . *unless . . .*

"Hey, Freya," little old Nettie purred, her gravelly, elderly tone soothing me to my core. "I know it's past nine at night, and that new receptionist that I just can't *stand* refused to call you until morning. I owe it to you to let you know now."

Oh God . . .

"Ethel died, Freya."

The phone slipped through my slick fingers, easing between my trembling legs and disappearing from view. I heard Nettie call my name—once, twice, maybe three times—and I had to force myself to pick the phone back up, to say something, *anything . . .*

"Are you sure?" I croaked, nearly choking over my own words.

"Officially pronounced ten minutes ago. I'm so sorry, Freya. You deserved to know tonight, not whenever they decided it was right. They'll take my phone privileges away, I'm sure. I don't even care. Ethel was important to me, and she was important to you. You need to know that she loved you as much as her son."

Nettie rambled on a bit more as I sat in silence, back uncomfortably bent, head buried between my knees as I rocked back and forth in a fetal position on the bed. It was impossible—*I'd just seen her!*—and Raiden was bound to walk in the door at any moment.

"Nettie, thank you for telling me," I suddenly interrupted, disrupting her speech. "I have to go, okay?"

"Okay, Freya. Godspeed. You'll be okay."

"Yeah. Okay. Bye," I mumbled, ending the call before Nettie could reply. I tossed my phone forward, watching as it tumbled from the bed and onto the floor with a shy *thump.*

Raiden reentered then, nearly tripping over a trio of frenzied dogs on his way in. His smile faltered when he laid eyes on me, brows pulling together in concern.

"Freya? What is it?"

Your mother is dead your mother is dead your mother is dead your mother–

"She's dead," I said, a shaky hand clamping over my mouth to stifle my sobs. Raiden's face fell, chest inordinately heaving as he struggled to comprehend the statement. I didn't even have to clarify who it was. He just knew.

"No–" he whined, shaking his head from side to side.

He crawled into my arms, his hot tears soaking through my clammy skin as he unraveled within my embrace. It wasn't *entirely* a surprise—she'd been sick for a long time—but the timing was certainly less than satisfactory.

Raiden wouldn't have been able to see her again anyways. To the best of the general public's knowledge, he was dead—reduced to ash and dust by the tragic fire that presumably claimed forty-six lives.

Only, the fire didn't kill anyone at all.

Raiden did that.

We lay in a sniffling silence for what seemed like an eternity, swollen, bloodshot eyes glued to the chipper cartoons on the television. At one point—well after midnight—I presumed, I finally asked him what was really in the decorative urn.

"Sand," he said, slipping his fingers between mine. "It was your dad's idea. Your parents wanted to make sure no questions arose, especially from my parents. Well, my dad. That was the hardest part, you know. Making the people who raised me believe that I was dead."

"I'm sorry," I whispered, pressing a kiss to the top of his hair. "I wish we didn't have to leave. I wish you could've seen her one last time."

"I wish a lot of things went differently," Raiden admitted, burying his nose within my neck. "I'll never forgive myself for killing all of those people, Freya. It keeps me up at night. It eats at me."

"I know," I cooed, continuously kissing the top of his head. "Listen, I have something to show you. It might cheer you up a little."

Raiden tore out of my arms, eyes widened in wonder as I eased off of the bed. The aging springs in the mattress whined at my sudden absence, and I felt a hot, scarlet blush raid my cheeks when Raiden playfully whistled at the sight of my nearly bare backside.

"Oh, fuck off," I teased, glancing over my shoulder to view his boyish grin. I shuffled through the mess on top of the dresser, desperately weeding through an abundance of dissimilar items before eventually locating a small stack of letters.

With a grin, I rejoined him on the mattress; bending over the side to turn on the dainty lamp on the bedside table. A soft yellow hue enveloped the room, earning a dissatisfied stare from a sleepy Bear as the dog blinked several times to adjust to the sudden light. Kelso and Mimosa seemed unbothered by it, and were instead curious of what was in my hands.

"They were originally for me, but they're about you. I think you'd appreciate some of them," I said, handing the letters and cards over to him.

"I didn't know people still sent stuff like this," he mused. "I feel like people got lazy after the internet and would just send some meaningless message. These are meaningful, you know? Like they care?"

I simply nodded, fingers knotted around the hair tie circling my wrist. I yanked and pulled at the elastic, a sudden tightness enveloping my chest as Raiden stumbled upon a letter from Jordan.

He paused, silently studying her incredibly posh penmanship. I was suddenly very aware of the fact that she had laid with Raiden in this very same bed.

"I'm surprised you kept this one," he chuckled, swiftly scanning over the note. "She acts like we actually dated or something."

"That one date must've meant a lot to her," I murmured, avoiding Raiden's stare. He brushed the letters aside, arms outstretched to claim my dismissive frame. He knew how much I despised Jordan—she was a lovely girl, but the thought of her with him just made me queasy—and for some reason, he found it rather amusing.

"Want to know a secret?" Raiden purred, pulling me into his arms. His palm found my cheek, curled thumb tracing circles along the flushed skin as he studied my sad stare. "The sex sucked."

I couldn't quite stifle the snort that emerged from my nose, a lively laugh tumbling off of my lips as Raiden chimed in. His lips finally met mine, tender fingers trailing along the bruised flesh of my neck. A low groan slipped off of my tongue when his mouth met the surface, and suddenly, he stilled.

"Freya?"

The blood turned to ice within my veins. I'd almost forgotten about the evidence of his birth mother's magical assault on my neck until now. After all, before this moment, we'd spent most of our time in near darkness—the room weakly illuminated by the brand-new television. But now, with the bedside lamp on, it was all on display—the deep, purple contusions, perfectly shaped like greedy fingers.

"It's fine," I lied, silencing his queries with a kiss. To my dismay, he pulled away, refusing to remove his gaze from my injured neck as he brushed my hair over my shoulder to view the damage.

"They look like fingers," he observed, gently caressing the surface. "They're fresh. This happened today, didn't it?"

"Yes," I breathed, readily recalling the mystic experience. I still didn't fully understand how it happened, but the marks on my neck proved that somehow, it had.

"Who did this to you, Freya?" Raiden hissed through gritted teeth. "Was it Vole?"

"No!" I rasped. "Vole saved my life!"

"Saved you from *what?"* Raiden's features hardened, gentle touch still glued to my neck as he demanded an answer—only, how could I even tell him? How could I reveal that I knew everything that he didn't? That I'd met his birth mother, seen his biological father, watched the way he entered this wicked world?

"Raiden, please–"

"Tell me right now!" Raiden exploded, tearing his hand away from my neck. I watched as his fingers curled into furious fists, and Mimosa woke from her deep slumber to emit a small whine. She always hated when he raised his voice, as rare of an occasion as it was.

I stood to my feet, anxiously pacing the tiny space between our bed and the dresser as my fingers restlessly tugged at the strap of my bra.

"Vole and I tried to find you," I said, studying my feet as I shakily walked. "When we thought you were dead. They can communicate with the dead, and they traveled past the veil. On their way to find you, they found your mother."

Raiden's jaw went slack. "*She* did this to you?"

"She was angry," I stammered, massaging my sore neck. I could still feel her claws, the way they sunk deeper and deeper and *deeper* . . .

"I didn't want to tell you. I didn't want you to know about her. She's nothing like you, Raiden. She's wicked, vile. *Evil.* She had every intention of killing me, but I don't think she was able to. This was the closest she got."

I omitted the details about his becoming, for what reason I wasn't quite certain. Perhaps to save him from the knowledge of his sinful existence, or potentially to save myself from reliving it.

"I'm so sorry, Freya. I wish you never tried to look for me. I wish I'd come before all of that happened," Raiden rambled, beckoning me back onto the bed. "I don't want to know anything about her. Not even her name, if you know it. She means nothing to me. She is not my mother. My mother was Ethel Crow, and she was a beautiful, faultless woman."

"Yes," I whispered, smiling sweetly as I clambered onto his lap. "Ethel was your real mother. She's your only mother, forever."

"I love you, Freya. I'm sorry I wasn't here to protect you," Raiden said, peppering soft kisses along my forehead. "I'm never going anywhere ever again. You'll never be rid of me."

"Good," I mused, capturing his lips in a quick kiss. "These past six months have felt like Hell. I know it isn't real, but it really did. I never want to feel that kind of pain ever again."

"We're going to go back to where you came from," Raiden whispered, leaning over to turn off the light. "Back to Italy, where your soul belongs. We're going to be happy, Freya. I promise. I'm going to do everything I can to make up for what I've done."

I settled into his embrace, breathing in the sweet scent of his skin. I wanted to pinch myself again—to remind my soul that this was actually happening. I spent so many days in agony, wishing I could have one last touch, a final hug, a kiss goodbye.

"Kiss me," I whispered, dancing my fingers along his jaw. With a grin, he obliged; suctioning his lips to mine as he breathed life back into me.

Right there, in that moment, wrapped up in love in one another's arms atop the mushy mattresses of our conjoined beds, surrounded by a triad of sleeping dogs and the pleasant buzz of the television—all was well.

It always would be.

twenty-seven

SIX YEARS LATER

Ten tiny fingers, ten little toes.

A gummy giggle, enchanting green eyes.

I nearly melted at the sight of her—four months old and just now finding her toes—and I couldn't help but pepper loving kisses along her cheeks, earning another enthusiastic laugh from the sweet baby in my arms.

"Someone keep an eye on Freya, I think she may try to steal my daughter," Brennan announced, snapping a pair of silver tongs in my direction. His husband, Elden, only laughed, stealing a kiss from my aging brother as he commanded him to turn over the lamb on the grill.

Don't let it burn for God's sake.

"It's not my fault you two make such pretty babies," I snipped, tickling Chiara's tiny baby belly with the tips of my fingers. To my complete amusement, she giggled once more, fat fingers reaching down towards her toes.

"It wouldn't hurt if she took one of them, Bren. I mean, you have three other kids that'll keep you on your toes," our father chirped, taking a generous sip from his bottled beer. On his lap was Brennan's oldest child, a son named Meo, who I named myself. He was nearly six and would talk your ear off until it bled. He was highly intelligent and had a deep fascination with astronomy, so much so that his grandparents got him an overpriced telescope for his fifth birthday.

The other two children—a three year old girl named Abra and a two year old boy named Ludo—were busy with Grammy Gaia in the kitchen, helping her make some side dishes like fagioli al fiasco, potato salad, and sauteed swiss chard.

It was a warm Sunday afternoon in the coastal Italian town of Portofino. Brennan and Elden lived more inland in a spacious country home big enough for their army of littles, whereas my parents purchased a petite property overlooking the Ligurian Sea.

Raiden and I settled directly in the middle of them both, in an inexpensive cottage down the street from our favorite café. There was just enough space for us and the dogs—Mimosa and Bear remained, Kelso passed on three winters prior—and we even added a needy, vocal cat called Jasper, who insisted on sleeping on Raiden's chest every night.

We spent every Sunday at Momma and Dad's seaside property, watching the royal blue waves crash along the shore and the boats weave in and out of view. I sat lounged in a cozy, coral chair, a sleepy Chiara dozing off in my lap as Meo rambled to my father about Jupiter's moons.

I caught a glimpse of my mother as she craned her neck out of the open kitchen window, fluttering floral curtains tickling her shoulder as she called out to me.

"Raiden's home from the hospital!"

My heart swelled three times its size within my chest, a wide grin easing across my mouth as I ushered a sleeping Chiara into Elden's open arms. I felt like a kid on Christmas morning, quickened pulse drumming against my throat as I skipped around the front of the home to meet an exhausted Raiden, dressed to the nines in dull blue scrubs. His trademark lengthy, brown locks were pulled into a secure bun at the base of his skull, and I swore that I could see the black bags beneath his tired eyes from yards away.

"Oh, honey," I murmured, arms outstretched as I approached the sleepy man. His expression instantaneously brightened at the sight of me, palm flattening against the curve of the car door as he slammed it shut.

"Well, aren't you a sight for sore eyes." He beamed, melting into my open embrace. His lips met my neck, placing petite kisses along the surface. My skin raised in response, goosebumps coating my exposed flesh as Raiden chuckled at the sight.

"I love when that happens," he said, running the pads of his thumbs along the scaly skin of my arms. "Is dinner almost done? I didn't get to eat my lunch. It was a long day at the office."

"My healing hero," I mused, meeting his lips with a quick kiss.

"Last time I checked, the power of healing was in your hands. I'm just an ordinary nurse," Raiden replied, snaking his arm around my shoulders. "Please tell me Momma made swiss chard. I've been craving it for days."

"You know damn well she did," I said, unable to tear my stare away from his handsome features. I toyed with his lazy fingers, smoothing my forefinger along the cool rings as we marched around the back of Momma and Dad's lovely home. Raiden outwardly sighed at the sight of the sea, his stiff stance instantly relaxing as he pulled his hair loose from the hair tie.

"This view will never get old," he announced, a toothy grin tugging at his lips as my brother skipped towards us, enveloping Raiden into a burly bear hug.

"Nurse Raiden has arrived, and just in time for some perfectly grilled meat!" my brother cheered, thrusting his greasy tongs above his head in triumph.

"Don't get cocky now, Bren. We all know the master griller is Elden," Raiden teased, earning a lighthearted punch from my younger brother.

The family flocked towards the outdoor wooden table, complete with a lively, yellow umbrella that reminded me of the beach. Elden was busy rubbing sunscreen on a protesting Meo while Momma marched outside with the side dishes, assisting Abra in carrying a heaping basket of fresh baked buns.

So there we sat—a family of ten—thankful to be alive despite life's circumstances. At the head of the table sat an empty plate accented with a red rose, reserved special for Grammy. Even after all this time, we always left a spot for her, regardless of her presence within Raiden. We knew she was always with us as long as he was, but it felt right to still set out a plate for her, as if her soul could pull back a chair to sit and watch.

Halfway through the meal, Raiden volunteered to bottle feed a finicky Chiara, stepping away from the table as he bounced the beautiful girl in his arms. I glanced over my shoulder to watch him—his stunning silhouette framed with the endless blue sparkle of the sea—his disorderly curls waving in the wind as he fed our niece. He always had the biggest smile spread across his face every time he held one of Brennan's children, and the sight warmed me to my very core, for it came so naturally to him, and I almost felt guilty for not making him a father.

After all, we could never have any biological children of our own. The mix of our blood was unheard of, and it wasn't something we planned to experiment with. Instead, Raiden spent the weeks before our big move recovering from a vasectomy, and I did my duty of donating my eggs to a clinic in our Canadian hometown. Somewhere out there, tiny Araedian children emerged from my donated eggs, surprising their parents with energies and power once unheard of to the mostly ordinary folk.

I planned to do another donation in the fall, and maybe even a third somewhere down the road before my fortieth birthday. With my generous donations and Brennan's inability to stop reproducing, the Araedian bloodline would live on long after our numbered days, despite the De Mörka's plans to snuff us out. Instead, their legacy would die with Raiden, erased from the world as if they never even existed at all.

Mere days after Ethel's passing, Raiden's father shockingly followed suit, making Raiden an orphan at only thirty-two. It was a difficult few weeks following both the news and his sudden return home, but the both of us managed. We spent most of our time bundled up in bed, my job at Sunflower Inn basically forgotten, along with a quite rude Zoey and an unbelievably irritating Cheltsey. Our remaining days in Canada were blissfully spent, and the familiar town that harbored so many memories was nothing but a distant memory to us.

For now, we simply existed, living out our remaining years on the coast of Italy, keeping one another company in the best of ways. I kept my healing to a minimum, especially when it came to Raiden, for his soul was finally his own once more, and the idea of snatching bits and pieces of his being like before was enough to permanently scar me. I no longer felt his pain or pleasure, instead, it was all my own. It was a relief to say the least, and instead, I left the healing to him, cheering him on as he worked hard day in and day out to care for the injured and the sick. Meanwhile, I spent most of my days volunteering around the community, and my favorite pastime involved teaching kids English at the primary school down the road.

I reminisced on the very first time Raiden had touched me following our severed bond—the first time I truly felt him without the overwhelming presence of his own pleasure. The way his lips upturned at the sound of my sighs, the gentle curls of his fingers, the torturous tickle of his tongue. He took his time, showing me what it was like to experience my own amatory sensations instead of a blend of both. He ensured that I was satisfied and spent, and I could still envision the cherry flush of his cheeks, the pillowy surface of his lips, all red and swollen from my teeth.

Raiden never made me question how loved I truly was.

When night fell and Brennan's babies were snoring beneath the bundled blankets on the grass, I took my rightful spot on Raiden's lap, nestling my nose against the hollow dip in his neck, the very same one that I'd seen sliced open in an alternate timeline. Only in this one, it remained unblemished, unmarred. The perfect, pale surface had never felt the sting of a rusted blade, the warm flow of rushing blood. The only evidence that remained was his scarred palm, physical proof of Grammy's selfless sacrifice.

I laced my fingers around his bony wrist, drawing his hand upwards towards my face as I placed a sealed-lip kiss along the raised flesh. He purred in response, nudging his nose along the surface of my brow as he muttered a series of sweet nothings, along with a hearty proclamation of love.

We kissed once more, and I gazed up at the stars; losing myself in their twinkling appeal. Raiden's fingers danced along my jaw, lips softly waltzing along my skin as he pulled me close.

I smiled, twisting my neck to meet his slack stare. He looked so effortless—so *stunning*—and I wondered how I ever got so lucky. For a split second, I pondered over the thought of what my life would be like if Grammy hadn't given her life for his. If Momma didn't turn back the clocks and manipulate time to save the man who tried to murder her family.

They saw the good in him—the good I always saw from the moment I met his malnourished, youthful self at the gas station.

"When you zone out like that, where do you go?" Raiden whispered, fingers weaving between mine.

I glanced back up at the sky, admiring the starry, cloudless night. I breathed in Raiden's welcoming scent—a mixture of nicotine and a medley of lavender and oak cologne.

This was home.

His lips tickled my jaw, and I completely unraveled within his tender touch.

"The rings of Saturn," I said, squeezing his hand as his lips finally met mine.

Just like the ones circling your fingers.

acknowledgments

Every written story of mine seems to stem from my unconscious mind. As cliché as it may sound, my mind works best at rest, (thanks, anxiety!), and these wonderful stories are born the second I wake.

Within my slumber, I had a vision—a grand, gorgeous estate, a lively party, the presence of magic, and most importantly, blood. It transpired to an awful, murderous mess, and my dream-brother (who turned into Brennan on paper) fought tooth-and-nail with my male best friend. We all seemed to harbor some sort of magic, and I watched with worry as the pair painfully fought.

Thus, *Scarlet Sunday* was born. Only, my dream ended a tad-bit differently (we may touch back on that later).

I'd like to start off with a massive thank you to my editor, Lauren Short, who worked countless late nights to ensure that *Scarlet* was as perfect as possible. Your pure devotion and endless adoration of this story has warmed my heart. You can find her on twitter at @Laurencsho.

To my cover designer HL Macfarlane, who is a fellow author, and most importantly, a friend. I came to her with a sloppy cover design and stunning images, and she took on the challenge and created the most perfect, professional cover. You can find more of her services at maclanternpublishing.com.

To Nicole Scarano, the designer of my bloody beautiful chapter headers and section breaks. Her work completed *Scarlet* in more ways than I thought possible. She offers flawless formatting and graphics, and you can find her on twitter at @NicoleRScarano.

To my very first readers, who helped me shape the story into something truly magical, and provided me with flawless feedback. Thank you for transforming me into the author that I am, and assisting me in my continuing growth. To my husband Tyler, who always listens to my crazy ideas, and isn't afraid to tell me if something is just downright silly. He came up with the whole "banishment" theme, and he was (mostly) responsible for Grammy's fate, so please direct all hate mail to him. Totally joking. Sort of.

To my number-one girl (and wifey) Cheyenne, who has been by my side morning and night for three years and counting. She is a talented writer and most importantly, she is the best part of me. Thank you for always being a shining light in my life, and helping me through both the good times and bad. I look forward to spending an eternity with you by my side.

To Mom and Mimi, my number-one supporters and most loyal fans. Admittedly, I feel my face go hot everytime I imagine my grandmother reading some of the dark and filthy stuff I write. I apologize in advance for the "shut up and fuck me" line. Please never bring it up or I may die.

To Cassidy, my late childhood best friend. The fourteen years we spent together will never be enough. I just know you'd absolutely adore Raiden, and you'd tease me endlessly about all of the fluff. I think about you every single day.

And to you, my reader. Thank you for reading *Scarlet Sunday* from cover to cover. Thank you for giving a little author like myself a chance. I am forever thankful for you, and I hope that I've managed to entertain you for a short time. Please don't hesitate to reach out to me, and to leave reviews on Amazon, Goodreads, and wherever else you see fit. Your feedback helps me improve for every tale to come.

Find me at:
Instagram – @alyssadicarloauthor
Facebook – facebook.com/alyssamdicarlo

a note

Oh, you're still around? *Lovely!*

As promised, I wanted to give you guys some insight to the original ending of *Scarlet Sunday* (well, the ending I experienced in my dream, that is).

Originally, Freya and Raiden were supposed to remain entirely platonic. Just super-duper close best friends. Well . . . you see how that ended up. I blame the Raiden inside my mind, he was pretty persistent with how much he loved her, and he was sure to let me know right around the time I wrote the family dinner scene (thanks for completely changing the story, Rai).

I actually intended to follow my dream, where Raiden was in love with Freya's brother, Brennan. Their fight scene was not only dramatic, but rather intimate, and extremely charged. It ended with Raiden kissing Brennan, (before being stabbed in the back by Bren), and I fully intended on following that storyline until I realized that Raiden was actually in love with Freya instead.

Oh well. Regardless of how the story wound up, (and how comical it must be to hear me ramble), I'm beyond proud of what my characters and I accomplished. *Scarlet Sunday* is extremely special, and I love every piece of it. I took a leap of faith with the fantasy elements, something way out of my comfort zone, and I poured hours of planning and research into my writing. If only you guys could see my notes.

Just kidding, no one wants to see that scribbled mess.

If you're still here, you're cool as fuck. I like you. Thank you for going on this journey with me!

Much love.
Lyss

www.ingramcontent.com/pod-product-compliance
Lightning Source LLC
Chambersburg PA
CBHW030340310726
48979CB00001B/114
* 9 7 8 1 7 3 3 2 4 8 0 4 4 *